HIGHLAND
BEAST

HIGHLAND BEAST

SONS OF SINCLAIR

HEATHER

USA TODAY BESTSELLING AUTHOR

McCOLLUM

Entangled Publishing, LLC
644 Shrewsbury Commons Ave., STE 181
Shrewsbury, PA 17361
Visit our website at www.entangledpublishing.com.

Amara is an imprint of Entangled Publishing, LLC.

Edited by Alethea Spiridon
Cover design by LJ Anderson, Mayhem Cover Creations
Stock art by Mihail Guta/Shutterstock,
Meinzahn/GettyImages, and kamchatka/Depositphotos
Interior design by Toni Kerr

Print ISBN 978-1-64937-077-8
ebook ISBN 978-1-64937-344-1

Manufactured in the United States of America

First Edition May 2023

AMARA

ALSO BY HEATHER McCOLLUM

To Logan, my dear golden-hearted boy.
And for those who feel the massive weight of the
world's expectations.

SCOTS GAELIC/FOREIGN/OLD ENGLISH WORDS USED IN *HIGHLAND BEAST*

air adhart – onward

aon – one

aon dha trì – one, two, three

àlainn –lovely

beò – alive, living

blaeberry – similar to blueberry but softer and juicier, grown in Scotland

blaigeard – bastard

boireannach brèagha – beautiful woman

cac – shite

daingead – dammit

dhà – two

dòchas – hope (name of Bàs's horse)

fuil – blood (name of Joshua's horse)

gu cath – to battle

jack – penis

magairlean – ballocks

mattucashlass – double-edged dagger

mo chreach – my rage

molaibh Dia – praise God

sgàil – shadow (name of Gideon's horse)

sgian dubh – black-handled dagger

siuthad – go on

tolla-thon – arsehole

trì – three

yard – penis

BOOK OF REVELATION

1   I watched as the Lamb opened the first of the seven seals. Then I heard one of the four living creatures say in a voice like thunder, "Come!"

2   I looked, and there before me was a white horse! Its rider held a bow, and he was given a crown, and he rode out as a conqueror bent on conquest.

3   When the Lamb opened the second seal, I heard the second living creature say, "Come!"

4   Then another horse came out, a fiery red one. Its rider was given power to take peace from the earth and to make people kill each other. To him was given a large sword.

5   When the Lamb opened the third seal, I heard the third living creature say, "Come!" I looked, and there before me was a black horse! Its rider was holding a pair of scales in his hand.

6   Then I heard what sounded like a voice among the four living creatures, saying, "Two pounds of wheat for a day's wages, six pounds of barley for a day's wages, and do not damage the oil and the wine!"

7   When the Lamb opened the fourth seal, I heard the voice of the fourth living creature say, "Come!"

8   I looked, and there before me was a pale horse! Its rider was named Death…

At Entangled, we want our readers to be well-informed. If you would like to know if this book contains any elements that might be of concern for you, please check the back of the book for details.

PREFACE

"The boy's been breeched for a year," Father's voice boomed. "'Tis time he learns his role and begins his training."

"George," Aunt Merida said. "Ye are my brother and I've stood by ye while ye've mourned Alice—"

"Don't say her name!"

Bàs Sinclair clasped the bunch of wildflowers in both hands as he stood silently outside the library door, shifting so each of his eyes got equal time peering through the crack. His palms felt damp and cold as his fingers curled around the stems.

"I stood by ye as ye've told everyone how your boys are God's four mighty horsemen," Aunt Merida continued. She was a brave woman, the only person Bàs had ever seen stand up to his warlord father. Had his mother been as brave?

"But Bàs is only five years old," Aunt Merida said. "'Tis bad enough ye named the lad Death, but to give him that…that hideous thing to wear…" Bàs could see her flapping her hand out to the side, but he couldn't see at what she was pointing.

"He is Death," Father said, his voice eerily calm. "'Tis the end of days when blood will soak the land, and the Lord wills me to send evil to Hell."

"And what if ye are the evil one?" Aunt Merida

said, her words snapping. "Raising your sons to be vicious and cruel and ignoring your daughter."

Bàs shifted again so he could see his large father. George Sinclair was built like the Highlands: rugged, stony, huge, and without warmth. His face and arms were scarred from many battles, and his bearded mouth was usually twisted in a cruel frown. He was the fiercest warrior in all of Scotland and seemed to Bàs like one of the angry gods in Gideon's Greek book.

"This is a cruel world, sister," Father said. "And I will train my sons to win against it."

"He would rather pick flowers and rescue birds from fallen nests, George. Ye cannot give him that. He won't sleep at night."

"Then he can get up and pace the hall with me sipping whisky."

"Bloody hell, George," Aunt Merida said.

His father didn't sleep well? Bàs loved to sleep, curling up in his warm bed in the nursery. He was the youngest, so the room would remain his, which suited him. It had a rocking horse and Cain's old chessboard. Bàs didn't play chess, but he used the figures to make up little stories about having lots of friends and going to festivals.

Bàs's breath caught in a quick little gasp as his father's gaze turned toward the door, specifically the crack in the door where he stood. "Come in, lad," Father called.

Despite his wildly thumping heart, Bàs pushed the door open with his knuckles while still clutching the floppy daisies and bluebells. He kept his gaze on his father. Joshua said it was always a good idea to keep Father in your sights in case he decided to attack. Bàs didn't know exactly what that meant, but he didn't look away.

"'Tis time for ye to begin your battle training, Bàs," he said.

Aunt Merida waved Bàs over, so he came, the flowers before him. He'd planned to put them on his mother's grave that morning but had been called into the castle from the field by his father's general. Bàs stood as straight as he could before his sire. Father's bushy eyebrows pinched inward as he glanced at the bouquet. He didn't say anything but turned to pick up something from the table.

"Starting tomorrow, son, ye will begin to train with the wooden sword with your brothers."

"Aye, Father," Bàs said dutifully.

George Sinclair turned back to him, holding something Bàs did not dare to look upon because Aunt Merida said it would cause him not to sleep.

"Ye were born the Horseman of Death," Father said.

Aunt Merida made a strangled noise, and Bàs's arms started to tingle. He inhaled slowly. Gideon said whenever he started to tingle or saw stars he should remember to breathe evenly. That would keep him upright. And, since Father could attack at any time, he must stay upright.

The rush of Bàs's exhale was loud in his ears, but nothing could block his father's voice. "Ye became the Horseman of Death the day of your birth, the day your mother died giving ye life. 'Twas why I named ye death, Bàs."

He'd known that was his name, and he remembered well the surprised looks people gave him when they learned it. Hannah had said that's why the other children didn't play with him, because of his name. Not because there was anything wrong with him.

George Sinclair thrust what he was holding toward Bàs, and his gaze instinctually dropped to it. He gasped. The skull looked human, polished white like it had baked in the sun after ravens had picked it clean. The lower jaw was missing. What remained was the nose bridge, dark eye sockets, and skullcap.

"The back is cut away so ye can wear it," Father said.

Bàs looked up at his father's dark eyes. "I don't want it," he said, proud that he'd kept the tremor out of his voice. "I like to sleep."

Aunt Merida snorted, and his father cast her a glare before shoving the thing toward him. "Take it, boy."

"I…I don't want to be death," Bàs said.

His father frowned down at him. "And I didn't want to lose the woman I loved more than my life and this whole damned world." His father looked up at the vaulted ceiling as if Bàs's mother might be hovering there, and then met his son's gaze once more. "Ye will take this mask made of an enemy's skull, and one day ye will wear it into battle as the fourth horseman, Death. Ye will be the most brutal of all my sons, with battle ax and sword. People will cringe at the sight of ye riding toward them. For ye are Death, Bàs Sinclair, the executioner for our mighty clan."

"I am?" Bàs's voice did shake then.

"Aye, lad," Father said, once again shoving the

skull toward him. He leaned closer, bending so he could meet Bàs's eyes evenly. "Your *mother* was your first execution."

Bàs's breath stopped in his chest as his whole face pinched, trying to stop the tears that would not be stopped. They poured hot from his eyes, down his cheeks. His hands opened, and the white daisies and bluebells fell from his sticky palm to the floor as he took the bleached skull from his father.

CHAPTER ONE

> "The lean and hungry wolf,
> With his fangs so sharp and white,
> His starveling body pinched
> By the frost of a northern night,
> And his pitiless eyes that scare the dark
> With their green and threatening light."
> A BOOK OF HIGHLAND MINSTRELSY

Bàs Sinclair knelt in the smoothed dirt raked around his rock garden. His skull mask, made from an ancient Sinclair enemy, sat discarded among the delicate bluebells and daisies that he'd encouraged to grow around the outer perimeter. He hadn't yet cleaned the blood splatter from his tunic nor taken his horse, Dòchas, to the creek to wash the green stain from his brilliant pale gold coat.

"May God forgive me for fulfilling my duty. Judge well and with mercy, dear Lord, the soul I sent to ye this morn." He pulled a rock from a pouch made from the slack of the woolen plaid wrapped around him. There was dirt and a drop of blood on the gray stone. He set it in the garden with the rest of the monuments to his victims, his gaze sliding over the hundreds of rocks set in a wavelike pattern. All of them were gray except for the few white stones set near the center block of pale white marble.

He bowed his head. His eyes closed, and he felt the familiar press of his friend against his leg. Without looking, Bàs slid his hands through the wolf's thick coat of fur.

"Amen," Bàs murmured.

He lifted his head. "Did ye miss me?" he asked, staring into the wolf's amber eyes. The wolf pressed his nose into Bàs's side, showing his affection. Bàs wrapped one arm over the beast and hugged him. "I missed ye, too, Beò." He scratched the top of the wolf's head and stood, stretching tall to work the aches from training the previous day out of his shoulders.

Bàs's gaze turned to the polished monument that he'd set in the center of his garden, which he'd spent several years carving to look like the face of a sleeping woman. Leaning over, he brushed his hand over the cool stone, dislodging some dirt from a dried leaf stuck to it. "Good eve, Mother," he murmured. *I am sorry*. He prayed the apology every time he walked by his monument to Alice Sinclair.

She was your first execution when she died birthing ye. Even with his father dead these past three years, his sire's words still made Bàs's gut tighten. He turned, scooping up his mask, and walked toward the fast-flowing creek that cut through the woods behind his cabin. Beò trotted next to him. His silent friend.

A mournful cry in the distance stopped his wolf. Beò tipped his black nose upward, sniffing the cool evening breeze. He let out a short bark and trotted into the woods. Perhaps he knew the pack howling not too far off. As a lone wolf, his friend was vulnerable, but he was the largest wolf Bàs had ever seen in these woods. He'd come home with scratches at times but nothing serious.

Bàs stripped off his dirty shirt and plaid and padded down the slope into a pool of cold spring water that eddied off the main creek. Using the soap his sister, Hannah, made for him, he washed, scrubbing hard at the evidence of his trade. The scars from battle remained, as did the hard stone of remorse that he pushed down in his gut. The blood splatter, dirt, and sweat broke free from his large body to be swept downstream. If only wickedness could leave him so easily.

Thou shall not kill. And yet he killed. It was his duty to kill enemies and those proclaimed as guilty. He was the mighty Sinclair Horseman of Death, hired executioner most sought throughout northern Scotland. People sent for him to deliver swift justice, beheading in one swing with his infamous ax or a whistling arc of his sword.

Bàs scrubbed his body with the scratchy horsehair brush until his skin was rosy and nearly raw, as clean as he could make himself with soap and water. He climbed out, shaking his head, and rubbed his hands down his bristled jaw.

One of the barn cats trotted toward him. "Daingead," Bàs murmured. The cat held a small red squirrel in her mouth, its tufted ears unmoving. The cats were forever offering him sacrifices or dinner, neither of which he wanted.

"Drop it, Banshee," he said, but the cat continued

to bring the despondent creature in her jaws. She set it down before him, but it didn't move. He scratched the cat's head. "I wish ye wouldn't do this."

He picked up the little squirrel. It was a young female, and there wasn't any blood dripping from an open wound. Could it be scared to death? Bàs rubbed her briskly. He'd seen Ella, his brother's wife, blow life into an unmoving foal once. They'd all been shocked to see the desperate act work when the horse started breathing on its own.

Standing there naked, the cold water drying on his skin in the twilight, Bàs held the little squirrel close to his face. He squeezed the sides of the creature's mouth so it would open and blew very gently into it. He let the air back out and repeated it twice more, watching the creature's wee chest rise and fall.

The squirrel jerked in his hand. "That's it, beastie," Bàs murmured and grabbed a rag from his belt on the ground where he'd left his clothes. He wrapped the squirrel, holding it close to his body for warmth. His cat, Banshee, rubbed against his legs in a figure eight pattern, purring loudly.

The squirrel's eyes blinked open, round and full of fright. Bàs smiled. "Ye'll be fine. But ye must stay away from the cats, my friend." Holding the squirrel against his chest, he looked down at the hunter. "Go on, Banshee," he said. "And stop killing things unless ye plan to eat them." But he knew the cat would continue. It was in its nature. Was killing in Bàs's nature? Apparently, yes.

With his free hand, Bàs scooped up his kilt, belt, and tunic and walked to the door of his cabin. He pushed inside where his two young wolfhounds leaped around in crazy circles to greet him. The squirrel remained frozen in panic as Bàs set it on a counter near the hearth, still wrapped up in the rag. Peeking out, it emerged to scamper up into the exposed beams that held his high ceiling aloft.

The dogs, Artemis and Apollo, jumped around Bàs as he balled up and threw his dirty tunic at the door. He grabbed a clean one. "Let me dress," he said, smiling at their antics. Cats showed affection with offerings while these two wanted only to tackle and lick him all over. Every animal was special in its own way. Bàs respected them more than humans who killed their brothers and sisters without remorse, and certainly not to fix an empty stomach.

Wasn't he as terrible as the worst humans? Perhaps if he were to feed his victims to his animals there would be more honor in it. He snorted at the horrid thought. He could imagine the looks of the people watching the execution as he dragged off the body, explaining it would feed his wolf.

Bàs opened the door for the two dogs, and they bounded out. "Leave the chickens be," he called after them as they scattered the small flock pecking around his garden. The one rooster flapped his wings, daring the pups to come close. Bàs had seen an angry rooster once peck a dog's eye nearly out.

It was a wonder there weren't more disasters within the haven of his home with so many different animals milling about. Somehow, most seemed to know that this was a kill-free region. His wolf had been raised here, and Bàs had taught him to hunt away from home. Perhaps that was what Beò was doing now.

Apollo and Artemis chased each other around the perimeter of the yard encircled by thick brambles. Several of the cats watched, backs arching if the dogs came too close. The chickens pecked and scratched, looking for bugs and worms, and his horse, Dòchas, nibbled at the shoots of new grass.

Bàs closed the door, standing on his covered porch, and bent to open the smaller doorway he'd put in for the beasts. The smaller door sat, hinged, inside the extra-large door he'd built to fit his tall body. 'Twas an advantage of building one's own home. He could have a door within a door if he wanted.

That way the squirrel could leave when it was ready, and the dogs could run back inside. Bàs glanced at the lowering sun and jogged down the steps. He must still check the henhouse for eggs, find his goat who wandered, feed his shaggy coo, and make sure her calf was well. Then he'd check his traps farther out and wash and stable Dòchas for the night. He didn't mind the work, though. His animals were more family to him than his brothers and sister—well, maybe not his sister, Hannah. She cared for him a great deal. He wasn't sure why. Perhaps she just pitied him.

A long wolf cry stopped Bàs on his way to the coop. It was close, a single note that tugged at him. Turning, he cupped his hands around his mouth and let out a long howl in return. He'd practiced with Beò enough to sound very much like the real beast. Lowering his arms, he waited.

"Where are ye?" he asked, his gaze scanning the summer-green foliage of the forest outside the high bramble surrounding his home. From the same direction, a lone howl grew again, extending long to carry. Beò was calling him. Bàs surged into a run. As he ran past the porch, he snatched the ax from its block and sprinted into the woods.

Arms pumping, ax clutched, Bàs leaped over fallen trees and crashed through bramble as he surged toward his friend. Artemis and Apollo barked with excitement, keeping stride with him through the forest. Bàs knew these woods as well as any animal, a mile in each direction. The river cut a path through the earth to wind across the property that ran the border between Sinclair and MacKay lands.

The muted sun was falling, slicing shadows through the thick forest. Bàs could see Beò ahead, standing on his hind legs, his front paws propped on a thick, heavily limbed tree. At the wolf's feet lay a woman, unmoving and crumpled on the ground.

"What the bloody hell?" Bàs murmured as he slowed to a jog, coming onto the scene. The dirt and last fall's leaves were churned up as if a pack of wolves had danced under the tree. He crouched, pushing the dogs back from the woman, and set his ax down.

Reddish-brown hair lay in haphazard waves around an oval face splattered with a thousand freckles. She looked like a picture he'd seen of Carpo, the Greek goddess of autumn, with hair the color of changing leaves. Long lashes lay under her closed eyes, stark against the pale smoothness of her skin. Bàs brushed the hair from her face, but she didn't stir. His fingertips picked up a gentle exhale from her parted lips. *Alive.* He released the breath he hadn't realized he'd been holding. The beautiful woman lived.

A quick survey of her exposed skin showed no bite marks. His hands slid along her limbs, straightening them gently to test for fractures, but everything seemed correctly attached. *So smooth.*

When he slid his hand under her head, blood stained his fingers. "Daingead." He muttered the curse. He turned her to the side and found a gash where her head had hit a rock. The gash should be stitched closed back at his cabin. Yanking another long rag looped over his belt, he gently bandaged the wound, tying the rag across her speckled forehead.

Beò whined, running over to him and then back to the tree where the two dogs circled, sniffing. Bàs stood. "What is it?" He looked up.

"Holy Lord," Bàs whispered, for up in the tree, tied to the thick limbs with rope, was a swaddled bairn. The rope was loose enough that it lay tipped on its side so he could see the bairn's face. Its wee eyes were closed, but it breathed. Bàs looked back to the unconscious woman. "Did ye fall from the tree after tying it up?" The wind rattled the leaves but gave no answer. How else would the wee bairn get in the tree?

Bàs hurried to the trunk and reached up on his toes. His fingers could just touch the woolen cloth nearly eight feet overhead. Despite the tilted position, the bairn was secure and seemingly asleep.

Beò trotted to the woman to stand over her, growling when Artemis and Apollo came close.

"Daingead," Bàs cursed when he glanced back and saw the blood on his friend's leg. He went over to examine it. "Ye defended her, didn't ye?" Even though the woman hadn't suffered a wolf bite, Beò had.

"We best get her back to the cabin," Bàs said, shoving at Beò to move so he could pick her up. Carefully, Bàs slid his arms under her, lifting her soft form easily. Beò ran back to the tree and made a yipping sound up at the baby. The dogs joined in, their barking breaking the quiet of the forest. The bairn's eyes opened in alarm.

"Mo chreach," Bàs said. Could he carry the woman and bairn without touching the bairn? Or dropping it? Bairns were breakable and died easily. One wrong move could bring an end to the wee life tucked in the blanket tied safely in the tree. It was probably better off tied there than balanced in his arms.

He looked down at the muddy, wet woman in his arms. She must have forded the river. "I'll take the lass back to the cabin and then come back for the bairn," he said. Beò looked at him, tilting his head as if he questioned his plan. Sometimes Bàs thought he did.

The bairn made a soft sound, like a whimper. What would Hannah do? His sister was wise when it came to caregiving. *Daingead.* "Hannah wouldn't leave a bairn tied up in a tree, would she?" He huffed. The knots could come loose.

Bàs set the woman on the ground where Artemis and Apollo shoved their wet noses along her arms and legs. Bàs traipsed back to the thick oak, grabbing the lower branch to pull himself up. Bark was scuffed away, showing the lass had climbed quickly, the toes of her boots digging into the trunk.

Using his arm strength to balance, he braced himself over the bairn. It was a wee thing, but its eyes were wide, staring up at him. Its mouth made the smallest *O*. Bàs's cheeks puffed out with his exhale.

He tugged on the knots holding the fragile bundle until the rope fell away, thumping on the ground beneath. Aye, the knots might not have held if the bairn moved or the wind blew. Bàs pulled it against his chest and lowered them, setting the bairn on the ground.

He looked at Beò. "I'll carry the mother. Ye carry the bairn."

Beò sniffed the swaddled wee person who stared up at the wolf's large muzzle with curious courage. The bairn made a noise, and the wolf jumped back, circled the mother and child, and then trotted away toward Bàs's cabin. The pups followed him.

"Ye forgot the bairn," Bàs called after the wolf and shook his head. "Some friend ye are."

• • •

Darkness gripped Shana Drummond while a dull ache thumped through her head in time with the pounding of her heart. *Take him. Save my little Edward.* Ivy's words shot through the darkness, and Shana tried to hold onto them. She realized the babe was in her arms, and she began to run blindly, trees on either side of her, their limbs reaching out to snag her like gnarled fingers.

The howls of wolves made her trip, but she caught herself before she dropped Edward. A chattering filled the air, but she couldn't see from where it came. It sounded like all the animals of the forest were snapping and barking at her heels.

Shana shook her head, trying to rid herself of the terror. The chattering grew louder, insistent. Shana tried to open her eyes, but they felt leaden. She inhaled fully, squeezing her eyes to clear them, and blinked.

Whiskers and bulbous black eyes filled her view. She released the scream that she'd tried to push forth in her dream. The creature lurched back and then jumped right on her head. Its claws grabbed her scalp, and its tail swatted her face as it scampered down her body to launch itself into the air.

Shana pushed up on an elbow, squinting against the pain in her head, and gasped as a man surged through the door. His broad shoulders and tall frame filled the opening even though the door was strangely huge and out of proportion with the world. Legs braced and hands fisted, the man looked ready to battle. Wavy brown hair reached his shoulders, and a clipped beard hugged his strong jawline.

His intense eyes scanned the room and then stopped on her. "Ye screamed."

Shana tried to make sense of the scene. Everything looked out of proportion, larger somehow, making her feel small and dazed. She pointed to the scampering creature as it climbed the log wall into the rafters. "You have a squirrel in your house."

He stared at her as if that wasn't an answer. She

blinked, trying to clear the dizziness gripping her. "Squirrels don't live in houses."

"The squirrel was here before ye," he said. "She'll leave when she's ready."

"Edward?" Shana pushed farther up in the soft bed, the covers rolling down to show she still wore her wet gown. Memories of fording the freezing river, Edward above her head, made her shiver. Lord, her head hurt.

The man pointed toward a wooden box filled with straw. "'Tis in there. Looking a lot like the Christ child in the manger."

"Is he well?" she asked, struggling to rise. She pushed onto her feet, and the room seemed to wobble.

The man strode across to her before she could inhale. He steadied her. "Ye fell out of a tree, hit your head, and were trampled by wolves."

"The wolves. Oh God," she whispered. How had she survived? "I remember them under the tree. My foot slipped, and I..." She touched the back of her head and felt a tied bandage. "Am I bleeding?"

The man's large, warm hand clasped her upper arm, keeping her standing straight. "Ye were. I put two stitches in and applied a poultice."

She concentrated on breathing evenly, trying to take in his words. They were thick with his northern accent, and the world still seemed unclear. "You saved me from wolves?" she asked. "Me and Edward?" What type of man could battle off wolves? The white line of a scar showed through his clipped beard along his jaw, making him look fierce. "You fight wolves and win," she whispered, her eyes wide as they stared at each other.

"'Twas Beò who saved ye from the wolves," the man said and helped her across the room. "I carried ye and your bairn back here, because the pack would have returned." He helped her over to the wooden box. "And it wouldn't be right to leave a bairn tied in a tree by itself."

Shana's focus cleared as she looked down at her sister's newborn babe. Edward's eyes were open, and he began to fuss. Shana gathered him to her. "Poor thing. You must be hungry."

"I sent word to my sister to come help with the bairn and to make sure ye are both well."

Panic jumped through Shana. "Your sister? No one can know we're here." She looked about the room and then at the man who stared at her with intense calm. If she wasn't so worried about protecting Edward and saving herself, she might consider him handsome despite his frown. He was certainly large and muscular. "Who are you and where am I?"

His eyes looked dark in the low light. "Bàs Sinclair. My cabin, which sits on the Sinclair Clan and Mackay Clan border."

Shana was new to the region, having come to help her sister with the birth of her first child. She shook her head. "Beò saved me, and you're named Bàs? Do you know Gaelic?" She'd studied it before traveling so she'd be able to communicate with Ivy's new family and friends if they spoke only the ancient language.

"Aye."

"Beò means alive and Bàs means death," she said. The man must go by a shortened version of

Sebastian, sounding like Bàs but really being Bass.

The man turned away, walking to the hearth to add another square of dry peat. "I've been told," he said, his voice a low rumble.

Her head ached, but the floor began to feel solid under her feet once more. She dipped with Edward in her arms and swayed to comfort the babe as she watched the man straighten at the hearth. Lord, he was large, his muscles thick with use. Even his hands seemed large and capable of crushing walnuts without aid. "My uncle was named Sebastian, too," she said to break the silence. "He wanted to be called Bass, but his mother wouldn't let him call himself something that sounded like Death."

Edward continued to fuss, clearly hungry. It had been hours since Ivy had last nursed him.

"'Tis hungry," Bàs said, nodding to the babe.

"Edward is a he," she said. "And I have no way to feed it, him."

"Ye don't have milk?" he asked, his gaze dropping to her breasts.

The perusal seemed innocent but sent a slight tremor through Shana. She was alone in the woods with this huge man and someone who could scare off a pack of wolves. *Sweet Mother Mary, keep us safe.* She straightened her shoulders. "I'm not his mother. Do you have goat's or cow's milk and bread? I can make up pap. And a bladder that I can poke a hole in to feed him unless you know of a wet nurse nearby."

"There's no one nearby," he said, the words sounding ominous.

Shana froze in her swaying, and her heart

pounded in the awkward quiet of the cabin.

"But," the man said, "my sister will come. She knows how to feed human bairns."

Human bairns?

The man leaned against the live tree trunk running up through the ceiling of this house made of logs. Every movement he made, including leaning, was full of stealth and grace. "Why is wee Edward with ye and not his mother? He looks quite fresh, new to the world."

Shana swallowed. She shouldn't tell him everything, but a bit of the truth was needed or he'd pry more and possibly alert the authorities. "His mother is my sister, and she begged me to take her babe away to safeguard him."

"Who would harm a bairn?" Bàs's face hardened so much that Shana pulled Edward closer to her chest. It was as if the man had donned an expression that promised death. *Like his name.*

Shana let out a ragged breath, watching him for any sign of lunging. "Her husband thinks the child is not his." True or not, the child shouldn't die, and neither should her sister. The circumstances around Ivy's marriage to the brute who beat her to give him an heir wiped away her sin in Shana's eyes.

She stared back at Bàs, waiting for his judgment. But he merely walked back to the hearth. "The bairn is safe here."

"Not if people know he's here," she said, stepping around the table to put it between them.

"All beasts are safe here." He stirred the contents of a small cauldron set over the fire. "As long as they have a name, that is."

Movement at the door made Shana's stomach clench so hard, she couldn't breathe. She clutched Edward against her as a huge wolf pushed inside through a smaller door. *Holy Lord!* "The pack's found us!"

The beast trotted directly toward her, and she raced across the room to Bàs, screaming. She clutched his arm with her free hand, dodging behind him to hold Edward between herself and the man's back. It was a broad back, full of muscle, from what she could feel as her hand slid down his shoulder and spine. She pressed Edward between them, trying not to squash the child while wishing to crawl inside the man. Could this mountainous Highlander keep them from being ripped apart by the beast?

"We can fight him together," she whispered, inhaling the fresh scent of him as she pressed her forehead against his back. The warmth and strength emanating from him gave her more courage. Edward and she had survived so far. And, somehow, she knew, even without knowing him, that with this man she could survive anything. "Just tell me what to do."

CHAPTER TWO

"A mother should take her babe to her breast
when 'tis born and not use a wetnurse. Wet
nursing opens the possibility that the child will be
exchanged with another, that the child will love
the wet nurse more than the natural mother, and
the child may adopt an undesirable trait and bad
physique from the wet nurse."
ADVICE FROM JACQUES GUILLEMEAU,
THE NURSING OF CHILDREN, 1600

Bàs spun toward the door when the woman barreled
into him, circling behind as if hiding from a battalion
of Norsemen. Her voluntary touch surprised him,
rooting him where he stood. The warmth of her
hands through his tunic reminded him of one of
Banshee's soft kittens. The strength in her voice
showed that she was ready to hiss and fight even
when flooded with fear.

"'Tis Beò," he said and looked over his shoulder
to see her head bent over the bairn, her palm resting
on him. Despite her head injury and probable
bruises from hitting the ground, she was spry and
courageous when defending the bairn. "He saved ye
from the wolf pack."

Beò circled the manger, sniffing the scent of the
bairn they'd rescued.

She raised her face. "But he's a wolf," she yelled.

He stuck a finger in that ear to stop the ringing.

"Aye, but he's *my* wolf." He turned toward her and looked down into her wide eyes. "He won't harm ye. He doesn't have a taste for human flesh." She moved to the side of him, the bairn held in her arms.

"Have you asked Beò if he has a taste for human flesh?" She nodded toward the box he'd found for the bairn. Beò circled it, sniffing. "He seems pretty interested in Edward's cradle." She pointed to the box and then grabbed his tunic sleeve.

Bàs pried her hand off his shirt to hold. He paused, waiting for her to yank it away, but she didn't. Her fingers were slender but strong, roughened from work but not cracked from harsh work. "I promise, lass," he said. "The beast won't harm ye or the bairn." Slowly, he guided them over toward Beò, and Bàs ran his fingers through the wolf's thick coat. "He's quite fond of—"

Scratching claws and a growl heralded his two dogs as they smashed together, trying to be the first one in through the small door. The noise startled the squirrel, making her jump off the table, onto the floor, scurrying to reach the tree he had built his cottage around.

Artemis ran right for the squirrel. Apollo barked and pranced, trying to get Beò to play while the wolf stared at him with what Bàs imagined were amused eyes. The woman pulled her hand away, sheltering the bairn against her chest, and pushed backward until the cabin wall stopped her.

Bàs put two fingers in his mouth and whistled in short bursts. Both dogs ran directly to him, and Beò followed sedately. Bàs produced two small scraps of dried fish, and after making the dogs sit, gave them each one. Bàs threw a third to Beò who caught it in the air, gobbling it with a snap.

"Siuthad," Bàs said and shooed all three out of the cabin with large sweeps of his hands. "Like I said, no harm will come to anyone with a name." Normally Bàs avoided learning people's names or anything else about them. An executioner never knew when he'd be called to perform his duty, and he didn't want the attachment. It was a thin line between executioner and murderer, and his name rule kept him from falling over it. At least that's what he told himself.

"I hope ye have a name."

"Shana." Her eyes were still wider than normal. She watched the canines pushing out through the door, ignoring the squirrel who was tame by comparison.

Shana. He rolled the name around in his mind. It suited her wild spirit.

She still wore the damp, rumpled, mud-stained gown in which he'd found her. Her hair was reddish brown with streaks of gold from the sun. It was long and wild as if tossed and tangled by sprites to puff out around her oval face. A multitude of brown freckles fell across her forehead, nose, and cheeks like flaxseeds flung onto a fertile field. Her lips were perfectly shaped and full of expression. The lass was beautiful in a natural way and unique, and she'd let him hold her hand.

He cleared his throat. "Like I said, ye and your nephew are safe here from the animals. Ye may stay to heal from your fall, and I can speak with my brothers about protecting the child and your sister."

"No," she said, starting a sway and jiggle dance that he'd seen Cain and Joshua do when holding their bairns to soothe them. "If others know we're here, word will get back to him."

Bàs didn't answer. Instead, he found the small jug of milk he'd steamed that morning over the coals in the hearth. "'Tis some coo's milk, and I have bread." He grabbed a leather flask with a narrow neck. "I use this to feed baby animals when they're fresh to the world and unable to suckle their mother. 'Tis clean."

Her gaze rested on the flask and then slid back to his face. "You feed baby animals?"

Bàs didn't answer. No one, besides Hannah, knew about his love for animals. The creatures were safe from his brutal duty unless they were considered food and did not acquire a name. Where he avoided people, especially fragile ones like infants, he could relax with Beò and his pack of animals at his cabin deep in the woods. He could be himself, more beast than man. His animals didn't require explanations, nor did they wait for him to answer questions about why he didn't remain at Girnigoe or touch bairns or interact with people. Sometimes Bàs wished he could become a beast, killing only to eat. Actually, he wished it most of the time.

"I mean…" She stared at him, her brows pinched. "I can't imagine you… You feed baby animals?"

He must guard his tongue. People had ideas about who he was, and he didn't correct them. *Bringing fear, my son, is your purpose. Fear and death.*

Bàs set the items on the table. "Use the flask or

not," he said and strode across the main room of the cabin and out the human door that fit him just right.

He inhaled the cool air that blew in with the night. His hawk, Bruce, would have arrived at Girnigoe Castle by now. Like Cain's falcon, flying over the battlefield with scraps of fabric in his talons to signal action, Bruce had learned to ferry messages back and forth to the Sinclair holding on the sea. Would Joshua or Cain bring Hannah with darkness falling? Probably not. Packs of wolves roamed at night, and neither brother would want to risk a horse or Hannah. They'd probably come at dawn, which meant he had two houseguests for the night. Well, three if he counted the squirrel.

He rubbed a hand down his face. "Betty," he murmured. There, the squirrel had a name, too. But the name that kept echoing through his head was Shana.

• • •

The door remained closed, but Shana kept an eye on it. When was Bàs Sinclair going to return? And would the wolf and dogs follow him? She'd mixed the crumbled bread in the warm milk to make pap, a poor substitute for her sister's milk. But Edward had guzzled the warm pap and was now sleeping in the manger that Shana had dragged to the side of the small bed where she'd woken.

There was a staircase in the back corner of the large room and a quick climb up had revealed a chamber with a very large bed in it and three pallets along the wall. Did Bàs share his bedchamber with the dogs and wolf? *He's kind to little helpless things.*

"Pshhht." She exhaled through her teeth. "They aren't little and surely not helpless." But Edward was. And so was her sister, Ivy, whom she'd had to leave behind. Shana would never have done so if her sister hadn't begged, swearing that her husband would kill the child because he knew the babe wasn't his. "Oh Ivy," Shana whispered.

Erskine was a horrid, cruel man who had wed her sister to beget heirs, heirs the man couldn't seem to father. Ivy said he had mistresses, and none of them had borne him any children. Yet, he raged at Ivy to give him an heir.

She'd met the kind apothecary in town, trying to find herbs that she could give to Erskine to make him more potent, and she'd fallen in love with him. When she became pregnant, Erskine had been pleased. That was until someone told Ivy her husband knew the babe wasn't his. Ivy told Shana Erskine had stared at her with silent rage, not talking to her the last few days before the birth. *He'd looked like he was deciding what to do with me and the babe.* And Ivy was convinced Erskine had decided to kill Edward.

"I have to go back for her," Shana whispered, looking between the door and her nephew. Her sister was the only family she had left after their parents had died. But where could she leave Edward where he'd be safe? Surely, not here with a wolf who liked his scent, even if Bàs said he wouldn't bite.

The wolves below the tree had snapped and howled, sending gooseflesh over her arms. Fumbling with the milk vessel, she reached to catch it, falling from the tree. Why hadn't she been mauled? She shivered at the thought.

Beò saved ye from the wolves. Beò, the biggest wolf she'd ever seen, had fought off a pack of his own kind to keep her alive? She couldn't imagine it.

Rap. Rap.

Shana startled, rising from the bed where the squirrel, who had apparently been creeping nearby, launched itself to scurry up a beam into the rafters.

"Come in," she called.

Bàs opened the door, and she realized he'd cut it to fit his size so he wouldn't have to bend. "How tall are you?" she asked.

One brow rose, his forehead pinched in confusion. "Taller than all but one of my brothers," he said.

She nodded even though that didn't answer the question at all.

He looked at the manger. "Did the bairn eat?"

"Yes," she said. "Thank you."

"I have a chicken plucked and ready to roast." He grabbed it from off the porch, along with a woven basket of vegetables. "Are ye hungry? Head injuries can make a man sick in the stomach."

Her stomach growled with hunger, and she rubbed a hand over it. "There's your answer."

He strode toward the hearth. "Ye've built a fine fire."

"I used the wood and peat you had stacked."

Bàs had already spitted the bird outdoors and coated it with some herbs. "Do you have a kitchen garden?" she asked.

"Aye. Herbs, garlic bulbs, and vegetables," he

answered as he set the chicken over two iron props. Muscles across his broad back showed through the thin fabric of his tunic as he worked before the hearth, and he wore the woolen plaid wrapped about his narrow hips like the Highlanders she'd met here in the north. His long hair was tied back with a leather thong. It was wavy, brown, thick, and well cared for. In fact, he was cleaner than most of the people she'd met while visiting her sister.

"I thought *all* creatures were safe here," she said, walking over to Edward. The bairn was sleeping peacefully, making small bubbles with his exhales.

"All creatures with *names*," Bàs said. He glanced at her over his massive shoulder. "I don't name my eating chickens, or any of the hares I catch in my snares, or the fish I catch."

She met his stare and felt a pull, as if she'd been caught on a line like one of his unnamed fish. She looked away, snapping the tether. "Thank God my sister named her son before we left," she said.

Bàs turned back to the fire where he emptied turnips and carrots into a black iron pan. "I wouldn't have eaten him," he said drily. "But Beò may have."

Shana stared at the back of his head, and he turned. The corner of his generous mouth hitched upward in a type of grin, and she found herself smiling in return. The action relaxed the aching muscles in the back of her neck.

Once the spit was set over the flames and the pan was sitting in the glowing coals off to one side, he straightened. "I have bread and ale as well. No wine."

"How about whisky? Do you have any of that?"

she asked, half jesting.

He studied her, his piercing gaze meeting her own. Bàs had the most interesting face. Handsome, yet something lurked in the lines, something painful, sorrowful. As if he mirrored all the anguish in the world. His brows rose. "Aye, I have whisky, but lasses don't usually partake unless they want to get drunk. Do ye want to get drunk, Shana?"

Did she? Then she could forget about the terrible adventure in which she'd found herself caught. When she'd set out from her village south of the Moray Firth, she'd been so excited to help her sister with the birth and early months of her first child. Shana had practiced midwifery for years and was happy to help Ivy with this frightening task of bringing life into the world.

When Shana didn't answer, Bàs walked over to a corked clay vessel and poured some pale amber liquid into a small cup. "In case ye decide that ye wish to get drunk. 'Tis smooth so it shouldn't make your head ache any more than the cut and lump ye already have."

His northern accent remained steady, giving away nothing of his emotions or thoughts. It made her want to look inside his mind at what he was thinking. He turned the spitted chicken and shook the vegetables in the pan.

Shana picked up the whisky and took a little sip. It was smooth, but it still made her cough.

"'Tis still strong," he said.

"I took just a sip." She set the cup down with a *clunk*. "No need to worry I'll get fuddled and…try to ride your wolf like a horse."

His mouth turned up into a true smile, lifting some of the darkness from his face. With it, he looked younger and roguishly handsome. "Poor Beò wouldn't know what to do."

He'd probably eat her, that's what he'd do. She glanced at the door. "The wolves that were under the tree, the ones he saved me from... Do they prowl these woods?"

Bàs stood, crossing his arms over his broad chest, his legs braced apart in a way that made him look like nothing could topple him. "At times. Usually, the packs stay outside Beò's territory, which runs to the river ye forded. This time of year, they are full of rabbits, deer, and squirrels. But aye, ye need to be wary."

She frowned. "Edward and I are fortunate then."

"'Tis best to carry a weapon if ye head into the woods. Do ye know how to shoot an arrow or throw a dagger?"

"I practiced with arrows as a girl."

He tipped his head to a set of arrows in the corner. "My sister has a smaller set. I'll send another note when my hawk returns, asking her to bring it for ye to practice with."

"You have a bird that takes letters to her?" Shana perched on the edge of the small bed.

"Aye. Hannah will come in the morn." Hannah, who knew how to feed human babes, someone who could take care of Edward.

"You are sure she will come?"

"Aye. She's always ready to help when called upon." He looked back at the hearth. "Can ye turn the chicken every once in a while and tend to the vegetables?" he asked. "I need to settle the animals for the night."

She nodded and watched him walk across the room and out the door. He whistled outside, and Shana hurried to one of two glassed windows where she watched the dogs and wolf trot behind him toward the barn. The man moved more like the wolf than the playful dogs.

Bàs Sinclair was full of deadly grace. He was beautiful in a wild way. His muscles, long bones, and sinew worked together in perfect motion. And he was honorable, saving them both without any insinuation about payment. Edward would be safe here under the man's protection and his sister's care.

He disappeared into the barn, and her gaze shifted to the deepening shadows beyond the bramble that surrounded the yard. Out there were wolves, the kind who ate you whether you had a name or not. And that was where she must go.

• • •

The smell of fire-roasted chicken lingered in the air as Bàs finished his portion. Shana ate heartily despite watching the dogs who patiently lay near the door.

"Your wolf stays outdoors?" the lass asked.

"He went to hunt on his own," Bàs said.

"Oh."

"He'll return to sleep. Upstairs with me."

She glanced toward the stairs and nodded. "The wolf had bites on him? From the wolf pack?"

"Aye, but I washed and put salve on them."

She glanced overhead. "The squirrel has a bite mark, too."

"Betty?"

She looked back at him. "The squirrel is Betty?"

He shrugged. "She needed a name."

"Of course," Shana said. "Well, Betty has a bite that needs to be washed and treated before it festers."

Damn Banshee must have bit down hard enough to pierce the little beast's skin. Bàs sighed. "Have ye ever tried to catch and treat a squirrel?"

"No." Her nicely arched brows pinched together.

He hadn't yet seen her eyes in daylight and wondered what color they were. "'Tis not an easy thing to do," he said. "Catching her will be nearly impossible."

"You have snares set in the woods, don't you?" she asked.

"I suppose I could set one in here, but then we'll have to hold her without her biting the bloody hell out of us."

Shana grinned, and the softness it brought to her features was startling. "Are you afraid of a squirrel?" she asked.

"Aye. And if ye've looked closely at their teeth, ye would be, too."

She laughed then, making his hand pause halfway to his mouth with his cup of ale. The sound was almost musical. "Brawny, powerful, brave Highlander afraid of some little teeth," she said.

Her words warmed him. He set his cup back down with a *clank*. "Big teeth, able to crack acorns," he said, showing his own set. He stood to retrieve some chicken for Apollo and Artemis. "But I'll help ye, and when you're shredded by those *little* teeth, I'll stitch ye back together."

"You said you had ointment already made. And we will need clean water and rags. Maybe we can get some honey to rub on it."

"She'll bite off the rags and lick the honey."

"Well, we have to try," Shana countered.

He agreed but treating the one cat bite would probably create a lot of squirrel bites to then tend.

Bàs fed the dogs and locked them out of the house, closing the critter door so Betty couldn't escape and the dogs couldn't run in to cause more havoc. The bairn continued to sleep, and Bàs set up a snare that would hopefully catch Betty's leg or tail.

"Now to wait," he said, adding a block of peat to the fire.

"Maybe we should go outdoors," Shana whispered. "So she'll feel free to roam." She moved her slender fingers in a circle to indicate the room.

Bàs nodded and glanced up at the rafters where Betty was running along in a sporadic race back and forth.

The night was cool after the heat of the August sun, and a breeze rustled the leaves surrounding his cabin. There was enough moonlight that they didn't need a lantern. "We should stay close," he said as Shana followed him onto the porch.

"So we don't get attacked by wolves," she said, peering into the darkness beyond.

"So we can hear if Betty starts flopping around when she's caught," he said. "And snapping those vicious teeth to gnaw her way out."

"I've never seen such a big man be afraid of such a small creature."

"Ye've never been bit by one of those small creatures, have ye?"

"No."

"Well then." He lifted an imaginary cup. "I raise my ale to ye surviving your first squirrel attack tonight." It was easy to banter with Shana. Although none other than Hannah and now his sisters-by-marriage had ever talked with him before, Shana was different. *Because she doesn't know who I am.* Once people knew he was Death, they turned away.

Bàs pointed to the swinging bench he'd hung from two chains at the end of the porch.

Shana sat at one end, and he took the other, both staring out at the darkness around the cabin. He touched his feet down, pushing to start the swing swaying back and forth. He didn't say anything. Once she knew he was the Horseman of Death, executioner of the damned, would she talk with him again? Would she hate him for his sins?

"You live out here all alone?" she asked.

"Hardly alone," Bàs said. "I live with the beasts. Dogs, cats, Beò, a coo and her calf, chickens, my hawk, a goat, and now a squirrel named Betty if she stays."

"That sounds lonely to me." He didn't answer. The swing squeaked softly on the chains, reminding him to oil the spots that rubbed.

"Why don't you live with your brothers?"

Bàs leaned back to stretch his shoulders. "I prefer to live out here with my animals." He watched Banshee and her mate trot out of the barn, probably going on a nocturnal hunt. "Animals are simple while men are not. In truth I would rather be a beast," he murmured. Then he wouldn't be having this conversation.

"But most animals are dangerous," she said, "and living alone could see you killed. Whether from an attack by a wolf or a vicious squirrel."

She jested, at least somewhat. But the question had been asked by his brothers and sister for so long that Bàs found it only annoying. He rested his hands on his thighs, focusing his attention away from the soft woman next to him, reminding himself that she would not stay for long.

"Man," he said without looking at her, "is the most dangerous animal of all. The most crafty and brutal." He let his feet rest on the porch so the swing stopped. "Men lie, and their main purpose is to kill. They squabble and war, sometimes for food but usually for vengeance, power, or gold."

Shana exhaled long. "You have a very sorrowful outlook on the world."

"When the world isn't so sorrowful, I will view it differently," he said, crossing his arms, his hands tucked in fists against opposite sides. "I have seen the darkness in the world: blood, pain, grime, and death. 'Tis sorrowful."

"I am a midwife," she said, and he noticed that she'd also crossed her arms. She stared out at the night. "I have seen the beauty of life coming into the world, and there is blood and pain and grime. But I guard against death."

"Ye guard against death?"

"Yes. I'm a midwife," she repeated. "I guard

against death. Every mother who puts the life of her child and herself into my hands… I guard them against the cruel specter who steals people from this world, causing such grief."

Bàs sniffed and looked off into the darkness, his chest tight with disappointment. "We are opposite then, in every way." She would hate him even more if she ever found out what he was.

Bang. Thump.

Their gazes snapped to the door for a second before they leaped up. Shana shoved the towel into Bàs's hands and ran for the door.

"I thought *ye* were going to tackle the beastie," he said as they rushed inside.

Betty was caught by the back foot. She thrashed about, terror on her face. Would it have been better for her to die of a tainted cat bite than suffer such fear?

"Get her," Shana called, dipping the rags into the heated water on the hearth.

"Calm down, vicious beastie," Bàs called and threw the towel over the squirrel. "I'm not going to hurt ye. I saved ye this past day." He caught her under the towel, pinning her to the floor. "Work the snare off her foot, too," he said.

"The bite is on the inside of her back leg, so you have to open the towel some," she said.

"Daingead," he murmured, trying to pin Betty's head and upper half without hurting her. She twisted while Shana slid the tight string off her foot.

"Don't let go," she said and pushed the towel up until the red welt of a puncture was visible on the squirrel's inner thigh. Shana washed it with warm water and a bit of soap.

"Hurry," he said as he felt Betty twisting out of his grip.

The bairn in the manger began to cry, and Shana glanced between him and the small package of ferocious revenge squirming under Bàs's hands. "Betty first," he said, his voice overriding the bairn's.

Shana poured a dash of whisky on the red sore and pressed a glob of yarrow mixed with honey over it. "Done," she yelled, yanking back her hand as Betty broke free.

Sharp incisors cut into Bàs's palm as he yanked back. But Betty was far from done. She hurled her little body at his chest, grabbing hold of his tunic as if he were a tree to climb, and ran up, leaping onto his shoulder and then head before jumping off to grab hold of the rafters.

"Bloody hell," Bàs said, staring down at the blood welling up from tooth holes.

"She bit you?" Shana asked, striding over to the bairn.

"Of course, she bloody bit me," he said. "I had her trapped under a towel."

Shana lifted the bairn, settling him against her shoulder. "At least we've done what we can for her bite. Cat bites are often fatal."

"How about squirrel bites?" Although, he'd been bitten before, trying to release squirrels that got into his snares when he didn't need them for food. He grabbed up the cloth, dunking it back into the warm water and washing his hand.

Hannah had shown him how to clean wounds so they were less likely to fester. His sister had taken care of him as a child, always hiding his illnesses or weaknesses from their father, who would have raged against Bàs for them. Bàs had learned quickly how to stay as healthy as he could to do his duty. Good food, daily training with heavy stones, running with Beò, little whisky. He did it all. The only part of Hannah's stay-healthy regimen that Bàs couldn't follow no matter how hard he tried was getting a good amount of peaceful sleep. He couldn't remember a night that he'd slept through when he wasn't ill from some fever.

Shana came over, still holding Edward. "I'll help."

Bàs backed up instinctively, preferring not to touch the wee bairn. If it died, he'd surely be blamed. "Ye have your hands full."

She walked away while Bàs rinsed the bite. She set the bairn in its manger and hurried back to Bàs's side. "At least you can wear a poultice without wiggling out of it." She lifted the pot of yarrow and honey. "Here," she said, setting the poultice back down. Her hands were small compared to his, but she cupped his hand, patting the wound dry.

Her fingertip slid over his skin, and he felt his blood rush faster. She touched around the wound. "She really bit down hard," she murmured as she squeezed each hole, making fresh blood come forth.

"When the enemy has ye pinned, a warrior must use every weapon he has," he said, watching her sponge off the fresh blood before dabbing on some honey. "Betty is a warrior."

"Our soldiers might do more damage in battle if they bit," she murmured, her face tipped down. The firelight tinted the waves of her hair even redder with strands of gold throughout.

Bàs inhaled the scent of the yarrow poultice, but also a sweet smell. "Rose?" he murmured.

She glanced up as she wrapped up a gauzy cloth with mashed yarrow in it. Their gazes met, and lightning splintered through Bàs, the thudding of his heart like thunder. "Just yarrow," she whispered.

"I smell rose as well."

Her gaze slipped downward. "'Tis my soap. I brought it from home. It has roses from my mother's garden mixed into it."

She looked back up, reconnecting, studying him. Were her eyes blue? Maybe green? His sister and Aunt Merida were the only women who didn't look away when he stared back. It felt...odd. It felt good.

"Where is home?" he asked. "Where ye make soap with roses from your mother's garden?"

She blinked, and he noticed how her eyelashes curled, but then looked back down at his hand. "It should heal without a problem if you keep it clean and reapply the poultice and honey twice a day for several days." For a long moment they just stared at each other, Shana still holding his hand, as if it were the most natural thing in the world.

The fire crackled loudly in the hearth, and she looked up at the rafters. Betty sat contorted, her toes spread wide at the end of the foot she held in the air while she licked the honey off her wound. Shana released his hand. "We should probably get a tincture into the squirrel in case she licks off all the ointment."

Bàs crossed his arms, the spell between them broken. "I'll let ye catch her for that."

Shana snorted. "I'll put it in a piece of food that she'll eat."

The fire snapped, the bairn whimpered, and Betty scratched up above. And all Bàs could smell now was roses.

CHAPTER THREE

"People whose professions revolved around death were people that the rest of society did not want to associate with. So executioners were typically consigned to the fringes of society—and even forced to literally live at the edge of town."

LIVE SCIENCE

Shana's eyes opened to darkness. *Where am I?*

She pushed up on an elbow, glancing around in the dark at the interior of a quaint cottage. She jerked in surprise as a little body leaped from the end of her bed, climbing quickly up the wooden walls. *Betty.* Shana glanced at the manger where Edward was sleeping. What had woken her?

Creak. Creak. She glanced up at the ceiling, which was the floor for Bàs's bedchamber. *Creak.* Someone or something was walking up there. Footsteps on the stairs kept her alert. They sounded like bare human feet, not wolf claws.

Bàs appeared at the bottom, his gaze going directly to her. "I woke ye?" he whispered.

"It could have been Edward or Betty," she whispered back, pointing above where the squirrel perched.

"Pardon," he said. "I'm going out on the porch. Ye should go back to sleep. 'Tis the middle of the night."

"And you?"

Bàs glanced at her from the open door. "I don't

sleep well." He stepped out, shutting the door.

Would he stay out there the rest of the night into the dawn so that she couldn't leave without him knowing? Shana needed him to sleep so she could sneak back to save her sister. In Ivy's weakened state, Shana must move quickly, but she didn't dare bring Edward. He must stay here with the caring warrior and his sister who could feed human bairns. Just until Shana could return with Ivy. If she told Bàs, he'd either stop her from going or want to go with her. And they couldn't leave Edward without care. No, she'd go alone.

Shana wore one of Bàs's large tunics while her dress dried over a chair by the fire. She padded over to the shelf where Bàs had taken down the dried yarrow. Clay jars sat in neat rows, and she began to sniff them. The quiet man had his own apothecary here in his cottage. Who would come to him out here for cures? His animals?

Bàs Sinclair was a mystery. Add the mystery to a handsome, honorable man, and no wonder Shana couldn't stop thinking about him or the feel of his strength under her touch.

She took an empty clay goblet and mixed some wine with valerian root, along with a dollop of honey to make it more palatable. She set the goblet in the coals to warm the drink. This could help him sleep well into morning.

Wrapping the quilt that he'd given her around herself, she took the goblet to the door, opening it. No wolves paced along the porch. Only a single, quiet man sat on the long swing at the end, his head tipped back.

"I brought this for you," she said, holding out the cup to him.

He leveled his face. "Thank ye." He took it but didn't drink. "Ye should go back to bed."

"I will." But she sat next to him on the swing. He was close to the center so that her leg brushed against his thigh. His chest was bare, his only covering being the plaid wrapped like a towel about his waist. If she weren't there, would he be sitting here naked?

"Do ye ever look at the stars?" he asked.

He hadn't moved over, and she didn't either, feeling the warmth of his body next to hers. "Yes."

He tipped his face up again, pushing the swing far enough out that the porch roof didn't block the sky. "Take a look."

Shana leaned back, resting along the wooden slats of the swing. A brilliant tapestry of stars lay scattered in patterns in the circle left open from the surrounding tree canopy. "They are like diamonds on a velvet black gown," she whispered. "Beautiful, rich, and not within my reach."

The stars glittered like a million sun drops on a windy lake. She picked out some of the familiar constellations but much of the sky was blocked by the swaying trees. When she tipped her face level again, her breath caught, because Bàs was staring at her. In the darkness, he seemed quietly untamed, like his beasts.

"I'm sorry I woke ye," he said. "I walk a bit at night."

She pointed at the goblet still in his hand. "The drink will help."

"I've tried many potions and drinks made for sleep, and they help but a little. But thank ye." He tipped the cup up, drinking it down without even asking what was in it.

She pulled his hand over. "Your poultice isn't staying in place." She untied the scrap of fabric around it, adjusted and retied it. "There."

His hand was heavy, but it was warm. The gentle strength in it that had held the squirrel without hurting her was evident. She stroked over the tied poultice, smoothing the wrinkles in the wrapping. He was so handsome and brave. She was drawn to him like he was a fire in the hearth on a chilling winter night. It had been a long time since she'd felt any sort of attraction toward a man. "Why don't you sleep?"

Bàs slowly pulled his hand from her, and she missed its weight. "My dreams are often dark. They've plagued me most of my life."

"Oh," she said. "I am sorry for that. Have you tried v—"

"'Tis the way things are," he said, and she frowned at the defeatist tone.

"Things can change," she said.

His gaze was in shadows, but it still held her there. "Thank ye for the drink." He set the empty goblet on the wooden porch and tipped his head back to look at the stars.

Shana needed to get him to sleep so she could sneak away at dawn, but right now she also just wanted to soothe him. This mighty man who'd saved her and Edward. He didn't sleep well. Why?

She swallowed and wet her lips, opening her

mouth to let the tune of the lullaby out.

"*Lavender's blue, dilly dilly,*
Lavender's green.
When you are king, dilly dilly,
I shall be queen."

It was a familiar song meant to soothe babes to sleep. Shana used the refrain to tie her own words together.

"*The night is dark, dilly dilly,*
The stars are bright.
Your eyes are heavy, dilly dilly,
Your thoughts are light."

Bàs turned his head to watch her sing, their gazes connecting with darkness wrapped around them like woven blankets. The words flowed out softly in perfect notes even though something tugged at her heart, threatening to steal her breath. His strong features drew her, his lips parted gently as if he might join her song. But he stayed silent, watching, listening.

"*Banish the shadows, dilly dilly,*
From your dark dreams."

Shana's hand rose to his face, pausing briefly before sliding her thumb across his cheek above his short beard.

"*Rest in the promise, dilly dilly,*
That you are seen."

She leaned in the slightest bit, but they were suddenly together, their lips mere inches apart, as if the breezes or shadows had pressed them closer. It had been so long since she'd been this close to a man, one who made her heart flip about and the heat rush through her blood.

Her lips remained open on the last note, and her eyes closed as she felt his warm mouth brush against hers. The kiss was gentle and strong and ignited the heat within her into a fire. But suddenly he pulled back, and her eyes fluttered open.

Black eyes glittered from the darkness, the shadows cutting lines across his hard face. Her breath caught in her throat as he met her gaze. "Lass, I don't want to be seen." He stood and walked into the cottage, leaving her alone on the swing in the night breeze.

• • •

Lavender's blue, dilly dilly, lavender's green. When you are king, dilly dilly, I shall be queen.

Bàs woke to the smell of yarrow and the refrain of the lullaby in his ears. Light was streaming into his bedchamber window, and the room was empty. He inhaled and realized his cheek had been resting on his injured hand, where Shana had secured the poultice with her strong but delicate fingers. *Shana.* He could still feel the touch of her lips across his.

He'd stolen the kiss, the notes of her song wrapping around him, pulling him in, breaking the bonds he kept on himself. Her song was like a siren's spell that was broken only when he realized the words. The words reminded him that he'd never tell her who he truly was. They were as opposite as the bluebells that grew in his gardens and the skull that had been thrust into his hands.

Bàs inhaled fully and blinked at the light. Since when had he ever slept past the break of dawn?

Maybe her song truly was a spell. Beò, Artemis, and Apollo were already up and out of his room. Had Shana let them out? He threw his legs over the side of the bed and found a clean tunic. Betty's bite didn't ache so much, so his plaid was easy to wrap around his hips, and he belted it in place.

What should he say to Shana when he saw her this morn? Should he apologize? For kissing her? For leaving her there alone on the swing in the dark? One simple press of the lips was becoming very complicated, very quickly. He snorted. 'Twas his first kiss ever. Simple or not, he'd always remember it.

He carried his boots down the stairs into the quiet room and glanced around at the emptiness. "Shana?" he called. The petticoats, smock, and stays she'd hung to dry were gone.

Betty chattered from up high as if explaining all she'd seen that morn. If only he understood squirrel chatter.

Hiccup.

Bàs spun on his stockinged heel toward the sound.

Hiccup.

It came from the manger. Setting his boots down, he walked over as quietly as if he were sneaking up on a dangerous animal. The bairn, Edward, was awake and stared up at him with wide blue eyes. Little bubbles formed on his lips.

Hiccup.

"I will find your aunt," Bàs said and walked to the door, swinging it open. "Shana," he called. The bairn required Shana and would save him from the awkwardness of having nothing to talk about except the kiss. Should he admit it was his first? Joshua, who seemed to know all about lasses, would probably say nay because it would set her to wondering why he'd never been kissed before.

Several birds flitted between the trees, and Bruce, his hawk, sat on the porch swing. Bàs had meant to send a second message about the bow and arrows, but Hannah would be here soon from the brightness of the sun. "Shana," he called louder, but no one answered.

Beò trotted over with Apollo and Artemis following.

"Where's the lass?" Bàs asked them. The dogs wagged their tails. Beò seemed to contemplate his question but remained mute as always. "Daingead," he murmured. Could she have been taken by whomever had sent her fleeing? With the wolf and dogs here, no one could have gotten close without Bàs hearing. He looked out at the nearly invisible lines he had set in the brambles that ran to bells in his cottage. They weren't cut or pulled.

Bàs ran to his stables, ignoring the rocks jabbing into the bottoms of his feet. Dòchas stood patiently in his stall, probably wondering why it was past dawn and he still hadn't been fed. No Shana. After a quick circuit of the surrounding bushes, he ran back inside the cabin to brush off his feet and jam them into boots.

Edward fussed in his manger, and when Bàs peeked at him he saw the bairn had spit up white milk. Bàs grimaced. "Bloody hell." He ran to grab a cloth on the table. There was a slip of paper from the small stack he kept for writing notes for Bruce to carry to Girnigoe Castle. He snatched up the note and the rag, running back to dab at the bairn's mouth.

Hiccup. More poured out. "Good God," Bàs said, wiping faster at the curdled foam, turning the cloth around so he wouldn't just spread it over the bairn's face. He tipped Edward gently on his side, careful not to touch his skin. Could bairns choke on their own vomit like men when they'd drunk too much?

The bairn rolled completely, smashing his little face into the blanket over the hay. He wiggled around with his hands caught in the swaddling cloths, his cry muffled. "Bloody… What do…? What the hell do I…? God help me," Bàs said, his half sentences popping out loudly, causing Edward to cry out, his lips pressed into the blanket. Could bairns smother themselves with their faces turned down? "Ye *want* to die, don't ye?" Bàs asked, accusation heavy in his voice.

Edward answered with another *hiccup*, and Bàs tipped him back with the rag. There was white vomit on the blanket and hay stuck to the bairn's wet cheek. "Shite," Bàs said and ran to get a clean rag. When he leaned into the manger to wipe more vomit off the bairn's face, he got a strong whiff of the very thing he'd just murmured aloud. "Shite," he said again.

Turning, he looked up at Betty perched above, her tail flicking this way and that like the sporadic beat of a drum. "Where's the lass?"

Bàs stepped back, looking at the ground where he'd dropped the paper from the table when Edward decided it was time to empty his wee body at both ends. The bairn cried in the background while hic-cupping, Betty chattered above, and the dogs ran in through their door. But all Bàs could do was focus on the words that struck terror through him.

Watch Edward. Don't let anyone take him. I will be back. I trust you. Shana

• • •

"She left her bairn?" Hannah asked, her eyes wide and her mouth twisted with judgment.

Bàs rubbed the side of his jaw. "Edward is not her bairn. He's her nephew."

"But still," Gideon said, "the bairn was put in her care by the mother. And she left it in the hands of quite literally death." Bàs's brother paced the interior of Bàs's cabin. He hadn't been inside since he helped Bàs build it several years ago. No one ever came there, and he never invited anyone.

Hannah cast a frown toward Gideon.

"I didn't tell her who I was," Bàs murmured. "And I'm not convinced she abandoned him." Bàs looked at the bundle in Hannah's arms. She held the pap bottle easily so that Edward could suck down the meal she'd cooked up of crushed oats and chicken broth. "Shana said she'd be back for him."

Could his kiss have scared her away? Bàs scrubbed his hands down his face. He wouldn't tell Gideon and Hannah about the kiss. If it got back to Joshua, Bàs would never hear the end of how he made a girl risk wolves to escape his kisses.

"The note didn't say when she'd return," Hannah pointed out.

Hannah and Gideon had read the note when they'd arrived to find Bàs trying to wash the foulness off the bairn while he still lay in the manger. Thankfully, Hannah had swooped in to soothe the poor thing, wash him, and wrap him in fresh swaddling blankets. Bàs had emptied the soiled hay from the manger and fetched some fresh from the barn.

"Only that she trusts ye to watch the bairn," Gideon said, shaking his head. "Did she not see that ye dislike bairns even if ye didn't kill the wee thing with a touch?"

"He doesn't kill bairns with a touch," Hannah said, her words like sharp daggers thrown at Gideon.

"Well, Bàs thinks he does," Gideon retorted.

"I don't necessarily…" Bàs's voice trailed off. "'Tis just…safer if I don't touch fragile things."

"Nonsense," Hannah said, smiling down at Edward. "You saved him and his aunt from wolves, and bairns are not that fragile." She set the pap bottle down and lifted Edward over her shoulder. "You need to remember to pat his back after feedings to release the bubbles in his belly. Otherwise, he will spit it back up."

"*I* need to remember?" Bàs asked, panic tightening his gut. "I'm not going to feed him or hold him. Death is part of me." He shook his head. "My touch could kill him."

Gideon placed his hand on Bàs's shoulder. "I don't believe that, brother. We're not the horsemen Father taught us to be."

Bàs looked at Gideon, the third oldest of the four brothers, the one raised to judge and proclaim justice as the Third Horseman of the Apocalypse.

"Weren't ye telling me at Christmastide that we are the horsemen and must remain the horsemen to keep Clan Sinclair strong? That we must perform the duties assigned to us?"

"And I've since realized that…" Gideon moved his bottom jaw back and forth as if it ached. "That I may have been incorrect about my statements before."

Bàs held up his hand where the gold ring encircled his finger, proclaiming him God's Horseman of Death. "'Tis even etched in gold."

Gideon hadn't put his Horseman of Justice ring back on since taking it off when he turned his back on the law to save the woman he loved. Even though he was the one to commission the rich gifts for each brother and Hannah.

"That merely proclaims you as the horseman," Hannah said, "in battle. You cannot make this bairn or any bairn or person die by touching them. No one has that much power."

Bàs wouldn't bring up the awfulness of his youth, the times he'd been blamed for someone dying. That he'd looked at them or touched them leaving chapel or somehow breathed death and disease on them. Then there was that one summer when their second aunt came to visit with her children. How disease took most of them away from the living after playing with Bàs. Even if she refused to say it, Hannah must remember how George Sinclair had boasted about the deadly touch of his youngest son.

Up above, Betty chattered as if arguing with him, too.

"New beastie?" Gideon asked.

"Her name is Betty," Bàs said. "Banshee bit her, and I saved her."

Gideon smirked. "So we won't be seeing a squirrel pelt hanging from your belt, since it has a name."

"How many animals do you have now?" Hannah asked, lowering Edward onto the clean blanket placed on the fresh hay in the manger.

"A few," Bàs said. Beò ran off whenever he sensed people, except Shana. If he counted all of them, including the egg-laying chickens, at present he had fourteen animals.

Gideon leaned over the manger to stroke Edward's cheek. His brother would be having his own bairn soon with Cait, his wife, due this fall. "I think ye like beasts more than ye like men and women."

"I do," Bàs answered.

Hannah made a little noise of annoyance, and he turned to his dear sister. "Except for ye, Hannah, but my brothers rank below my chickens."

"The ones ye name or the ones ye eat?" Gideon asked, a smirk on his face.

"The ones I name," Bàs said. "Which is a good thing for ye." Bàs's jest fell flat with the worry in his voice.

Gideon crossed his arms, his smile fading, as he walked back to look out the door into the yard. "We could track her."

"I'll determine her direction," Bàs said, "but I'd like to give her a chance to return on her own. Prove that she wasn't abandoning the bairn."

Gideon nodded. "Give it three days, and then we go after her."

"I cannot watch the bairn for three days on my own," Bàs said, looking to Hannah. "It will surely die."

Hannah glanced up at Betty. "If you can take care of an injured squirrel and nurse wild animals, you could take care of a single human bairn."

Bàs shook his head. "Nay, I won't. I can't. Ye need to take him to Girnigoe."

Hannah exhaled, knowing he spoke the truth. He'd kill Edward in three days. "I'll take him," she said, "*not* because I believe you can't keep him healthy and happy, Bàs, but because he will be all mine for a few days." She smiled, bending over the bairn.

He bent forward in relief, resting his hands on his knees. "Thank ye."

Hannah began to gather the bairn's pap bottle and extra blanket and looked to Bàs. "Come home in three days, with or without the aunt, and we'll decide what to do then."

Could he wait three days? If she left a note, she wasn't carried off. But Bàs couldn't free the feeling of danger from his bones. *Shana, where did ye go, lass?*

CHAPTER FOUR

"I heard say the executioner was very good,
and I have a little neck."
ANNE BOLEYN, MAY 1536,
THE MORNING BEFORE HER EXECUTION

"Edward was doing quite well on the pap," Hannah said, "but Viola Finley, who is running the Orphans' Home, is also nursing him along with her bairn, Henry."

"That's generous of her," Bàs said as he paced before the hearth in Girnigoe Castle's Great Hall. It had been two days since Shana had disappeared, and Bàs wasn't planning to wait another. He'd tracked her to the river she'd forded before, and it looked like Beò and the dogs had accompanied her that far, but she'd continued heading south. Could she be from the Sutherland or Ross Clans?

"Viola keeps Edward only to feed him, but I take him the rest of the time," Hannah said. She glanced to where their brothers Cain and Joshua stood near the table. She walked past Bàs, squeezing his arm. "I think Cain has another job for you while we wait."

Ella, Cain's wife, came into the hall, holding her daughter, Mary. The bairn was growing fast. Cain had proclaimed proudly how she'd taken her first steps, sending a rider to tell Bàs. Ella had stepped in a day later to rescue her wee lass off the back of a pony when Cain tried to give her a first riding lesson.

"Ella," Bàs said, striding over. The little girl reached for him, and he instinctively stepped back. "Morning, Mary," he said, nodding to the blond-haired cherub. His gaze snapped back to Cain's lovely wife, who'd been the leader of the Sutherland Clan before handing off the duty to her young brother.

"She doesn't bite," Ella said, shifting the girl to her other hip.

"Aye, she does," Joshua said from the table.

"Only when her uncle is stealing her poppet," Ella called back.

Joshua pointed toward the little girl, his brows high. "She's a fighter, that one, and her Uncle Joshua is going to teach her to be fierce."

Ella rolled her eyes and looked back to Bàs. "What is it?"

Bàs ran a hand up his forehead. "Could ye send word to Kenneth at Dunrobin Castle about the bairn's aunt being missing? Her tracks show her headed south."

"I already have," Ella said, and her sorrowful look told him the answer before she spoke. "And he hasn't heard of a midwife named Shana helping her sister give birth. He's asking outside the village now."

"I've sent word to Alexander Ross at Balna-gowan Castle," Cain said, walking over with a missive in his hand. "But he's not very responsive."

"He's still being an arse after we stole back our ten head of sheep he raided," Joshua said.

"She could be the sister of someone living apart from a village," Hannah said, taking Mary from

Ella's arm to snuggle. The wee girl giggled and threw her arms around Hannah's neck as she kissed all over her plump cheeks.

Bàs's gut remained tight. "I truly believe she'd have come back unless something or someone is stopping her. She risked her life to get the bairn to safety." He shook his head. "She wouldn't abandon him."

"We will send out scouts," Cain said. "Ye can join them, but first I have a job for ye." He held up the missive. "Gideon would like us to honor the request of the Oliphant chief. Apparently, there's been a child murdered, and he requests an executioner with the backing of God to see the punishment through."

Cain handed him the letter that gave only brief details of a newborn being smothered. The thought of the helpless creature fighting its way into the world only to be snuffed out immediately made Bàs's hands fist. Bairns were innocent like animals. Smothering a newborn was murder at its worst.

"Gideon's trying to lure the Oliphants into becoming an ally in case King James decides to listen to his uncle's lies about us up in Orkney," Joshua said, crossing his arms, his face fierce.

"Aye," Bàs said. "I can go from here."

"You brought your mask?" Hannah asked from her crouched position where she held Mary's little hands so the wee one could practice walking.

Bàs watched the lass wobble but catch herself. "My ax, sword, and mask are always with me," he said, his voice rough.

"Which is probably why ye sleep alone," Joshua said, making a comical face that was a mix of pity and laughter. Bàs's second-oldest brother had made the rounds before settling down with his wife, the queen of an Orkney tribe descended from Norse royalty. And now he was determined to find a woman for his youngest brother.

"I don't sleep alone," Bàs grumbled.

"Dogs don't count," Joshua said.

Bàs turned on his heel, irritation and worry over Shana mixing to spur his temper. "The letter says as soon as possible, so I'll go now," he said, glancing back at Joshua. "I have the need to kill someone."

Joshua laughed. "Father would be proud."

Cain threw his fist out, knocking into Joshua's arm. "Hold your tongue."

Normally Joshua's teasing didn't bother Bàs overly, but today his brother's words burrowed down through his core. A fast ride on Dòchas and the execution of a murderer of bairns was just the thing to soothe Bàs's temper so he wouldn't punch Joshua.

Dòchas surged under Bàs's legs, the two of them working as one to fly across the land. The stain from grasses that Bàs rubbed onto Dòchas's golden coat gave him a green tint. He hadn't had time to wash it off from the last death he delivered. With his polished ax in hand, all he had to do was pull on the skull mask to complete the look of surging death.

Even if he and his brothers were not actually God's Horsemen as written in Revelations, they certainly played the part. Sometimes the impression of them leading their four armies of white, bay, black, and pale green horses made the enemy back down without a single blow. One could justify that George Sinclair's insistence that his boys were the

Four Horsemen of the Apocalypse, and the efforts they employed to keep up the ruse, saved lives.

Bàs played his part like he had since the day his father started teaching him how to frighten people with silence, an intimidating stare, and his skull mask. Not to mention the incredibly sharp and swift ax and sword Bàs could unleash without hesitation. Judging someone guilty was the task for his third-oldest brother, Gideon, as the Horseman of Justice. Bàs's purpose was to follow orders and bring death.

Although he'd never shirked his duty, some kills were easier than others, like when a man smothered a newborn bairn. Bàs leaned over Dòchas's neck and let the wind wash away his worry over Shana. If he didn't see her again… Well, it didn't matter, really. They were too far apart in their duties and philosophies to ever grow close.

He snorted. Grow close? It was a ridiculous hope that he would ever grow close to someone. Aye, Shana had kissed him, but she hadn't known what or who he was then. Bàs imagined fear tightening her lovely features, fear and horror over what he was, and as if sealing a tomb, he pushed the thought of Shana down in the pit of his stomach.

The miles disappeared under the fleet horse's hooves, and Bàs arrived on the outskirts of Wick Village, south of Girnigoe and Sinclair lands along the coast. His father had wanted to take over the Oliphant lands but hadn't gotten around to conquering the clan before he was killed in battle with the Sutherlands.

Bàs slowed Dòchas to a walk to pull off his tunic. The tattoos of the horse on his arms and the ax on

his back marked him as the Horseman of Death. He
reached around to find his skull mask that tied to a
special hook built into his saddle and put it on. The
hard bone of the enemy's skull pressed under his
cheekbones, the woven cording holding it flat up his
forehead and over his head. He'd chiseled away as
much bone as he could inside as a child, and Hannah
had added leather so it would fit snug when he was a
lad. Since he'd grown, he'd removed the leather,
which left the bony ridges hard. The discomfort was
familiar now, as familiar as the feel of his blade cutting through a criminal's neck.

"Time to do our duty, friend," he said, patting the
horse's neck.

Bàs walked Dòchas toward the first thatched cottage of Wick. A young lad was playing in a puddle
outside the open door when he spotted Bàs. He
froze, standing with one leg raised to make a splash.
"Mama!" he yelled and tore into the house, the door
slamming.

Bàs ignored the child's fear and rode along the
path as it wound into the center of Wick. After the
execution, he'd ask the chief to question his clan
about a midwife helping a sister give birth.

All along the road, people peered from behind
shutters, curtains, and doors as he passed. The sound
of a child crying in fear tugged at his heart. He welcomed the tightness because it proved his heart was
still human and not turned to stone like the rocks he
placed in his garden.

Bàs stopped in the center of town. Several groups
of men had gathered, silently waiting. Bàs, skull
mask in place over the top half of his face, hefted his

ax in the air with two hands spread along the handle. "The Sinclair Horseman of Death is here to send a murderer of a bairn to stand in judgment before God. Bring forth the villain."

He lowered his arms and watched a man run toward Old Wick Castle east of the town, right on the sea cliffs like Girnigoe. If Chief Oliphant had the murderer in chains, it shouldn't take too long to bring him to the raised platform, which they'd already erected. Bàs turned Dòchas in a tight circle and watched the growing crowd. Most were silent and thankfully none were children, who should not be witnessing the bloody mess of a beheading.

The wind blew the leaves. Otherwise, all was silent. Not even the birds sang in the heaviness. Several women came out of their cottages to stand beside their husbands, but no one approached Bàs. He wouldn't have spoken to them anyway, even though the skull mask left his jaw free. His only purpose was to send the criminal to stand before God. Speaking would make him seem more human, so his father had discouraged it.

Bàs heard the crunching footfalls before the runner rounded the curve in the road. He stopped several yards away and looked to Bàs, breathing hard. "The chief and his guards are bringing the condemned." He gave a quick bow to Bàs. "I can hold your"—he swallowed hard—"mount while ye do your duty, milord."

Bàs dismounted, thudding to the ground where he snatched up a gray rock in his fist. Tucking it into his sash, he straightened to his full six-foot four-inch height. A small gasp rose when he raised his ax overhead, which made his large muscles bulge in case anyone thought he hadn't the strength to dispatch the villain. With measured steps he climbed the stairs onto the platform, propped his ax against his tall, laced boot, and crossed his arms to wait. He'd put the rock down before he swung. There was usually a splatter of blood, but if not, he'd still take the rock back to his garden.

The few children who arrived were shooed away, but he saw several of them peeking from behind houses. He recognized a warrior or two whom he'd met at festivals in the competitions. The Oliphant warriors were proud and worthy, another reason Gideon wanted them to form an alliance with the Sinclairs.

The crunch of boots came closer, but Bàs stared straight ahead. He didn't need to see the condemned man's face. Even the guilty showed up in Bàs's dreams to torture him. Remembering the faces made the nightmares more real.

The chief of the Oliphants stopped next to him. "Horseman of Death?" he asked, his voice carrying. Bàs gave one slow nod, and the stocky, bearded man continued. "You will send this woman to Hell today for killing my son and my wife."

A woman? Bàs's heart began to thump harder. He'd killed women before, but they were much fewer and not prone to killing bairns. Was she mad? Had she been properly questioned by a neutral party? Had she confessed?

Before he could stop himself, Bàs turned his face to the condemned being dragged up the steps. And he knew in that moment, her face would haunt his nightmares forever.

Shana. Her eyes were swollen. *Green*. They were green in the light of day. Her lip was swollen, too, and her golden red hair was wild about her beautiful oval face covered in brown freckles. "The babe died in childbirth," she called out, her voice cracking. "And you…" She glared at the chief. "And you will go to Hell for killing my sister."

• • •

Shana yanked her hand from the brutal hold of the guard, but she knew her chances of escape were gone. With the heavy sorrow of being told by Erskine Oliphant, her sister's cruel husband, that Ivy was dead, Shana had barely enough energy to walk to her execution. Only the woman who'd attended Ivy's birthing, Janet Bell, was permitted to stand by Shana as any type of comfort. And now that Shana was there, staring into the bony skull face of death, her knees buckled.

Death reached out as she fell to the platform, catching her arm in a steadying grip and helping her rise. Janet hurried up the steps to stand next to her. As Shana looked up at the skull before her, her breath caught. She stared into the bony eye sockets where human eyes stared back. "I did not do this crime," she said. "Search my eyes for the truth."

Erskine spoke behind her as she continued to stare into the skull's dark hollows, meeting the executioner's gaze. "I have caught the midwife responsible for my son's death. Her negligence also killed my dearest Ivy. Implements of witchcraft have been found in her belongings."

Several gasps came from the crowd at Erskine's lies, and she swallowed past the lump in her swollen throat. No one would believe her, and there wasn't time to form a plan.

Shana had survived the trip back, running directly to Liam Ross's apothecary shop. She'd sought to tell him that his son lived and to get his help in freeing Ivy from Erskine Oliphant's grip. Instead of the chemist letting her into his shop, Oliphant guards opened the door. Liam had vanished from town, and the guards easily overpowered Shana, dragging her to the castle to stand in judgment before Erskine.

Shana hadn't even been able to explain her side. "Where is my son?" was all Erskine had demanded. And she'd refused to tell him that the babe was safe at the border of MacKay and Sinclair lands with Bàs, the gentle warrior who loved animals and his sister who must now protect Edward.

Shana rubbed her face, grimacing at the bruise she felt on her jaw where Erskine had hit her. Soon all her pain would be gone, but little Edward would have no family. "Lies!" she yelled out to the crowd. "This man killed Ivy, his wife, after his son died during childbirth. He wanted a son so badly he took his fury at God out on my sister in her weakened state. Erskine Oliphant is the one who should be executed today."

"Shut your mouth, woman!" Erskine shouted and raised his fist for another strike.

Shana squeezed her eyes shut, waiting for the punch that might blessedly knock her unconscious so she wouldn't be aware when the ax cleaved through her neck. She heard Janet gasp.

"Bloody hell, let go," Erskine said, and Shana opened her eyes.

The huge executioner held Erskine's fist in his hand, forcing it down by his side. "Ye will not hit the woman," Death said, his voice quiet and even. The accent was thick, and Shana looked at his build. Large biceps and thick calves, he was a deadly warrior through and through. His voice was familiar, and her heart picked up speed. *No, he can't be.*

"I will do whatever I want to her!" Erskine yelled. "She killed my son and wife."

"Who judged her guilty?" Death asked, and Shana's eyes widened as she stared at him.

"I did!" Erskine said. "And ye are Death, not a judge but an executioner." He snapped his fingers, and the large guard grabbed Shana out of the executioner's grip. The guard shoved her toward the tree stump that was set up to serve as a block, and Janet hurried after her to put a prayer book in her hands.

"May God keep ye," Janet said, her eyes wide, and stepped back so the guard could force Shana to kneel before the block.

The wood felt hard and bruising under her knees, and her heart thudded with panic. Shana's breath rushed in and out so fast that she saw stars. Holding the small prayer book between both hands, she rested her elbows on the stump. *Oh God, help me. I must help Edward. I must avenge Ivy. Please, God.*

"Has she made a confession?" Death asked.

Perhaps it was her panic that made him sound familiar. Was God blessing her with some hope to get her through this ordeal?

"She refused," Erskine said, another lie.

"Does she have the coin to pay the executioner?" Death asked. Executioners were expected to be paid by the victim to ensure a quick and relatively painless death.

"She has no coin," Erskine said, knowing that would mean she might be hacked to death by an insulted henchman.

"I will ask if she forgives me," Death said, his voice coming closer.

Shana leaned into the stump, thankful she'd been allowed to use the privy before being dragged from the castle or she'd surely be pissing herself. Not that it mattered. Once she was dead, everything would leak from her.

She gasped softly when she felt the breath of Death at her ear. Instead of a cold wind, it was warm. "I swear to ye, I will not harm ye, no matter what I say or do. I swear it, Shana."

Shana couldn't breathe as he moved away. She closed her eyes, her body trembling. With a forced inhale, she said, "I forgive you, executioner." A mumble of the people rose and fell before her.

"I am the Horseman of Death," the executioner called out, his loud and piercing voice startling her so much, she dropped the prayer book.

The guard shoved her body forward so that her neck sat directly over the block, her chin hanging over the edge as she held herself propped there. The raw wood scraped against her throat, and she swallowed hard.

The executioner continued to talk, his voice

booming like thunder over the gathered crowd. "God guides my ax, for I am his messenger." And then he began to recite the lines from the Bible in a way that sent all the hairs on Shana's body to stand on end.

"When the Lamb opened the fourth seal, I heard the voice of the fourth living creature say, 'Come!' I looked, and there before me was a pale horse! Its rider was named Death…"

The crowd was hushed, and Shana's heart flipped and pounded behind her ribs. Stars sparked behind her eyelids, and she fought to hold onto the executioner's whisper. *I will not harm you.*

"So, behold on this day, God's judgment," Death called out.

Shana squeezed her eyes shut, trying desperately to hold onto the memory of the gentle kiss that had warmed her, a memory full of hope that had kept her strong in Old Wick's dungeon. *I am sorry, Bàs.* She'd promised to return. Would he think she'd lied? Would he curse her?

She inhaled slowly, concentrating on the brush of his lips against hers in the night.

The Horseman's boot rapped on the wooden scaffold as he called, "God guide my ax!" The swing brought a breeze, making her curls tickle her face.

Whack!

CHAPTER FIVE

The executioner employed to behead the
sixty-seven-year-old Plantagenet heiress, Margaret
Pole, was "a wretched and blundering youth who
literally hacked her head and shoulders to pieces in
the most pitiful manner." It took him eleven swings
of his ax to finally behead her.

EUSTACE CHAPUYS, AMBASSADOR TO THE
HOLY ROMAN EMPEROR, 1541

Bàs stood still, his hands clasped around the handle
of his ax as it reverberated, embedded, next to the
stump where Shana clung. It had cleaved through
the hard oak board of the platform.

Shana let out a small yell, resting her head on the
stump, her shoulders moving with her fast breathing.
Bàs could see her shaking, and he hated it. He hated
everything about the fear and lies and everything
that made him who he was. But, right now, the
Horseman of Death must save her.

"Ye didn't hit her!" Erskine cried. "Swing again."

"I have never missed a neck in my entire life,"
Bàs said, his voice loud above the crowd. "'Tis the
guiding hand of God that saves this woman. God has
judged her innocent of these crimes and turned the
course of my blade."

A loud murmur rose within the courtyard, and
Bàs reached down to pull Shana up from kneeling. It
was a tribute to her courage that she hadn't swooned.

With his other hand he yanked the ax free of the platform.

"Then I will do the deed," Erskine said, pushing forward.

Bàs, skull mask still in place, spun toward the Oliphant chief while pulling Shana to him and raised his ax. "Another step closer, Erskine Oliphant, and we will see if God sends my blade straight through your heart." His words halted the man.

Bàs kept his gaze on Erskine but his voice carried over the village center. "If any harm comes to this woman, after God has deemed her innocent, I will slaughter the person who commits that crime." His ax swung out toward the crowd as he extended his muscle-strong arm. Several people stepped back as if they thought he would throw it at them. "And if any of ye allow this woman to come to harm, I will come to ye during the night while ye sleep and slice your heads from your shoulders."

Gasps came and several people ran from the scene. Erskine had the ballocks to stand indignant before him, his hate-filled gaze on Shana.

"Get out of my way," Bàs said. There were four armed guards standing between him and Dòchas. Would Erskine force him to slaughter on the stage before his people?

Erskine spoke with a lowered voice. "I have Ivy. If ye want to see her alive again, ye must return with me to the castle."

Shana's gaze snapped up to his. "She's alive?"

Erskine shrugged. "Maybe. She was when I put her down in the dungeon two days ago."

"Bring her out here," Bàs said.

"I will do no such thing," Erskine said. "And I have a guard ready to strike her through if I don't come back."

The man was probably lying, but Bàs felt the strength return to Shana at his words. Her renewed vigor came from hope that her sister still lived, and hope was often stronger than self-preservation.

"I need to tend her," Shana whispered. "She just gave birth and could be dying this minute." She pulled away from Bàs.

He could throw her over his shoulder and battle their way to his horse to ride her out of Wick, but she would never forgive him. There was already enough hatred piled on his soul that he didn't relish earning more.

Fury prickled up inside him. Fury at Erskine for nearly making him commit a mortal sin of killing an innocent. Fury at himself for everything he was created and trained to be. Fury at the situation in which he had found the lass only to lose her again. It pierced him with a thousand needles, making him itch to slash Erskine and all his loyal men.

"Your refusal brings war to your people," Bàs said, his words clear and full of warning. "War led by God's Four Horsemen."

"Ye and your brothers are as mortal as the rest of your clan," Erskine said.

"The MacKay, Sutherland, Flett, and Sinclair clans combined," Bàs bellowed. "We do not allow innocent women to be threatened, abused, or killed without retribution."

Dòchas's ears flicked at the volume of his voice. Bàs rarely yelled, and the tension was making the horse ready for battle. Bàs and Erskine stared at each other while Bàs tried to devise a plan that would carry Shana to safety, but no scenario seemed likely to succeed. It was true he was a fierce warrior and could take ten or more Oliphant warriors on and still walk away. But there were at least thirty armed men waiting to do Erskine's bidding, and Shana would be right in the middle.

"I'm not leaving without my sister," Shana said and walked across the platform toward the guards. The woman who'd dared climb onto the platform with Shana hurried after her. Shana's back was straight, her head held high in defiance even though she nearly tumbled down the steps, her hands grabbing hold of the one crude rail. He could see them shaking either from the near death or her mistreatment at Oliphant hands.

"I will kill anyone who harms her or her sister," Bàs said, his words so full of death that they sounded almost like a growl.

Shana didn't look back. Her hands clung to her skirts as she started to walk along the path leading to Old Wick Castle. "Take me to my sister, who is clearly still alive," she said loud enough for people to hear. "God did indeed save an innocent woman today." Two of Erskine's guards strode quickly to her sides.

Bàs slid his sword out to hold in his left hand while his ax became an extension of his right. "And ye, Erskine Oliphant," Bàs said, drawing the man's sneering gaze. "If any harm comes to that woman, ye will meet death in the most painful way possible." His gaze shifted from Erskine's belligerent face to his guards. "Same with any of ye." His teeth clenched, lips pulled back to match the upper jaw of the skull he wore. "Now get the fok out of my way."

Erskine made the safest choice to step aside, as did the two remaining guards. In an easy throw of his leg, that he'd practiced since he was the age of five, Bàs mounted Dòchas with his blades still out. With a clench of his knees, the horse leaped forward, spinning around to race north to bring war down on Erskine Oliphant.

War to save Shana.

• • •

Shana's chest hurt with the pure mortal terror of the execution reprieve. *It was Bàs Sinclair.* It was Bàs, the kind man who saved squirrels. The man who looked at stars and couldn't sleep. The man who'd kissed her so gently. *The Horseman of Death? He's a bloody executioner?* He was death, the very thing she avoided, battled, and hated with every ounce of her being, ever since she'd lost so much to it.

Would he have killed her if she hadn't met him the night before? Did he save her only because he knew that Edward was alive? She'd sang to him, held his hand. She'd bloody kissed him! *I kissed Death!*

Shana's mind spun with her pumping blood as the guards led her down a set of stone steps into darkness. Only a flicker of torchlight below marked the bottom.

"Ivy?" she called, but the word seemed swallowed up by the damp chill pressing in on her. She heard nothing but the occasional drip of water on stone. The smell of mold and wet waste made her choke. She held her breath as she hurried off the last step toward the bars locked in the stone ceiling and floor. "Ivy? Where are you?"

"Shana?" The voice was weak, but it was there.

A gust of relief came from Shana. "I'm here."

Ivy lay on a pallet on the floor of the cell. A single window above let in light and air, which was surrendering the heat from the day. She turned toward the guards. "Bring us blankets, water, and untainted food." They didn't move. "Now, or if you think the wrath of the Horseman of Death sounds vicious, wait until you see what I can do if she dies from lacking simple things." Hopefully the darkness hid the bruises Erskine had given her, reminding the guards that she hadn't strength enough to back up her warning.

The one guard murmured something in Gaelic and marched back the way they'd come. Shana shook the bars. "The key." The remaining guard grabbed it off the wall and went to the door. As soon as he unlocked it, she ran to Ivy, lowering down to the pallet where her sister lay. Ivy was pale, her eyes searching Shana's desperately with a question she could not ask. Shana leaned into her ear. "Edward lives and is safely away from here."

Ivy exhaled, her eyes flickering shut. "Thank you," she whispered, but it sounded too much like a farewell.

Shana pulled off her cloak, laying it around Ivy, covering her with her warmth. Brushing back her hair, Shana could feel the heat of a fever. Left in the dungeon, she would surely die, even with warmth, food, and drink. She needed clean warm water and herbals.

Behind Shana, the key clicked. She spun, almost expecting to see the specter of death creeping up to take Ivy away. But it was just the guards locking her in.

"Liam?" Ivy whispered.

Shana tucked her cloak around her sister. "I don't know where he is."

Ivy nodded, a grimace of pain or fear cutting across the once lovely features of her face. Shana found her hand in the folds of the cloak and squeezed it, but it felt lifeless. "Hold on a bit longer," Shana said. Although Shana wasn't sure if any help was coming.

Your refusal brings war to your people.

That's what Bàs had said. Did that mean he would return with an army of Sinclairs? Could the Horseman of Death bring them the chance for life? Could the man who'd kissed her so tenderly bring war down on hundreds of people? She closed her eyes, not knowing what to pray for.

• • •

Bàs and Dòchas tore across the two wooden drawbridges that led to the inner bailey of Girnigoe Castle. Bàs swooped down, landing on the ground before his horse had completely stopped, and ran to the doors.

The door banged against the wall as Bàs strode inside. All three of his brothers were present, along with Hannah, holding Edward, Aunt Merida, and Cain's wife, Ella.

Joshua pulled his sword. "What the bloody hell?"

"My God, Bàs!" Aunt Merida yelled, her palm flattening over her heart.

Gideon rose from the table where he had parchments laid before him.

"What's happened?" Cain asked.

Bàs met his oldest brother's gaze while his breath rushed in and out. "I've declared war on the Oliphant Clan."

Silence.

Bàs noticed several warriors from the bailey had followed him in. No one said anything for a long moment.

Joshua was the first to speak. "Ye can't do that." He looked at Gideon. "Can he do that?" He looked back at Bàs. "Ye can't do that."

"It depends," Gideon said.

Bàs looked to Hannah, who held the bairn against one shoulder. "I found Shana." Her eyes widened.

"The bairn's aunt?" Ella asked, going over to Edward.

"Aye." Bàs's gaze shifted between Cain and Gideon. "She didn't return because that bastard, Erskine Oliphant, is holding her. She was the one I was sent to execute this morn, judged guilty without a trial by the chief alone for the murder of his son and wife."

"That man's a stubborn fool who cares little for his people," Aunt Merida said, shaking her head.

"Chief Oliphant doesn't know his son is alive?"

Hannah asked.

Bàs cupped the back of his head. "Shana didn't tell him. She was willing to die over giving Edward up to Erskine. And at the end, Erskine admitted that her sister, Edward's mother, is still alive in the dungeon at Old Wick Castle. And yet he was having me execute Shana for the death of his wife and son."

Ella gasped softly. "Just having given birth. The new mother is in a dungeon."

"She could already be dead," Merida said, her face pinched with anger.

"Did ye execute the lass?" Joshua asked, crossing his arms.

"Of course not." Bàs dropped his hands. Joshua could be such an arse.

Everyone stared at Bàs. "Is that the first execution ye've ever refused to do?" Cain asked, his voice quiet.

Bàs's gaze slid to his chief and oldest brother. "Aye." Heat crept up his neck. If Cain was anything like their father, he would rage and strike against Bàs instead of the Oliphant Clan. But Cain was not George Sinclair.

Aunt Merida's hands came together as if in prayer as she glanced heavenward, her lips moving silently. Was she glad for his disobedience? She'd always argued against Bàs's father about Bàs's role in the clan. Beseeching her brother not to make Bàs into a detested executioner, shunned by everyone inside and outside their clan.

"Where is the lass now?" Gideon asked, his brows tight with thought. No doubt he was trying to understand the tangle Bàs had tossed in their laps.

"She ran to the castle instead of fleeing with me," Bàs said. "To save her sister if she can."

"Valiant," Joshua said. He unfolded his arm to point at Bàs. "And ye declared war."

"If they don't hand over Shana and her sister, Ivy, alive, then aye," Bàs said.

"Ye don't have that authority," Gideon said. "To speak for the clan and our allies."

"I will—" Bàs started but Gideon cut him off.

"But ye have every right to declare war against another as a man and to ask others to join your cause." Gideon nodded.

Behind Bàs, Keenan Sinclair, a warrior and friend, stepped forward. "I will join the Horseman of Death's war on Erskine Oliphant and any who support him."

"As do I," another said.

"And I," a third said.

Bàs nodded to them and met Keenan's gaze. The man had been a friend since childhood, one who never encouraged whispers behind Bàs's back.

"We ride with the pale green army in battle," Keenan said, "so we will ride again with Bàs Sinclair."

Bàs's clenched fists opened, his fingers stretching as if ready to grab his sword. Shana had a much better chance of coming out alive if it wasn't only him slashing his way into Old Wick. He'd always been surrounded by death. It consumed his life, but now he was very much consumed with trying to keep someone alive. This was completely new to him.

"I'm old, ornery, and seek vengeance against any abusing husband," Aunt Merida said, having dealt with one of her own. "Put me in the battle, and I'll cut Erskine down myself."

Gideon looked to Cain. "Looks like we'll be gaining another territory." Cain nodded, and Gideon gave Bàs a lopsided grin. "I will write up a declaration of war on Erskine Oliphant and his supporters for injustice against the common people." His hand went out to the parchment on the table. "And forget the contract for an alliance."

His third brother loved everything to be official on paper. Bàs didn't care. He just wanted to help the innocent woman he'd almost killed. The woman who'd given him his first and probably only kiss.

Would I have killed Shana? Would he have questioned the crime and judgment if he hadn't saved her the other night? The thought squeezed the breath from his lungs, and he shook it off. He could hate himself later, but right now he must act.

"How are we getting the aunt out of the castle?" Ella asked.

Cain frowned more than when he'd heard his brother had dragged his clan into a war. "We?" He shook his head. "Not *we*." He indicated his brothers by turning his finger around in a circle to encompass them. "The four of us will get the two women out of Old Wick."

"You need a woman," Ella said, "to get inside if you're going to do it with stealth. I can dress as a maid in the castle who is bringing food down for the prisoners."

"I can, too," Aunt Merida said.

Bàs's jaw dropped open, and a quick glance at his other brothers showed the same expression.

"Kára is probably a better warrior than me," Ella said, "but she's large with child, and Cait is not far behind her."

"I can help, too," Hannah said.

"No," Bàs said.

"Nay."

"Nay."

Followed by "bloody foking nay," from Joshua. Hannah frowned at them all.

"Wee Edward needs ye to look after him, Hannah," Aunt Merida said. "Ella and I will sneak in."

"Pardon, Merida," Ella said, "but I have quite a bit of combat training in case things go wrong. I don't want to worry about getting you out, too."

Cain looked like he'd half choked on a mouthful of old fish. "Ye are still nursing Mary."

"Hardly," Ella said. "She's eating more than nursing these days. And I'll only be gone the night." She looked eager. "I'll go get on my trousers."

"I must make a plan first," Cain said, chasing after her as she strode toward the steps, and the two of them disappeared above.

"Cain," Bàs called after him, but he didn't return. When the two of them disappeared together, often they didn't come back for a long time.

"They won't be tupping," Joshua said. "Cain's too worried that Ella will get her way, and Ella looks bloody determined to sneak single-handedly into Old Wick to get them out. The two will be cursing, not kissing."

Aunt Merida pointed at both Gideon and Joshua. "See what happens when a lass is tied to the house with a bairn after she's used to adventuring." She jabbed her gnarled finger at Joshua. "Kára is at your cottage with wee Adam and a belly full of another, while ye're here drinking ale with your brothers." She shook her head.

"And planning war," Joshua said, his eyes opening wide as he gestured with a snap of his arm toward Bàs.

"Mark my words," Merida said, "Kára will be out declaring war on someone after this next bairn is born just to get out of the house."

Bàs ignored them, staring at the corridor where Cain had charged after Ella. No matter what Cain decided, he was going to act tonight, before Shana died. Because the thought of that brave, beautiful woman lying pale and unmoving was too painful to consider.

• • •

Ivy slept. Shana had managed to get ale and bread into her, changed the cloths between her legs, washed her the best she could, and warmed her with the heat from her own body. They'd been left alone in the dark, cold dungeon after the drink, blankets, and food had been sent. Janet Bell, Ivy's friend, had retrieved the prayer book and sent it down as well, although there was hardly light enough to read it.

Luckily, Shana hadn't heard or seen any vermin sneaking around the shadows ready to bite. Did Bàs help rats, too? A squirrel was close to a rat, wasn't it? No, Betty had big, frightened eyes and a poofy tail, although she certainly could bite.

The executioner had no bandage around his hand. Would Bàs have taken it off not to look weak in anyway? Not to look human? She rubbed the back of her knuckle against her dry lips, remembering the kiss. She'd wanted more, much more. She dropped her face in her hands, tipping to her side to lie next to Ivy, falling into a fitful sleep.

She woke with a start, pushing up, her eyes going to the only source of light. She went to the window, breathing in the air that wasn't tainted with dampness, mold, and old birthing blood from her sister. It was close to dawn, the sky lightening to a dark blue. Was Bàs out there somewhere?

I swear to ye, I will not harm ye, no matter what I say or do. The eyes she'd seen in the holes of the skull were intense and full of emotion. It was the man who cared for dogs, cats, a goat and cows, a hawk, and injured squirrels. A man who wouldn't eat any animal who had a name. She closed her eyes, shaking her head slightly. How could a man who cared for the smallest of creatures be such a killer?

The squeak of a rusty hinge signaled that someone was at the top of the dungeon steps. She hurried to Ivy and lay on her side against her back as if she still slept. But light footsteps on the stairs made Shana turn, her gaze focused on the darkness. A thin, tall form wearing breeches appeared at the bars. Even though Shana couldn't see their features, the person moved like a woman. Shana sat up, watching her retrieve the key hanging on a hook across the room.

"Who are you?" Shana whispered.

"Ella Sutherland, Lady Sinclair of Girnigoe

Castle, and we need to get you and Ivy out of here."

"Sinclair?" Shana murmured. "Are you from Bàs?"

"He's my husband's brother."

"And they sent you?" Shana was trying to understand. "'Tis too dangerous. Erskine—"

"I'm not alone," Ella said, coming inside and straight to Ivy, "and I didn't give them the choice to leave me at home." The woman's voice held rebellion.

"'Tis almost dawn," Shana said, glancing at the window where the dark blue lightened. "They will see us escape."

The woman's beautiful face brightened with a slight smile. "That's the plan."

A sniffing sound came from the barred window, making Shana spin toward it to see a large canine head. "Beò?"

"You know Bàs's wolf?" Ella asked.

"He saved me once," Shana said, gently shaking Ivy.

"We didn't even know he had a wolf," Ella said, and bent over Ivy. "We will need to carry her out of here if she won't wake."

"Will no one stop us?" Shana asked, lifting her sister under one arm while Ella lifted under the other.

"Where are we going?" Ivy murmured. Her legs stiffened, trying to hold her weight.

"Somewhere safe and warm," Ella said.

"That sounds wonderful," Ivy answered, propelling her legs forward. Shana and Ella lifted Ivy one step at a time, climbing out of the dungeon. "Edward?" Ivy whispered.

"He's there, too," Ella said.

Ivy gave a little sob, her legs moving faster. They got to the top, and Ella halted them inside the door leading to the rest of Old Wick Castle. She maneuvered Ivy to stand to the side against the wall with Shana. "Now we wait," Ella said. "It won't be long."

Before Shana could ask for what they were waiting, a deep horn sounded somewhere outside. "Give it a moment," Ella said, her voice soft. Loud voices came from the other side of the door, and Shana's heart leaped in her chest. She clung to Ivy, holding her up as Ella let go. The door flew open, and Ella caught it before it could slam into Shana and Ivy.

As the guard ran through the opening, Ella ducked low, tripped him, and shut the door. In the darkness, Shana heard him grunt all the way down the stairs until he thumped at the bottom. He didn't make a sound after that.

Ella cracked the door. "'Tis clear," she whispered. "Come."

Shana felt Ivy steady herself, and Ella came back to her other arm. All three of them managed to slide out of the door without any guards running into them. "They should still be out," Ella said, peeking first into Old Wick's Great Hall. "Any others will have run outside." She and Shana helped Ivy walk out of the corridor, and Shana's inhale stuttered as she looked at several men lying back in their chairs. One was even laid out on the floor. "They're only sleeping," Ella said, and Shana wondered to what type of women Bàs's brothers were married.

They moved across the room past slumbering warriors and around the long tables, and Shana realized Ella was heading toward the kitchen at the back of the castle. That must have been how she got inside. A woman coming in to help with the morning meal would have been much less suspicious. Erskine would never expect a woman to breach his walls, since he thought all women dull and cowardly. He'd apparently never met Lady Sinclair.

Two of the kitchen maids stood against the wall near the hearth, their eyes wide with panic. Ella shook her head. "Come with me then, if he will blame you for the slumbering men." Both maids followed them out the back door into the kitchen gardens. The smell of rosemary and thyme mixed with the scent of late summer roses as they hurried across the path toward the walls.

"Did you put something in their drink?" Shana asked.

Ella turned her face to her and smiled. She had long dark hair that swayed along her back in a thick braid and fine features despite a few scars that proved she'd been a warrior. "A little sleeping concoction from Orkney Isle. Very tasty in honey mead, from what I hear, and quite powerful."

The five of them moved toward the back wall where thick morning mist tumbled over the top of the sea. The maids gasped, clinging to one another, when Beò trotted around the corner straight toward them.

"He's friendly," Shana said.

"He's also the only way Cain would let me sneak inside Old Wick," Ella whispered. "Bàs said he'd protect me and also sniff out where they were keeping you even though we guessed it would be the dungeon."

The wolf stopped before Shana as if they were old friends and not that she'd, up until now, screamed whenever he came near. Shana held out her hand for him to sniff. His wet nose touched her skin, and then he continued toward the wall surrounding Old Wick.

"The only way out is through the portcullis at the front," Shana said.

"We made another way," Ella said.

"We?"

Before she could answer, the quiet of early morning was broken with a bellow. Shana felt Ivy jerk at the sound of her enraged husband. "Speak your demands!" His voice came from the bailey before the castle. Silence followed, an eerie silence that swirled with the mist around them. The fog was thick enough that Shana wondered if another Sinclair woman had wielded magic to create it. She shivered but sent up a prayer of gratitude for whatever help she could have to save Ivy.

Against the back wall was a board tied to two thick ropes that had been lowered inside the gardens. "You and Ivy sit on it," Ella said and took another, thinner rope, tying it around Ivy. "Don't let her fall off." Ella turned them around to face the wall. "Use your legs, Shana, to push out from the wall as they pull you up. If you fall against it, 'twill scrape you."

"If 'tis war ye want, 'tis war we begin!" Erskine yelled from the front. Still there was no reply. The silence sent gooseflesh up Shana's arms. It was as if Erskine had gone insane and was yelling at trees in the mist.

Suddenly the rope jerked, and the board began to rise. "Let them know we have two more lasses to bring up," Ella called quietly.

Obviously, there were others helping despite the silence. Rather quickly, the board rose. "God save us. God save us," Ivy whispered over and over as she held on to her side of the rope. Shana kept her arm around her weak sister and her feet walking up the wall. Would Bàs be on the other side? Or the executioner?

But when she got to the top where a ladder had been laid, she didn't recognize the men standing on a narrow strip of land outside the wall. The strip was about six feet wide and covered with slippery grass. Beyond that was the sheer cliff face dropping into the choppy sea. To the right the land widened, leading into a sparse wood that opened into a meadow beyond.

Ivy gasped softly. "Look," she said, her face turned toward the meadow.

Shana lifted her gaze from the angry sea below, and her inhale stopped. The mist hovered in spots, snaking around the thick oaks and white birches. No birds sang. No people moved about with the waking day. But men sat on horses. Hundreds of men, maybe a thousand. In between trees, clogging the road leading to the castle, out as far as Shana could see, there were warriors sitting on horses. Gray horses with a green sheen clustered closest to the wall where she and Ivy paused. Then a wedge of red horses, then black, and then white on the farthest side. But what caught at her frantically beating heart were the four warriors seated on horses at the front of the armies.

Only her perch on top of the wall afforded her the view.

The four men were huge and silent, mounted on their chargers before the closed portcullis. Their bare arms were muscular and tattooed. The warrior on the white horse wore a crown. The warriors on the red and black horses were bareheaded but held their swords ready. And the warrior on the pale green horse, the very executioner who'd saved her, wore his skull mask and held an ax in one hand and a sword in the other.

A thousand men sat on horses in the dawn mist, but not one made a sound. Even the horses seemed turned to stone as they waited for a signal to attack. The Horseman of Death had brought war to Clan Oliphant, exactly as he'd promised. *Bàs Sinclair?* Was it really him leading this force? Was the kind man from the woods truly a harbinger of war and death?

CHAPTER SIX

"The whole secret lies in confusing the enemy, so
that he cannot fathom our real intent."
SUN TZU, THE ART OF WAR

Sitting straight and ready on Dòchas, Bàs kept his
face toward Erskine Oliphant where the man raged
on the other side of his portcullis bars. Because of
the bloody skull mask, Bàs would have to turn his
face to the right to see along the wall where Cain
and he had lifted Ella during the night. And he
would rather die than ruin the rescue. So he had to
rely on the training of the Sinclair, Sutherland, and
Mackay forces that now surrounded Wick, the town
and the castle.

Cain had been correct that Erskine's men would
concentrate at the front of the castle. Even the warriors in the watchtower looked forward toward the
armies fanning out from the front of the gate. Since
Old Wick's wall did not have a walkway built along
it, and the earth dropped into the sea at the back,
they didn't patrol the circumference of the wall, giving the Sinclairs a perfect place to quietly pull Shana
and her sister over to freedom.

Lord, please let her be well. He'd have reached
her sooner, but Cain had insisted on waiting until
the dawn mist was rising from the grass. Bàs admitted that it did make an eerier picture, but he worried
that his threats earlier might not have deterred

Oliphant guards from harming Shana. His hands tightened around the hilts of his weapons, his well-honed muscles hot and ready from holding them aloft.

Erskine fumed and yelled like a bairn having a rage. "Bloody hell," one of the men inside the walls yelled, and Erskine backed up, his arms flailing.

"Kill it," Erskine yelled, and Bàs instantly knew what had frightened the blustering fool.

Without waiting for a signal from Cain, Bàs yanked his throwing mattucashlass from his boot and snapped it toward the gate with practiced aim. The blade shot through the bars toward a guard who'd raised a gun in the gatehouse tower. The dagger hit the man's hand, making him yelp and drop the weapon. Another guard scrambled to pick up the gun, but another blade flew from Cain, turning perfectly to impale the wooden post beside the man's head in warning. Beò trotted out, unopposed, between the bars to rejoin Bàs.

"Bloody big wolf," Joshua whispered, looking down at Beò, who circled Dòchas.

"Shhh," Gideon said under his breath.

The horses, except for Dòchas, shifted uncomfortably in the presence of the wolf, but their riders controlled them. Beò might be a distraction, but Cain had appreciated another warrior, even a wolf warrior, being on the grounds of Old Wick when Ella insisted on climbing inside. It was easy enough for Beò to enter through the bars in the darkness. And Beò could sniff Shana out if she wasn't being held in the dungeon. He'd let him sniff the rags he'd used to revive her in his cabin.

Erskine hurled more insults and threats from behind his pointy-toothed iron portcullis. Along the right flank, a screech like that of a falcon cut through the trees and mist, which was the signal from one of his warriors that the lasses were outside the wall. Bàs drew in a full inhale.

Cain held out his arm for his real falcon to land. The Four Horsemen stood before the barred portcullis where they began their biblical quotes, one by one down the line of four.

"There before me was a white horse," Cain said, his voice rising above the army, stopping Erskine's tirade. "Its rider held a bow, and he was given a crown, and he rode out as a conqueror bent on conquest."

"Then another horse came out, a fiery red one," Joshua said, his voice deep and fierce. "Its rider was given power to take peace from the earth and to make people kill one another. To him was given a large sword."

"Shut your bloody mouths!" Erskine yelled.

Gideon sat tall and still on his mount. "I looked, and there before me was a black horse. Its rider was holding a pair of scales in his hand."

"Witches, all of ye," Erskine said.

Finally, it was Bàs's turn. The words were etched on his mind, practiced since the age of five and perfected once his voice deepened. "When the Lamb opened the fourth seal, I heard the voice of the fourth living creature say, 'Come!' and I looked, and there before me was a pale horse. Its rider was named Death and that rider is me." The words seemed to resonate in the air, even muting Erskine for a time.

Cain spoke. "War will descend on Erskine Oliphant, his land, and his people if anyone tries to undo what has just been done." Without any outward signal, Cain turned his horse, Seraph, in a tight circle, and then Joshua, Gideon, and Bàs followed one after another.

"What has just been done?" Erskine yelled, but no one answered. In stately precision, like the ancient Romans whom Bàs had read about while learning Latin, the lines of warriors turned to ride away, the flanks watching in case any Oliphant was foolish enough to try to strike their backs.

"Answer me, dammit," Erskine called, but each brother headed to the front of his army.

Breaking through the trees, onto the moor beyond, Bàs yanked off his mask, his gaze searching the riding force. Pristine white Seraph veered across the armies of bay, black, and pale green-gray horses toward Ella. Cain reached his wife, sweeping her onto Seraph to gallop forward, his arms around her as if he'd feared he'd never hold her again.

The horse she'd been riding had an unknown woman on it dressed simply, like a maid. A Sutherland warrior, riding with Bàs's army, came beside her, guiding her mount beside another warrior holding a second maid. But any questions about who they were slid from Bàs's mind as he spotted Shana.

She was smashed between Keenan and a pale woman who must be her sister. Keenan held them both, using his knees to guide his horse, but Shana still clung to Ivy with both arms. Bàs veered toward them, slowing his speed to come even.

"I will take them to my cabin. No one knows where it is," Bàs said.

"She needs medicines," Shana said above the thunder of hooves.

"Ivy will heal at Girnigoe Castle then, with Edward," Bàs said, slowing his horse so that he and Keenan walked, horses flying past them on either side. "Kára's aunts are there with my Aunt Merida, who will see her well. I would have ye come with me to the forest."

"Why?" Shana asked, and the fear he saw cross her face made his gut clench hard. The feeling was sudden and sharp, like a kick delivered by a horse. He'd never vomited from self-hatred and fought back the nausea so he wouldn't show his weakness.

"Because I wish to speak with ye. To explain." Even right next to her he'd had to yell the words to be heard over the horses. "I will take ye to Ivy then."

Without waiting for her agreement, Keenan raised his fist, which signaled another Sinclair warrior to stop beside him. "Take the ill woman to Girnigoe. Gently." The rider pulled Ivy across from Shana as she tried to cling to her.

"No," Shana said, but Keenan caught at her hands. "Ivy," Shana cried out.

"She will be better in their care," Bàs said, and reached for Shana. Instead of coming across to him, Shana's fist snapped toward his face. He could have dodged it easily or caught her knuckles in his grip. But he didn't. He let her hit him in the eye. Light and pain exploded through it, but he didn't flinch.

She shook her hand as if she'd hurt herself. "You

lied to me," she yelled. "You said nothing."

His injured eye would swell, and he didn't wish for Keenan to know everything about this private matter. "Come with me," he said. "I but ask for an hour, and I will ride you briskly to Girnigoe." He glanced at Keenan. "If I do not bring her within two hours of this moment, bring a contingent to my cabin to rescue her from Death."

Shana had smudges of dirt on her forehead and cheek, and her lips looked dry. Had Oliphant given her anything to drink? Her green eyes narrowed into a glare. "And you expect me to believe I will be safe with you, after you almost killed me?"

Bàs couldn't hold her gaze with the truth twisting his conscience. He looked over her head. "I have no defense. I can swear to ye now only that I will not harm ye."

"You swear? On your soul?" she asked. "Does an executioner even have a soul?"

Bàs swallowed down the pain of her words and lowered his gaze back to her eyes. "I swear on my mother's soul."

What did she see in his eyes? Agony? Whatever she saw must have been enough, because she let him lift her across without striking again. Shana fell back against his chest as they surged forward, and Bàs inhaled the warm essence of her. Even with the smell of a dank dungeon clinging to her, she smelled sweet to him. He exhaled through his nose, pushing the scent away, knowing she'd never allow him to appreciate her sweetness.

• • •

The cold spring water quenched Shana's throat and mouth as she drank from the cup Bàs handed her. She sat in a chair at the square table in Bàs's cabin. Betty ran around in the rafters, stopping to peer down.

Bàs looked up at the squirrel. "She doesn't want to leave," he said as if trying to break the tension between them.

Shana ate some oatcakes he'd set before her but didn't say anything. If Bàs wanted to talk to her, so be it, but he couldn't make her talk to him. Not after he ignored her demands to go with Ivy. She kept her bruised knuckles in her lap, taking small pleasure in the darkness marking Bàs's swollen eye.

"I must take care of Dòchas and my other animals," Bàs said and walked out of the cabin.

Shana snorted softly and looked up at the curious squirrel. "He rides me out here to talk and then goes outdoors without saying anything of consequence." With her stomach less empty and her mouth washed free of dust, Shana wanted to get the putrid smell and dirt from Erskine's dungeon off her skin. There was probably a bathing tub at Girnigoe. Here in the middle of the forest, she'd need to use the cold stream that cut through the land. With another huff, she stood, scraping the chair along the wooden floor, and walked out of the cabin.

Bàs stood under the trees. His head was bent as if in prayer. *Well, he certainly needs to pray for forgiveness. Horseman of Death. Good Lord.*

Shana stepped off the porch and walked closer. Bàs's face was tipped down toward an area made up of rocks, hundreds of them. The rocks were mostly gray and set in intricate spirals that ran far enough apart to make paths through the design. The swirls radiated out from a large, carved white marble stone sitting upright in the middle.

The carving was the face of a woman with long, flowing hair, her features cut in smoothly sanded lines, her eyes closed. The carving was beautiful, riveting, and pulled at Shana's heart until she felt the press of tears behind her eyes. "Who is she?" she asked, breaking her silence.

Bàs rested his hand on top of the carving. "My mother."

She didn't know what she expected him to say, but it wasn't mother. "Did you carve it?"

"Aye," he said and turned away, walking toward the barn.

Shana stepped along the curved path of the garden marked with stones. Most were common rocks, but there was an area around the central carved stone where a few white stones sat. A sense of reverence weighed heavily in the garden where flowering mosses grew in between and over some of the rocks. If a church were held outdoors, this sacred place would be one, and it would be dedicated to Bàs's mother. He hadn't mentioned her being at Girnigoe to help Ivy. Had she died?

Near the stream, Bàs wiped a wet rag over his horse, washing off the green to leave a pale golden coat. It was as unique as its master, the Horseman of Death and leader of the calvary of pale horses for the Sinclairs. The man who'd kissed her so tenderly. The man who'd almost taken her head.

The scripture quotes from Revelation that Bàs

and his brothers had recited before the wall of Old Wick had sent chills through Shana. That fear had turned to anger as he insisted she go alone with him. Now her curiosity overrode everything else. She rubbed her arms as she studied the tall, broad-shouldered man. A tattoo of a horse's head sat on his muscular upper arm. When he bent to wash his horse's leg, his long hair moved so she could see the tattoos of an ax and a skull on the spread of his upper back.

Shana couldn't help but notice the defined muscles in his legs, showing from under the woolen wrap around his narrow hips. Bàs Sinclair was all power, deadly power contained in a thoroughly conditioned body, ready for war and ready for killing. And yet, he'd saved her, spared her, rescued her, and kissed her. The various parts of him did not fit together.

Shana stepped across the grassy area to stop before Bàs and his horse by the stream. "Why didn't you tell me who you are?"

He didn't look up, taking a dry rag to wipe the horse's coat. "People fear me when they know. I didn't want ye to fear me."

"People have every right to fear you," she said. "You kill people. And not only as a warrior in battle, but you wear a skull mask and carry an ax. You color your horse pale green and call yourself the Horseman of Death!"

Her eyes widened. "Bàs is not short for Sebastian, is it?" He didn't answer. "My God, your name is actually Death."

Shana realized her hands were flopping about as she spoke and dropped them to her sides, waiting.

Bàs continued to wipe his horse, the green coming off on his rag. "Aye."

"Aye?" she repeated. "To what part?"

His hand stopped and his face turned to her. The tightness there, like a man tortured, brought the same press of tears back that she'd felt staring at his mother's sculpture. "All of it," he said. "I am the Horseman of Death, executioner for Clan Sinclair."

Her mouth opened as she stared at him, chill bumps rising again on her arms. Despite his words, the look in his eyes made her heart ache. Suddenly, she could imagine him a little boy mourning his mother. There was sorrow, remorse, and resignation reflected in his eyes. It was as if Bàs Sinclair had surrendered any hope of joy in life.

"Did you ride down from a cloud as a man already grown?" she asked. "Did you have wings?"

Some of the remorse in his face softened. "I don't remember anything like that. I do remember picking flowers as a small lad, and I've been told…that I was a difficult bairn to birth."

"As a midwife, I've helped many women with difficult births. Even when the child is twisted inside, 'tis not the babe being difficult but the body and babe not aligned."

She glanced at the white rock in the garden. "Is that what happened to your mother? Did she die from your birth?"

Bàs met her gaze without blinking. His eyes were a deep blue, piercing, and intense even with one of them swollen from her punch. "Aye," he said. "She was my first execution."

He took up the horse's reins and began leading

him toward the stable. Shana stared where he had stood, watching the water in the stream bubble and churn over rocks. *First execution?* A babe executing his mother?

She turned, her hands sliding down her cheeks. Bàs's broad back was corded with muscle, his steps strong and graceful like a predator. Her mouth opened as her fists clenched, and she yelled across the yard at him. "That is the most absurd thing I've ever heard!"

Bàs paused but didn't turn around. Shana ran after him, yanking his arm to look him in the face. "What devil told you that?"

"My father."

She stared, mouth open. Slowly her brows rose. "You didn't name yourself death. Your father did, didn't he?"

"'Twas within his right as my father," Bàs said.

Her heart clenched as she imagined a small Bàs with blond hair standing before a monster of a man saying, "You killed your mother. You are nothing but death."

The face she stared at hardened. Bàs's jaw was naturally square, but everything seemed more rigid. "I don't ask for nor want your pity, Shana," he said. "I merely wanted ye to know who I am and why I was wielding an ax yesterday when ye were brought forth."

He tried to turn away, but her fingers curled into his arm. His skin was warm despite the mid-morning coolness in the air. "Would you have killed me yesterday if Beò and you hadn't found me and Edward before?" Shana held her breath. If he said no, would she believe him? If he said yes, could she forgive him?

"I don't kill many women," he said but didn't look at her.

"But one who had killed a babe and a helpless mother?" she asked. "Isn't that what Erskine accused me of?"

Bàs exhaled. His eyes closed for a moment and then opened to meet her gaze. "I hope that I would not have, but…I do not know." He stepped away, and she let him go.

I do not know. It was honest. It was horrible.

Shana watched Bàs disappear into the barn and walked back to the garden, peering down at the many rocks. The statue of Bàs's mother was ethereal and lovely. One or two of the common granite stones had dark spots clinging to them. She crouched to look closer, turning one of them with her fingers. The dark stain marked underneath where the rain could not wash it away easily. Blood?

She dropped the stone, yanking her hand back, and straightened. Her gaze followed the lines as she walked among them. Hundreds of rocks spaced precisely, set in the dark forest dirt. This wasn't a rock garden dedicated to his mother.

This was a memorial to all the people the Horseman of Death had killed. Her hand rested on her pounding heart as she looked to the barn. Could such turmoil live inside a man without completely changing him into something dark, something evil?

CHAPTER SEVEN

"Then the two women departed from her, and she kneeling down upon the cushion most resolutely, and without any token or fear of death, she spake aloud this Psalm in Latin, In Te Domine confido, non confundar in eternam, etc. Then, groping for the block, she laid down her head, putting her chin over the block with both her hands, which, holding there still, had been cut off had they not been espied. Then lying upon the block most quietly, and stretching out her arms cried, In manus tuas, Domine, etc., three or four times. Then she, lying very still upon the block, one of the executioners holding her slightly with one of his hands, she endured two strokes of the other executioner with an axe, she making very small noise or none at all, and not stirring any part of her from the place where she lay: and so the executioner cut off her head, saving one little gristle, which being cut asunder, he lift up her head to the view of all the assembly and bade God save the Queen."

ROBERT WYNKFIELDE 1587
THE EXECUTION OF MARY, QUEEN OF SCOTS

A blue and rose-hued chaffinch flew before Dòchas as Bàs steered him through the woods above the moor leading to Girnigoe Castle on the rocky coast of the North Sea. Shana rode before him, silent since her outburst outside the barn.

He'd forced her to come out there with him to talk and then he'd spent his time hiding from her. He frowned fiercely over her head, his gaze trained on the familiar castle in the distance. *What the bloody hell did you think would happen?* That she'd kiss him again? He almost snorted over the ridiculous thought.

He'd been somewhat successful in that Shana had talked to him again even if her words were full of vengeance and fury. Those were better than the pity he'd heard in her voice and seen in her eyes. It was all bad.

But, honestly, what had he expected? Forgiveness? Understanding? He didn't deserve any of it. He should have let Shana ride with Keenan to Girnigoe.

"Did you have a rock for me?" Shana's voice broke through the stillness of the forest.

"Rock?"

"For your garden. All those stones represent the people you've executed, or am I wrong?"

He paused, staring out at a few birds swooping down from the thick summer foliage. "I...dropped your rock on the platform as soon as I saw ye," he said.

She didn't turn around but shook her head. "Are the white rocks different?"

"They are in remembrance of those who have died without me executing them."

Shana twisted in the saddle to look up at him. "Your mother's effigy is in white."

He met her rich hazel eyes. They were the perfect shape with long lashes around them. "Those who died without me executing them with my ax or sword," he said.

She huffed from her pert nose and faced front again. "You didn't execute your mother, Bàs. I'm a midwife and I've…" She shook her head. "So, I know better than your father. And Bàs is a stupid name for anyone. I'm calling you Sebastian."

"'Tis not my name."

She shrugged. "And you didn't ride down from Heaven as the Horseman of Death, either."

She sounded irritated, which helped him relax. Irritated at him was far better than fearing, hating, or pitying him. His arms brushed hers as he held the reins loosely. He could have controlled Dòchas with his knees, and his horse knew the way to Girnigoe, but holding the reins gave Bàs a reason to keep his arms around her. She was warm and soft and, most importantly, she didn't seem as afraid of him as she'd been when he'd taken her from Keenan. Maybe it was good that he'd insisted. His swollen eye was well worth every single word she spoke to him.

"Hold on," he said as they broke from the forest onto the moor. Her fingers reached forward, clutching the pommel before her, but Bàs wouldn't let her fall. His arm curled around her middle, holding her securely between his thighs as Dòchas surged forward. Her reddish-hued hair flew in his face, making his grin return. He didn't need to see his way to his home, so he reveled in the whipping tendrils of Shana's hair and the warmth of her body while they flew across the field of late summer wildflowers and grasses. He could almost imagine her wanting to be there in his arms.

He pointed past her toward the ocean where the fortified castle sat that was his clan's seat of power. "Girnigoe Castle," he said, his lips near her ear. Two drawbridges, a moat, the ocean behind it, and a ten-foot-thick wall made the castle impenetrable.

"'Tis huge," she called, the wind whipping her words away, tugging her hair.

"And protected."

Dòchas's hooves leaped over the dry peat, instinctively knowing where the holes and boulders were that might trip him, until he slowed before entering the village. Bàs led the horse through the winding path between thatched and slate-covered houses toward the first drawbridge into the castle. Several people came out to watch him proceed, but no one raised a hand to him, and several children hid behind their mothers' skirts.

"The sea protects Girnigoe on one side, and we have two moats with drawbridges before the inner bailey," he said.

"Old Wick has the sea at its back and only a single wall," she said.

"Which is easily breached."

Bàs nodded to several warriors as he walked Dòchas by them. Keenan nodded from where he stood by his horse as if he'd been about to ride out to rescue Shana. Bàs returned the nod but frowned at his friend and continued, Dòchas's hooves beating a dull song as they rode over the wooden bridge.

"Bàs Sinclair, Horseman of Death!" Thomas yelled down from the gatehouse, announcing him. The title made the muscles up the back of his neck ache. *Stupid Thomas.*

Dòchas clopped across the second bridge. They were both lowered, so Cain didn't consider Erskine Oliphant a threat. No doubt, scouts were riding the boundaries, ready to carry news of a moving army.

Bàs halted Dòchas in the bailey before the doors to Girnigoe keep. "Is Edward here?" Shana asked.

Bàs dismounted, reaching up to encircle her waist and lifting her easily down. "Aye, unless he's at the Orphans' Home where the mistress there has been nursing him with her own son. Ella Sinclair will also be inside."

"I hope Ivy's milk has come in," Shana murmured and turned toward the doors as if ready to run inside, but then she stopped, looking back. "Are you not coming?"

Did she desire his presence? Bàs waved over a lad from the stables, who ran to take Dòchas's reins, and caught up to Shana.

They walked through the entryway, along another corridor that was lit by sconces secured to the walls, and then into the Great Hall where excited voices filled the space. If there'd been music, Bàs would have thought it a celebration.

"'Twas easy enough to pour the whole sleeping draught into the ale," Ella said, smiling at Joshua's very pregnant wife, Kára. "And it knocked them right out." She looked toward the stairway that was empty. "Gertrude and Charlotte were very brave to serve it. I couldn't leave them there to face Erskine's wrath."

"Of course not," Cain said, pulling Ella into his arms, holding her against him. The worry over Ella's safety had deepened the lines of his face as if the morning had aged him. He didn't look likely to let her go even when she kept talking, her hands shooting out around him with her excitement.

"I can see how you were able to make Joshua sleep," Ella said to her sister-in-law, her words somewhat muffled by Cain's grasp.

Kára patted Joshua's chest as he gave her a playful glare. "You could have stripped all the men naked, and they wouldn't have woken," Kára said.

Joshua snorted and lifted under her knees to spin her slowly around. "Maybe I let ye strip me naked while I was awake the entire time." He kissed her soundly and set her back down, steadying her, since her balance was off with the huge belly before her. This would be their second child. Their first, Adam, was toddling around the room with Mary, Aunt Merida and Hannah watching them closely.

"Thank you all," Shana said, "for going to such efforts to save us."

"And no casualties, save for Bàs's eye," Joshua said.

Kára gave him a kick in the shin. He frowned, rubbing it.

Ella pulled away from Cain and walked over to squeeze Shana's hands. "Ivy is above in a comfortable room with Kára's talented grandmother and aunt tending her. I'll take you there."

"And Edward is—"

"Up there, too," Gideon said, "with my wife, Cait. She can't get her fill of bairns." He smiled, probably because Cait was pregnant, too, with their first child.

Cait had softened Bàs's third brother like Ella and Kára had softened his other brothers. What would Father think of that? Bàs guessed he would spit with fury and make them run out in the cold rain naked to battle one another until someone was bloody and they were all covered with fresh mud.

"I'll take ye up," Bàs said, but Ella tugged Shana along.

"No place for a warrior," Ella called back, and Bàs was left behind. He watched them walk together, Ella still in her black breeches and Shana in the same ruined gown he'd found her in under the tree.

"Hannah?" Bàs said and she turned his way, a chubby wee Mary wiggling in her arms. "Can we find another set of clothes for Shana and her sister? Their gowns are in poor repair."

"I have a supply of clothing for just such a need," Hannah said, her smile fading as she studied his face. "I'll find something for them after I tend your eye."

"Keenan said Shana's punch had some power behind it," Joshua said, a huge smile across his face.

Bàs slid his hand over his puffy eye. "She was... angry."

"For not telling her ye're the Horseman of Death or because ye forced her to ride back to your cabin alone?" Joshua pressed.

"Forced her?" Hannah said, her face aghast.

"Just to talk for a moment," Bàs said and threw his arms out to the room. "Without all of ye listening in and adding unwanted comments."

"Unwanted comments?" Joshua said. "I'm sure he doesn't mean me."

"Bloody arse," Bàs murmured and let Hannah push him down into a chair.

. . .

"Are you well, Ivy?" Shana asked as she sat on the edge of the bed, holding Ivy's cold hand. In the two hours that Bàs had abducted her to his cabin to talk, the ladies of Girnigoe had given Ivy a warm bath, plenty to drink, medicinal herbs, and a bowl of chicken stew.

Ivy smiled at Shana but quickly looked back at her babe, lying swaddled next to her on the bed. "I'm much improved thanks to you and these kind women."

"You're already responding to the feverfew," the older lady named Hilda said. She seemed to oversee the room. "And nothing is torn below." She glanced up at Shana. "Thanks to an experienced midwife."

"You're much stronger after holding your babe again," the second lady, named Harriett Flett, said from the other side of the bed. Shana's sister stared at her swaddled babe, refusing to look away.

"He's doing fine indeed," the woman named Cait said to Ivy. "You can try to nurse him if you'd like."

Ivy glanced from Cait to Shana. "I would like that."

"It can weaken the body," Shana said, looking to the wise women. "I've seen it with some new mothers."

"We'll keep watch," Harriett said. "But let us give the sisters a chance to rejoice together in their freedom."

"I'll find some more soup and tarts to bring up," Cait said. "A nursing mother needs to eat well." She smiled and left the room, the two elderly ladies following her.

After some maneuvering of Ivy in the large bed, Edward latched on immediately, already having been nursed by the other mother at the Orphans' Home. Ivy looked up at Shana with big watery eyes. "Look what I can do, Shana." Happy tears leaked free.

Shana smiled with her, touching her nephew's soft head. "Perfect."

Ivy wiped her eyes. "Liam Ross is his father." And all the joy seemed to drain from her face, leaving her pale. "Do you know what's happened to him?"

Shana settled on the bed next to her and shook her head. "The maids said they hadn't heard his name mentioned in the hall at Old Wick."

Ivy exhaled, her eyes shutting as if she were saying a little prayer. "Maybe he got away."

Or Erskine had already killed him. But Shana kept that possibility tucked inside. "Did Erskine know about him? Who he was?"

"I don't know," she whispered. "I told Erskine the child was his own, but then Janet, my friend there, said she overheard Erskine talking about the babe being someone else's." She shook slightly at the memory. "I do hope Janet hasn't suffered from my escape. Erskine knows she was my friend. He's likely questioning her."

Shana squeezed Ivy's hand. "We must pray she is well. Maybe the Sinclairs can help get her out of Old Wick, too."

Ivy looked up at Shana, her eyes glistening with

emotion. "I thought Erskine had killed you. He said he was having you executed by a horseman from God for stealing his son."

"Even though he knew Edward wasn't his?"

Ivy nodded. "I know he would have killed him, my beautiful wee boy." The tears leaked out. "Both of us." She squeezed Shana's hand. "We are so fortunate that you convinced the Sinclairs to rescue us. How did you do that? In two days' time?"

Bàs Sinclair, that's how. "God showed us favor, Ivy. There's no other explanation for the three of us sitting here in warmth and comfort behind many walls and drawbridges surrounded by warriors from so many armies…" She shook her head. "I have no other explanation." *I kissed him.* Was that the explanation?

"The Sinclairs are stronger than King James himself." Ivy whispered the treasonous words.

Shana nodded. She'd never seen a royal army, but she couldn't imagine it being fiercer than the one that had rescued her and Ivy that morning, all of them completely silent except for the words of the Four Horsemen. Shana shivered at the memory of their resonating voices reciting verses from Revelation. And the complex man who'd rescued her from wolves in the forest, whom she'd punched in the face without repercussion, was the fiercest of all.

• • •

Ivy and Edward had slept through the night next to Shana after Shana had bathed in warm fragrant water. It had soothed her muscles and rid her of the dankness that had clung to her from Old Wick's dungeon. She'd even washed her long hair and let it dry into curls before the fire.

It was well past dawn now, and she'd heard people walking outside the room she and Ivy were sharing. So Shana ventured out, wearing a simple gown over a clean smock that Bàs's sister, Hannah, had provided.

The curved wall of the winding stone staircase was cool under her hand as she slid it along the stone. She reached the bottom where light from the Great Hall cut into the corridor.

"I'm telling ye, let's bury the lass," Joshua said, making Shana stop inside the hall. "It worked for us." He nodded to his wife, Kára. "Bury her, and Erskine will believe she's dead." The large, tattooed warrior flipped a hand at Gideon. "Have Osk walk the beaches until he finds a dead seal or big fish to lay underneath. It'll stink like a decaying body."

"No one is burying my sister," Shana said, her voice making them all turn her way.

"'Tis just a ruse," Kára said. "But we can come up with a better, less terrifying solution." She held her hand before Joshua's mouth to stop him from saying anything more. Joshua growled and grabbed his wife's hand, kissing the palm in a way that made it obvious the couple would have many more children together.

"Has Erskine or the Oliphant Clan reacted to yesterday?" Shana asked, her gaze seeking out Bàs. He stood like a powerful sentry, his arms crossed and his mouth firm. His gaze met hers with determination and something else. Regret? Apology?

"We've had a messenger bring a letter this morn demanding Ivy's return," Bàs said. "And yours, to be punished for Edward's death."

She exhaled in relief. "Erskine still thinks the babe is dead. Thank God."

Bàs's brothers looked at one another. Cain stood near the table, his arms crossed. "Ye should know, lass, that the Oliphant Chief has sent a report of the death of his son and abduction of his wife and sister-by-marriage to King James in Edinburgh."

"For what purpose?" Shana's gaze returned to Bàs, who walked across to stand next to her. It was a subtle yet powerful gesture that said he supported her. She was grateful, but she was still angry about him forcing her to go to his cabin yesterday and didn't move closer to him despite the silent pull she felt.

Cait's husband, Gideon, who had spoken as the Horseman of Justice, cleared his throat. "Erskine is making trouble with the crown. He knows his Oliphant forces are not enough to go up against our massive army alone, and he knows we have alliances with the Sutherland Clan and my Mackay warriors at Varrich. In truth, we are strong enough to take the crown from King James if we acted. Erskine is saying that we are strengthening our numbers to do just that."

"Will King James bring his army here?" Shana asked, her hand at her throat. "Demand that Ivy be returned to that monster of a husband?"

"Over my dead, shrieking body," Bàs's aunt, Merida Sinclair, murmured then raised her voice.

"The lass has been through enough."

"Next thing you know, he'll be branding her," Ella said, rubbing a splotch on her jaw. Her gaze connected with Merida's.

The older woman gave her a little nod. "Which we won't allow," she said, her gaze snapping around to Cain.

Cain exhaled. "Of course not."

Joshua sniffed. "The burying-her-with-a-dead-seal idea doesn't seem so ludicrous now, does it?" Kára shushed him.

Shana felt Bàs's arm brush against hers, but she kept still. *He didn't tell me who he was.* But then the same voice reminded her, *And you didn't tell him who you were.*

She crossed her arms, which put more space between them. "Is the king not afraid of the Four Horsemen?" Shana asked. "You all seemed to frighten the Oliphants enough yesterday."

"The king is wary of us," Gideon said, studying her until Shana felt like he was searching her for some ulterior motive. "He visited in January to see our strength, most of which we hid from him to abate his concern. If Oliphant exaggerates our strength even a bit, James will worry again."

"Erskine Oliphant mentioned the involvement of witchcraft in his letter," Hannah said. Bàs's sister stood near the hearth, holding a little boy who was yet to be breeched.

"And James is obsessed with hunting witches," Ella said.

Bàs shifted, crossing his own arms. "We proved our loyalty when he was here last. Surely he knows we could have allowed his death back then but saved him against the enemies in his midst."

Gideon rubbed a hand down his clipped beard. "Kings have short memories and see traitors everywhere." He looked at Shana. "And James doesn't uphold the idea of divorce, even in the worst circumstances. He may side with Erskine, at least about sending your sister back to her marriage. And there is real danger if he thinks ye are a witch."

"James has asked us to journey back to Orkney," Bàs said. "To bring his traitor uncle to heel after proclaiming himself king of Scotland." He looked directly to Gideon. "Remind James of that."

Hannah walked over from the hearth, swaying with the boy up against her shoulder. "For now, though, we will focus on getting Ivy strong. I think she did a good thing, sending Edward away. Erskine thinks the boy is dead, and we should continue with that ruse to protect him."

"Ye could go to Edinburgh yourself," Bàs said to Gideon.

"No, he cannot," Cait said, her hand going to her rounded belly.

Gideon pulled Cait into him, kissing her forehead. "I'm not going anywhere right now." He looked to Bàs and then Cain. "Let's see if my letter keeps James out of this."

Shana's gaze took in the room of young couples and children. She and Ivy had brought turmoil to the Sinclair Clan. The hollow feeling of guilt grew inside her.

She glanced up at Bàs's face. He frowned at a man walking inside the Great Hall. A clergyman, from the robes he wore. Shana's heart leaped faster.

"Pastor John?" Cain said.

Shana grasped onto Bàs's arm without thinking. "My sister is not dying. There's no need for you to attend her."

The young man paused, a pinch of confusion in his brows. "I'm here for Bàs, not your sister. However, if she needs me to pray with her, I can visit. I was going to ask if her son was christened yet."

Shana released her breath. Realizing that her fingers were clutching Bàs, she dropped her hand. "She's sleeping right now, and no, Edward still needs the church's blessing."

The pastor nodded. "I'll come back with my holy supplies once my other business is finished."

"What's brought ye then?" Cain asked.

"'Tis old Hamish."

"Has his time come to die?" Bàs asked.

Pastor John nodded. "He won't settle down to it, though. I think he needs your help."

Shana's eyes widened. "What kind of help?" Did the Horseman of Death execute old warriors? Lop off their heads as a mercy?

"Of course," Bàs said and strode toward the doors without answering her.

Hannah lay Adam into Joshua's arms and hurried over to Shana. She threaded her arm through hers. "Come with me to see."

"I don't want to see this," Shana whispered, planting her feet on the stone floor. "I am a midwife and abhor death."

Hannah didn't respond except to drag her along

with her out of the keep. For such a slender woman, she was incredibly strong. Their slippers crunched on the pebbles in the bailey. Several men nodded to them as they passed, and Hannah called greetings up to the gate tower as they walked across the bridge. Ahead, Bàs and Paster John turned to follow the lane around a stone cottage. "'Tis not far," Hannah said.

"How will your brother help him?" Shana asked.

"He will help him die," Hannah said as if her answer was praise indeed. "He is quite good at it."

Shana half snorted with a dark laugh. "He is the Horseman of Death."

Hannah kept her face straight ahead. "He is so much more than that," she said, her lips tight.

CHAPTER EIGHT

"In Early Modern England, death was viewed
indelibly through the analogue of Christianity. The
deathbed was a spiritual drama, a battle for the
dying individual's soul between the forces of God
and the demons of Satan. If the individual died
well, peacefully, with family and priest, then
salvation was assumed to be theirs. A bad death,
alone or in agony or without a holy man's
sacrament, was to be avoided at all cost."
HISTORIC-UK.COM

Bàs ducked to enter the dimly lit home of Hamish
Sinclair, a distant great-uncle who had fought along-
side his father and grandfather.

"Elsie," Bàs said, nodding to Hamish's daughter.
She'd been taking care of the aging man since his
wife died several months ago.

"He's in the bedroom, being as ornery as he can
despite falling asleep every few minutes," his daughter said. Bàs could see the strain in her face, the
wetness in her eyes. Hamish had experienced some
type of attack inside his body last year while he was
riding. He fell from his horse, and Aunt Merida had
thought he'd die rapidly. The old man had hung on
but couldn't walk, which made him even more blus-
tery to everyone except his wife.

"If he's sleeping more and more," Bàs said, "it
shouldn't be long now."

Elsie nodded, giving him a sad smile.

"How are you doing, Elsie?" Hannah asked, and Bàs noticed that she'd followed them to the cottage. Shana stood next to her inside the doorway. Why had Shana followed? She'd made it very clear that she was opposite to him. She brought people into the world. *While I take them out of this world.* The thought tightened a familiar ache although he tried to ignore it. This was who he was. Opposite of the beautiful lass whose kiss he'd never forget.

"'Tis hard," Elsie answered Hannah and crinkled her apron in her chafed hands. "He hasn't eaten for days now."

Pastor John took Elsie's hand. "I will pray over him whether he wants it or not."

"Thank ye, Pastor. If he manages to lift anything, make sure to duck."

Bàs forced his focus back to his task and entered the one other room in the cottage where a big bed sat against the back wall. It was dark with the windows covered and a single candle burning in a glass lantern. The tang of sweat, piss, and discontent soured the air.

The old man lay with his eyes shut, his chest rising slowly. Would Hamish go peacefully in his sleep? Not likely. Not when he held so tightly to life with anger. Bàs's father had been the same way. Many of the old warriors were.

They wanted to die fighting on a moor against foes, saving their families.

They wanted to die with their swords in their hands, not in bed with their blades propped in the corner.

Bàs walked to the windows, pulling open the inside shutters, and daylight lit the room along with some fresh air.

"Cover the damn windows, Elsie," Hamish said, his voice thin on a shallow breath.

"A warrior doesn't hide in the dark," Bàs said. "He comes from the shadows into the light to protect his kin and clan."

"I ain't hiding," Hamish said, his voice a bit stronger as he squinted open his eyes. "I'm dying. Alone in a bed." Bàs could hear the repugnance in his whisper. And then he coughed, a rattling, hacking cough, and Elsie ran to prop another pillow behind his back.

"Don't fuss," the old man said between coughs that seemed painful.

"Then stop coughing," Elsie replied. She brought him something to drink, holding it to his lips.

The cleric came in but didn't say anything. Hamish glanced at him. "Ye give me no comfort, Pastor. Go on now."

"The Christ will welcome you with open arms, Hamish Sinclair," Pastor John said.

Hannah and Shana stood quietly outside the door of the bedroom, watching, listening. What was Shana thinking? Her lovely features gave nothing away. If she was repulsed by the lurking of death, she could leave, but he had a calling to honor.

Bàs picked up the sword from the corner of the room and went to the bed. "A Sinclair warrior dies with a sword in his hands." He lay the sword next to Hamish and took up the old man's hand, laying it over the handle.

Hamish's gnarled fingers wrapped around it. "'Tis an old friend," Hamish whispered. "Loyal to the end."

Bàs straightened and crossed his arms, his legs braced in a battle stance. "Ye've conquered the foes here, those who would threaten your clan. Ye are a brave and honorable warrior, and now 'tis time for ye to battle against any devils trying to get into heaven."

Pastor John cleared his throat. "I don't think—"

"Shhhh," Hannah said, cutting into his correction.

"And Margie?" Hamish asked, his eyes closing as he exhaled a long breath.

"She will be waiting there for ye with open arms." Bàs glanced at Pastor John. "Like Jesus, but with her blaeberry tarts for ye."

Hamish's lips opened, his hand clutching his sword where his thumb stroked the smallest bit over the wrapped leather at the handle. "I would not have her see me die this way," he murmured.

Bàs inhaled, and the scent of the sick room made him frown. Even with the windows thrown open, air did not cleanse the sourness. "Ye're right," Bàs said. "A warrior dies staring up at the sky."

"Aye," Hamish whispered. "With mist on his face and honor in his heart."

The man linked the idea of dying outdoors with honor. Bàs looked at Pastor John. "I'll take Hamish. Ye bring his pallet." Without waiting for permission, he slid his arms under the old man's legs and back. He wore an old tunic that covered him down to his knees. It was stained, and underneath the man felt like a pile of hollow bones that weighed nothing.

"Where are ye taking him?" Elsie asked, her eyes wide.

"Where a warrior dies," Bàs said. "Outside."

"Where everyone can see him?" Hannah asked.

"If they want." Bàs continued out of the room, careful not to hit Hamish's head. The man seemed to be asleep again, his eyes closed. Would the Horseman of Death kill him by moving him? It was still better in Hamish's mind than dying in a sick bed. Would Shana agree?

Bàs carried him out the front door. The day was pleasantly cool, the sun muted by the low clouds. Rain might come. He paused and spotted a patch of open sky surrounded by trees behind the cottage where it was relatively flat. He glanced back where Pastor John, Hannah, and Shana lifted the stripped mattress tick while Elsie ran out with clean sheets to place back on it once they set it down. "Over here," Bàs called.

Several villagers paused to watch the strange procession. Even though Bàs had sat with numerous warriors as they died of age and infirmity, he'd never brought one outdoors. But it seemed right, and he let his gut lead the way. Dignity and familiar things that brought him joy was what Hamish needed as he moved on. 'Twas what Bàs would want.

Elsie covered the straw-filled tick that the other three had laid onto the ground. "There," she said, "'tis clean now."

Shana ran back toward the cottage. Had she decided to leave?

Bàs laid the old man down on the fresh pallet, covering him with the quilt he'd probably shared

with his Margie through the half century they'd lain
under it together. For a moment, he watched to see
Hamish's chest rise with breath. Bàs released his
own breath when he saw the evidence of life. His
touch hadn't killed the fragile man.

"Here." Shana came into the clearing carrying
the warrior's heavy sword by grasping the hilt with
two hands, the sharp tip pointed at the ground.

"Thank ye," Bàs said and grasped it, too, his fingers brushing hers. She didn't move away for a
moment, looking into his face as if studying him. The
smooth space between her brows pinched, and her
eyes looked greener in the light under the trees.

"What are ye doing with old Hamish?" a voice
called from the path and the spell, or whatever held
their gazes, was severed.

She turned to look at the elderly man in the road.
"He's not executing him," she called.

Old Angus laughed and walked toward them. "I
didn't think he was, but fighting the Horseman of
Death would be a good way to go."

Shana stared at Angus and startled when Bàs
took the sword from her hands. "Oh. Yes."

Had she really thought he would end Hamish's
life with violence? Bàs placed the sword on the bed
and wrapped Hamish's hand around the hilt. Eyes
still closed, Hamish took what seemed like a long
full breath.

"Bàs felt he would be more comfortable outdoors," Elsie said.

The older man, Angus, walked up to stand next to
Bàs. "Comfortable, eh?"

"A warrior like Hamish wants to die outside with

his sword in his hand," Bàs said.

Angus crossed his arms and frowned. "Hmph. I suppose if one can't die in battle, 'tis the next best thing." He nodded and dropped his arms. "What say ye, Hamish, ye old war horse?"

Hamish didn't open his eyes, but his mouth relaxed, almost into a smile.

"Well, I'll sit with him a spell," Angus said. He glanced over at Pastor John. "Let Sean and Iain know. They'll want to come over." Pastor John nodded and hurried away.

"I'll get ye a chair, Angus," Elsie said, retreating to the cottage.

"Much obliged," Angus called. "Sean and Iain will want some, too."

Bàs strode toward the cottage and realized that Shana followed. "I'll get the chairs," he said. "If ye want to go back to the castle, Hannah can walk with ye. This may stretch well into the night."

"Like a birth," she said.

"I suppose." He glanced her way. "Those waiting want the person, whether new or old, to get on with it, but 'tis up to God and them to decide on the timing."

She nodded, her mouth relaxing. "I'll stay for a bit," she said, and followed him back out with a chair as he carried two more.

He set them in a semicircle around the bed and nodded to two younger warriors who'd stopped by at the sight of a man lying on a pallet outdoors.

Angus lowered himself into a chair, and Bàs steadied it so it wouldn't fall over while he settled. "And then," Angus continued without acknowledging Bàs's help, "Hamish brought his sword down on the bastard's skull. I swear I heard it crack the man like a roasted nut."

The two young warriors chuckled while Hannah held a hand to her mouth. She'd grown up around such stories and would find them as funny as the men.

"Taught him to respect his elders," one of the younger warriors, Jacob McGinty, said.

"Aye, it did." Angus laughed heartily. "Ye agree, Hamish?"

Hamish didn't move, except for a finger over the hilt of his sword. Angus pointed at it. "Aye, he agrees."

Bas motioned to the two young warriors to follow him back to the cottage. Elsie had been sleeping on a single bed in the front room. Bas lifted her pallet off the cording and deposited it on the big bed in the back room. "Let's take this out so he's off the dirt," he said. The three of them carried the smaller bed out to the clearing where several younger warriors had stopped by to see what was happening.

"Aon, dha, trì," Bas called, and the group of men lifted Hamish and his pallet onto the smaller bed frame. The edges of the tick flopped over each side, but at least Hamish was higher up so Angus could look him in the face without almost tumbling out of his chair.

"I brought the whisky," Sean Sinclair called as he hobbled toward their group on a cane. His leg had lost all feeling from a slice in battle five years back.

"Lying fool," Iain said, "I'm carrying the whisky."

"But 'tis my whisky," Sean yelled back. "Ho there, Hamish," he said, settling in one of the chairs.

"Hell of a good day to die."

Iain came over, looking closely into Hamish's face. "Hope ye ain't dead yet. I just brought the whisky."

Shana stood beside Bàs, and he heard her inhale quickly. "His eyes moved," she whispered.

"There ye are," Iain said as Hamish's eyelids lifted halfway, and his mouth twitched at the corners of his dry lips. He didn't say anything, but he seemed to take in the gathered people around him.

"Ye are outside, Da," Elsie said. "So ye can see the sky."

Hannah pointed at a dark cloud overhead. "I hope it doesn't rain."

"No matter," Angus said, leaning back in his chair and quickly straightening when he felt it start to topple. "Rain on a dead man's face is a good thing. Washes him clean of this earth."

"Amen," Pastor John murmured on Bàs's other side.

Hamish's eyes raised to the sky that showed through the circle of trees. "He knows where he is," Shana whispered.

"Aye, the dying know more than they show," Bàs said, and his breath caught as her fingers brushed against his.

She looked up at him. "You...understand death."

He couldn't get over how green her eyes looked. It was as if they'd changed to match the trees above her. "Not all of it is bloody or sorrowful," he answered. "Some 'tis a mercy."

"There was this one time before the battle at Craigmin Bridge, where Chief Sinclair, George the old devil," Iain said, having found his own chair and pulling it right up to Hamish's bed, "told us to ride south to wait in ambush."

Sean laughed. "So Hamish said 'why when I can just look at the bastards across the moor and run them through?'"

Angus slapped his knee. "He was one of the few who could turn George Sinclair's mind from a battle plan."

Tales about his father's stubborn nature and war-like ways were legendary and painted the man in a heroic light. Bàs had learned quickly that there was little truth in legends. But holding Shana's hand helped him remember some of the good in his father. George Sinclair rarely lost a fight, or if he did, he came back full of revenge.

A few of the mid-aged warriors stopped to listen to the three old men talk around Hamish, each of them coming forward to share their own tales of the man. Bàs could tell from the small sounds Shana made when a particular story made her want to laugh or was not for ladies' ears. Elsie brought out tankards of ale, and two warriors carried out the table from indoors. One man ran home, returning with buns and berries that his children had picked.

"Pass that whisky around," Iain said, indicating the flask.

"'Tis more potent outdoors," Angus said, making the young warriors look at him like he'd lost his mind. "'Tis true," Angus said and worked his way out of his seat." Standing, he pointed to each of them. "Ye take a few drams of whisky indoors, and ye can still walk about, chatting, maybe doing a jig if a tune starts up, but the moment ye step out-doors…" He staggered to the side as if drunk. "The fresh air knocks ye right over."

Iain slapped his knee and laughed hard. "Aye, 'tis that blasted fresh air that does a man in every time he tries to walk home."

"And here we all are in the fresh air already," Sean said, snorting.

The young warriors laughed, and the flask was sent around. When it came to Bàs, he held it out to Shana. "Would ye like a sip?"

"With all this fresh air about, ready to knock me over?"

He allowed a slight grin. "I will keep ye upright if ye wish to sample."

She sniffed the strong liquor and took a little sip. It made her nose scrunch, but she swallowed it down with a small cough. "'Tis strong."

"But smooth." Bàs took a swallow, passing it along.

The stories became bloodier, and Hannah drew close. "Perhaps we should go back to the castle," she whispered.

Shana glanced toward the men and then back to her. "If you could check on Ivy and Edward, I would like to stay a bit longer."

Surprise opened Hannah's face, but she nodded. "I'm sure Bàs can see you safely back," she said, glancing between them.

"Thank you," Shana said. She turned as the men around Hamish erupted in laughter, and Sean leaned over to gently punch Hamish's thin arm.

"And that lass became his wife," Sean said. He

tapped his friend's hand where it rested on the sword. "And Margie will be waiting there for ye, old friend."

"She'll probably scold ye for being late," Iain said and passed the whisky to Sean, who took a swig and then yanked a cloth from his belt to squeeze his red nose. Iain patted his back.

"'Tis a process," Bàs said softly, and Shana nodded next to him, keeping silent.

The day wore on with people coming up and leaving, but the three old men got up only to piss and eat. Angus's short stay had become a vigil as the three men regaled the younger with stories of their heroics on and off the battlefield with Hamish. Whether he was truly their ringleader or only an active participant, they were making him out as the hero.

Hamish's hand moved less and less through the day, and he didn't open his eyes again, but that didn't stop the stories. Someone had found chairs for Shana and Elsie, and Bàs sat on the ground beside them. Ella and Cain, and then Joshua and Gideon, had come down from the castle to join for a couple hours, bringing as much food as they could carry for what had become a party to celebrate Hamish and his feats of valor. When the light began to dim, Joshua built a fire to keep the discussions going. Sometimes there would be silence as men thought until one of them remembered a story or couldn't be comfortable in the silence.

Bàs had no problem remaining quiet and letting others talk. He watched for Hamish's chest to rise and fall, all the while aware Shana hadn't left. His eye throbbed now and then, a reminder that Shana wanted nothing to do with him.

The night breeze blew the smoke away, and a gentle rain began to fall. Elsie ran inside to grab her cloak and another blanket to lay over Hamish.

"I'll walk ye back," Bàs said to Shana.

"What will they do, all of them?" she asked, looking around the small circle.

"They've spent half their lives in rain, training or battling." Each man opened the woolen sash that lay over one shoulder to his waist and laid it over his head. "Our cloaks are part of our plaid. Rain doesn't bother. And 'tis washing Hamish's face."

"Oh," she said, looking around at the shrouded men. Not one left.

Bàs hesitated and then opened his sash wider. "Ye can come under if ye wish to stay." His stomach tightened when she didn't move, and he dropped his arm. *Fool.* He glanced to see how many of the men had just witnessed his rejection.

"By the tree where there's no mud yet." Shana's words brought his gaze back to her, and he forgot to breathe as she beckoned him over.

He followed her to sit at the base of an oak, and he threw his sash over both their heads, making a tent. The space underneath filled with his warmth and her scent. *Strawberries.*

Bàs's heart thumped hard in his chest. No one had ever sat so close to him before, not even his sister when she was tending some wound. And Shana leaning against him was nothing like a sister, not with her warmth and softness calling to him. All of it brought back the feel of her kiss that first night together. *That was before she knew what I was.* The thought made him stiffen, but he didn't move, not even to breathe, until his chest ached. He didn't want to do anything that might cause her to move away.

All around, the men, their sashes draped over their heads, lifted their tankards as the rain tapped harder on the leaves overhead. Their voices rang out in the darkness, a song of battle and valor, of sorrow and love for kin and clan. Even if their voices were ragged and out of tune, they hit the words and beats together like they did marching out to war on campaign. Even and strong, the voices melded, and Bàs opened his mouth to sing the next verse.

"See! They're in disorder!
Comrades, keep close order!
Ever they shall rue the day.
They ventured o'er the border!
Now our foes fly before us!
Vict'ry's banner floateth o'er us!
Raise the loud exulting chorus
Sinclairs win the field."

Shana leaned into Bàs's shoulder, her head finding the side of his arm. His words stopped but then he continued, not wanting to shatter the moment. He was thankful she could take some comfort from him. He continued to sing with the men as they kept vigil, waiting for death. Shana's hand moved to lay on his leg, resting there naturally. His pulse raced as if, in this place of death, a place he'd always dwelled in some way, his heart was waking.

It was terrifying.

CHAPTER NINE

"The ancient Celts had very deliberate rituals regarding death—they believed the best death was one earned in combat or warfare. They knew that they would be reincarnated and the "other" world they went to was just a resting place till they lived again.

Bodies were washed and wrapped in a burial cloth—and often as not burned—but bodies or ashes could be put into minutely measured tombs/ resting places—stone chambers or simply covered with stone and/or earth. Sometimes personal objects were buried with them."

A SHORT VIEW OF SCOTTISH FUNERAL TRADITIONS
BY TOM DORAN

"Hamish! Ye dead man?"

Shana's eyes opened to a gray dawn. She inhaled and smelled damp forest and woodsmoke and realized she was pressed against Bàs's hard chest. Her back ached, and a foul taste coated her mouth from not washing her teeth.

"He ain't breathing," someone whispered. It was Sean who'd taken a spot in the bed, right up against Hamish. He inched away with a groan and nearly rolled off the floppy tick. Ian caught him and helped him stand.

"But his eyes are open," Angus said.

Shana pushed up from Bàs, who released her

from his sash so she could straighten against the aches in her hip and back. She rotated her shoulders to work out the stiffness. "I fell asleep," she murmured, wiping her mouth with her hand. She hoped she hadn't breathed foulness on Bàs.

"'Tis good. Ye missed some of the more scandalous tales," Bàs said, looking down at her as she ran her fingers through the tangled mess of her hair, which had frizzled from the rain. "Hamish led quite a wild life before Margie settled him down."

Angus drew a horn from beside him and struggled to stand. One of the younger warriors helped him. Once he was up, Angus waved him off and held the horn to his lips. He blew, and the deep sound resonated in the dawn.

A younger warrior drew a horn and blew, joining Angus. Cain, Joshua, and Gideon had returned sometime during the night and two of them lifted horns to blow. And then another man ran up with his horn, and another until nearly a dozen horns blew a note that blended into something of a wail. It sent shivers up and down Shana, making gooseflesh pop up on her arms.

Bàs helped her stand, his fingers warm. After a long moment, when more in town gathered, some shirtless and half dressed, the horns stopped, and everyone stood in silence. Were they praying? Shana added her own.

Dear Lord, send Hamish to Margie's open arms. And Jesus's, too, although Hamish really wants to be with his Margie and her tarts. Amen.

She opened her eyes as the men began to move. They worked in silence. "I need to help," Bàs said.

"Of course." Shana let his sash fall away from her.

Bàs, his tunic damp and stuck to the large muscles of his back and shoulders, walked through the path the men made for him. Hamish's eyes were still open, and Bàs gently closed them. He made certain the man's hand was wrapped around the hilt of his sword, which Bàs had told her he'd be buried with.

Elsie stood alone, clutching her hands, and Shana hurried over to hug her with one arm as they watched the men wrap Hamish's body in the sheets and Pastor John murmur words over him. They left his face exposed to the cloud-heavy sky.

"'Twas a good death," Angus said, and a murmur of agreement rose to hover over the glade. No one seemed to want to leave even though many had been there all night in the cold and wet.

Bàs turned to the people. "Thank ye all for giving Hamish the death a warrior deserves." Nods came from them all. Bàs unsheathed his sword, holding it up with the point toward the sky. "Farewell, warrior Hamish of the Sinclair Clan. May ye live forever in Margie's arms."

All around the circle, men drew swords, or if they didn't have one, they held their fists up to the sky. Bàs's voice shot out as he thrust the sword tip high. "Air adhart!"

Shana jumped as the power behind the words snapped like lightning out of him. All the muscles of Bàs's arm were contracted, bulging against his damp tunic.

"Air adhart!" the others repeated, their voices flying high above the trees.

"Onward." Elsie murmured the translation.

Bàs lowered his sword, and the others followed. He looked out at them. "Now 'tis time for the living."

People slowly dispersed, walking down the curved path lined by stone walls. Angus slapped his hand on Bàs's shoulder. "When 'tis my time, take me outside like Hamish. Sean and Iain, too."

"I'll see it done," Bàs said.

Angus nodded, his mouth screwed up in a half smile. He and his two friends walked off together, taking their time so Sean wouldn't feel like he was slowing them down. Joshua followed as if making sure they reached their cottages. Gideon and Cain walked together back toward the castle.

Pastor John signaled four stout warriors to lift and carry Hamish away. "Will they take him to the church now?" Shana asked Elsie, who watched from beside her.

"Aye." She smiled despite her tears. "Pardon." Elsie ran over to Bàs. She looked like she wanted to throw her arms around him but stopped herself. She clutched her hands instead. "Thank ye, Horseman," she said. "Ye made his dying something of beauty."

Bàs nodded. "He was a good man, a strong man. If ye need anything at all, send for Lady Sinclair up at the castle. I am certain Lady Ella will be by today to help ye with his belongings and remind ye that ye may stay here in Girnigoe."

"Thank ye," Elsie said.

He walked past her to Shana. "I'll take ye back to your sister."

Shana and Bàs walked together up the winding

path, the cold morning breeze making her clutch her shawl closer. Her stomach growled.

"There will be food up at the castle, and then ye should rest today," he said.

"Will you return to your cabin?"

"I have animals to care for at home," he said.

"And you don't like being at Girnigoe."

Bàs glanced at her, and their gazes met. "The place holds no fond memories for me." He looked forward again. "I don't like crowds, and my animals need me."

The thought of him leaving felt heavy like the clouds overhead.

He walked her up to the doors but stopped. "Will you not come inside?" she asked.

"'Tis best I get back before I fall asleep and the dogs, cats, and Betty go hungry. Ilsa needs to be put out to graze so she has milk for her calf." His head tipped to the side as he stared at her. "Your eyes were green, but now they look blue, a gray-blue."

"They look green when I'm upset," she said with a small grin. "Blue or gray when I'm more at peace. I suppose 'tis odd."

"Mine are always blue," he said.

She focused on his swollen eye where red spilled over into the white and cleared her throat. "I…am sorry I hit you. I don't usually resort to violence."

He met her gaze. "Because ye bring life, Shana Drummond, and comfort. I deserved your violence."

But hadn't he also given comfort to Hamish, his daughter, and all his friends? "Well, I am still sorry," she murmured. "Here." She uncurled her fingers, holding out her hand. A rock lay in the center of her palm. "For your garden. For Hamish." It was a white rock with a little sparkle to it. "I found it last night. I thought it might do for his stone."

Bàs slowly took it, his fingers brushing her palm. The sensation shot right through Shana with a shiver that reminded her of the fluttering feeling inflicted by his kiss. *He's the Horseman of Death.* The thought made the shiver of heat turn icy.

"Thank ye," Bàs said.

Death had stolen so much from her in the past, and she'd turned her back on it. The heavy weight of sorrow had nearly suffocated her before, and she'd spent years learning to help others evade it. Death was the enemy.

He is death.

With a ragged inhale, she turned and walked toward the solid doors of the keep.

• • •

His wolf sat watching Bàs set Hamish's white stone in a place next to the slightly larger one for his father, George Sinclair.

His eyes slid from right to left over the patterns of stones, some bits of blood still clinging to them, others washed clean. So many lives gone by his hand. Most of them were warriors, but a good many were executions, executions that he hadn't questioned, finding it easier to do his duty without asking about the judging of the condemned.

Bàs knelt before his mother's stone and bowed his head. "Would I have killed her?" he whispered. "Executed Shana without asking her crime? Because

Oliphant requested the Horseman of Death?"

He listened to the breeze in the trees. The branches and leaves gave no answers. Even Apollo and Artemis lay quietly and Beò, as usual, sat guard in silence. *Would I have killed her?* He wanted desperately to say no, but he truly didn't know the answer. The weight of not knowing pressed against his chest.

A branch snapped in the distance, and Bàs stood. Beò rose and trotted toward the sound, the young dogs following him, having decided to be part of his pack.

No one came close to Bàs's cabin without his protective animals being alerted. He also had twisted cording tied between trees in various places that would trip those who didn't know to watch for them.

"Beò?" a woman's voice called. "I hope that's you."

Shana? Was she alone?

Artemis and Apollo barked, their tails wagging. Keenan Sinclair pulled his horse to a stop at the edge of Bàs's clearing, Shana on the back, her arms holding his middle. The sight of her hugging the rugged warrior turned Bàs's gut, which had leaped at the sound of her voice.

"Why have ye come?" he asked, striding over. His eyes narrowed on Keenan.

"She asked me to bring her," Keenan said, his brows rising slightly in question. At what? The anger Bàs couldn't hide from his usually apathetic stare? Or the fact that the woman who'd fought so hard *not* to come to his cabin before had requested just that?

Shana swung her leg over the horse's rump, her

blue petticoat following in a wide drape as she
jumped down. Bàs's arm shot out to steady her as
she landed. "Erskine sent men demanding Ivy and
me back," she said. "I thought you should know."

Bàs looked to Keenan.

"Twenty armed men," Keenan said, answering
the silent question.

Bàs's gaze slid back to Shana. "Are Ivy and her
bairn well?"

Shana looked between the men. "Ivy is growing
stronger even over this night and day. And Edward
is nursing from her without issue."

Bàs nodded in thought and crossed his arms.

"Your brothers are discussing what to do," she
said. "Without you there."

Bàs rarely added to discussions concerning clan
politics. Having accepted his role in the clan as a
child, he'd learned to keep his opinions separate
from his actions. His three older brothers had always seemed eager and competent in deciding
what should be done to keep Clan Sinclair the
strongest in northern Scotland, perhaps all of
Scotland.

Bàs was called in to frighten and kill, not decide.

But this situation had begun with him declaring
war on the Oliphant Clan. He should be part of the
discussion.

"I'll come," he said. "Keenan, ride back and let
my brothers know that nothing should be decided
without me." Keenan's brow rose higher, along with
his grin. The warrior had always ridden with Bàs and
his army of pale green horses. "I but need to secure
my animals," Bàs said.

"Mistress," Keenan said, "I can return ye to Girnigoe."

"I can ride with Bàs," Shana said.

"I'll take her," Bàs said at the same time.

Questions lurked in his friend's gaze, questions for which Bàs had no answers.

"Then I'll ride back with your message." Keenan turned his gray horse around and trotted into the woods the way he'd come.

Shana and Bàs watched him go until only they, Beò, and the dogs remained in the clearing before his cabin.

"What did ye hear that made ye ride out here?" Bàs asked. "With Keenan?"

Keenan probably volunteered when she mentioned wishing to come. Shana was unique and lovely with her red tousled hair and scattering of freckles across her face and neckline. Her greenish eyes were perfectly set with long lashes and displayed her emotions easily. Her smooth skin and high cheekbones would attract any man. And Bàs couldn't stop thinking about the softness of her generous mouth.

Her lips pinched gently. "I fear they want to send us back."

"Ye heard them say this?"

She shook her head. "Only that it was one possibility to stop a war with King James."

"So, James *is* involved?" Bàs had met the tall, opinionated king at the new year when he came to Varrich Castle to test Sinclair loyalty.

"Erskine is involving him," she said. "That was part of the message that his riders brought with his demands." She shook her head. "As soon as Ivy can travel, I'll take her and Edward somewhere safe, perhaps to France."

The vision of Shana, her red hair whipping around her face as she grew smaller, standing at the rail of a ship sailing away, flashed in Bàs's mind. "I'll talk to my brothers. The Sinclairs are strong enough to protect ye and your sister and nephew."

"Even against the king of Scotland?"

He didn't answer.

• • •

Bàs's horse had been washed free of the green stain, revealing a coat that shown so pale yellow that it looked golden. Shana rode before Bàs as the horse moved swiftly and smoothly through the forest where some of the leaves showed hints of fall's approach. "It's as if he flies when he runs," she said and watched the horse's ears twitch. "And his coat shines."

"Dòchas shimmers when he's not playing the mount of the Horseman of Death," Bàs said, his deep voice from behind. "And he's trained since he could walk to fly across the moors."

She leaned forward and slid her hand along the horse's neck, feeling the strength under the golden-hued coat. "What does his name mean? Dòchas."

There was a long pause as they skirted some sharp gorse bushes, their yellow flowers giving warning to the long thorns. "It means hope," he said.

"Hope," she whispered, feeling her throat tighten. The man who rode so powerfully behind her had suffered. It revealed itself in little signs. Yet he was also the strongest man she'd ever met, as if each strike against his soul had honed him into the deadly horseman he portrayed. She shivered.

"Ye're cold," he said, draping the sash of his plaid around her like he had during the vigil.

They emerged from the forest, and Dòchas broke into a gallop that felt like the rolling of waves under Shana. With Bàs's plaid wrapped around her, holding her to his chest, she did not fear falling. Bàs and his horse moved as one across the land studded by gray boulders and clumps of bluebells, yellow buttercups, and purple thistle. A few sheep, sheared earlier in the summer, ran from them, bleating a warning. A small herd of Scottish coos roamed about, lifting their large, horned heads to stare at them from behind shaggy tan hair.

A bit of sun broke through the low clouds to shine over the moor, and for a moment Shana found herself lost in the beauty of it all. It was nothing like the gray stone streets of the town she and Ivy had grown up in south of Edinburgh. Here, riding the Highland wind, safely tucked next to a fierce warrior who had already saved her life three times, she felt free.

"Thank you," she called out, the wind snatching the words away.

The moor gave way to the village before the massive stone Girnigoe Castle, which sat clinging to the rocky seacoast, and Bàs slowed his horse. Even though Shana had stayed two nights there, the sight of the castle, fortified by ten-foot-thick walls, a dug moat, and two drawbridges still caught her breath.

Who could possibly breach this place? Could King James? And how many would die if he tried?

Shana's stomach flipped as she felt Bàs lean into her. His voice came at her ear, low words without emotion. "I don't deserve your gratitude." The absence of sorrow, anger, teasing, or stubbornness made her turn to his face. Lord in Heaven, he was handsome. A short-cropped beard followed the squareness of his chin and jaw, framing a full mouth that she didn't imagine smiled much. His brows were furrowed as he looked out toward the road his horse followed.

"You saved me from the wolves and from Erskine Oliphant," she said.

He looked down, his eyes holding the emotion that was absent from his voice. It stopped her breath. "'Tis a blessing that we met before I was called to your execution." His lips parted as if he'd say more, but then he didn't, his gaze going back to the path before them.

Shana turned forward. They both knew what he would have said. She'd said it with accusation before. He might have killed her without questioning Erskine. He'd have been doing his duty as the Horseman of Death.

You wouldn't have killed me. The thought sat on her tongue, but she didn't release the words, because she didn't know if they were true. *He's death. I am all about life, and I hate death.* She shook her head in silence at the huge chasm between them.

Several men who she recognized from Hamish's vigil nodded to Bàs as they passed. A few women stood outside their homes, churning butter or hanging tunics from a line. They didn't retreat, but many of the children hid in the folds of their mothers' petticoats, peeking out to glimpse Bàs. They were afraid of him, and studying the women's faces, many of them were, too.

Keenan stood beside the raised portcullis. "I gave them your message to wait until ye arrived before making decisions," he said, his gaze moving to her. Did he care for Shana?

Keenan met her gaze. "Ye are well, mistress?"

Could Bàs's friend think his touch was dangerous, too? "I'm quite well," she answered, and gave him a tight smile. Bàs moved on and she whispered, "Bloody arse."

Bàs snorted the smallest bit. "Ye don't like Keenan?"

She glanced at him and caught the softening of his mouth. The hint of a grin sat in the corners. It was a crack in the unemotional mask he always wore. "He's your friend and yet he questions if you did anything to me."

Bàs's grin faded. "I am the Horseman of Death, Shana, and he would protect ye from it, from me."

She huffed. "We must shake that notion from your clan."

"Why?" he asked, his brows pinching between his clear blue eyes.

The question made her blink. "Because you aren't merely death, Bàs Sinclair, even if that's your name."

"It's all I've ever been. 'Tis my duty, my purpose."

She snorted and turned forward again as they rode over a second drawbridge and into a bailey paved with flat stones.

Bàs dismounted and reached up, his large hands going around her middle to lift her down. They were strong hands, spanning her waist, and she wondered how warm they would be on her skin if she weren't wearing a bodice, stays, and shift. The thought made her pulse race, and she pressed a hand against her heart before dropping it back to the folds of her skirt.

They walked without speaking toward the large doors leading into the keep. Everything about the Sinclairs was large: their horses, their castle, and their horsemen. Keenan caught up to them to flank Shana's other side.

Bàs's three brothers stood in the Great Hall on either side of a long table. Cain was the eldest and chief. Joshua was known as the Horseman of War, and Shana had certainly seen how he liked to cause mischief. Gideon was the brother who dealt with all the legal matters and had a way of staring into you that made you want to confess even your smallest sins. He could have been a priest on the continent.

All the brothers wore a tattooed horse's head on their arms, which were bared in their shorter-sleeved tunics that they must wear during the warm days of August. The men were of similar stature, brawny, tan, and fierce, but Bàs, with all his swinging of his ax, seemed the largest.

Joshua crossed his arms, frowning at Bàs. "Ye order us not to discuss clan matters without ye, little brother?"

Bàs kept striding toward them. "Not when they have to do with me."

Shana walked with him, Keenan too. Hard expressions and Bàs's fisted stride increased the tension in the room.

Joshua's brows rose in a teasing look that warred with the tightness of his mouth and fists. "We've never had a disaster caused by ye before, little brother. Gideon didn't have a procedure drawn up for the occasion."

Shana stopped several steps behind Bàs as he continued right up to Joshua. Fists at his sides as if ready to fly, Bàs stood straighter, huge shoulders rolling back almost as if he unfolded to his true towering form.

Bàs spoke succinctly in his brother's face. "Call me Death, or Bàs, or younger brother, but if ye held your tongue long enough to look, there is nothing little about me."

CHAPTER TEN

"Let us have nothing so much in minde as death.
At the stumbling of a horse, at the fall of a stone,
at the least prick with a pinne, let us presently
ruminate and say with our selves,
what if it were death it selfe?"
FRENCH PHILOSOPHER, MICHEL DE MONTAIGNE
(1533–1592) FELT THAT WE SHOULD THINK ABOUT
DEATH CONSTANTLY TO PREPARE FOR ITS INEVITABILITY.

Bàs stood before Joshua, waiting for his older
brother to strike. Two years ago, Joshua would already be swinging, but since returning with his wife
from Orkney Isle, the Horseman of War wasn't so
predictable. Either way, Bàs wished Shana was
standing farther back.

Joshua's nostrils flared, but then a grin crept over
his lips. "It seems all parts of our *youngest* brother
have grown, including his ballocks."

"Enough," Cain said, but Bàs kept Joshua's gaze
until his prickly brother turned to the table.

"We don't need a war inside Girnigoe as well as
outside," Gideon said.

"I'm not the one who declares war without discussing it with my chief first," Joshua said, glancing
at Bàs over his shoulder. "Some of us have families
to protect now and must think before we drag others
into war."

Gideon cleared his throat, his mouth twisted

slightly. "Attacking a royal garrison on Orkney Isle pretty much did that, Joshua," he said, referring to Joshua's adventure the previous year.

Across the hall, Gideon's wife, Cait, walked out from the arched stairwell with Cain's wife, Ella, who held their daughter, Mary. "At least I don't feel like I'm going to retch all the time now," Cait said.

She and Gideon had announced her pregnancy last month. With all these bairns coming to Girnigoe, the focus of the Sinclair Clan seemed to be changing. Perhaps *that's* what they should be talking about.

Gideon left their tight circle to stride over to Cait.

"What's wrong?" Cait said when she gazed into his face.

"Nothing yet," Gideon said.

She glanced at the brothers by the table. "Whatever it is, Gideon is not running off to the Edinburgh court until *after* this babe is born."

Cain walked over, kissing Ella and then Mary on the forehead. The bairn reached for him, her plump hands grasping in the air until he lifted her. The bairn immediately tugged on the thin braid fashioned in his hair that ran along his jawline. When he pried it from her fingers, she latched onto the gold ring he wore on his right hand, proclaiming him the Horseman of Conquest.

Bàs's thumb slid against his own ring, the one with an ax etched into one side and a skull on the other. Another reminder that he was Death, something he'd never questioned while his father lived.

"Perhaps we brothers should go to the library to

discuss this…issue," Gideon said.

Both ladies frowned. "If it affects the whole clan, we should be part of the discussion," Ella said. Guilt tugged at Bàs. He would be responsible if any of his brothers died in a war he started.

"And Rhona is in the library letting the children pick out books to take back to Varrich," Cait said, her mutinous gaze on Gideon.

Joshua dropped his arms, sitting at the table. "Well, our *youngest* brother is ready to lead our clan in the war he started."

"I did not say that," Bàs said. Joshua was such an arse, and even more so when Kára wasn't around.

Ella walked over to join Shana. "Which is deserved, from what Ivy has told me. Erskine Oliphant is a monster." Ella looked to Cain. "He may not have branded his wife, but he abused her every month when her courses came, proving she wasn't pregnant."

Cain swore under his breath.

Gideon looked to Shana. "Mistress, ye need to know that Erskine Oliphant has accused ye of being a witch. He's sent word to King James that ye took his son and sacrificed him to Satan, then stole his rightful wife away, and that the Sinclairs are harboring the two of ye."

"A witch?" Bàs said, his fists pounding one on top of the other.

"Erskine is crafty, using an accusation of witchcraft to gain the king's attention." Cain held Mary casually over one shoulder, his frown fierce as he looked out at the group. "King James wages war on sorcery, hanging or burning those accused without proper investigation. He thinks witches prevented his young bride, Anne of Denmark, from crossing the North Sea to reach him. 'Tis said he's writing a book describing witches and how to find them."

Gideon held up a parchment. "And he's found a woman who swears she heard Shana Drummond chanting and saw her take the bairn, wrapping it tightly and running away with him into the woods."

They all turned toward Shana. She crossed her arms. "I've never chanted anything, but I did take Edward away at Ivy's insistence that Erskine would kill him because he'd been told the child isn't his." Her gaze moved from Cain to Gideon. "My sister's only crime is that she tried to find a way to stop her monthly beatings by getting herself with child with another man."

"Who is Edward's father?" Cait asked and sat at the table opposite Joshua. "And where is he? He should be helping your sister, not abandoning her and his son."

Shana glanced toward the stairs as if worried her sister would hear. "His name is Liam Ross."

Bàs shook his head when Cain looked his way. "I haven't heard of him."

"Nor I," Gideon said. "But the Oliphant Clan is large."

Shana exhaled long. "She stopped seeing him as soon as she knew she was pregnant, trying to distance herself from him to protect him." Shana cupped her cheeks as if reliving Ivy's explanation. "When Ivy's friend told her Erskine knew he wasn't the father, Ivy begged Liam to leave the village."

"Without her?" Joshua asked, his words

snapping. "He's a coward then." For someone who wasn't the judge of the clan, Joshua was quick to disapprove.

Shana clutched her hands before her. "She convinced Liam that his leaving would protect her and the babe, that she could convince Erskine the babe was his."

Silence in the hall was broken only by Mary fussing to be let down to practice her new skill of walking. Ella took her, holding her wee hands, guiding her as she toddled. "Perhaps something should...*happen* to Erskine Oliphant," Ella said, glancing at Cain.

Cain let out a small growl. "Ye are not sneaking over there in the middle of the night to assassinate him."

"Ye aren't either," Gideon said, pointing to Cait, who had opened her mouth. "No matter how well ye climb."

Cait gave him a playful glare. "I was going to suggest we women pay the Oliphant Village a visit," Cait said. "See what the wives say about the chief, if there are others who would like to see a new chief in his place. What type of support Erskine has and if any of them really believe Ivy's sister to be a witch."

"Nay," Gideon and Cain said at once.

"A woman heavy with child would hardly be seen as a threat," Joshua's wife, Kára, said, walking out from the alcove, her stomach protruding. She had one hand pressing on her lower back and one holding her unbreeched son on her hip. "I could waddle in there and back out without a single guard paying me any attention." She looked at Joshua with a broad smile.

Joshua jumped up to go to his wife. He scooped Adam from her and escorted her to the table. "Ye can go," he said.

Kára's brows rose in surprise, and Joshua kissed her on the mouth.

He threw his arm around her shoulders, locking her to his side. "But I will be there with ye every step of the way. Waddling in and out."

She snorted. "Now *that* won't attract attention at all."

Bàs glanced at Shana. Reddish hair around her shoulders and the freckles across her smooth-looking skin painted a perfect resemblance to a Highland fairy he'd seen depicted in one of Gideon's books. Could a witch hunter see her otherworldly beauty as evil, her freckles as witch's spots?

Distress in Shana's features twisted Bàs's gut. "What do ye think, Shana?" he asked. In his years of silence, he'd learned the importance of listening, not only to words but to inflections and postures. The way Shana stood, her back straight, her face tight and pale, there were things inside her, ideas swirling about.

"Ye have firsthand knowledge of the village of Wick and the castle," Bàs said. "And of Erskine."

Shana tipped her chin upward, and he noticed how much taller she was to his sisters by marriage. She crossed her arms, holding tightly to her elbows. "Ivy and I will not be responsible for civil war, pitting the Sinclair Clan against the crown." She shook her head. "We will take Edward and leave here on our own, without aid from the Sinclairs."

Bàs's chest squeezed, making his voice rough. "I

will not have ye sacrifice yourselves to the wolves. I'll go with ye."

"We Sinclair brothers are the Four Horsemen," Joshua said, frowning. "Not three. Ye cannot go."

Incredulity tightened Bàs's face. "Ye're reported dead on Orkney. We're already three."

Joshua, Adam draped over one arm, threw his unburdened arm wide. "No one believes a dandy Stewart killed me. Only James believes that shite." The bairn kicked and laughed as he tried to reach his toes peeking out from his long infant gown.

"Keep the foul words inside around the babes," Ella said.

Bàs stared hard at Joshua. "Then James will also believe that Shana and her sister are under the protection of the Horseman of Death. I will carry them away where they will be safe."

Joshua pointed at Bàs, his brows high. "Ye aren't turning your foking back on this clan for…" His gaze slid to Shana.

Kára, anticipating the trouble Joshua's tongue could cause, snatched Adam from Joshua's arm. The bairn had been the only thing holding Bàs back. He took two strides toward his arse of a brother, his fist pulling back. *Crack!*

Pain burst in his knuckles as they collided with Joshua's hard jaw, throwing him backward. Joshua didn't fall, but he did stumble, either from the impact or the surprise. Bàs had never struck any of them before. He saved all his fury for battle. Even his executions were performed without emotion.

"Bàs?!" Hannah yelled from the doorway as she strode into the hall, pushing her hood back off her head. "You're fighting with Joshua? What's going on?" Her gaze slid about the people standing with wide eyes. Even Cain seemed stunned where he stood behind Joshua as if Bàs had performed some trick of magic.

Bàs kept his fists before him as he watched Joshua, judging whether he would come at him. The surprise on his older brother's features as he rubbed his chin turned dark, his nostrils flaring under dark, pinched brows. He charged forward, and Bàs's heart stopped as Shana jumped before him.

• • •

Shana closed her eyes, waiting for the impact of a charging bull. "Stop!" she yelled.

"Stop!"

"Stad!"

"Bloody hell!"

One and two-word exclamations filled the hall, punctuated by one of the babes crying out at the sudden frenzy. Before Shana could open her eyes, steely arms grabbed her, pulling her off the floor and swinging her behind him. She opened her eyes as her feet touched down. "Shana!" Bàs stood, staring her in the face. "Ye could have been killed."

Her heart pounded with the truth of his words, making her voice breathless. "Rather I die than be responsible for tearing this clan apart."

Joshua's hard words came from behind Bàs, air funneling in and out of his nose so hard she could hear it. "If I'd killed ye, lass, there'd be no saving this clan."

Her breath came quickly as she stared up into Bàs's tortured face. He'd already lived a life of pain, and she couldn't add more. "We will be fine," she said to him. "Ivy and I will go south to our childhood town."

"Nay," Bàs said, shaking his head.

Keenan stepped up beside her. "I'll take them, keep them safe."

Instead of looking appeased or relieved, Bàs's face hardened even more as he turned it to his warrior. "Ye will not. If Shana leaves, *I* will take her."

Keenan exhaled, and he nodded once slowly, stepping back. There was nothing but respect and wariness in the warrior's expression.

"No one is going anywhere right now," Ella Sinclair called out. Hannah had taken Mary from her, and Ella walked around the large form of Bàs and took Shana's arm. She patted it. "They are rough and rowdy lads sometimes." She glanced at Bàs. "Although I've never seen Bàs violent outside battle." She tugged Shana along toward the stairs. "Let's check on Ivy and Edward. She was asking for you earlier."

Shana looked over her shoulder where Bàs watched her. Kára blotted some blood from Joshua's lip while he stood with his hands fisted. Hannah had ahold of Bàs's arm as if to stop him from running after Shana. Cain and Gideon stared after her, their faces tight with concern. Concern that their brother was willing to leave their clan for her after they'd only just met? How could he consider it? How could she allow the idea to take root in her, chasing away the chill of worry?

She took a deep breath as she climbed the steps behind Ella. "He feels guilty he was sent to execute me," Shana said. "That he may have done so without question if he hadn't met me and Edward first. 'Tis why he's acting protective now."

Ella stopped, leaning against the spiral staircase to look down at her. "Bàs doesn't let us into his thoughts and feelings. He's remained apart and quiet for the two years I've been here, and Cain says he's been like that for a long time. When his father started making him kill and people showed their fear of him." She gave Shana an odd smile, her arched brows bending. "'Tis nice to see him reacting." Her smile turned into a sly grin. "And 'tis always a good day to see Joshua knocked around a bit." She started to walk again. "'Tis good for him. He's got his father's temper."

"Does Bàs have his mother's then?" Shana asked as they continued up to the landing.

"I was a child and an enemy to the Sinclairs when Alice Sinclair died, but from what I have heard, the woman had a generous heart and could calm the fury right out of her husband. The day she died, George Sinclair lost his mind to grief. Everyone around him took the brunt of his anguish, most of all his sons."

"Most of all Bàs?" Shana asked. "Because she died giving birth to him?"

They'd stopped outside the bedroom Ivy was using, and Ella met her gaze. "Yes, I fear so. Bàs hasn't forgiven himself for living when she died giving him life."

Shana's heart felt sick. She touched Ella's arm,

squeezing it gently. "I'm certain that Alice Sinclair doesn't blame him, and given what you've said, she likely would have given her life for her babe. I know I would have for my babe."

Had Shana said too much? Her past wasn't exactly a secret, but she didn't talk about it without reason. Before Ella could ask her anything, Shana pushed into the room. The sight of Edward nursing against Ivy loosened the heartache she felt, and she smiled. "I'm so happy to see you well," Shana said, going over to the bed.

Ivy had lighter hair than Shana, and more delicate features, taking after their mother. She smiled up at her sister. "Thanks to you helping me with the birth and…afterward." Her smile faltered at mention of being thrown from the childbirth bed into the dungeon.

Ivy glanced around Shana to Ella. "And thanks to you for breaking us out of that terrible place."

Ella smiled, nodding. "I'll leave you two and go see if Joshua's getting his arse kicked. Just because Bàs is quiet doesn't mean he's easily beat. In fact, I think he's the biggest of all four of them," she whispered as if Cain might overhear.

The door shut, and Ivy frowned at Shana. "What's going on between the brothers?" She carefully lifted Edward up over her shoulder, patting his back.

Shana sat at the edge of the bed. "Erskine has accused me of witchcraft and killing Edward to satisfy Satan or some such nonsense."

Ivy's eyes opened wide. "Do the Sinclairs believe you're a witch?"

"I don't think so, but Erskine's sent his accusations to Edinburgh, and King James is apparently vicious in his hunt for witches."

"He thinks Edward is dead?" Ivy asked. The babe released a burp, and her sister switched him to her other breast.

"Yes."

"We could leave here then," Ivy said. "Take my babe and run."

Shana nodded and leaned forward to squeeze her sister's arm. "We need to get you strong enough first." She took a full breath, glancing toward the door. "Then the two of us and Edward will leave."

CHAPTER ELEVEN

"[I will] faithfully and diligently exercise the said
office according to such cunning and knowledge as
God has given me. [I will] 'not suffer a labouring
woman to name any than the true father of the
child' nor 'allow any woman to give birth in secret.'
[I will have] 'two or three other honest women
present,' who, along with the midwife, could
demand to know the name of the child's father, to
report to the magistrate.

EARLIEST KNOWN MIDWIFERY OATH,
ELEANOR PEAD, 1567

"Hitting Joshua," Hannah said, shaking her head as
she poured a diluted tincture over the broken skin
on Bàs's knuckles. His sister had taken care of him
like a mother since he could remember, always hiding any of his weaknesses or illnesses from their
father, who would've railed against Bàs if he'd
known. Hannah had nursed away the coughs he'd
seemed prone to and had treated all his cuts and
scrapes so they wouldn't get tainted.

They sat in the Great Hall together near the
hearth where the morning's fire had burned down to
coals. Cain stood at the table peering over Gideon's
shoulder as he composed a letter to King James.
Hannah dabbed at the dried blood. "You know
Joshua's head is as hard as a boulder," she said.

Bàs had grown up with Joshua and his irksome

comments, but when he'd insinuated that Shana wasn't worth him leaving the clan, something had snapped inside Bàs. He didn't say anything but let Hannah apply a balm over the cuts and bruises.

She glanced up at him even though her head was bowed. "You like her, Shana Drummond."

"She's innocent of Erskine's slander, and her sister is in dire need of help, too."

Hannah looked back at his knuckles, taking a strip of clean cloth to bind them even though Bàs didn't think they needed it. "She's bonny with all those freckles and fiery hair," Hannah said. "I've never seen the like. And she's terribly brave to help her sister, going back for her after getting her son to safety. Noble and brave."

Bàs's chest felt tight, and he had to swallow past the boulder in his throat before he could reply. "And I almost beheaded her." His voice was soft, but Hannah straightened, meeting his gaze.

"But you didn't."

"But I could have."

She shook her head, reaching forward to squeeze his arm. "But you didn't. You saved her. You have nothing for which to chastise yourself, Bàs."

He met her familiar gaze. "Have I killed other innocents? Because I didn't know their stories and didn't ask?"

She squeezed tighter, her lips in a thin line, but she didn't answer.

The door slammed open in the entry, and a villager rushed inside. His head turned this way and that and then he ran over to Cain. "Mistresses Hilda and Harriett are helping John Mackay's wife at

Varrich in her birthing and my Liza has spilled her waters. Someone said the lass ye rescued from the Oliphants is a midwife."

Bàs stood. "Aye, Shana's a midwife."

John clutched his hands before him, pumping them as if in desperate prayer. "Please get her. Liza says she's going to die with this bairn. 'Tis her seventh. Says she's too old." He shook his head. "I can't carry on without her."

"I'll send her right down," Hannah said, hurrying toward the steps.

Gideon handed the man a small cup of whisky, looking a bit pale himself. His wife was pregnant for the first time, and they all had been told how mad their father went when he lost his wife.

The men stood around silently, each lost in their thoughts.

If I'd killed Shana, would I be responsible for John's wife dying, too? Bàs rubbed his jaw at the ache under his clipped beard.

"I'm here." Shana's call preceded her brisk walk forward, setting things in motion. She wore a clean gown of soft green wool, her thick hair plaited to fall over one shoulder. There was no panic in her face. Only a fierce determination.

John beckoned with wide gestures. "This way, mistress."

"I'll accompany ye," Bàs said.

"I'll help, too," Hannah said, hurrying with them out through the entryway into the bailey where the shadows of night were growing.

Shana's arm brushed Bàs's as they bent together under the partly lowered portcullis. The touch was brief, but he sought to remember the pressure and the feel of his pulse quickening. He'd tuck away each touch into his memory for when he was once again alone. *Maybe you'll be with her.* Impossible when their two worlds were so opposite. *She'll never forgive me for—*

"Last eve we helped Hamish leave this world," she said, interrupting his dark thoughts. "And this eve we help a new life in."

Maybe that's why he felt drawn to Shana. Because she brought people in to make up for him taking them out. That and she was an exceptionally beautiful lass who he realized smelled of strawberries. Aunt Merida's or Hannah's soap. It suited her.

John stopped before the door of a squat cottage on the west side of the village. Instead of opening it, he ran to the side window where the shutters were cracked. "I brought the midwife, luv."

His statement was answered with a groan. "I'm dying, John," a woman yelled from inside the house. "Because ye did this to me again."

The man blanched, jumping back from the window. He turned to Shana, shaking his head. He lowered his voice. "If 'tis my Lizzy who dies or the bairn, let the bairn go, but save Lizzy."

"Has she had trouble in the past?" Shana asked.

John shook his head. "Six other bairns without a problem."

Lord, if the woman died, John would have to raise all those children on his own. Bàs couldn't imagine it.

The door was yanked open, and a lass who looked barely old enough to have a child herself

waved Shana and Hannah inside. She was probably
John's oldest daughter, Jean. Her eyes were wide,
and she wore an apron that looked wet and wrinkled
as if she'd been wringing it in her hands.

Bàs walked up to John and let his hand fall heavily on the man's shoulder. Bàs would have said
things like "It will all be well" and "You'll have a
healthy bairn tonight," but the truth was no one
knew for certain with such a dangerous task as childbirth.

• • •

Shana's gaze swept the dim room. It was stuffy and
hot and smelling of damp herbs and birthing waters,
and she nearly choked. "Open the windows," she
said.

"And let in the specter of death?" asked the girl.
"He's standing right outside the door with Da."

Shana frowned, but it was obvious the girl was
frightened and overwhelmed. "Bàs will not harm
anyone in this room, but the lack of fresh air will."

The girl ran to the shuttered windows, throwing
them wide. "What ye doing?" the woman lying in the
bed asked. She looked to be middle-aged with fine
lines at the corners of her eyes and gray just starting
near her temples. Sweat beaded on her face.

"She said to open them," the girl called back.

"Who are ye?" the laboring woman asked, pushing up in the bed, but before Shana could answer,
the woman's face pinched in obvious pain.

"I'm Shana Drummond, a midwife." She walked
over, looking to the girl. "Is there hot water?" The

girl nodded. "Good. I need hot water by the bed, a bar of soap, a clean piece of rope, fresh sheets, and a sharp knife that's been heated in the flames."

"Put another knife under the bed to cut the pain," Hannah said. The old advice worked only if the mother believed it.

"Ye're a midwife?" the woman asked. "Ye barely look old enough to have a bairn, let alone deliver one." A low groan followed while she puffed out her cheeks.

"Let the air out," Shana instructed. "Don't hold it. I've helped deliver fifty-three babes." Shana pulled a chair up close to the straining woman. "And you've had several," she said, nodding to the girl who struggled with Hannah to lift the cauldron off the iron spider in the hearth.

"I've had six bairns," she yelled, her gaze snapping toward the window that was open halfway. "I was supposed to be done, but here I am with number seven." She raised her voice. "And it's going to kill me, I tell ye. Tear me asunder." Her eyes looked wild enough that Shana thought she might believe her dire prediction.

"What's your name?"

The woman sniffed back what could be tears. Sweat matted her hair, and her smock looked stained. Her hands were red, and she wrung them in the crumpled quilt.

"Lizzy. Lizzy Gilroy."

"And I'm Jean," the girl said and jumped back as some of the water sloshed over the lip of the cauldron as they set it down. "My little sister is with the neighbor lady, and Da said all the lads had to find somewhere to go while Mamma labors."

"Mistresses Harriett and Hilda are helping with another birth right now," Hannah said. "But Shana is here to help. And me of course, although I've only helped birth horses."

Lizzy looked at Hannah. "'Twill give ye nightmares." Hannah's eyes widened, but she didn't move.

"Pish," Shana said, waving her hand. "It can be beautiful."

"Well, ye've never had one squeeze out of ye," Lizzy yelled.

"Actually, I have," Shana replied evenly. "And it was hard and frightening, and because of that I swore to learn how to help other women through it in the easiest way possible."

Shana gently squeezed the woman's arm. "Lizzy." She waited until the tired mother met her gaze. "We are going to get you through this. Your body knows what to do and so does your babe. You've done it before."

"I'm too old to do this," she said and blinked, but a tear still escaped.

Shana caught her hand with both of hers. "You are a warrior woman, Lizzy." That caught her attention, and Shana smiled reassuringly. "We women are strong enough to bring life into the world, and you've done so six times. You're courageous and strong."

"I don't feel courageous and strong," she said, her voice low as her brow puckered like she might cry.

"Men riding out into battle don't always feel courageous and strong, either," Shana said.

"They don't?" Jean asked.

"No." Shana stroked her hand. Touch could be a powerful tool to reassure the mother. "Sometimes they are tired or nauseous or afraid they won't make it through."

"I feel nauseous," Lizzy said softly, her hand clutching Shana's.

Shana kept her gaze. "They may even worry over a grown child who is riding with them. That they might not be strong enough to bring that child home."

Tears suddenly broke from Lizzy's eyes, and she sucked in a fast sob, squeezing Shana's hand. "John said he wants me to live, not the bairn," she said. "But…" She glanced at her round stomach, her other hand running lovingly over it. "I loved the little lad or lass from the time they kicked me inside."

More tears came, and Shana felt her own gathering. The unbidden memories of her past twisted up inside her like a whirlwind. The silent, limp babe. The brief *I am sorry for your loss*. The bitterness of still having to go through the pain and healing when she had the emptiness of loss weighing down on her.

Shana managed to keep her own tears back except for one, feeling its hot trail down her cheek. She let out a long breath, nodding gently. She cleared her throat. "I understand that well," Shana said, wiping the one tear away.

Lizzy looked at her. "Yer bairn?"

Shana shook her head, and Lizzy squeezed Shana's hand back. "But," Shana said, "when I lost my son at birth, I vowed to learn everything I could to give babes and warrior mothers every chance under heaven to make it through their own battles."

She took a steadying breath to fortify herself. "I've learned how to preserve life, whether new life or more experienced life," she said, referring to the mother.

Lizzy nodded quickly. "Aye, I believe ye did."

Shana smiled. Reliving her own horror to help this woman trust her was worth the pain the memory brought. "Very well, Lizzy Gilroy, warrior mother, let's get this battle won."

• • •

When I lost my son…

Bàs moved immediately away from the window after he heard Shana's words. He'd never been an eavesdropper, preferring to know as little about others as possible. He avoided all attachments, not knowing if he'd be called to execute them or someone they loved.

But he'd heard, and the words moved through his mind like a serpent, creating more questions as he and John paced outside the window for over an hour. Shana Drummond had lost a son. *Had she been married? Was she still married?* She didn't wear a ring, but not everyone did. *Had she run away? Was her husband dead?*

"Gu cath!"

Bàs straightened suddenly as the war cry flew from the half-open window. John grabbed his arm, holding on as if fear had struck him mad.

"Did…" John started, realizing he clung to the Horseman of Death's arm and dropping it, and pointed at his cottage. "Did someone in there yell 'to battle'?"

"Gu cath!" came another voice.

"Gu cath!"

"Aye," Bàs said over the continued war cry from within. The women's voices rose, punctuated by a drawn-out groan.

"Breathe." Shana's voice called, echoed by another, probably Hannah. "Yell it out," Shana said, and a voice filled with primal power washed forth. "Gu cath!" The war cry sent chill bumps up Bàs's nape.

John stumbled on his feet, and Bàs grabbed him, helping him sit on a stump. Again, the cry came, and several other voices followed with it, all of them hollering as if they rode fiercely into the melee of battle.

The two men stared at the window, but neither of them would go near it. What the bloody hell happened inside a birthing chamber? Bàs had helped many horses be born in their stables. Even with difficult births, the horses didn't yell war cries. An army of barbarians would stop in their tracks if hit with such a sound, coming from many raised voices with such power.

"Waaaaa!"

"The bairn," John said, standing, his hands fisted by his sides. Several minutes later, Hannah stood at the window, pushing it open with one hand while she cradled a bairn in her other arm.

"'Tis a healthy girl," she said. The bairn yelled her own war cry, making Bàs smile.

"Lizzy?" John asked, not willing to even look at the babe. Had his father refused to look at Bàs when he knew his wife lay dying? Bàs's smile faded abruptly.

Hannah glanced behind her but then turned to smile at the nervous man. "Lizzy is a warrior woman to be extremely proud of."

"She ain't dying?" he asked, his hand clasped onto Bàs's arm again as if his world were tilting.

"Not if Shana and she have anything to do about it," Hannah said and ducked back inside.

"Thank ye, Lord!" John yelled and threw his arms around Bàs, pinning his arms to his sides.

A rumble of laughter came from Bàs with such relief for the man. Bàs caught sight of Angus walking farther down the lane. The old man nodded to him, and a sense of calm seemed to claim Bàs. "Aye, 'tis balanced," he murmured. And it felt good.

John released him and ran to the door but stopped, his hands out to the sides as if he didn't know quite what to do. "Can I come in?" he yelled.

The door opened but the daughter blocked the space. She held her chin high and met her father's gaze. "'Tis women's work, Da. Ye'll have to wait. Mama's a warrior woman and needs to be washed and rested." She closed the door.

John turned around slowly, a look of surprise across his face. But it changed to joy, and he laughed, running to the window. "Ye are a warrior, Lizzy! Ye always have been. Love ye, lass!"

"Love ye, too, ye randy arse," she yelled back, making him laugh harder.

The door opened again, and Hannah came out. "I am going to gather some food and a fresh smock from up at Girnigoe," she said. "'Tis fortunate I keep a supply of extra clothes."

"I'll help," Bàs said, striding next to her.

"Thank ye, milady," John said as he plopped down on his stump, wearing a grin that reminded Bàs of someone who'd drunk too much whisky.

Hannah kept quiet as they walked, her shoes crunching. She glanced at Bàs. "Were you listening at the window?"

He didn't say anything for several strides. "We could hear the war cries."

Hannah snorted softly and smiled. "'Tis quite empowering. Shana decided that Lizzy needed to treat birthing like a battle, a battle for life instead of a battle for death."

"That was wise," Bàs said, pride filling his chest. Not that he had any claim on Shana, but she was extraordinary, like he'd known from the start. *Lost my son.* What had she been through to make her so wise?

"She's brilliant," Hannah said and glanced at him again, her smile dimming. "But did you hear her speaking about her past?"

He strode without answering, only his boots and her slippers crunching on the pebbles lining the path. Finally, the words came out. "She lost a son."

"Did you know?" Hannah asked.

He shook his head without looking at her.

Hannah put her arm through his. His sister, who usually felt fragile, walked with strength as if the birthing had filled her with power, too. "'Tis best not to let questions fester. Shana has a past like each one of us." She looked up at him. "The past creates who we are." She patted his chest. "As you know." They continued toward the gray fortress where his past had created the Horseman of Death.

• • •

"Go on now," Ivy said, her eyes half closed. "Edward was up a lot last night, so I'm taking a much-needed nap with him."

Shana turned from the arched window. "You're certain?"

Ivy waved a hand toward the door and yawned, turning on her side to face the sleeping bairn who was next to her on the wide bed. Rolled blankets surrounded him on the other sides to keep him from falling off in case he was suddenly strong enough to roll.

"We'll be well," Ivy said. "You're all rested and bathed and looking lovely. You should be with people, not stuck in here all day."

The day before had been a day of recovery after being up with Lizzy Gilroy and her babe most of the night after the birth. Shana had slept and bathed and eaten up in the room with Ivy and then slept another full night while the rain and wind swept around the castle. It was finally clear, although puddles dotted the bailey under their window.

"Very well," Shana said, glancing at her sister and nephew. Edward hadn't really disturbed Shana during the night, except that his cries spurred dreams of her own lost boy. She'd heard her small son crying in the dream even though she held him, his eyes and mouth clearly closed, his skin a dull gray color. Melancholy felt like lead in her chest.

Taking her cloak with her, Shana walked down the winding stairs. Had Bàs returned to his cabin in the woods? She hadn't had time to talk with him since before the birthing.

"Good morn," Kára called out as Shana entered the Great Hall. She sat next to Cait and Ella at the long table.

"Glad to see you down," Ella said, waving her over. "Here are some of our cook's delicious tarts, along with ham and eggs."

"And warm bread," Cait said from behind her hand as she finished chewing.

Shana walked over. "You're all alone this morn?" Were the men out preparing to war against the crown? Because of her?

Ella made room for her along the table. "We have no further news from the Oliphants or King James. The men are out training with their horses on the north field."

"As they normally do," Kára added. "I would be training myself with daggers, but my time is coming near." She indicated her large belly. It seemed like she might be due any moment, from the size.

"Is the babe moving well inside?" Shana asked, sampling the delicious fare.

"With ferocious kicks," Kára said, smiling. "I fear he or she will have Joshua's temper." The look on her face showed that she didn't mind. She glanced behind her and then lowered her voice. "My grandmother and aunt are midwives in the village, but after your amazing help with Lizzy Gilroy, I wonder if perhaps you could attend me."

"And me," Cait said. "When my time comes this winter."

"You heard about the birth?" Shana asked. Had

they also heard what Shana had revealed to help Lizzy? That Shana had birthed and lost a babe herself?

Ella took up her mug of morning ale. "By sundown yesterday, Lizzy had told everyone in the village how encouraging you were with her, how you'd helped her rally her spirits like a coward forced to head to battle." She lifted her cup, saluting Shana, and smiled broadly. "You're likely to have every pregnant woman in the area asking for you."

Shana looked to Kára. "I've overstepped? With your aunt and grandmother?"

Kára waved off her concern. "They've had their hands full and could use some help. With the men not warring, they've been busy making babes." She laughed, patting her belly.

"I'd be happy to help," Shana said, "while I am here."

"Once this is cleared up," Ella said, "we'd be happy to have you and Ivy stay on at Girnigoe."

"Or in the village of Varrich," Cait said. "That's where Gideon and I live. He's the chief of the Mackay Clan there where I run a school and an orphanage. We're in need of a knowledgeable midwife."

Where the Oliphants had been suspicious of her talents, these ladies seemed to embrace Shana. "Thank you, all of you. I will speak with Ivy about where we will live…if all this mess gets resolved."

Ella laid her hand on Shana's arm and squeezed gently. "*When* this mess gets resolved. Not if."

Shana released her exhale. "Ivy and I will not be responsible for a civil war," she said under her breath. Glances between the ladies revealed their worry as well.

"Hopefully it won't progress to that," Ella said with a grim smile.

"We've seen enough war," Kára said, and a far-off look came into her eyes. "The brothers will avoid it if possible."

"If we must," Cait said softly, "Gideon has formed alliances with enough clans to rally an army of thousands who are not fond of James and his policies."

Shana's eyes opened wider at such treasonous talk, but up here in northern Scotland, several days' ride from Edinburgh, one could speak one's mind without being thrown immediately into traitors' prison. Shana had lived south of Edinburgh with her husband, Ben Blair, near her old family home where tongues were held tighter.

"You said that the warriors are out training?" Shana asked.

Kára spread some honey on a thick slice of bread. "Yes, and Bàs is with them. Even though he's ridden to his cabin during the day, he's returned to Girnigoe these last nights." She took a bite and smiled at Shana.

"Odd that," Ella said, tilting her head as she looked at Shana. "I've been trying to get him to stay the night here for the last year, but he rarely does. Only when something keeps him here past dark, and he doesn't want to risk his horse with wolves roaming."

"Something seems to be keeping him here," Cait said with her own smile.

Shana felt her cheeks warm, but the thought of

Bàs remaining here for her made her feel lighter. She felt safer when he was near, which was ridiculous considering who he was, what he was.

Ella stood. "Let's walk outdoors to the training field, and you can see why the armies of the Sinclair horsemen are so feared and respected." When Shana stood, Ella looped her arm through hers. "I fought against them before," Ella continued. "And there are no warriors in Scotland fiercer and more experienced."

"Watch for the mud," Cait called after them. "It poured buckets last night with that howling wind."

Ella pointed out various buildings and defense structures as she led Shana across the puddle-strewn bailey. They crossed two drawbridges and under the raised iron portcullis. "I have a horse named Gilla who is being exercised by one of the men today."

Shana looked at the lovely woman with deep brown hair. Even with the curves that came with motherhood, she looked fit. And she was obviously brave enough to sneak into Old Wick to release her and Ivy. "Do you ride with the men in battle?"

"I used to, but now I spend more time with my bairn, Mary. I do join them out on the practice field daily, but I wanted to make certain you weren't left to wander about this morn."

"I didn't mean to interrupt your day."

"You're doing no such thing." Ella looked at her. "And if you have anything to do with the light I've seen in Bàs's eyes these last two days, then I owe you much more than a day off my horse."

Shana looked outward as they followed the path winding through the thatched cottages. "I had noticed that there is heaviness, a sadness, in his eyes."

"Hannah says it's been that way since their father gave him that skull mask at the age of five years."

"Five?" Shana asked, her gaze snapping to Ella.

Ella shook her head. "George Sinclair was a monster. My mother's husband fought him his entire life. They were both stubborn and powerful war chiefs. But George Sinclair became a madman after his wife died in childbirth. He forgot that Hannah existed and turned his four sons into the Horsemen of the Apocalypse."

"Naming Bàs Death," Shana whispered. The trees gave way to a relatively flat meadow where hundreds of men and horses moved in mock combat. The air was moist with low clouds that moved under a blue sky, casting shadows across the army. Most were shirtless, their kilts sitting low on their hips as they practiced turns, thrusts, and controlled swings of their mighty swords on and off their horses. Some battled with wooden swords against one another, striking with deadly force if they'd been using steel blades.

"They train mostly in their four units, white, bay, black, and pale green horses as described in the Bible," Ella explained, pointing them out, and Shana could see the horses arranged in areas together.

"The pale green horses are really white or gray?" Shana asked. "And then dyed somehow?"

"Yes," Ella said. "Any gray-colored horse and some white are assigned to Bàs's army. Before battle, the warriors paint their horses with a dye made from field greens." She pointed toward the far-right field. "Some leave it on, letting it wear off naturally. Others wash it off, like Bàs does to Dòchas, who has a gorgeous golden coat."

"The armies, separated by color, certainly make them look like the Four Horsemen," Shana said. She pulled her cloak tighter around her arms against a shiver as she imagined the four different armies barreling down on her.

"The brothers have been playing their parts since their mother died twenty-some years ago."

"Bàs starting at age five?"

Ella nodded, her look sad. "His father started off by having him wear the skull and memorize the words from Revelation."

"He didn't make Bàs kill anyone as a child, did he?" Shana's gaze stopped on the tallest of the warriors riding a golden horse against another gray horse. Each rider held spears that looked like their noses were snubbed instead of pointed.

"Hannah says that their father tried to get Bàs to kill animals, but he refused, even when he was whipped for disobedience."

Shana's fist pressed into her chest. "I can't imagine Bàs ever killing an innocent animal." Tears swelled in Shana's eyes, tears of pity that she'd never show to Bàs, but this far away he couldn't see even if he noticed her watching.

Ella gave a dark laugh. "Hannah says their father continued to order him to kill animals until Bàs finally snuck up on George Sinclair with a blade one night while the man was drinking whisky before the fire."

"What did he do?" Shana asked and held her breath as she turned her gaze to Ella.

CHAPTER TWELVE

Regarding the *Sgian Dubh* dagger
(pronounced skian doo)

"The derivation of the name of this little 'weapon' is
open to discussion. Traditionally the handle was
made of black 'bog wood'—wood that had long lain
submerged in a bog, and that's certainly an obvious
origin. Others point to the fact that originally it was
a hidden knife and therefore rather sinister
and used for 'black deeds.'

In rougher ages it was secreted in the oxter—the
armpit—and could be withdrawn for use in a flash."
TARTANS AUTHORITY WEBSITE

Ella gave her a wry grin. "Bàs held the razor-sharp
edge of a sgian dubh against his throat."

"My Lord," Shana murmured.

Ella nodded, her brows arched high. "Bàs told his
father that he would rather kill him than any animal
he put before him. His father was happy his son had
found some boldness and laughed as he grabbed
Bàs, knocking him down. But after that, George
Sinclair didn't bother him about animals."

Shana turned back toward the field. "And now
look at him. I don't think anyone could knock him
down."

"He's filled out his frame even more over this

past year," Ella said. "With muscle, and when he stands straight, he is taller than his brothers. Although I doubt any of them would admit it."

A gray horse broke away from the army and galloped toward them. Keenan Sinclair stopped several yards away. "Milady Ella," he said and nodded first to her. "Mistress Shana. Would ye care to ride today? Come see how we train?" He breathed heavily from exertion.

"I should get back to the keep," Ella said. "Mary will be rising from her morning nap, and Merida let me sleep in this morning by taking her, so I don't want to burden her." Ella motioned to Shana. "But you should go closer, maybe over there." She pointed to the back corner of the field closest to Bàs where another forest stretched out.

"I'll take ye," Keenan said. He grabbed his tunic, throwing it on over his head, and reached down a hand for Shana to take. She put the toes of her boot into the stirrup and rose to sit behind him. "Hold tight," Keenan said and waited until she hugged his middle before tapping his horse.

Shana gasped as they shot off like a cannon across the field. She kept a tight grip around the Sinclair warrior to stay seated. He dodged men on the ground practicing hand-to-hand combat and turned to race up the edge of the field to stay out of the way of the horses.

"Shana?" Bàs's deep voice caught her ear, the one not pressed against Keenan's broad back. The horse slowed, and she relaxed her hold enough to look around. Bàs rode toward them, pulling up beside them. He was shirtless, his chest rising and falling with heavy breathing. He leaped down from his golden horse and raised his hands to her.

The muscles of his biceps bulged easily as he pulled her from the back of Keenan's horse, setting her gently on the tufted grass. His skin was tanned by the sun and stretched over his chest and shoulders in smooth ridges, showing the muscles underneath.

"The lass wanted to get a better look at our practice," Keenan said.

Bàs frowned his way. "Ye can get back to practice then."

Keenan nodded and pulled off his tunic again, exposing his own muscles. They seemed to flex as he leaned back, securing the tunic to the back of his horse.

"Thank you for bringing me closer," she said.

His mouth curved easily into a smile as he straightened. "I enjoyed our short ride together, Shana." Without looking at Bàs, he turned his horse in a tight circle, lifted his sword, and charged back into the mix. Lord. Were all the Sinclair warriors built like Highland mountains?

She thought she heard Bàs curse and turned back to him. His features were hard. He cleared his throat, his face softening. "Ye are well?"

"Yes. I'm rested, bathed, and fed. Like a well-cared-for babe." She smiled softly, feeling a tremor of awareness being so close to him. And even though there was a field of men who could see them, none were close enough to hear their words or notice the appreciation in her gaze.

Shirtless, the sheen of sweat across Bàs's muscles

emphasized them even more. Several scars sat in white lines across his chest and arms in contrast to the tan skin. A light brush of hair ran across his chest, and the ridges of muscle going down his stomach disappeared under the low edge of his plaid wrap. "Keenan asked if I'd like to see the training up close, and Ella thought I should go."

Bàs's eyes narrowed. "He has quite a number of lasses chasing after him."

Shana frowned. "I'm not one of them."

Bàs crossed his arms, his legs braced. Shana could imagine him in battle, a fierce warrior executing his duty with efficient skill. "He's like a dog sniffing around ye, looking for a mate."

She snorted. "If he comes too close, I'll bite him." She showed her teeth.

Bàs's brows relaxed, and the sides of his mouth softened into a grin. "He'd be quite surprised. Do ye bite often? 'Tis something people near ye should know."

She laughed softly. "Not usually."

"Pardon," a man said as he ran up. "Shall I practice with the pale horses or the black?" The man was young, his short beard sparse in spots. He smiled at her, his gaze appreciative enough to make her cheeks warm. "Mistress." He bowed his head to her. "I am Osk Flett, Kára's brother."

"Ye can work with Derek." Bàs stepped in front of Shana, blocking her from Osk's view. Bàs cupped his hands around his mouth to yell at a man drinking by the edge of the forest. "Derek, work with Osk on hand-to-hand technique." The warrior nodded and corked his bladder.

"I should let you practice," Shana said, looking to the forest line near them. "I'll stand there out of the way."

"Good day, mistress." Osk nodded to her and ran toward Derek.

"When ye wish to return to the castle just wave your arm, and I'll take ye," Bàs said.

"I'll make sure not to let Keenan sniff around me anymore." She walked off, holding her skirts up to step through the damp wildflowers and moss. Shana reached the trees and leaned against a large trunk where the sun had dried the soft green moss growing up the side.

Bàs walked among the warring men, pointing, nodding, or showing a better way to move in combat. She'd never watched men in battle before. The turns and footwork made it look almost like a dance, a lethal one with strength and force in each step.

Bàs was obviously the teacher, and the men respected and listened to him. Farther across the field, Shana picked out his three brothers overseeing their armies, too. The clouds continued to fly across the sky as Bàs walked comfortably within the melee of men and gray-green horses. The men swung, turned, dodged, and even wrestled their opponents to the ground.

When Bàs reached Keenan, who was parrying with another man, Bàs said something, and the man traded his wooden sword with the steel one Bàs had been carrying. So Bàs was going to practice, and he'd chosen Keenan as his opponent.

Shana's clasped hands rested under her chin, and she gasped as Keenan swung first, trying to take Bàs by surprise. Bàs easily blocked the assault, shoving Keenan's sword off with his own. From the distance, Shana could see the different styles of battle. Where Keenan kept his gaze and strikes centered and quite offensive, Bàs met each one but didn't advance. After long minutes, Shana noticed that Keenan's chest was heaving with exertion where Bàs was mildly going along as if it truly were a game.

"He's letting Keenan tire himself out," she said to herself.

Several men had stopped to watch. If any came too close, Bàs would swing around, sword raised to strike. But he always got back to Keenan before the man's next lunge. Keenan was a large man, too, but not as tall as Bàs. The muscles in Bàs's arms, back, and shoulders were impressive, yet he didn't have the bulk that would slow him down. *Graceful*. That was the word. The man was graceful in his movements, like a predator toying with his prey. His footsteps were always light so he could spin and duck and leap out of the way while Keenan's movements became clumsier as he fought.

Finally, Bàs crossed his sword with Keenan's, coming face-to-face. Shana couldn't make out any words, but Bàs's expression turned from calmness, close to boredom, to ferocity. Teeth clenched and eyes sharp, his lips moved, releasing words a second before his leg swept out with such power that Keenan was thrown backward as he fell. Arms spread out on impact, Bàs walked over gently, touching the tip of his wooden sword to Keenan's chest.

Bàs had obviously won, but instead of holding it there for all to notice, Bàs threw the sword aside and offered his hand for Keenan to grasp. The fallen man lay there for a few seconds, his chest rising and falling quickly before taking it. Bàs pulled him up and several men patted Keenan on his back. Bàs said something to him. Whatever it was brought a grin to Keenan's face, and he nodded, grabbing up his sword again.

Shana felt like she'd just witnessed some sacred interaction of the male human animal. Was it the same as women gathering to test their baked tarts against one another at a festival? She snorted softly at her musings, her gaze drifting and latching onto Bàs as he mounted his golden horse. He glanced her way before running the horse back and forth across the field against various men as if they met in combat. She held her breath every time they came together.

Dòchas needed as much training as the men, and Bàs led him through intricate patterns that helped the beast nimbly dodge other horses and swords. Bàs didn't even hold the horse's reins, using his knees and the pressure from his legs to guide the horse.

A movement along the line of the summer-green forest caught Shana's eye. "Holy Lord," she whispered, edging around the tree as if to hide. The large gray and white wolf stood inside the tree line, watching the training. Several horses closest to the beast hedged away, surprising their riders who quickly brought them under control. Before the men could look to the forest, the wolf was gone.

Shana clung to the tree as she watched the massive wolf emerge from some bramble deeper in the forest but closer to her position. *Please be Beò*. Her gaze scanned the woods, made darker by the gathering clouds, but she saw no other wolves. Bàs's wolf roamed the forests alone from what he said. It was the pack that had sought to eat her with Edward.

The wolf moved closer to the edge again, head turning slowly as if searching for Bàs. Its nose lifted, sniffing the wind, but, surely, it must be bombarded by smells from all the men and horses. Shana watched him step out of the woods and then retreat, over and over. "You are trying to find him," she whispered. "Why?"

Shana walked out from the tree and onto the meadow. Bàs was riding toward her end of the field, and she raised her arms, waving them high. Turning her head, she didn't see the wolf anymore, but kept her arms moving. Dòchas's thundering hooves snapped her face forward. Bàs pulled his horse around in a tight circle to stop him. "Ye wish to go down?" Bàs asked, breathing hard. His posture was straight and ready for any attack as if he still trained out there with his men.

"No," she said, looking into the woods and then back at him. "Beò was here." She pointed to where she'd last seen him. "He kept going out and then back into the woods as if he was looking for you."

Bàs frowned, dismounting, his boots thudding on the ground hidden by daisies and tall cornflowers. "Beò stays away from people."

"I think it was him. He was alone. No other wolves."

Bàs held his fingers to his mouth and let out a long, high-pitched whistle. Dòchas's ears twitched, but he stayed still beside him. From out of the dense middle trotted the wolf, right toward Bàs.

Bàs spoke in Gaelic to his friend as he bent to examine him. Shana held her breath. It still amazed her that a wild wolf could form such an attachment. Bàs ran his hands over the predator's face and neck, even checking underneath. Still crouched, he looked to Shana. "I don't feel any wounds, but something is wrong to bring him out here, especially with all these men nearby."

He straightened and watched Beò trot deeper into the trees. The faithful animal turned to look over his shoulder at him. "Something must be wrong at home."

"At your cabin?" Shana asked.

"Aye." Bàs looked at her. "I'll ask one of the men to take ye back to Girnigoe."

She was shaking her head before he finished speaking and went to Dòchas. "I'll go with you to help," she said. "It could be Betty."

"I don't think Beò would search me out to help the squirrel." Bàs walked over but didn't mount.

Shana stuck her boot into the stirrup, which pushed her petticoat up to an indecent level. Luckily, the horse blocked her from the field. "Another animal could use my help." Shana straightened, lifted herself up the side of the tall horse, and threw her leg over, tucking her petticoat under her spread legs. She looked down at Bàs. "Are you coming?"

Bàs grabbed his tunic off the back of Dòchas and threw it on before mounting the horse. He settled behind Shana, and she breathed evenly to calm the hard *thump* of her heart at his nearness. Bàs Sinclair was brawny, lethal, and as graceful as any courtier she'd seen walking with royalty before Edinburgh Castle.

And she was riding off alone with him into the forest, following his wolf.

He's more than Death. She repeated the words, feeling the rightness of them, and realized she believed them.

...

I should've ridden her down to Girnigoe.

Bàs chided himself for the twentieth time as he neared his cabin, slowing Dòchas. But the fact that she wanted to go, so different from the last time they'd been here, made him unable to say nay.

Beò trotted ahead, stepping nimbly over the ropes that Bàs kept strung between trees to alert him of any visitors. "Do you see anything wrong?" Shana whispered.

"Nay," he said, his mouth near her ear. He couldn't help but inhale the fresh strawberry fragrance that had been teasing him the whole ride. Combined with her natural warmth, it made Shana smell like a fresh baked tart.

One I'd like to devour.

He led Dòchas through the bramble-flanked path that allowed easy access to his yard. Beò paused ahead in the center of his clearing and looked back at him as if wondering why he'd stopped. "Doesn't look like there's any danger," Bàs said.

"Except from the mud," Shana said. Water stood about the yard in puddles and small lakes, and the tall grasses along the riverbank were all brushed down, showing how the river had breached.

"The rains last night were fierce," he said. Bàs dismounted. All seemed quiet, especially with Apollo and Artemis back at Girnigoe Castle. Banshee and one of the other cats ran out of the barn, coming up to him. "Do you two know what's amiss?" he asked. The cats slid around his legs, purring.

"I'll look around," Shana called.

"I'd rather ye stay up there and be prepared to ride Dòchas back to Girnigoe if needed."

Apparently, she didn't agree. She leaned forward and threw her leg over the horse's rump, preparing to slide down. Bàs caught her waist, helping her land without scraping herself on the saddle.

"Thank you." She adjusted her blue gown. It looked like it'd been brushed clean at Girnigoe, and a bonny edge of white lace showed from the low neckline, teasing the skin above her ample breasts.

He turned away before he did something that would shock her or worse, make her afraid. *Daingead*. He needed to get ahold of himself. Joshua had kidded with him that he was so stoic that he'd never warm to a lass, but Bàs felt very warm, even hot, anytime he was near Shana. The memory of their brief kiss played over in his mind so often that he could still feel the warmth of her on his lips. But then the memory of her fearful face staring at him on the scaffold replaced the heat with ice. He could never make up for causing that fear in her.

She walked toward the cabin. "I'll check on Betty if she's still here."

"Someone could be inside." He leaped onto the

porch, throwing open the door before Shana could reach it. Betty skittered along the rafters. He made a quick circuit of the upstairs where his bed seemed untouched.

When he thumped back down the stairs, Shana was looking upward, her chin tilted back, exposing the lovely column of her neck. "Only Betty is here," she said. "She looks healthy enough."

Why had Beò risked himself to find Bàs? He trudged across the clearing, splashing with each step, toward the barn that sat on the bank of the river that was gushing along, swollen from the rains. His eyes opened wide. "Ilsa!" he called to the Scottish coo. The river had broken over the bank and swept away the back part of the barn's fence. "Iona!"

"What is it?" Shana yelled, splashing after him, her skirts held high.

"The river has swept into the coos' barn," he said, running to the front of the structure and throwing open the doors. Beò trotted inside and then back out, standing watch.

"The cows must have been washed downstream in the storm surge when the river swelled over its bank," she said.

"Bloody hell," Bàs said and grabbed their halters off the nail in the barn.

Shana gasped. "The calf." Iona was only four months old and vulnerable to predators and the rushing waters. Her mother, Ilsa, could survive as long as a pack of wolves didn't surround her.

Bàs threw an arm out to the river and looked at Beò. "Where are they?" The wolf trotted toward it. Shana followed behind Bàs as he ran after the wolf.

Bàs kept slowing and glancing behind him to make sure Shana wasn't in trouble. Even holding her skirts up, they dragged in the mud as she sunk.

She shooed him ahead. "Don't wait for me. Find that babe."

"Yell if ye need me," he said over the rush of the water. "Don't get too close to the bank. 'Twill give way."

"Go on!" She shooed him again, and he took off after Beò, leaping over increasingly large puddles and dodging trees that gripped the soggy banks with knobby roots washed clean by the raging river, as if they held on for dear life.

For long minutes he followed the swollen river until water had risen to flood the forest floor, creating a wide estuary.

Ahead, a low bellowing rose over the rushing water. "Ilsa!" Bàs yelled. He tore forward, dodging a thick tree. "Ilsa!" She stood mired in muck with Iona next to her. Bàs let out a huff of relief. "Thank ye, Lord," Bàs said, lifting his feet high as the mud sucked them into the boggy area. Old leaves floated by, lifted from the forest floor, and the tops of ferns were tugged by the slower water flowing over the land.

Ilsa bellowed again. Her eyes were wide under the long hair, and Iona huddled near her, mewing in a higher voice.

"You found them!" Shana called. "Are they stuck?"

"I'll see," he said, pulling his legs up one after another to climb closer to them. He hadn't thought to grab a rope. *Mo chreach!* Ilsa weighed a thousand pounds. When he reached the spot where they stood, Ilsa's legs were muddy but not mired where she stood on a buried plateau of rock. She remained there because Iona was stuck.

"There now, mama," Bàs said, his voice calm as he approached. He slipped her large, soft halter over her nose, avoided her horns, and buckled it in the back.

Ilsa snorted, her thick tongue curling out to lick her gray nose. She tossed her head upward, her curved horns thrusting about, and snorted again. Bàs dodged her horns as she lowered her nose to her calf who stood beside the rocks mired up to her belly.

"Ilsa must have followed her down the river," Shana said from a spot six feet back. "What a good mama," she called.

Beò trotted around them, staying on firm ground. His smart friend had known the cows would be attacked by wolves that night if they weren't rescued today. The water and Ilsa's horns would hold the pack off only so long.

A sucking noise came with each pull of his boot from the mud, and Bàs came up to Ilsa, scratching the wide part of her nose where the hair lay in a stringy mess. "How long have ye been out here?" She snorted again, glancing down to make sure Iona was still there.

The calf weighed a bit over a hundred pounds from what Bàs guessed the last time he lifted her. The mud would add to the weight, but where Ilsa would be impossible to get out without ropes and men, Iona should be easier.

A gasp behind him made him turn in time to see

Shana land hands first on her stomach. "Shana!"

"Blasted mud." She slowly relaxed there on her stomach but kept her head up with her elbows squishing into the mud. "My foot stuck in it."

Her dress lay in the dark reddish-brown soup of river water and floating brush. He traipsed back to her, grabbing one arm at the same time she tried to roll onto her back.

Feet stuck in the thicker mud, Bàs wobbled, thrown off-balance. "Mo chreach!" He hit the muddy water with a splash. His eyes shut right before his face went under.

"Bàs!" Shana yelled.

He pushed a hand down, his fingers squishing through the soft, cold dirt to raise his head. Turning onto his side, he wiped a hand over his wet face, probably smearing more mud on than he removed. They looked at each other, and Shana's lips curved upward. She brushed a dirty finger over her nose. "You've got a little dirt on your nose."

Laughter pushed up from deep inside Bàs, coming out with a natural smile. "Ye do, too."

Her eyes opened wide, and she gave a shocked frown. "Do I? Where?"

He laughed harder and crawled closer, one of his boots staying behind in the mud. He reached Shana, pointing at her nose. "There." She wiped it, her smile returning. "And there." He pointed at her forehead.

"How about my cheeks?" she asked.

They were close, both lying in the mud with cold creek water running under and around them as if they were boulders in this shallow inlet. His hand rose, and he slid his thumb across a little leaf stuck to her cheek. "Aye," he said, his smile fading at the intensity in Shana's gaze.

They stared at each other for a moment. Bàs felt pulled to her. He inched closer, staring at the greenness in her eyes. The light of the trees enhanced it. Even covered in mud her beauty wasn't dimmed at all. Her lush lips parted, and he drew in a shallow breath, his heart pounding as hard as during intense training.

He wanted so badly to kiss her again, just one kiss. He leaned closer, and by some miracle Shana didn't pull back.

CHAPTER THIRTEEN

"If I could be anything in the world, I would want
to be a teardrop because I would be born in your
eyes, live on your cheeks, and die on your lips."
MARY QUEEN OF SCOTS, 1542-1587

Shana's eyes closed, her heart beating hard as she
waited for whatever this yearning between them
would bring. Another kiss like the one that plagued
her thoughts?

Moooooo! Ilsa bellowed.

Shana's eyes snapped open, and her gaze shifted
past Bàs. "Is she in trouble?"

Bàs's face was so close to hers. He paused, as if
frozen in the air. He'd been about to kiss her, and
she'd looked away. *By the devil!*

Before she could stop him, he exhaled and rolled
to his side in the mud, sitting up. "Nay. She's ready to
see her calf out of this muck."

Disappointment made the mud stickier as Shana
slowly pulled up onto her feet, her petticoats clinging to her legs with what felt like fifty pounds of
mud. "You lost a boot," Shana said, watching him
trudge back over to the cows.

"Maybe ye could find it while I dig this calf out."

They both began to push mud about, getting
dirtier with each stumble. "I will never get the grime
out from my fingernails," Shana said, her voice surly,
although the mud was only part of her annoyance.

As she watched him work to save the cows, Bàs didn't seem at all like Death. Executioner was the role he played for his clan, but it wasn't him, it wasn't the kindhearted man who risked all to save his cow and her babe. The anger at finding out his secret, in the worst way possible, had receded, and it seemed that unbidden heat was growing in its place. The cold water helped to cool her ardor, and she shivered as she waded over to the boot.

Shana frowned at the boot and yanked the oval rim, grunting. Slowly it slid up through the suction of the mud until it gave way. She yelped as she landed on her arse, but it was free. "Got it!" She struggled to stand and then held the boot high. "Victory!"

Bàs stood next to Ilsa, his hand on her side as he smiled at Shana. "A successful outcome in our campaign against the vicious mud monster," he said.

She chuckled, glancing down at herself. "I think I've still succumbed." She was completely covered with dirt, bits of leaves, and clinging mud.

Bàs shoved against Ilsa to get her to move away from the calf so he could dig around her babe's short legs. Ilsa snorted but stepped over, the rock base beneath giving her the leverage to pull each leg up from the muck.

"Can ye come around to the firmest ground and tug Ilsa up onto dry land?" he asked over the rush of the river beyond them.

"I'll try," Shana said and watched Bàs yank a long strip of wool from his plaid, turning to Ilsa to tie it to the halter he'd buckled onto her.

Shana retreated to dry land and walked around the flooded plain as far as she could and then waded back to Ilsa. The cow turned her head, and Shana dodged her curved horn as she grabbed for the flapping end of the woolen strip. "Come along, Ilsa," Shana said, tugging.

Ilsa snorted and turned her head back to Iona. Shana gasped as her strength pulled her once again to the muddy floor of the forest.

"Go on," Bàs said, his voice firm as he shoved the cow, his shoulder pressed into her side. "I'll get your bairn."

With another snort, Ilsa turned to Shana, who'd struggled upright, and took a step forward. "That's it. Come on, mama coo," Shana said, using a soothing voice.

Iona bellowed, and Shana dodged Ilsa's horns again as her head swung back around, but Shana was ready this time and dug her heels in. The calf cried as Bàs hugged her hard in a squat. He lifted the calf slowly straight up, the mud sucking at the little hairy legs as if not wanting to let go of its catch. Bàs held all four legs together as he scooped her against his chest. The water made his tunic stick to his skin, outlining the mounding of his muscles as he carried the calf slowly through the flooded area.

"Move, Ilsa," Shana called, pulling hard at the huge Scottish cow. The ground kept shifting under Shana's feet. She fell to her knees once but pushed back up, slowly leading Ilsa to drier ground. Bàs reached it first and lowered the calf. He held Iona as she tried to run back into the muck to reach her mother, letting go once Shana had led her out. Iona ran right under Ilsa, shoving her nose against Ilsa's udder and then suckling.

Bàs stretched his arms. "Iona's grown. I'd say she's closer to two hundred pounds now, at least with mud all over her."

For a moment, Shana stared at the show of masculine strength standing before her. Covered in mud and water, Bàs looked like a god formed of granite and earth. What would it be like to be surrounded by all that strength? The thought of Bàs's body against hers made chill bumps rise along her body, her nipples hardening.

"Aye," Bàs said. "I think ye have the right idea."

Shana's mouth opened, her brows rising. "Right idea?"

He pointed up the stream. "The storm must have washed away the fence, and they were swept downstream. 'Tis bloody lucky that Iona didn't drown."

Shana shut her mouth, swallowing against the dryness there. "And Beò came to find you."

His fingers brushed Shana's as he took the muddy sash from her that was tied to the mama cow. Each touch was a teasing jolt.

"Let's get them back," he said.

The shadows had grown longer through the forest as they led Ilsa along, Iona following eagerly. A soreness was settling into Shana's muscles, and she rubbed her shoulder as they stopped before the barn. The day had turned warm, and with all the activity and mud covering her, she felt sticky. "You don't have a bathing tub," she called after him as he left the cows to disappear inside.

He'd dumped buckets of fresh river water over the cows to get the worst mud off and was fitting them with clean halters. "I can take ye back to

Girnigoe for a bathing tub," he said, glancing at her. "I bathe in the creek."

She looked over to it rushing along. The clear water beckoned. "I'll wash up a bit there then," she said. Did he bathe nude? Certainly, he did while living out here alone.

"I'll join ye after I put them in Dòchas's stall."

Join her?

Bàs must have realized how that sounded because he quickly added, "Farther down in the deeper pool." He glanced at her, and she swore she saw a red hue infuse his face.

It was such a human reaction, and it warmed her. The Horseman of Death blushed. There really was more life to him than death.

. . .

Bàs watched Shana lower onto the bank of the rushing creek. Her arms were coated in semi-dried mud, and her dress was stained and wet. Her hair lay in a tangle over one shoulder, tied loosely to keep it out of her way. "Ye know how to swim, don't ye?" he said.

"I do."

He lifted the tunic over his head, pulling it off. "Because the bank is slippery and could give way if 'tis too saturated."

Shana rubbed her arms through the sleeves of her ruined dress. "I'll take care. 'Tis cold, so I'll just wash my face and arms and what bits of hair I see with mud in it." She glanced down at her muddied gown and sighed. "I guess I'll take the petticoat off to try to wash some of it."

His brows pinched. She must be cold. "I can still ride ye back to—"

"The creek will do."

"I don't have any strawberry soap," Bàs said.

She tipped her head. "You know I like strawberry?"

His gaze met hers. "I could smell it on ye before."

"Oh," she said, the conversation suddenly awkward.

Bàs picked up a bar from a tin he kept near the creek. "This one smells of …" He held it to his nose. "Pine and lemon, maybe rosemary."

When he looked at her, her gaze flew upward to his face, as if she'd been looking lower. He glanced down to make sure his plaid was still around his hips. It was.

She strode up to him, and Bàs found himself holding his breath. He had very little experience with women, since they were all afraid of him. And even though both Joshua, with his graphic descriptions, and Gideon, with his foreign book about tupping in all sorts of ways, had schooled him in the art of coaxing pleasure in a lass, Bàs hadn't put it into practice.

She stopped before him. "Any soap will do," she said.

Every muscle in his body tensed. *Should I kiss her?* Or would she punch him in the other eye? In the darkness that night that seemed so long ago now, she hadn't known who he was, the role that he played in life. Back in the mud, he'd thought she might want a kiss, but then she'd looked away.

They stood only inches apart now, and he stared at the natural curl to her lashes. They were light from her coloring and harder to see far away, but up close he could see them swoop high over her bluish eyes.

He leaned closer. "Yer eyes are blue now."

She blinked, which accented how her eyelashes fanned up and down. "I must be at peace then."

"Do they always change colors like that?"

"I haven't studied them enough to know."

"Have ye had anyone else study your eyes?" he asked, watching the subtle changes in her face. "A man perhaps?"

She glanced down but didn't back away. "I guess you heard, or Hannah told you what I told Lizzy during the birth." She looked back up at him, a sad smile on her lips. "I was married young, to a soldier named Ben Forbes. He died while I was pregnant."

A part of him relaxed in relief. She wasn't married, but he hated the pain she must have felt. "And the bairn, too?" he asked.

Her lips tightened, and she gave a short nod. "During the birth."

"And that's why ye became a midwife? To help other women and bairns?"

She nodded fully. "The physician who was sent to help me rushed the delivery when it should have been handled delicately. My son died from his ineptness and rough handling. I didn't fully know that then, but I've learned much since."

His hand settled on her upper arm. "I am truly sorry, Shana. The pain ye endured with your husband dying and then your bairn. Ye are a strong woman to continue an upward life rather than drowning in bitterness."

She snorted slightly. "I'm bitter at times, but I try to move forward instead of dwelling on what might have been. That can eat you up inside." Her finger touched his chest as she said it and then she let it drop.

"So…" He hesitated. "That's why ye chase away the specter of death with such dedication." She was all light while he was all darkness.

The space between her brows pinched. "I'm dedicated to the women and babes who need proper medical care," she said as if correcting him. It was a subtle difference, but he wasn't wrong.

She glanced down and then back up into his face. "Losing my babe was the worst thing to ever happen to me. I carried him fully and mourned him bitterly." She laid her hand over his arm. "And I would have given my life for him." She shook her head. "Without blaming him the smallest bit."

His mother might not blame him for her death, but Bàs surely did. His chest ached, reminding him to inhale. "I…I will bathe downstream where the water is deeper." He rested the lump of soap in her hand. "Just take care ye don't slip."

"I will," she said. Her rose-colored lips opened like she would say more, but then she turned to walk barefoot along the grassy bank. She pulled the tie from her red hair, letting it fall haphazardly around her shoulders. Brilliant and fiery.

His hands curled inward, clenching as if he wished he were holding fists of her silky tresses. When she glanced back at him, he turned, walking

toward the lower pool of creek water where he usually bathed.

The clear water burbled loudly over the rocks
and stones that made up the creek. The crystal clear-
ness of it enveloped him to the waist, his bare feet
gripping the loose river stones below. Once all the
way in, he removed his wrap, letting the water wash
the mud from it. He'd have to stretch it to dry, or it
would shrink up to his ballocks. He scrubbed it between his hands and threw it onto the grassy bank.
Another lump of soap sat there with his scrubbing
brush of coarse hair, and he took both.

Bàs sunk into the stream, moving to the deeper
pool where the water emptied. He ducked under
and stood, letting the water cascade off him, taking
some of the mud and sweat. He rubbed the soap
over his head and ducked under to rake one hand
through the length, working against the snarls.

He rubbed the soap lump over the brush and
went to work, scouring his arms and chest with the
harsh brush until his skin burned. The coolness of
the water healed it as he sunk under to rinse, using
some of the soap bubbles to wash all his other parts.
He made sure to wash the healing bites from Betty.
Was Shana bathing her naked arms upstream? If it
were warmer, she might have taken a full bath. He
could imagine her hair floating all around her lovely
face as she floated, her breasts breaking the surface,
her white thighs resting just underneath.

Hand on his jack, Bàs bobbed up and ducked
under again, the water filling his ears. As he sur-
faced, he heard the yell.

"Help!"

He turned, and a body crashed into him. Churning legs, wet linen, and flailing arms attacked him at once. He dropped the brush, catching Shana's arms. "I've got ye, lass."

He lifted her against his body, and she sputtered, coughing and sucking in air. "I lost my blasted footing." She grabbed hold of his shoulders, her feet kicking against his shins.

"Ye aren't good at taking care," he said as he watched her try to slap her water-darkened hair back over her shoulders. It had tumbled forward and covered half her face.

She squinted her exposed eye at him and slapped back the rest of it. "I'm usually quite good at it."

"I don't know about that," Bàs said, keeping her buoyed. "Within the last week, ye've fallen from a tree, were nearly eaten by a pack of wolves, were captured and imprisoned, and nearly drowned."

She opened her mouth as if to refute, but then closed it. "It's been an unusual week."

Her chest rose and fell as she fought to catch her breath. Her gaze dropped to his chest. "Your skin... 'tis red."

He glanced down where his scrubbing had rendered him red. "I use a bristled scrub brush to wash with."

"Why?" Her fingers touched his chest where he knew that some of his hair had also been plucked away by the abrasive force he used. Her touch was tentative, as if she worried it hurt him.

"It takes dirt and...blood off well," he said, trying to control his unruly jack that didn't seem to care how cold the water was when Shana was up against him.

"And skin and hair," she said. "Doesn't it hurt?"

It did. "I don't mind it."

She slid her hand down his chest. Her lips were parted as she looked up at him. "Blood and mud come off with a lighter touch. You can wash well without the bristles."

"I don't think I can," he said. The painful brushing somehow washed away the gruesomeness of whatever killing he'd recently done. Even when he wasn't coated in blood and spit and sometimes entrails and sinew, the scrubbing helped clean away the memories of it.

"'Tis easy," she said. Her feet slid against his under the water, resting on top of them. Her other hand came up to join her first, lying against the muscles of his chest. She stroked them down. "I'm afraid I dropped your soap, but even the water can work."

She stopped a bit lower than his waist, surely realizing he wasn't wearing his wrap to bathe. Her hands washed upward to his shoulders, sliding along their upper breadth to work down his arms. "Such large muscles must ache at times with all you do."

"Aye," he said, watching her. His hands found her waist under the water, holding her against the current that continued around them, tugging her smock. The breeze blew through the leaves above, adding to the sound of blood rushing in his ears and water around them.

She swallowed, gazing up at him. "Bàs."

"Aye?"

"I have no maidenhood to protect. I'm a widow.

A woman who's birthed a child."

Her words gripped his breath like a fist. A surge of heat rushed up inside Bàs. Had she been feeling the same pull he'd felt?

For a moment they stared at each other. Her waiting, and Bàs waiting to see what would come out of his mouth. "Lass, I…I would not dishonor ye."

She drew closer, and the warmth of her body pressed into him, her abdomen against his jack. "'Tis no dishonor when a mature woman wants you to touch her. Asks you to touch her."

Her hand rose to his cheek, her thumb stroking across it where he knew an indentation sat from the years of wearing the skull mask, having it bump and press into his face. She didn't recoil from it, the evidence of who he was.

"Are ye asking me to touch ye, Shana?" he said, his body poised and unmoving. He was like an arrow nocked and drawn back.

"Yes, I—"

Bàs's face lowered to hers before she could finish her words, his lips finding hers. He touched them with gentleness, not wanting to scare her away. But she wrapped her arms around his neck, rising and slanting her face to his. Her lips sealed against his in a hot kiss filled with promise.

Bloody hell, he wanted her. He wanted to lay her down and touch her in all the places Joshua said he should touch a lass to make her moan. To see and kiss the curves he felt pressed against him.

Without breaking the kiss, he stooped and lifted under her legs to pull her up from the water. She was so soft, and his heart thudded in his chest. His toes found purchase as he carried her to the bank, kissing her deeply. He broke the kiss, and Shana looked bewildered. Bewildered was good, wasn't it?

"I just need to set ye on the bank," he said, his voice gruff with heat. He lifted her, setting her there in her smock, which clung to the curves of her body, revealing what was underneath. She didn't hide herself but stood there, her nipples hard under the white linen.

Bàs climbed easily out of the river, and her gaze dropped to take him in as he straightened. He saw her swallow, and waited. Shana stepped up to him, a tentative smile on her lips. Without a word, she pulled him down for a kiss. Bàs lifted her into his arms, and her fingers caught in his hair, holding his head as she kissed him fiercely. With a growl of want, Bàs marched toward the cabin. Balancing her on one knee, he threw the door open.

A scampering reminded him Betty had become a lengthy visitor if not a permanent resident, so he headed straight up the steps to his bedchamber. With his dogs at Girnigoe, nothing moved when he entered the room, closing the door behind them. The air was warm from the summer sun and still held the fresh scent of wood.

He kept kissing Shana as he lowered her feet to the ground. She smelled of lemon and rosemary and tasted of fresh creek water.

"Holy Heaven," she murmured, her hands sliding from his neck to his shoulders. "I want you." She squeezed his large biceps. "All of you."

Her words shuddered through his body, making his jack harden even more. No one had ever wanted him before, in any way. He was death, something people avoided or completely turned their backs on.

He inhaled along the skin of her neck, kissing below her ear. "I want to make ye moan, Shana," he whispered there.

"I do, too," she murmured, making him smile against her. Her hands slid to his naked hips. "This wet smock needs to come off." She shivered.

Bàs crouched to catch her hem and looked up her length. "Och, but lass, ye are lovely," he said. Her tresses were still wet but had started to dry from the breeze outdoors, curling around her face. She was glorious with her red hair tangled around her pale face, the brown freckles forming intriguing patterns.

He spoke as he stood slowly, watching her face as he lifted the wet linen. "I want to kiss every single dot on ye, lass."

Her breath came faster from between her rose-hued lips. "They cover every inch of my skin," she said.

A slow grin grew on his mouth. "And I will kiss every single one." He pulled the wet smock past her face and over her head. It made a *thump* as it hit the floor in a pile they both ignored as he drew her naked body against his own. Softness against hardness. The difference shot like liquid fire through his veins. He groaned as his hands glided down her straight spine and over her round arse. "Ye are so soft."

She slid her hands down his back and around to his front, dropping to his jack. "And you are so hard and…massive." She glanced down where his erection stood tall and ready. Was that fear in her eyes?

The thought sent an arrow of ice through him.

He pulled her hand away, kissing it as he leaned back enough to put space between their bodies. The absence chilled his skin so that it almost hurt. But he was used to discomfort. "We don't have to do anything."

She smiled then, looking up into his eyes. "I am no timid maiden, Bàs Sinclair. You are large everywhere." She inhaled through her nose. "Good Lord. And beautiful."

He was big, aye. He trained his body to respond to any physical threat by building his muscle and stamina, but he knew he was marked with scars, white nicks here and there along with a longer slash down one leg. The edge of his mouth quirked upward in a half grin, and he brushed her hair from her cheek. "Your idea of beautiful and my idea of beautiful are very different, lass."

He stroked her cheek. "This is beautiful," he murmured, leaning in to kiss her smooth, speckled skin. He took her arm while keeping his eyes on hers even though he knew the landscape of her body lay bare. He turned her arm so the pale underside lay upward and kissed a light path from her wrist to the back of her elbow. He followed his kisses with a light stroke up her arm. "This is beautiful."

Her smile had faded, replaced by parted lips and an intense look. Passion? He'd heard tales of it, but never thought he'd see it directed at him.

Slowly his gaze dropped, and his finger reached to slide along her long neck to her collarbone. The freckles were like stars lighting his way. "And this." Then his gaze slid to her breasts. Perfect pale orbs, the nipples peaked. "Beautiful," he murmured,

trailing his finger down between them to the softness of her gently rounded stomach that perched
between the flaring out of her hip bones.

His gaze raised to hers. She watched him, her
hands clasped in fists, but she didn't look like she
wanted him to stop or merely tolerated his touch.
Nay. She was flushed, her nipples pearled, her
breathing shallow. Bàs laid his whole palm on her
abdomen, rubbing along it to each hip before trailing his fingers lower. Eyes raised to Shana's, he
watched hers close as he slid between her legs.

Gideon and Joshua had made certain that Bàs
knew about what they called "the hidden gem" on a
woman. As Bàs grazed it, Shana sucked in her
breath. He slid against it again and felt her quiver.
He kneeled, his fingers moving past her most intimate spot to slide down the muscles of her inner
thighs. She was freckled there, too.

"The loveliest woman," he murmured and kissed
the inside of her thigh, his finger tracing from dot to
dot. When he rubbed her calves, she moaned. He
would massage her, outside and inside.

"Boireannach brèagha. Beautiful lass," he said
and worked his way back up the outside of her thigh
and hips until he stood again.

She immediately slid her hands down his chest to
his hips and stepped into him. She was taller than
most lasses, but he was still much taller, so she rose
onto her toes to press against him as if to test how
they fit together. The feel of her warm, soft, curved
body against his again reached inside Bàs, and the
river of fire he'd managed to keep a grip on swelled,
pushing past all barriers.

His arms wrapped around Shana, pulling her against him so there was no space between. Their mouths came together in hunger for each other. He lifted under her round arse, and she wrapped her legs around his hips, his jack pressing against her most intimate spot. He raised her up and down pressed to him, and she moaned against his mouth. She thrust, the crux of her legs wet.

"I want you, Bàs," she said, breaking the kiss for a breath, her hands sliding through his damp hair. She stared into his eyes. "I want you now."

Was this the begging that Gideon talked about? The one lass who'd lain with Bàs before had made no noise and didn't talk. Bàs liked it when Shana talked. He leaned in, kissing her neck. "What do ye want me to do, Shana lass?"

She slid her feet down to rest on the floor, her head thrown back so he had complete access to her neck. Straightening, she took his hand from around her back to the front of her, leading him down to the crux between her legs. Her fingers pressed him against her, farther still until he pressed inside.

Bàs groaned low, his breathing hard as he felt the wet heat of her on his fingers. He moved them, and she squirmed. "Yes, that, and more," she said, her hands finding his thick jack.

"Shana," he said, as breathless as she. Kissing her again, he walked them both toward the wall until the backs of her legs hit the bed. They fell together onto it, making it creak. He leaned over her, kissing her mouth until she broke away to whisper in his ear.

"Suck my breasts," she said.

He moved down her, kissing her skin, reveling in

her unique fragrance until he reached them and
drew a nipple into his mouth. Shana moaned, arching her back and then sliding her pelvis against his
thigh in a mating rhythm. He found her heat again
with his fingers, playing there while loving first one
breast and then the other. She continued to moan
and thrust upward as if she reached for her release,
something Joshua assured him he should strive for
before mounting a woman if possible.

Bàs stroked in a rhythm, his own jack throbbing.
She reached down to it and spread her legs across
the bed, wide. He should wait. Shouldn't he wait?

"Now," she said as if reading his mind. Apparently,
Joshua didn't know everything.

Bàs lifted her body, and she bent her knees, letting them fall outward. Splayed and ready, she was
the most beautiful creature he'd ever seen. He
leaned on his elbows over her, his forearms on either
side of her face. With one surge, he thrust into her
willing, open body.

Pleasure gripped him hard, and his groan mim-
icked her own. And they plunged into each other
again. Her hands found his arse, and she pushed,
encouraging a fast rhythm, her legs wrapping around
his hips.

"Oh yes, Bàs, oh my God, yes!" Her nails scratched
down the skin of his back.

Bàs pumped into her like a savage and caught
her mouth again with his. They were wild against
each other. He felt her hand go between them toward her mound, and he followed with his own,
replacing her fingers against her sensitive spot as
their bodies still pressed together in perfect rhythm.

Over and over, building toward oblivion.

"Yes, oh yes," she cried out, and he felt her body clench around him.

"Shana!" he roared, his whole body tensing as he released into her.

CHAPTER FOURTEEN

The urine of a woman with child will have a "clear pale lemon colour leaning toward off-white, having a cloud on its surface."

"A needle left to rust or a nettle turning black when placed in the [urine]."
MIDWIFERY TEXTS,
POSITIVE TESTS FOR PREGNANCY, 1552

For long moments, waves of ecstasy washed through Shana until their bodies began to slow.

Bàs rolled her to the side, using his leg to keep her against him. They stared at each other, breathing heavily. Bàs raised his hand to cup her cheek and brushed his thumb against her freckles. "That was… excruciatingly wonderful. Ye are wonderful."

He kissed her, and she wanted nothing more at that moment than to stay wrapped up with him. When he pulled back, she smiled brightly. "Definitely excruciatingly wonderful," she said and touched the small white lines from healed stitches on his upper jaw. She hugged him, and he pulled the covers over their naked, cooling bodies.

Over the years of being alone after Ben had died, Shana had learned how to find pleasure on her own. Ben hadn't known much when they'd married and had never driven her as wild as what she'd experienced with Bàs. It wasn't like Bàs had done anything different, known some sensual postures to make everything feel…more. But they'd come together naturally and intensely.

She turned her face to his and smiled. "You're staring at me." Reaching up, she smoothed the pinch between his brows. "As if you're pondering great things."

"Forgive me," he said.

She pushed up on her elbow. "For what?" Surely, he had known this was what she'd wanted, what her body had wantonly craved.

"Ye didn't release first. 'Tis supposed to be that way."

She blinked, pausing. "There's no supposed to be when two find pleasure with each other." She shook her head slightly. How could he apologize for giving her the greatest pleasure she'd ever experienced? "Tupping can happen many different ways."

"I know," he said. "There's a book from the east that Gideon has, written in an ancient language." He pushed up to rest against the carved headboard and righted the pillows for her to join him.

She followed, pulling herself up, the blanket clutched to her breasts. "A book?"

He crossed his muscular arms over his chest. "It has pictures. I can show it to ye."

Bàs Sinclair was a massive man, fully grown, old enough to have many lovers like so many men did before settling into a marriage. He was brutal on the battlefield and terrifying walking onto a scaffold with his ax. And he'd brought such pleasure to her, not rushing like an inexperienced lad bent on sating his lust.

Shana plumped the pillow behind her and looked at him. Reaching over, she touched his bottom lip and smiled. "How many women have you…touched, tupped before me?"

He frowned. "Did I not do something right?"

Her smile broadened. "You did everything right," she said, nodding. "Believe me. That was… Well, it felt better than anything with Ben, who was my only other experience."

His frown softened, but he still looked worried. "One," he said. "When I turned eighteen years old, Joshua thought to gift me with a lass for the night."

"She taught you how to touch a woman?"

He shook his head and rubbed the short beard on his chin that had brushed her skin, teasing it as he'd kissed down her abdomen before. The thought made her body clench again in want, and she shifted on the bed, pressing her legs together.

"The lass didn't speak. I found out later she'd been dared by her friends. No one wanted to touch the Horseman of Death."

Shana sat up straighter, forgetting to hold the blanket over her. "That's awful."

Bas pulled the quilt up as if to keep her warm. "She wasn't a virgin, and I did my best to do everything Joshua and Gideon told me to do, but she didn't make the noises ye made."

"Told you to do?"

He lifted his arms, stretching over his head, and the sight of his muscles bulging caught her full attention. She reached for one of his biceps, capturing it with her hand. The feel of the strength there, knowing it could be deadly, yet gentle too, made her lean into him again.

Bàs pulled her onto his lap as if she weighed nothing, and she set her arms on his broad shoulders. "Aye," he said, but she'd forgotten what she'd asked, especially as she felt him harden under her arse.

He smiled. "Ye forgot what ye asked me, didn't ye?"

Shana's cheeks heated, but she pressed her breasts into him. "You distract me with all this." She rubbed her palms over his chest.

He chuckled. "And ye distract me with all this," he said, pulling the covers off them.

She pressed into his warmth, and they lay back on the bed. He slid her to the side and bent over her, kissing her gently before pulling back. "My brothers have schooled me on the parts of a lass's body, parts that feel good if touched the right way."

She smiled. "Are you saying I should thank your brothers for what just happened between us?"

"Nay," he balked, but then laughed. "Nay." He rolled, pulling her over, until she was sprawled across his chest. "But if there are other things ye wish me to do, ye but need to ask, lass."

She grinned. "So, what does this book say?"

His brows rose. "'Tis not the words but the pictures."

"You need to borrow the book to show me." She kissed him. "But for now, let's figure this out as we go along." She snaked her hand down to find him. He was already hard, and she was beginning to ache again.

"There is one picture that shows the lass on top," Bàs said, a question in his teasing grin.

Without a word, Shana leaned in, kissing him as she spread her legs wide to straddle him.

• • •

Bàs brushed his nose. It tickled, and he opened his eyes to the dawn coming into the windows of his room. Shana was pressed into his side, her arm flung over his chest and her hair a tumbling mass of untamed curls. He didn't move and kept his breath even, trying to hold onto this moment.

Shana was fragrant and warm against him, her body relaxed in his embrace without a bit of fear that he could taint her as Death. The one girl who'd braved his touch had feared she would sicken and die afterward. At present, Shana didn't seem worried, which made Bàs not worry.

Jingle. Jingle.

Bàs tensed. One of his trip ropes had been grazed by something or someone, making the bells ring. Or Betty had hit them.

He listened, not willing to move Shana if it were merely a squirrel ready for breakfast.

"Brother!"

"Daingead," he whispered and began to shift Shana to the pillow next to her.

"What time is it?" she murmured.

"Past dawn, and we have a visitor."

She pushed up in the rumpled bed, and Bàs froze at the view. Her hair, which seemed like it would never be tame again, lay in tangled curls covering her bare skin, but her breasts broke through the red curtain.

"Brother!"

"Bloody hell," Bàs said, turning from the most precious sight, his jack already standing tall.

"Did you send your hawk with word to Girnigoe?" Shana asked, her eyes wide, probably imagining her sister's panic when she didn't return last night.

"Aye. Bruce returned without it last night." He'd rewarded the bird with part of their dinner of fish.

His front door banged below. "Brother, I need ye." It was Joshua, and he sounded alarmed.

Bàs opened the door to his bedroom, his plaid in his hand as he ran down the steps. "What's wrong?"

"Good God," Kára said, her eyes wide as she took in the sight of Bàs running naked down the stairs. She looked to Joshua. "So all you Sinclair brothers are built like randy bulls."

Joshua jumped before his wife. "Cover yourself," he said, frowning at Bàs. His gaze went up the steps, and then his brows rose high. "Is Shana with ye upstairs?"

Bàs wrapped his plaid around his hips when he saw Kára peeking out from behind Joshua.

"'Tis no business of yours," Bàs said.

"Well, she's not at Girnigoe," Joshua said, his head tipping back and forth as he glanced around the room. "And she's not down here."

"I am here," Shana said, padding down the steps. "Is something wrong with Ivy or Edward?"

They all turned toward her. She had the thin blanket wrapped around her over a very rumpled-looking smock that they'd forgotten on the floor.

Kára stepped out from behind Joshua. "They're well."

Joshua's mouth hitched up, twisting in a comical

smile, and he scratched the side of his bristled face. "Didn't mean to ruin your morning," he said.

"'Tis me," Kára said, her hand on her protruding belly.

Whatever crude teasing that was about to fall from Joshua's mouth dissolved as his face tightened with concern. "She's bleeding."

"Not much," Kára said.

"Any pain?" Shana came down and led Kára to sit.

"No, and the babe is kicking. I think my time is coming."

"Why not find her grandmother and aunt?" Bàs asked, buckling his belt to hold the plaid in place. "Instead of riding her all the way out here?"

"Hilda and Amma are at Varrich Castle," Kára said, sliding her hands over her stomach. "This was closer, and Joshua's quite concerned."

A chattering started above, and Kára looked up at the rafters. "You have a squirrel in your cabin."

"That's Betty," Shana said as if that explained everything. She looked toward Bàs and Joshua. "Perhaps you two can wait outside while I examine Kára." She smiled sweetly, but it was obviously a dismissal.

Bàs walked toward the door, grabbing Joshua's upper arm on the way out.

"So...?" Joshua drew out before they'd even stepped off the porch. "The fiery-haired sister. She's bonny. Did ye bring her to her pleasure first?"

"We're not having this conversation," Bàs said and strode toward the barn to check on Ilsa and her calf.

Joshua jogged after him. "'Tis important that the

lass feels good if ye want her to do it again, brother."

"Shana felt very good," Bàs said.

"Did ye use your mouth on her? Kára loves that."

They had come together again in pretty much the same way they had the first time except that she'd been on top for the first half. She'd found her release with his, but Bàs surely wasn't going to share intimate details with Joshua.

"Don't ye worry about Shana," Bàs said.

"I'm not," Joshua said. "I'm worried about ye. If she leaves ye for not making her moan and thrash about, she'll break your tender heart."

Bàs turned in frustration, the words huffing out of him. "She moaned my name over and over and thrashed about in pleasure and release. So ye don't—"

He stopped mid-sentence at the sight of Keenan and two more lasses staring at them from their horses across the quiet clearing, listening to every word.

• • •

"Did you bleed with your firstborn?" Shana asked Kára as she helped her sit on the small bed in the cabin's main room.

"My first babe, Geir, came early. There was a lot of blood," she said, her face tense. "But I had suffered some trauma." She shook her head. "This pregnancy is different, more like when I carried Adam."

"Try not to ride and walk much for the next few

weeks. The babe is likely to come soon, but we want him or her to arrive when they're ready, not because your body is ready to be free of this burden." She smiled, leaning in as if imparting a secret. "When you're with child, it's as if your body is taken over by the little beastie, and sometimes your body decides enough is enough."

Kára exhaled, her cheeks puffing. "I think my body is getting to that point. So much kicking." She shook her head. "This babe seems very big and temperamental. He reminds me of Joshua already."

Shana sniffed a laugh. "Kicking is good. Remember, though, that he will slow down inside right before birth, and that's natural."

Rap. Rap. Rap. "Shana? Kára? Are ye almost done?"

"Soon," Shana called back to Bàs.

"Because ye have a couple more patients waiting to see ye."

Shana looked at Kára, and then they both looked at the door. "I thought very few people knew where Bàs's cabin is in the deep forest," Shana said.

Kára began to stand, and Shana helped her. Kára smoothed the petticoat that jutted out from under her breasts with the fullness of her belly. "I didn't know where it was. I thought only the brothers, Hannah, and perhaps Keenan knew."

Rap. Rap. "'Tis me, Kára," Joshua said as he opened the door. He held one hand shielding his eyes as if he didn't wish to see anything disturbing. "Are ye done? There's a lass out here panting like she's about to foal any minute."

"Women don't foal," Shana said in passing as she

hurried outside.

"Whelp then?"

"We give birth," Kára said behind Shana, a frown apparent in her tone.

Shana went straight to the woman who was breathing heavily, holding onto Keenan. He looked at Shana, his face tightening with anger as he glanced down her smock. She'd left the blanket behind in the cabin. "Help me get her inside," she said, ignoring his condemnation. Had he guessed that she'd stayed the night with Bàs or had Joshua said something?

"A million pardons, mistress," the woman said. "'Tis my time, and I made Keenan bring me to ye."

"Are you also with child?" Shana said, glancing at a second woman who didn't look pregnant.

She shook her head, hurrying after them. "I but came along to ask ye about some herbs and such and about my wee Elsie who gets terrible nosebleeds."

Shana looked back at Kára. "Can you let Ivy know I'm safe and will return as soon as I help these women?"

"I will," Kára said.

Joshua held firmly to Kára as she walked to his horse and lifted her up to sit sidesaddle before climbing on behind her. "And I will be sure to let our brothers know that ye are safe and doing fine here, Bàs," Joshua said with a full smile for his brother.

"Bàs, could you start a fire inside," Shana called.

"Didn't mean to interrupt things here," Joshua said and had the audacity to wink at her.

Kára smacked his arm. "Leave her be." She smiled at Shana. "Thank you again."

Shana nodded and hurried inside.

"The bairn is coming!" the woman on the bed cried.

• • •

"Where is her husband?" Shana asked Bàs as they rode Dòchas slowly through the forest.

"He died last year when he fell from his horse training," Bàs answered.

"Last year? Then the bairn isn't his?" Shana asked.

He wasn't one to spread gossip, but he knew it would stop with Shana. "I think the father remained at my cabin with her," he said, glancing back to see the other lass, who wasn't pregnant, following behind on the horse she'd ridden in on.

"Keenan?" Shana whispered, twisting in her seat to look up at Bàs.

He met her eyes. They looked tired and quite green. "I've seen them together often. He will help her with the bairn if he is, and he'll help with the bairn even if he's not."

"Then he's a good man," she said, turning forward again. She wore the blue dress, which was still damp and very wrinkled, but it was better than showing up at Girnigoe in a blanket.

He leaned in toward her ear. "I'm sorry we were interrupted this morn. I would have liked to wake up leisurely together. Not with my brother hollering for me."

"Me as well," she said, relaxing into the shelter of his chest.

Bàs inhaled near her hair, which she'd tamed somewhat with a wide comb. They continued farther on while Bàs tried to ignore how her perfect arse rubbed between his legs.

"Would you stay with me?" she asked suddenly.

"Stay with ye? Tonight?" The Lord was answering his unholy prayers. "Aye."

"No," she said, still looking outward over the horse's head. "If I become with child? Would you stand by me like Keenan is with Millie?"

That was a question he'd never been asked, never even thought he'd ever be asked. "I... Shana." He shifted, leaning to the side. "Look at me."

Finally, she turned in her seat. Worry sat in her face. "Do ye regret last night?" he asked, his words soft.

The surprise that lifted her brows helped him draw breath. "No." She touched the side of his face, and he turned his mouth to her palm to kiss it. "Not even if your brother tells the whole town."

Bàs grinned. "Kára won't let him."

"But what if I become with child?" she asked again.

Bàs stared at her, bewildered. No one had ever come near him, let alone asked him to stay in their life. He was hated, feared, and avoided.

"You have no answer?" she said.

She tried to turn back, but he wouldn't let her. "Of course I will stay with ye, Shana," he said. She relaxed enough to meet his gaze again. "My only hesitation," he said, "is that I've never... Well, I never thought a lass would want me to stay with her, with or without a child. I am despised by the world,

Shana. I am Death. No one wants me to stay with them."

She frowned. "You are not Death, Bàs." She shook her head and huffed. "I'm going to call you something else, but Sebastian doesn't seem to suit. Do you have a favorite name?"

His finger rose to her brow to smooth the pinch there. "Nay, I do not."

"Gavin? Iain? Mathias? How about Rory?"

A smile relaxed across his mouth. "Ye can try any name, but I won't likely answer."

She huffed softly and turned forward again. "I'll try Sebastian again. Bàs could be short for Sebastian."

Bàs had always been his name, even before he knew his father was convinced he was the Horseman of Death. There was a time when Bàs believed his sire but, since watching his three brothers step askew to their duty as the Four Horsemen, Bàs had started rethinking what his role should be in the clan. Perhaps he didn't have to remain the executioner until he was finally killed himself. Maybe his life could hold more. *Much more.* The desire took root in his chest. It was fragile like a sapling, but it started to grow.

He inhaled against Shana's hair. His lips moved near her ear. "As long as ye let me stay with ye, Shana, ye can call me anything ye wish."

She squeezed his arm into her middle, adding to the lightness that Bàs felt spreading out within him. Could she possibly look past all the killing he'd done? Past the skull mask and slicing ax?

They left the forest, riding out onto the moor

leading down to Girnigoe and the village. The other lass, Margaret, came even with them. "Thank ye again, mistress. I'll get some raspberry leaves right away for a brew."

"I'll keep a lookout for the plant, too," Shana said, "and bring you some."

Margaret smiled sweetly. "I live with my ma. Lady Ella knows where." Her eyes flicked to Bàs. They widened slightly, and she snapped her gaze back to Shana quickly. "Good day, milady," she said with an uneasy smile and pressed her horse into a run toward the village.

Shana snorted. "If your name was Sebastian, she wouldn't have looked like that."

"I think it has more to do with my skull mask and sharp ax."

As he looked back out, he saw a rider coming up the hill, galloping. It was Gideon. "Hold on," Bàs said, pulling Shana tighter into him as they surged forward. It took little time with them both racing to meet each other. Slowing, they circled their horses. "What is it?" Bàs called.

"A woman has come from the Oliphant Clan," Gideon said. His gaze slid to Shana. "She seeks sanctuary from Erskine Oliphant. She says she's Ivy's friend."

CHAPTER FIFTEEN

"[I swear to] baptize any new-born, in the time
of necessity, using the accustomed
words and plain, pure water."
Part of the 1567 midwifery oath. The number of
baptisms by midwives with proceeding death
records shows that midwives were able to tell when
a newborn wouldn't survive.

CAMBRIDGE.ORG

Ivy's friend? Janet, the woman who'd helped during
Edward's birth? She was the only person Ivy had
mentioned as someone with whom she confided, and
she'd been the one to walk with Shana to the scaffold that dreadful day that Bàs had come to kill her.
No. Not Bàs. The Horseman of Death.

Bàs dismounted and lifted her down from
Dòchas, and they traipsed together into Girnigoe
keep. A woman sat before the hearth with Ella and
Hannah. She rose, turning toward Shana.

"Janet Bell," Shana said, studying her. "You seek
help from the Sinclairs?" The woman had lush dark
hair now that Shana saw it down. At Old Wick Castle,
she'd worn her hair back in a tight bun. Now it was
loose and fell around her comely face. She was young
like Ivy, and her dark eyes were pinched with fear.

"I didn't know where else to go," Janet said, coming forward to meet Shana.

"Do ye have no kin?" Bàs asked.

She shook her head, sending him a wary glance. "My mother died several years ago, and I never knew my father or his kin."

"Friends?" Shana asked.

Janet's face grew heavy with worry. "Ivy was my only friend." She glanced at the stairs leading above. "Is she… Is she well?"

"She is," Shana said. Janet was flushed, her gaze flitting about the room.

"So, the people of Wick know that Ivy and Shana live?" Bàs asked.

Janet's gaze stopped on him, and she nodded. "The village witnessed the four Sinclair armies. They know for whom you came. Despite Erskine's insistence, the town does not want the Drummond sisters back for fear of spurring the Sinclairs and your allies to revenge."

"Exactly what I thought," Merida said, coming from the hall leading toward the kitchens. "Do people want Erskine gone, too?"

Janet looked at her. "I don't believe so. He's strong and keeps the clan in order."

Ella snorted. "Leading through fear and threats does not indicate a good leader."

Shana agreed. "Has he threatened you?"

Janet's gaze dropped to the large squares of stone built into the keep floor. She nodded. "He thinks his son still lives and that he is being hidden here at Girnigoe."

"Did you tell him that you saw Shana carry the bairn away to sacrifice in a satanic ritual?" Gideon asked.

"No," she answered.

"Because someone did," Bàs said.

"I didn't," Janet said again and stepped back when Bàs looked at her. "Erskine probably lied to get the king's help," Janet said, her words tumbling over one another.

Shana could imagine Erskine lying to the king. Especially about something that unfortunately didn't require proof, only suspicion.

"Is that why ye've come to Girnigoe to seek sanctuary?" Bàs asked next to Shana. "Because he wants ye to back up his lie?"

Janet paused for a moment and then nodded and looked to Shana. "You and Ivy should run as far from here as you can."

Janet came up to Shana, taking her hands. "Perhaps he will forget about Ivy and stop raging. Divorce her. She could be free of him then."

"On what grounds?" Gideon asked from behind.

Janet glanced his way. "Adultery."

Janet knew Ivy had been having an affair? Could she know Edward was not Erskine's son?

No one said anything for a long pause. "I need to talk to Ivy," Shana said. "And see if she would like to see you."

Janet's face tightened. "Is the bairn alive?"

Shana met her steady gaze. "The babe died after it was born. I took it away because my sister could not stand the pain of looking at her son."

"He was alive when you took him," Janet said.

Cain stood beside his wife. "Ye told that to Oliphant?"

Janet held a hand around her throat as if she imagined a noose. "'Twas the truth I knew, but I would never have said anything that would hurt Ivy. She's my friend."

"I'll see if Ivy's awake," Shana said, hurrying toward the winding staircase. She cast a glance back at Bàs who gave her a slight nod. It wasn't an answer to anything, just support and acknowledgment that something seemed not quite right.

Rap. Rap. "Ivy, 'tis me."

"Come in," Ivy called, and Shana pushed through. Ivy was sitting up in the bed they had shared, nursing Edward. She smiled, but her brows rose high. "I heard that you were out at Bàs's cabin all night." Her gaze moved up and down Shana's wrinkled gown.

Shana took a deep breath. "Janet Bell is below."

Ivy's gaze snapped up to hers, and her smile dropped away as if she'd lost all feeling in her face.

"She's arrived to tell us that Erskine is raging and is convinced Edward survived. She seeks sanctuary here."

"He knows Edward's alive?" she whispered, as if the walls would report back to him.

"I don't know, but Janet thinks he lived. She saw me take Edward away while he was quite alive."

"She heard me begging you," Ivy said and looked down at her suckling babe.

"She says we should run away and not tell Erskine about Edward. That Erskine will seek a divorce under accusations of adultery, and you can be free of him."

Ivy's lips tightened. "But Erskine thinks…knows Edward is not his. Why does he want him so badly? If it was merely to kill him, us leaving Wick should be enough to satisfy his revenge."

Shana came to sit on the edge of the bed. "Perhaps he's realized that he cannot get a woman pregnant, but still wants an heir."

"If Edward is not Erskine's true son, the clan may contest. The chieftainship will go to another strong leader, because Erskine has no other blood relation as far as I know."

"Maybe Erskine plans to insist Edward is his, raise him as his own son."

Ivy sighed, setting Edward against her shoulder. "He knows Edward is Liam's. I can't imagine he would accept him as his own. 'Tis not his blood. Family bloodlines are very important to Erskine. 'Twas why he would never take an orphaned child as his own."

"How did he discover you were seeing Liam Ross?" Shana asked.

"Janet told me she overheard one of the soldiers telling him."

Ivy stroked the babe's little dark head. "Erskine wasn't even coming to my bed when I conceived. I did go to Erskine's bed after I realized, so that he might think the child was his." Her face was tight as if the memory of his touch made her nauseous.

Shana paced across the floor. "Could he think the child is his even if rumors say you were with another?"

"I won't let him have Edward," Ivy said. "He'll either kill him or abuse him like he abuses everyone in his life." She kissed the little head. "If Edward goes to Wick, then I go, too, to protect him."

And Shana would lose Ivy forever, and her

nephew. "You will both be in jeopardy," Shana said. "I can't let that happen."

Ivy looked at Shana. "It doesn't surprise me that Erskine's raging against Janet. She was my only friend there and was present at the birth. She also thought he would kill Edward. In fact, she gave me the courage to ask you to take him away."

"It sounds like Erskine has turned on her."

"Maybe she would be safe to tell," Ivy said.

Janet was an unknown. Even though Ivy had counted her as her friend, her sister had been desperate for companionship at the time. "The more people who know Edward is alive the more dangerous 'tis for him."

"All of the Sinclairs know," Ivy said.

Shana frowned. "I don't think they spread gossip."

"Maybe we need to leave soon," Ivy whispered. "Find a way to sail to France."

Her words were like arrows piercing Shana. How could she leave Bàs so soon after they'd come together, after he'd shared so much with her?

"What about Liam Ross?" Shana asked. "Would you leave without telling him he has a son?"

Ivy's face pinched as if in pain, and Shana's stomach clenched with guilt.

"I need to find him," Ivy said. "He's so strong and smart. He would take us to safety."

"He was an apothecary in the village?" Shana asked. Would he have gone far with his son and Ivy in danger?

"I met him when I went to find herbs that might make Erskine more potent. He was so kind and helpful. I think I fell in love with him." She shook her head. "I know I fell in love." She stroked her babe's back. "And I will do everything to keep our son alive and out of Erskine's cruel hands."

Shana came around. "Let me take Edward away so Janet can see you here alone."

"The cradle and all the blankets," Ivy said, letting Shana take him from her.

"I'll get Bàs to carry them out." The babe was sleeping, his little healthy body warm and soft. It made Shana's heart ache for the son she'd lost. "I'll do anything to protect you, little one," she whispered.

Shana looked to Ivy. "I'll take him up to the nursery where Ella's daughter and Kára's son are, and then find Bàs."

Shana walked to the door, opening it with her free hand.

"Good," said a voice in the dimness of the corridor. "A familiar face. I seem to have gotten lost."

Shana stood face to face with Janet. The woman's brows rose high. "I guess the boy lived after all."

. . .

Bàs paced in the Great Hall. "Something feels wrong."

"More so than us risking civil war to protect a woman we barely know?" Gideon asked.

Bàs turned on him. "And an innocent bairn along with the woman's sister who's been accused of being a witch. If James or Erskine get ahold of Shana, she will probably be hanged or burned."

Gideon held up his hands. "Pardon, brother." He shook his head slightly. "I speak before my conscience catches up to my tongue."

Cain scratched Apollo's head where he stood next to Artemis, the two large dogs standing ready as if they felt the tension in the hall. "Cait would deduct ten points," Cain said to Gideon, referring to Cait's tally to teach Gideon some tact.

Gideon crossed his arms, frowning at their oldest brother. "'Tis a good thing she's at Varrich teaching then." He turned back to Bàs. "And I agree. I think the woman really wants to see if the bairn is alive. She could be spying for Erskine."

Bàs crouched next to Artemis, stroking her shaggy coat. Dogs were a great calming influence and helped him think. "If Janet stays, could she live for a while at the Orphans' Home at Varrich?"

"I'll ask Cait," Gideon said. "That could keep her away from Girnigoe and the bairn but not send her back to Wick."

Bàs stood and glanced at the hallway where Ella had taken Janet to use the privy. "'Tis been some time," he said, feeling tension slide across his back and shoulders. "I'm going to find them."

Cain was already walking toward the archway when Ella came running out, colliding with him. "She asked for food, and I left her in the privy. When I came back, I waited, and finally knocked." Ella shook her head, her cheeks red. "She wasn't in there."

"Find her," Cain said and three of them took to the steps while Gideon jogged off outside, probably to circle the castle.

Bàs raced directly to Ivy and Shana's room. The hall was empty, but the door was cracked.

"Shana?" Bàs said.

"Come in," she called, and he pushed through to find Janet standing by the bed where Ivy held Edward.

Shana's face was pinched. *Bloody hell*. He strode to Janet, stopping before her. The woman's eyes widened with fear, but he didn't care. "Ye sent Ella to find ye food so ye could sneak about."

"I…I got lost in the corridors."

He lowered his face mere inches from hers. "What game are ye playing, Janet Bell?"

She swallowed. "If the child and mother truly disappear, Erskine will have to divorce her based on desertion and move on. Ivy and her child will be safe."

"Why is that your concern?" Bàs asked.

"Because…" Janet started, her words stumbling, her face red, "she's my friend."

"Janet is trying to help," Ivy said.

"Sebastian," Shana said. "You're scaring her."

Neither woman questioned the use of the strange name. Bàs's gaze shifted from Janet to Shana, and his gut tightened. There was anger on her face, but also a watchfulness that made Bàs take a step back from Janet. Could Shana be worried for the woman in the face of his anger?

Someone came to the door behind them. "There you are." 'Twas Ella.

"Bloody hell," Cain said, stopping inside the door.

Shana came before Janet. "You say you want Erskine to think the babe is dead?"

She nodded quickly, like a bird. "I'll keep the secret. I want them to escape, too. Erskine is mad. At the soonest possibility, Ivy, her sister, and son should sail for the continent."

Silence sat heavy in the room. Only Edward made small sounds while he lay in Ivy's arms.

Nay. It echoed in Bàs's mind. *Nay.* He wouldn't let Shana leave for the continent, trying to keep her sister and nephew alive at the hands of the French. But he said nothing, not before this woman whom he did not know.

"'Tis time to make plans," Bàs said, looking back at Cain. Plans to war against a man who would drive Shana from Scotland.

• • •

Shana opened her eyes to a lightening room. She'd slept next to Ivy, Edward between them. Was Bàs somewhere in the castle or had he returned to his cabin in the woods? They'd placed a pallet in the room for Janet, but a quick glance showed it empty.

Shana turned her face to watch the gentle rise and fall of Edward's chest. Were they safe here at Girnigoe? Would they start a civil war across Scotland? She closed her eyes for a moment, but it didn't block out the visions of battle and death that would follow. All because a tyrant wanted a son.

Please let Erskine turn away from Ivy and believe Edward dead. Please let King James be too busy to worry about a false witchcraft accusation in northern Scotland.

Until she knew Erskine wasn't pursuing them,

and the king wasn't coming to test them as witches, she must plan as if they were still in grave jeopardy.

Years ago, she'd believed the best circumstances would happen, and then her new husband, Ben, was sent to sea to die and her own son never took a breath. They were hard lessons, and she'd stopped believing the best outcome was probable. No. The worst outcome was usually the way fate worked. And that meant civil war, witchcraft trials, torture, and death.

Shana rubbed a hand against her clenched stomach and gently slid from the bed, fixing the blanket in case Edward suddenly learned to roll. She padded about the room, washing her face in the basin of clean water, brushing her hair, and dressing, thankful that Hannah had given her another gown while Shana's petticoat and bodice were thoroughly washed and pressed with hot irons.

This costume was dark green with an under petticoat of blue plaid. The wool was the softest Shana had ever felt. Luckily her stays, which tied in the front, were dry, and the new clothes fit her well. She tied her hair back in a long braid that lay over one shoulder and left her sister and nephew sleeping.

The corridor was quiet, and she stepped lightly down the stairs, coming out in the shadowed archway and into the Great Hall. The four brothers were standing there, along with their sister, Hannah, and their aunt, Merida. It was like a family meeting, and Shana pulled back.

Eavesdropping is in poor taste, her mother had told her long ago, but then taught her to do it anyway because *'tis also the only way one can learn things*.

"If ye fear James, I will take them to the continent myself," Bàs said. His strong back was toward her. He stood taller than the rest, and his frame was as broad.

"We don't fear James," Joshua said, his arms crossed. "We fear the death that will ravage this land if there's a civil war."

"Which we don't know will happen," Hannah said, her higher voice strong.

"Erskine Oliphant needs to be killed," Merida said, shaking her gray head. "Reminds me of Alec Sutherland, nasty bit of pig snot."

"I agree he should be replaced," Cain said, "but to do so after he's written to James could pull us into war with the crown."

Joshua shook his head. "War will bring too much death to the land, make us weak against England and France."

"The Horseman of War doesn't want to war," Bàs said.

Joshua glared. "Are you craving more kills, Brother Death?" he asked. Bàs didn't reply. "Ye do know that every one of those lives ye've taken has harmed others, their families. They've grieved or wondered what became of their son or husband or brother."

"Joshua, stop it," Hannah said.

"The swing of your blade slices through hearts of wives, sisters, parents," Joshua said, continuing.

Gideon exhaled. "And here we go."

"He knows," Cain said, his voice like thunder. "And ye know as well as the rest of us that Bàs has done his duty for this clan without hesitation."

"I do not wish to kill," Bàs said, his voice low, reined in. "But I would no more let Shana and Ivy be sacrificed as ye would give Kára and Adam to James to question and kill."

Joshua swore under his breath and rubbed the back of his head as if it ached.

"James is hunting witches like a man gone mad," Merida said. "If he thinks they are here, we will all be under suspicion."

"Midwives and woman apothecaries are often the first to be accused," Hannah said.

"With Kára about to give birth," Bàs said, "ye better hope James doesn't take away all the midwives."

Joshua raked a hand through his hair. "Daingead. We cannot have war right now."

Shana couldn't hold back any longer. She strode out from the archway. Let them realize she was eavesdropping. "I agree. That is why Ivy and I are leaving."

Bàs turned to her, his face hard but blank of emotion, as if he wore his skull mask. "Then I am leaving, too," he said. "Today."

CHAPTER SIXTEEN

"The commonest recommended method for bringing on a slow labour was to make the woman go up and down stairs and preferably shout out loud…. As the labour progressed, the woman was helped to the birthing stool, which seems to have been the most popular method for delivery… [Midwives] were advised to manipulate the birth canal by stretching and pulling. One reference stated that the membranes should be torn out with nails (of the hand). Cutting was common as were fissures after poor suturing, usually with silk."

CHILDBIRTH IN THE LATE 16TH CENTURY
BY LESLEY SMITH

Bàs rode Dòchas slowly through the forest, glancing back often at Shana, who rode with Ivy on another horse from Girnigoe's stables. Darra was a gentle mare, swift and sure, which was perfect for carrying a new mother with her bairn tied to her chest under a cape. That way no one at Girnigoe could say they saw her leaving with a bairn. Although with Janet Bell missing, Erskine might already know that Edward lived.

"I can't imagine Janet returning to Wick," Ivy said. Bàs stared ahead as she spoke. "Erskine will question and possibly kill her. She must have gone somewhere else."

"But why leave at all?" Shana asked.

"Perhaps she was taken," Ivy said.

Shana's voice carried easily through the woods. "There was no indication of a struggle. No horses are missing. 'Tis as if she walked away."

"Or was carried away," Ivy insisted.

"We will be safe out here," Bàs said. "There's only one easy way in and out of my yard, through thick bramble with inch-long thorns, and my place is hidden."

"And he has a wolf to protect us, and two huge dogs," Shana said.

We will stay hidden at my cabin. The argument with his brothers had ceased with him promising to remain at his cabin with the women until they could decide a course of action. It would probably take a week to find out if James was going to react to Erskine's accusation of witchcraft. And they weren't sure if Janet would report that the bairn was dead or alive if she returned to Wick. Gideon had sent a message to one of two spies he had living with the Oliphants to find out if Janet was seen there.

Artemis and Apollo trotted ahead and circled back only to run ahead again. Bàs kept his senses alert. He'd thought his cabin was secluded enough that no one could find it, but recent visits had proven that wrong.

"Is it much farther?" Ivy asked. "Edward is starting to fuss for a feeding."

"Past those brambles." Bàs pointed. "There's a narrow pass that avoids the prickers."

They walked between the bushes, and the way was clear. The bailey was also empty, the creek receded. Ivy's gasp behind him heralded the approach of Beò.

"He's Bàs's friend, his pet," Shana said. "He has many beasts about. They're all kind. You'll see. There's even a squirrel who won't leave his cabin."

"Who in their right mind lives with beasts?" Ivy asked in a whisper that still carried to Bàs.

"Someone who sees more good in them than in man," Bàs replied and dismounted. "Let's get ye settled inside."

Bàs spent the day fixing the fence that had floated away with the flooded creek, reinforcing it with rocks that would be harder to move. Ilsa and Iona wandered through the yard with the chickens. Banshee brought him a dead vole, and Beò watched everything from the porch. The dogs played about harassing the sheep and avoiding Gillian, the goat who tried to butt them with his small horns.

Shana, Ivy, and Edward would take the upper bedroom while Bàs slept, probably with Betty, on the small bed downstairs. He'd originally set it up for when he must nurse some animal all night, catching sleep when he could. What were the chances that Shana would join him there? He snorted softly as he stepped from the fresh stream, having scrubbed himself free of the day's grime. He'd forgone the hard bristled brush this time, enjoying the coolness of the water on non-burning skin.

His skull mask sat on a stump that he'd carved for it to perch upon. The half skull had been his constant companion through the years, his father always insisting on him wearing it when out. It was a powerful reminder that he was the Horseman of Death. Could ridding himself of the mask be enough to throw off his deadly role? *I could throw it in the river.* His glance went from the bulbous white bone to the swiftly flowing river. He'd never dared to even think of doing so before.

What would he be without it when the Horseman of Death was all he'd ever been? Was there something else in life that he could be? Just a warrior and healer of animals? How about a husband and father? The thought raced around him, making his stomach flip with something that might be giddiness.

At the sound of the door, he looked up at the porch where Shana emerged, a wooden bucket in hand. She saw him and turned his way, walking to the creek. "I need water to boil some of Edward's rags."

Bàs took the bucket and dragged it through the water, filling it. "We've had no time to...talk," Bàs said as he stopped before her.

"I know," she said, disappointment in the bend of her sweet lips. She glanced toward the cabin. "Do you think you can get Betty out of the house tonight?"

Hope swelled in Bàs's chest. "If that means ye'll join me downstairs, I'll see to it."

A smile slid across her lips. "You might have trouble with that." She turned, and he walked with her, a towel about his hips as he carried the water-filled bucket. She lifted his empty hand, the injured one. "This beastie doesn't seem to want to leave." Her finger slid over the puncture wounds that were only light red now.

"I'm a warrior and coaxer of beasts," Bàs said. "I think I can handle it."

Two hours later, Bàs looked up at the ceiling

where Betty scampered along the rafters. "Bloody hell," he murmured, followed by a quick prayer. *Help me Lord to free my house of beasts, at least at night.*

He'd set five non-lethal traps about the downstairs of his cabin. None that would hurt her, only catch her so he could evict her for the night. Boxes with food set inside should draw her in, and her body weight at one end would make the box shift, dropping the door on the front. He'd used them for years when catching sick animals that needed tending.

So far, Betty was proving infuriatingly smart. She'd take the food at the lip of the box but not traipse down to the other end to get the bait inside. Perhaps he should switch to the trap that would catch her foot or tail.

Bàs walked outside where both Ivy and Shana sat on a blanket in a patch of sun. Banshee lay atop Shana's petticoat purring loudly while being petted. The cat liked her enough that she would start bringing Shana dead voles and birds soon.

Shana's hair was down and unbraided, the curls moving naturally along her back as she turned to slide a hand along Banshee's back. The dogs played nearby, making Banshee's tail bristle every so often, and Ilsa munched on the summer grasses that Gillian hadn't already bitten down to the root.

He took a full breath, releasing it slowly. All was peaceful. He was content at that moment and felt himself grasping hold of it. The forest had always calmed him, his animals forgiving him and loving him unconditionally, more than he could ever do for himself.

What would it be like to have Shana there with him? Could she consider staying with an executioner, someone marked as the harbinger of death from his birth? He glanced over at the stone garden where his mother's carved face sat looking out. Merida had whispered to him time and again how his mother did not blame him for her death, that his father was wrong to name him so, that Bàs was kind and compassionate at heart. Was he?

To animals, aye. But people, especially those who killed and hurt others? Should he be kind to them? Or was he doing what must be done to protect the world? Where was the line drawn between protector and killer?

Bàs took a step toward Shana and Ivy when Beò charged into the clearing. Ivy gasped.

"'Tis Bàs's wolf," Shana said rising with her sister who was clearly shaken.

Bàs spent no time questioning the urgency, knowing Beò didn't run into the clearing unless in warning. He grasped a mattucashlass from his boot and drew his sword. "Someone comes," Bàs said. "Go inside."

Shana linked her arm with her sister's, and they hurried across to the porch when a horse galloped along the bramble-flanked path.

"Bàs!" Joshua yelled from his horse where he cradled Kára. His head whipped around. "Shana, 'tis Kára. Her waters broke."

Shana rushed down the steps. "And you threw her onto a horse?"

"He overreacts a bit," Kára said. Her face tensed, and she closed her eyes as pain seemed to take ahold of her.

Bàs ran over so Joshua could lower his wife gently down to him. The woman was swollen to capacity. Joshua jumped down. "I've got her," he said, taking her from Bàs's arms. "Her amma and aunt are away at Varrich. This was closer, and she prefers Shana."

"Don't tell my amma," Kára said, her face squeezing.

"Keep your breath going in and out," Shana said, ushering Joshua through the door. "On the bed down here. 'Tis closer to the fire and water."

"What the bloody hell are ye trying to catch in here?" Joshua said, glancing at the traps, one of them on the bed.

Bàs dodged them and plucked the one off the bed. "Betty needs time out of the cabin," he said.

"Who's Betty?" Joshua asked.

As if to make her presence known, the squirrel scampered up the logs on the other side of the bed. "The squirrel's still here?" Kára asked.

"It seems to be her home now," Shana said, glancing at Bàs. "Put a large pot of water over the flames. I need a sharp clean knife that's been run through a flame and a thin rope to tie the navel cord. And clean rags."

"I can help," Ivy said, standing in the doorway.

Shana looked to her. "No heavy lifting."

Ivy nodded and went with Bàs toward the hearth where he set her to stirring up the fire.

"Shouldn't she be hanging from something?" Joshua asked, looking up at the rafters as if Bàs usually had nooses tied there waiting to be filled by the condemned.

Shana sat next to Kára on the bed, talking softly to her about breathing and what the pains felt like. She glanced at Joshua. "That is up to Kára. Some women like to be down in the bed."

"Up," Kára said, breathing through another pain.

Shana looked to Bàs. "Can you rig ropes over the rafters or sheets?"

Bàs hurried to a chest, pulling out some sheets. He threw them over the rafters, making Betty chatter and scurry as if she thought he was trying to swat her off.

Kára let loose a long moan, one of pain and fear. Shana clasped her hand. "Kára." She waited until Kára opened her eyes and stared into hers. "You've done this before, and you have two healthy sons. You can do this. Your body knows what to do, and we are here to help."

She nodded. "Make sure she comes out safely."

Shana smiled. "A girl?"

"I think so," Kára said. "It feels different from Adam. "Bigger."

"That's why you're worried?" Shana asked, and Kára nodded, glancing at Joshua.

"And early," Joshua said. The Horseman of War's face paled.

Suddenly Apollo and Artemis rushed through the small door that remained open. Betty chattered and flew along the beams above, making the dogs look up and bark at the new game.

"Bloody hell, Bàs!" Joshua yelled. "Ye're surrounded by beasts."

Bàs opened the door and shooed the dogs out. "I prefer them to men."

"Maybe we should call you Beast instead of Bàs," Joshua said.

"I was thinking Sebastian," Shana called over the barking of the dogs. Both Joshua and Kára looked at her. Shana shrugged. "Sort of a longer version of Bàs, and it doesn't mean death. Because that's the worst name I've ever heard."

"John is worse. Or James," Kára said from her position on the bed. "And not Patrick or Robert or Henry." She looked at Joshua as if they'd been discussing names for their new babe. "And absolutely not Jean."

"Of course not," he said. "Whatever ye want, Kára." He kissed her damp forehead, pushing back her golden-colored hair.

Bàs secured the sheets so that Kára could loop an arm through each to help her stay up, her feet under her. Right now, she reclined on the bed, draped with the quilt.

"I need to check you," Shana said and waited for Kára's nod before lifting the quilt.

Bàs spun around to face the door.

"I'll leave," Joshua said.

"You need to hold me," Kára said, "help me stay up."

Joshua blew air from his cheeks. "Aye, my love."

Bàs stopped at the door. "Let me know if ye need anything."

Shana's voice stopped him. "I need you."

"In here?"

"Yes. The babe is coming quickly, and I can't waste time running to the door to holler for you. Stay inside."

"Do I have to…watch?"

"No," Kára said, stretching it out into a moan.

"Ye definitely don't want to see this," Joshua said as he lifted under his wife. "'Twill give ye nightmares."

Bàs heard a smack, and Joshua grunted.

Ivy, who'd been quiet by the fire, laughed. "Keep your gaze on the door. Women's work can be gruesome."

"The smells," Joshua said as if reliving it. "And so much blood and…more, flying out of the woman. Like bloated entrails bursting open."

"Good Lord!" Shana said. "What type of births have you seen?"

"Remember Calder swooning when he watched his wife, Brenna, birth wee Joshua?" Joshua said. "'Tis meant for only the strongest to witness."

"You look white as a bleached sheet," Ivy said, probably to Joshua.

Kára groaned low, a rumbling cry of agony like she was being ripped apart.

Flying? Did the bairn shoot out of the mother? Horses dropped their foals. Were human mothers different? He wasn't about to look. "Is it different from horses then?" Bàs asked, listening to grunts, groans, and the ropes of his bed creak as Joshua balanced on it to lift Kára.

But Joshua didn't respond.

"Bàs," Shana called. "Trade places with Joshua."

Bàs's stomach jumped up high, and he placed his palm on the door, wishing he were on the other side of it. "Me?"

"Before he passes out and drops her!" she yelled.

"I…I don't pass out," Joshua said, clearly sounding like a man about to pass out.

Bàs skirted the room, keeping his back to the bed until he was at the head of it. He stepped up on it, balancing, and took Kára's arms. Joshua sunk downward. "I've got ye," Bàs said.

Thunk. Bàs glanced over to see Ivy bending over Joshua. His brother's face was white, but his eyes were open. "That rat is staring down at me," Joshua murmured, and Ivy, Kára, and Bàs all looked up to see Betty watching like the spectacle was a wrestling contest or theatrical play.

Bàs took a full breath to fortify himself. "She's probably laughing at ye."

"Fok," Joshua murmured and made a rude gesture at Betty above.

Kára let out another deep groan, and Bàs swore he could feel it pulling up through her body as he held her securely in the sheets. Her hands wrapped around the lengths of cloth, her knuckles turned white with her grip. Thank the Lord, she wasn't holding his hand. She'd likely break bones.

"I see the head," Shana called, coming out from the quilt to smile up at Kára. "Head first is good."

Kára nodded, her breath coming too fast.

"Breathe slower," Bàs said, and Shana nodded to him. "Innnnn…" Bàs said and inhaled loudly. "Ouuuuuut." He exhaled. Kára followed, and Bàs glanced to the floor where Joshua was also breathing in and out with them, trying to regain his strength to stand.

"Stay down," Ivy said. "Until you're strong enough to keep up on your own. I'm not going to get in your way if you start to drop, and you don't want to hit the babe or mother."

Another cry started coming out of Kára, and it turned into a roar.

"That's it," Shana called from below. "One more push."

She pushed once more and Shana said, "I've got it. Bàs, lower Kára gently."

Out from the quilt came a bairn, covered in whitish gunk and blood. The cord tying it to Kára looked thick and gray like a bloated intestine. Lord, Joshua was right. Bàs took a fortifying breath, and the smells slammed into him.

Lowering Kára carefully onto the bed, Bàs stepped down and sunk to the floor to lean against it. He looked at Joshua and shook his head. "Ye're right. No place for a man."

Ivy snorted and ran over with wet and dry linens.

"Ye'll need new sheets," Joshua said to him.

"Consider these my gift to ye both, on the occasion of your child's birth."

Joshua smiled broadly and pushed up to sit, both brothers on the floor while Ivy, Shana, and Kára worked above.

"'Tis a girl!" Shana called, and a small sob came from Kára.

Bàs looked to see her smiling and crying at the same time, reaching for the girl. The bairn began to cry with vigor, and Bàs turned to smile at Joshua, who beamed. The brothers stared at each other for a moment, and for the first time ever, Bàs envied Joshua and the joy that radiated from him.

Kára groaned, and Shana came above with a

knife and clean rope. When she put the blade to the thick cord, Bàs looked away. "Does that hurt her?" he asked Joshua. "The cutting the...whatever that thick gray rope is?"

"I don't think so," Joshua said, struggling to rise, but before he could stand Ivy came over holding the wrapped bairn.

"Sit," she said, and Joshua thumped back down to lean against the wall beside the bed.

She leaned forward, gently laying the bundle in Joshua's arms. Bàs slid farther away instinctually, not wanting to touch it. He would never do anything to take away the joy on Joshua's face.

They both turned, though, when Kára cried out. "She has to birth the part that kept the bairn alive inside her," Joshua said with a grim face. He nodded as if he was full of birthing knowledge even though all the brothers had been helping horses give birth for years. "Best to keep your eyes on the bairn," Joshua said. He cradled the wee lass in his arms.

"Ivy, get more towels and water," Shana said, and Bàs turned at the steady authority in her voice. She looked up the bed at Kára. "Are there twins in your family?"

"No," she said.

"Twins?" Joshua asked, his eyes growing wide.

"Our father's grandmother is said to have been a twin," Bàs said.

Shana ducked back under the quilt.

Joshua looked at Bàs, his jaw slack. "Are we having twins?"

Bàs jumped slightly when Kára cried out. The squirrel scampered farther from the bloody scene below. Maybe a noisy birth would scare her from the cabin, although Bàs was certain he wouldn't be sharing that bed with Shana tonight anyway. After the gore of childbearing, he might never use that bed again.

Joshua rose, and Ivy took the bairn from him. "Are ye having another bairn, Kára?" Joshua asked, coming to Kára's face.

"I don't know," she said, her tone snapping. "How should I know?"

"'Tis in your body," he said, his tone slow as if instructing a student.

She glared at him. "'Tis not like I could feel four feet kicking me at once." She didn't say it, but "idiot" was implied.

Shana came above and smiled encouragingly to Kára. "Another head is crowning. 'Tis a double blessing."

Bàs slid away from the bed and stood. Kára's eyes were wide and blinking. She looked sweaty and exhausted and ready for a night of relaxing with a whisky before a fire, a hot bath, and bed. Not like she wanted to go through another painful delivery.

Shana came up to the top of the bed, dragging a chair closer to sit. She took Kára's hand. "This babe is working its way out. It's something your body and the babe will make happen, like the first."

"I don't have the strength to do it again," Kára said, and tears welled in her eyes with the words, as if saying them opened the dam.

"Then you rest, and the babe will come when 'tis ready," Shana said.

Kára's eyes squeezed shut through another wave

of pain. "I think 'tis saying 'tis ready."

Shana waited until the pain lessened and Kára opened her eyes. "Then your body is helping it along, so it will be quick."

"Ye can do this," Joshua said, leaning over Kára and kissing her forehead. "My warrior queen. The strongest woman I know."

She kept his gaze and gave a small nod before another wave of pain hit her.

"I'll check on the progress," Shana said.

Bàs stood. "Should I hold her up again?"

"Another position would be on all fours," Shana said, sliding out a blood-soaked sheet that made Bàs's stomach churn.

"That," Kára said, and Joshua helped her slowly roll. She groaned at the movement, and as she rose onto her knees, Shana placed a clean sheet under her. Somehow the position made it less horrifying.

"'Tis like a horse foaling," Bàs said.

Joshua nodded. "But don't ask her to neigh."

Bàs's mouth puckered, and he slid his gaze to Ivy who stared at him in horror as if he'd been considering it. "I would never ask her to neigh. Or any woman."

"Unless they wish to," Joshua added.

"Some wish to?" Bàs asked.

"Not while giving birth," Joshua said, rolling his eyes. "But maybe at other times, if they are playing about being chased. Like ye're a randy stallion and she's a wild mare."

"Stop talking," Kára said and huffed rapidly.

"Can I help?" Bàs asked. If not, he'd quietly exit.

"She said stop talking," Joshua said.

"She meant you," Ivy said. She still held the bairn and swayed gently with it.

Shana looked up at Bàs. "When I bring the second babe out, take the first and let Ivy clean the second."

Bàs's gut tightened as he glanced at the bundle in Ivy's arms. Fear gripped him hard, nearly cutting off his breath. Could he harm the infant? He'd held Edward minimally and not when he'd just been born. *You can't hurt a bairn simply by touching it.* Shana's words from before bored through his mind. *You are not Death no matter what your father named you.*

Bloody hell! Shana brought life. He brought death, no matter what she said. They were opposite in every way.

Shana looked at him when he didn't answer. Blankness froze on his face even though his mind was spinning through self-condemnation and regret. "Bàs? Hold her," Shana said. "That's all."

He nodded and kept his arms crossed so he wouldn't be expected to take her right away. Ivy moved closer to him. "Never held a babe before?" she asked.

"Not by choice," he murmured. He'd held lots of baby animals, but humans seemed the most fragile.

"'Tis coming," Shana called from behind Kára, and Kára let out another long groan. "One more push, Kára."

Joshua stood by her head, gently patting her shoulder and back as if not sure what to do. "Ye can do this, love," he said as she hung her head. She seemed to hold her breath for a moment and then she released a big exhale with a sloshing sound that made Bàs's stomach twist.

"That's it!" Shana said under the quilt. She pulled back, her hair brushed in wild disarray about her face. "'Tis another girl!"

Joshua leaned before Kára, kissing her face. The love there was tangible, like nothing Bàs had seen before. Again, jealousy slammed into him.

"Let me tie off this cord," Shana said, "and then Joshua, you help Kára lower to her side and then back."

"Kára's amma tied Adam's navel too tight," Joshua said. "So his jack is a wee thing."

"'Tis a girl," Kára said, "so she can tie it tight."

"Ivy," Shana called, and her sister thrust the first bairn into Bàs's arms.

"Keep her warm," Ivy said and rushed away to take the second bairn from Shana.

Bàs looked down into the first bairn's face. It blinked, looking up at him. She didn't seem frightened. Little lips moved as if wanting to suckle. "I think she's hungry," he called.

But no one paid any attention to him. Ivy worked on wiping off the second bairn, and Shana was busy with Kára, who'd returned to her back.

"Is there supposed to be that much blood?" Joshua asked. "'Tis like when I cut off an arm and the heart is pumping the man's blood out—"

"Stop talking," Kára and Ivy said at the same time.

Shana didn't answer him but felt Kára's abdomen through her smock. Like watching a battle, Bàs couldn't turn away. This was certainly Kára's battle.

"Her womb is not contracting to stop the bleeding," Shana said. "We need to encourage it through massage and nipple stimulation."

Joshua's brows rose in high arches, and he pointed his finger at his chest. "Should I stimulate her nipples?"

Bàs turned away, his gaze going to Ivy who worked on the silent bairn in her arms. Ivy's face was tight. "Come on, little one," she whispered, her tone frantic.

Bàs walked over. "What's wrong?"

She glanced at him, eyes wide. "I can't get her to breathe."

CHAPTER SEVENTEEN

"Some men, but chiefly fools, have Yards so long
that they are useless for generation. It is generally
held, that the length or proportion of the Yard
depends upon cutting the Navel string, if you cut it
too short and knit it too close in Infants it will be
too short, because of the string that comes from the
Navel to the bottom of the bladder, which draws up
the Bladder and shortens the Yard: and this beside
the general opinion, stands with so much reason,
that all Midwives have cause to be careful to cut the
Navel string long enough, that when they tye it, the
Yard may have free liberty to move and extend it
self, always remembring that moderation is best,
that it be not left too long, which may
be as bad as too short."

THE MIDWIVES BOOK OR THE WHOLE ART OF
MIDWIFERY DISCOVERED BY JANE SHARPE, 1671

Bàs stared down at the little girl in his arms and then
at the unmoving girl who Ivy had placed under a
clean blanket on the table. "Come on, wee girl," Ivy
said, rubbing all over the little one's body.

"Check the mouth," Bàs said, coming closer. As if
drawn to the quiet panic on this side of the room,
Betty chattered down from the rafters.

Ivy opened the bairn's mouth, wiping the inside.
"I don't see anything." She looked over her shoulder. "Shana, I need you."

"I'm a bit busy here," Shana called back. "Bring one of the babes back over to put to breast."

"I'm needed here," Ivy called back. The wee babe was taking on a slight bluish tint.

"I can suckle if I need to," Joshua said.

"Good God, Joshua. Stop talking," Kára said. "Are the babes well? I don't hear them."

"We have to do something," Ivy whispered. Tears filled her eyes as she ran her fingers over the wee lass's face, but the bairn didn't open her eyes or take a breath. "As a midwife, Shana can perform a baptism immediately to save the babe's soul."

Bàs glanced back up at the rafters where Betty watched and then back to the wee bairn turning blue before his eyes on the table. He'd revived Betty with his breath, and he'd witnessed Ella help a foal. "Here," Bàs said, thrusting bairn number one into Ivy's arms. "Take it to Kára."

Lord help me to help this bairn. His prayers roared through his head with the rush of his warrior blood.

Bàs slid the soft quilt down to expose the bairn's unmoving belly. He opened its wee mouth and covered it with his, blowing gently in. The belly extended. He stopped, letting the air release. Good. Nothing was blocking the airway. He did it again and then again.

"My God, what are ye doing?" Joshua yelled behind him.

Bàs continued to exhale his air into the bairn's little mouth and nose, letting it release. Shana was suddenly by his side. "She's not breathing?"

"Nay," Bàs said quickly before giving her his

breath. His entire chest was tight as if he were suffocating as well. *I'm killing her. Please God. Save her.*

Joshua was beside her. "What are ye doing?"

"He's trying to save your daughter," Shana said, her voice defensive. "So stay back."

The room grew silent as Bàs gave a couple more exhales. Shana laid her ear over the small chest. "I hear a heartbeat."

Relief kicked Bàs hard at the same time the bairn jerked, a faint cry wafting from its open lips. Bàs staggered backward as Shana rushed to take the bairn up in the blanket, rubbing it briskly like Ivy had been doing before.

Bàs's heart pounded in his chest, and he couldn't grasp a full breath. Panic had gripped him tightly, and now the relief poured through him so hard, he felt dizzy. He made it to the table and plopped down on one of the stools there. Betty hopped along the rafters over him, chittering.

Joshua hovered around the second bairn as Shana checked it, and Kára watched from where she held the first bairn to her breast. Ivy looked over at Bàs, her eyes wide as if he might very well be a witch.

"Is she breathing?" Kára called, emotion thick in her voice. Tears rolled down her cheeks unnoticed.

Shana looked over the bairn's wee head at Bàs. A gentle smile slid along her lips. "Yes, she's well. With help from your brother."

"How did ye do that?" Joshua asked. He shook his head. "Ye aren't death, brother. Ye are life and the best uncle a bairn ever had." Shana let him take up his second daughter, cradling her as he brought her over to Kára.

Shana walked to Bàs. She raised her hands to cup his face but stopped in midair. They were covered with dried blood. "I look like I've been in battle," she said, turning them this way and that.

Bàs stood and stroked his thumb over her cheek. "Ye have been in battle. Saving three lives."

Behind him Joshua laughed heartily. "Who will believe it? The Horseman of Death bringing a bairn back to life. 'Tis amazing."

"You might not want to phrase it that way," Ivy said. "Else King James will come after Bàs as a witch, too."

Joshua snorted. "He will have to get through me and my brothers first, which is impossible." With that, Joshua strode briskly across the room to Bàs and pulled him into a hug like a bear trying to crush its next meal, lifting him off the ground. "Anything ye want, I will get it for ye," Joshua said. "Anything for saving my lass."

He let Bàs down, and Bàs unfolded his shoulders. "Ye don't need to get me—"

"Anything!" Joshua roared.

"New sheets would be appreciated," Bàs said.

Joshua laughed and slapped him on the shoulder before striding to Kára and his two suckling daughters.

Shana returned from the pail of clean water where she'd washed her hands. Her smile was infectious. She came close and touched Bàs's face. "Believe me now? You're not dangerous to babes. There is more life about you than death." If they'd been alone, Bàs felt like she would have kissed him, but instead she ran her clean thumb over his lip. "You're extraordinary."

Bàs's heart swelled with her words and touch, the pride in her tone making him feel too overwhelmed to speak.

She smiled brightly and turned, hurrying back to Kára.

Bàs walked to the door and stepped out into the soft glow of twilight that had fallen across his protected clearing. He glanced at the polished white bone of the skull mask that sat on its perch in the yard. *I could throw it in the river.* He'd had the thought before, but this time it roared in his ears. *I could just be me, not the executioner.*

He stopped before the skull mask but then walked on to his rock garden where he often took his thoughts. He gazed at the sculpture he'd made of his mother's face.

The moss around her was soft and spongy, and he stared down at her. "Did ye see that?" he whispered and then tipped his face upward to peer through the clearing in the tree canopy at the darkening sky. "Did ye see that?" he said again.

He knew it didn't make up for taking her away from his father, from his siblings. But perhaps it showed that there was hope. Hope that death didn't consume him inside and out.

• • •

Shana softly closed the door behind her and stood on the dark porch. All was quiet inside the cabin, Ivy and Edward asleep above and Kára, Joshua, and their two daughters sleeping downstairs. She should be resting with Ivy, but Shana's mind was on the incredible man who'd given up his house for the discomfort of the barn. She hadn't seen him since he'd saved the babe.

"Miraculous," she whispered into the night. Exhaling into someone was not something Shana had been taught. The air that came out of a person was not the same that entered, yet it was able to feed a dying babe enough to get her breathing on her own. She must find out how he'd done it. At least that's the reason she told herself for visiting him in the night.

Her boots crunched on the gravel as she walked across the yard to the barn. She pushed at the gap of the barn's double doors and peeked inside. "Bàs," she called softly into the darkness. If he was sleeping, she wouldn't wake him. He'd had an exhausting day as well.

"I answer to Sebastian now." The voice came from above, and she tilted her face upward at a spark of light as he hit a flint.

"Do you?" she asked, smiling.

"Nay," he said. "I still don't think it suits."

She kept her gaze on the pinprick of light as it grew. "I believe Bast is a name, with the *T* on the end." She watched him set the flame in a glass lamp and shut the doors behind her.

"What does it mean?" he asked, and she saw him look down from a loft.

Good Lord, his features were so handsome. Compassion lurked there, a kindness that radiated from his heart past the scars and heavy responsibility he carried as executioner.

"I…" She hesitated, remembering what he'd asked. "I don't know."

Snort. Shana looked toward the noise and saw Ilsa standing along one wall with Iona sleeping under her. Dòchas stood in a stall, and a small goat stared at her from its bed of straw opposite Ilsa.

"The meaning behind a name is important," Bàs said, flooding the narrow stairs on one end with light from the lantern. "I'll ask Gideon. Surely, he has a book with the name in it. Would ye like to come up to my cozy nest?"

Shana's heart beat faster, and she walked closer, looking up at him. The lantern glow cast gold over his features, his longish hair loose. He wore no tunic, and his muscles sat corded across him. In the light, she could see the horse head tattoo on his upper arm, marking him as one of the Sinclair horsemen.

"Yes," she whispered. Why was she so giddy at the thought of joining him? She wasn't a virgin. And they'd already been together. But her stomach flipped a little as she set her foot on the first rung of the ladder. She rose, her face coming even with the floor above.

The swept planks of wood led over to a pile of fresh hay covered with wide blankets. There was even a chair and small table. "Do you sleep out here often?" she asked. He helped her stand away from the ladder with his hand under her arm.

"When Ilsa was birthing Iona, I wanted to stay close through the night," he said, straightening, and his head brushed the slanted ceiling.

"A warrior who sleeps with beasts," she said, smiling.

He shrugged his broad shoulders. "I feel more comfortable with beasts. When I was a lad, I wished to become one." He set the enclosed flame on the table. "When I grew old enough, I built this place, the cabin and barn, so I could live with them. No fear lurks in their faces when they see me. They don't worry over curses or my touch."

Shana's smile faded, and she stepped before him. "I don't worry over curses or your touch." She found his hand in the shadow and pulled it up between them, her fingers sliding between each of his. "You shouldn't either."

With his free hand, he slid the backs of his knuckles along her cheek. "With ye, I don't, Shana."

She slid her hands up his bare chest, marveling at the strength under the warm skin and sprinkling of hair. "You are beautiful, Bàs Sinclair." She looked up into his eyes. They were dark and felt like a place she could fall easily into. Fall or jump, fully knowing he would catch her. "With a golden heart," she said, stopping on his chest where it beat hard, surely in time with her own.

His face darkened. "Shana...the things I've done—"

"Have no place up here in your nest," she finished. "We all have past things we wish we'd never done. Some more than others. All we can do is move forward."

"But ye must know who I am before we..." His words trailed off, but he caught her face in his hands, staring down into her eyes. Warmth radiated off him, drawing her against him.

Her stomach flipped. "Before we...?"

"If we are to get closer, Shana."

She wasn't sure how they could become physically closer. Was he asking her to wed? Or hinting that they might in the future? The panic she'd felt the few times after Ben, when a man had tried to come close, reared up inside Shana. But she inhaled slowly through her nose, staring into the depths of this man's gaze, and her heart drowned out her instinct to turn away.

She leaned into him, feeling his stiffness. He seemed to hold his breath while he waited. For what? For her to run or at least pull away.

Shana did neither. "Before we become…closer," she said, "you can tell me of your sins, Bàs Sinclair, but not right now." She leaned up high on her toes and captured his face with both her hands. "Right now…" She lowered her voice. "I want you to kiss me until I can't think of anything except you moving inside me."

Merely saying the words made her body clench with want. Bàs's arms came up around her, holding her to him as his mouth came down on her parted lips. Heat flared inside Shana as she clung to him, this mighty man who'd been shunned with a thousand glances filled with fear and silent accusations.

"Och, but Shana lass," he murmured. "I am going to make ye moan so."

Her hands slid down the ridges of his stomach to the hardness that pressed against the confines of his wrapped plaid. Before she could tug the belt loose, her stays opened, and the heaviness of her petticoat dropped from her waist. She tugged his belt again, and felt the buckle release, and his heavy plaid dropped to the floor. He lifted her, setting her outside her fallen skirts and stays.

Shana pulled the tie at the top of her smock and wiggled her shoulders until the white lace slid off first one shoulder and then the second. It lowered until her breasts came out over the top.

"Lass," Bàs said, his deep voice full of an exhale. "Ye are all soft curves and heat."

She pressed her hips against his erection as he kissed the tingling skin of her neck. "And wet," she whispered, her lips bent toward his ear.

He rucked up her smock, his hand stroking the bareness of her backside before sliding to the front where she opened her stance. He touched her, and her legs nearly buckled. "Oh God, yes, Bàs," she moaned. Slowly he lowered her to the soft wool blanket over the hay.

"'Tis cold in the barn," he said, sliding his hand along her stockinged leg. "Keep them on, and your smock."

"I'm not cold with you," she said as he lay down next to her. But she forgot everything about clothing as his deft fingers found her again, stroking her inside and out. By the light of the lantern, she watched him kiss the insides of her thighs, which she'd spread wide.

When he parted her to look at her, he murmured something in Gaelic. She didn't know the words but the feeling behind them was reverence. A shiver of desire infused her, and she held her breath as he lowered his mouth to her hot body.

This was new to Shana, and the wet heat from his mouth strummed pleasure up through her core. "Oh yes," she murmured, her breath shallow as the tension built inside. Watching his head bent to her, loving her with his mouth and fingers, Shana had never felt or seen anything so giving, so loving. The pleasure built quickly, and she fell off the edge of sanity, letting his name out with a low groan. "Bassss," she cried between panting.

As wave after wave of pleasure made her body contract, he lifted her to kneeling on all fours. Instinctively she arched her back.

"Ohhhhhh…" she cried again as Bàs thrust into her from behind. He grasped her hips, pulling back and driving into her again and again. He breathed heavily near her ear, his one arm wrapped around her, holding her up against his powerful surging. Over and over, they moved. His hand slid to her hanging breasts, kneading them and rolling her nipples. The line of pleasure stretched taut all the way to their joining, and once again Shana felt herself falling over the edge.

Behind her, Bàs increased his tempo and let out a groan as he lay his body against her back and climaxed. She followed, the two of them joined in pleasure, his hands finding hers planted before her as he leaned over. Their fingers intertwined as they rode the waves of ecstasy together.

• • •

"Ella said you were only five," Shana said.

Bàs held her in the crook of his arm, her head resting on his shoulder where they lay in the loft of the barn. "Aye."

"How could he tell you something so horrific at that tender age?"

She didn't know George Sinclair. Even though Aunt Merida has said there was a time when his father laughed and sang, there was nothing soft or forgiving left in him by the time Bàs grew old enough to know him.

Guilt flowed like putrid sludge through Bàs. Not only had he killed his mother during his birth, but he'd created a monster in his father.

"He started by giving me the skull mask." Bàs remembered it vividly. The sweat in his palms had held some of the stems of the flowers he'd picked even though he'd released them when his father had thrust the human skull at him. "Bluebells and daisies," Bàs murmured.

She pushed up, leaning on her arm. "He gave you flowers with the mask?"

Bàs snorted darkly. "Nay. I had just picked flowers for my mother's grave, something I did almost daily. Bluebells and daisies were her favorites from what Cain could remember. I dropped them when he handed me the mask."

Bàs stretched his arms up, bending his elbows to pillow his head. "My training started the next day."

"Training to kill people?" She kept her voice even, but he could feel the tension in her body.

"He started with animals, but I refused."

She rested her hand on his chest. It was warm, a balm against the memories. "He must not have responded well to that."

"Nay, he did not." Bàs remembered the beatings. Once he'd been knocked unconscious and woke up with Aunt Merida and Hannah staring down at him. Even young, Hannah took care of most of the cuts and bruises he'd received from their father or later in training. Secretly, so Bàs would continue to seem strong and unaffected by physical harm.

He inhaled through his nose and looked up at Shana, reaching to slide a finger gently along her cheek. "But then I held a blade to his throat one night and told him I'd rather kill him than an innocent animal. He knocked the mattucashlass away, of course, but after that he didn't order me to slay innocent creatures."

She watched him in silence for a moment, the darkness hiding most of her expression. Which was good, because he could imagine then that she didn't look at him with pity like Hannah and Aunt Merida.

"When did you kill your first human?" She lowered to rest back against him.

"At birth with my mother." The comment rolled off his tongue without thought, a repeat of what he'd heard his whole life.

She leaned halfway across his chest. "You already know what I think of that."

He slid a finger over her lips. "I'd have saved her if I could have."

She stared hard at him, eyes lit by the dim moonlight. "As a mother who lost a babe, I tell you, she would rather you lived than she."

Bàs turned his gaze to the rafters he'd constructed of sturdy oak. "So many more people died when my father's rage at her death turned outward. And then he raised us to be the Four Horsemen of the Apocalypse."

She reached for his hand, squeezing it. "But you also made a safe place for your people and those under Sinclair protection." She shook her head. "You can't take on the weight of what your father did because your mother wasn't here to remind him to be a decent man. You can only go forward."

"As Death?"

She sighed. "I don't know. Maybe. When at battle. It keeps you and your men safer because people fear the prophecy. And the whole farewell to Hamish…" She gripped his hand tighter. "Death can be a comfort for some, and when you help them through it with dignity it raises up everyone around them as well. Takes the fear out of dying."

"Taking the fear out of death," Bàs murmured and snorted wryly. "My father would hate the idea."

She leaned in, kissing him gently on the lips. "Even better."

He chuckled softly, pulling her closer.

A comfort? He'd never thought of his role that way. He'd been only the bloody harbinger of death. Could he help those who must cross do so with honor and comfort? "I hadn't thought of helping people die well," he said, sliding his hand down her back, feeling the warmth of her skin through the thin smock she wore. "Ye are wise, Shana Drummond."

Lifting her leg, she slid it over him, where she could probably feel his hard jack. "I'm also not tired enough to sleep."

He chuckled, the sound coming from deep in his chest as if the weight his happiness was usually under had shifted. He rolled toward her, and her leg wrapped over his hip so her foot could rub against his bare arse. Pushing her gently, he leaned over her. Their breaths mingled as he hovered before her lips. His hand slid up her stockinged leg until he reached the naked skin of her warm thighs.

"Well then, lass, we need to tire ye out."

• • •

The gray morning light was coming through the one window when Shana opened her eyes. She took a deep breath as she tried to remember where she was. The hay crinkled under her as she rolled to one side, and she felt the mild aches of being loved. A smile crept across her lips when she saw Bàs sitting up, his bare back to her.

His hair was swept to one side, and she saw the outline of another tattoo high up under his neck. She sat up to run her fingers lightly across it. With his long hair, she hadn't yet seen it, and when they'd explored each other well, it had been dark.

It was a skull like the mask he wore, and an ax. The symbols of the Horseman of Death. It sent a slight shiver through her, not of sexual want and not of fear. Just awareness. Bàs Sinclair, for all his gentleness and giving, was a trained killer.

"Someone is riding through the briar," he said, his voice low. He rolled forward onto his feet and slowly rose, uncoiling into the mountain of strength he was. Scars and muscles stood out along his calves, thighs, and tight arse.

"Another woman who needs my help?" she asked, trying not to stare at his remarkable form.

"I'm not certain," he said, helping her stand. "Stay here while I check." He set a kiss on her lips and brushed one of her wild curls behind her ear.

"Don't go out naked or you'll throw her into labor," she said with a teasing smile.

He grabbed his woolen plaid, wrapping it deftly and cinching it around his waist with his belt. It wasn't pleated evenly in his haste. It rather looked like a woman who'd thrown on a costume in a rush not to be found naked with her lover. "You look ravished," she said.

He smiled at her from the ladder. "I believe I have been."

Shana's heart felt light, and her smile was broad and genuine. Was that love that tickled in her chest? *If we are to get closer.* His words from last night added to the happy giddiness she felt.

Bàs stepped out of the barn, and Shana quickly dressed as best she could, leaving her stays loose until Ivy could tighten them. She climbed down the ladder and smiled at the coos, goat, and Dòchas. "I surely hope you all slept through any noise you heard last night," she whispered, feeling her cheeks warm.

Shana pushed through the doors to a gray day. Heavy clouds overhead made the yard seem smaller, and the smell of rain permeated the cool air. She stopped. Even her breath stuttered to a halt as Bàs stood before a large man on a horse.

"I've come for Ivy and my son," the man said. "I am Liam Ross."

CHAPTER EIGHTEEN

Babies born in the 16th century were immediately swaddled, tightly wrapped with linens and swaddling bands to keep them warm and secure. Swaddled, they would sleep in cradles. The common man sometimes used a box, basket, or manger for a cradle, but the rich would have ornately gilded cradles for their babies.

Henry VII's household [had an] immense cradle for state occasions. Decorated with the arms of his house and filled with plush fabrics, at seven-and-a-half feet long and two-and-a-half feet wide, this monstrosity would have dwarfed a little princeling and kept his admirers well back.

MEDIEVAL CHILDREN BY NICHOLAS ORME

"Liam!" Ivy rushed down the stairs inside the cabin and hurled herself into the man's arms. He hugged her back, but his gaze continued to scan the room as if tallying the threats. His eyes rested on Joshua as he stood before the bed where Kára held their two newborn bairns.

"Where have you been?" Ivy asked, pulling back to smile up at him. "I was so worried."

"Aye," Joshua said, crossing his arms. "Where have ye been while we saved your woman and bairn?"

Liam Ross said he was an apothecary in the town

of Wick for the Oliphant Clan. But one look at this man, and it was clear to Bàs that he was a warrior. Large muscles and stature gave evidence of his strength building, but it was the way he stood ready, his gaze searching out threats that had thrown Joshua on the offensive. They stared at each other like two alpha wolves sizing each other up.

Shana stepped forward. "'Tis good he hid away, or Erskine would have killed him, and Edward wouldn't have a father."

Bàs walked to the hearth and threw some dry peat onto the coals from last night's fire. "Oh, I don't know about that," he said, turning back, his arms crossed. "Ye don't seem the type of man to let a wee rat like Erskine Oliphant kill ye. In fact, ye look like a warrior very able to handle any attack."

Ivy smiled at that. "You *are* strong," she said, looking up at him with something close to adoration in her gaze.

"Especially for an apothecary," Bàs said.

"Aye," Joshua said, suspicion heavy in the word.

"In this country, 'tis best to be physically prepared," Liam said. "And although I could definitely kill Erskine, a legion of his men…" He shook his head. "Nay." He looked down at Ivy. "Although it nearly killed me to leave ye in Wick when ye begged me to leave, and then I'd heard ye'd lost our bairn."

He'd heard Edward had died? And yet, when he rode into the clearing, he'd asked for his son.

Ivy shook her head, a smile broadening across her face. "I didn't lose him, Liam. I had Shana steal him away to safety. He's upstairs, fit and eating heartily."

Liam smiled, his gaze rising along the stairs. "I

wish to see him."

"I'll get him," she said, turning to race up the stairs.

"How did ye hear he was alive?" Joshua asked.

Bàs crossed his arms. "And how did ye find us?"

Liam glanced at Bàs and then Shana. "I had only hoped he'd lived. When I learned that Ivy was safely with the Sinclairs, I came at once to find her." He looked to Bàs. "I met your man, Keenan, at Girnigoe Village, and he gave me directions to your cabin."

"So ye haven't been to see Cain at the castle?" Joshua asked.

Liam shook his head. "I came straight here."

"Humph," Joshua said, glancing back at Kára but not relinquishing his battle stance.

"Here he is," Ivy called as she carefully descended, holding the bundled bairn.

Liam went to the stairs, taking the bairn from her. With Edward in his arms, he didn't look so dangerous, but from what Bàs had seen of his brothers around his niece and nephew, protecting one's bairn made a man dangerous indeed.

"And he's healthy?" he asked, his finger tugging the blanket down a bit to see the bairn's chest.

"Very," Ivy said. "Thanks to Shana."

"And Bàs and his pet wolf, Beò," Shana said, "saving us from a pack of wolves when we ran from Wick."

Liam looked around to Bàs. "Ye have a pet wolf?"

"He's more like a brother," Bàs said. "A wolf is no one's pet."

Crack.

"Bloody hell," Liam yelled, his hand going to his head, as a hazelnut bounced off and clattered on the wooden floor. Edward began to cry at the outburst, and Ivy pulled him away from Liam. "What was that?" Liam asked.

Bàs nodded to the rafters where Betty, her tufted ears quivering, peered down. "The squirrel apparently doesn't like ye."

"Squirrel?" Liam said, looking up. "What type of place is this? Wolves, squirrels living inside?" He turned to Bàs. "Do ye have trained bears walking the perimeter?"

Bàs allowed a grin. "Perhaps." He didn't, of course, but it was better for people to think it possible.

"Why don't we all sit down and break our fast," Shana said. "I'll make oatcakes and bacon, and Bàs can pull a fish from his snare on the river for me to roast." She looked expectantly to him. He nodded, and she went on with a smile. "After filling the hollow in our stomachs, we can figure out what to do next."

Liam continued to watch Betty cautiously as if she might have another nut to hurl while scampering across the rafters. Joshua turned to speak low to Kára and lifted one of his daughters.

"I'll bring in some trout," Bàs said. He walked out where a gentle rain fell, tapping on the leaves. Liam's horse still stood in the yard, unattended. The man had been so bent on seeing Ivy and Edward that he hadn't tied him or given him water after his fast ride. His ears twitched as Bàs walked closer. Lather bubbled out around his bit. Bàs raised his hand to take his reins, and the horse shied to the side. "Ho now," Bàs whispered, holding his palm up for the horse to sniff. Bàs stood still for a full minute, before the skittish horse inched his face closer, its nostrils flaring to take in his scent.

"There now," Bàs said evenly, and gently slid a hand down the horse's nose. As he ran his hand over the horse's jaw to the leather straps, he saw cuts at the corners of the horse's mouth as if the bit had been tugged harshly over and over.

"Bloody hell," Bàs murmured. He strode to the barn and opened the doors so Ilsa, Iona, and Gillian could come out. He grabbed a spare halter from a hook on the wall.

Bàs jogged back to Liam's horse and led him over to the gently sloping creek bank. He laid the reins over the horse's neck, looping it under to hold him while he slid the straps off over his ears, letting the bit fall from his mouth, and slipped the halter on. He ran his fingers along another cut where the leather had rubbed a sore. He let the horse dip down to the water, eagerly drinking. Bàs gently slid a hand along his side and watched the animal flinch again.

Anger tightened Bàs's stomach, and he glanced at the cabin. This horse had been hit and its bit yanked. He walked carefully around the horse, keeping one hand on him so he knew where Bàs was the whole time, and he saw welts along his rump from a strap.

When the horse raised his head from the stream, Bàs clicked his tongue, leading him into the barn and a second stall where he filled an iron holder with fresh hay and a pan with oats. "There ye go now," he said. As he turned away from the animal, his gaze settled on the cabin.

Liam Ross was a liar and an abuser of his horse. Fury rose to surge through Bàs's blood, and he drew an inhale through his nostrils as if he were about to charge into battle. *Learn the facts before you react.* Gideon's words of wisdom, usually to Joshua, kept Bàs from charging back to the cabin to throw Liam against a wall, yanking him around by the teeth until his mouth foamed.

Maybe the man had a good explanation. Maybe the horse was recently acquired from a terrible circumstance. Or maybe the man was a foking abuser of animals. And if he abused animals, Ivy and Edward were in jeopardy.

• • •

"Oh, Shana," Ivy said, her smile bright. "I'm so blessed." The sisters were upstairs with Edward where they'd helped each other dress.

"Yes, you are," Shana said. She returned her sister's smile as they gave Edward a bath with a bowl of warm water and a soft cloth. He fussed at being stripped bare, but they were quick, making sure all his parts and the stump at his navel were clean and free of taint.

"And now that Liam has returned, he will take us away from Erskine and we won't bring war to anyone."

Shana's smile faded. "You cannot marry him while you're wed to Erskine."

"I'll petition for a divorce based on me being an

adulteress and abandoning my marriage." She said it as if she hadn't a care for what people thought of her, which was certainly liberating but not common by any means.

"Do you think King James will agree to a divorce when petitioned by someone who's been accused of witchcraft?" Shana asked.

Ivy's smile faltered. "I don't know the mind of a king, but he won't be able to find us anyway. Liam will take us somewhere safe where we can raise our son as if we are married."

"Is that Liam's plan, too? Has he said as much?"

Ivy exhaled as she wrapped Edward in a clean blanket. "We haven't had a chance to talk since he arrived, but we did back when we first met."

"When you were visiting him in the apothecary?"

"Yes." She glanced at Shana. "He said he would take me away from Erskine, and we could have our own family. That he loves me beyond life itself." She looked so happy as she remembered their exchange that Shana didn't want to pose any more questions, at least not to Ivy.

"I'll leave you to nurse him," Shana said, nodding to the babe.

"Thank you, sister," Ivy said, settling onto the bed to put Edward to breast. "You have rescued me from the most horrible life and given me a chance at true happiness."

"'Tis always what I've wanted for you." Shana closed the door softly and stood in the darkness at the top of the stairs, staring at the wood grain. Ivy had come to live with Shana when Ben was killed. She'd been there when Shana lost her son at birth.

They'd cried together. And when their father had arranged a marriage for Ivy with a powerful chief, Shana had helped her sew her bridal clothes. Shana had only ever wanted happiness for Ivy, and she seemed completely in love with Liam Ross. Why then did Shana's stomach feel twisted and tight?

Walking down the steps, she smiled at Kára who was trying with Joshua to line the babes up to feed them at the same time. Kára huffed, looking at her. "God gave me two teats, so I should be able to feed them together."

"They both want milk at the same time," Joshua said. "If I try to hold Astrid against me while Kára feeds Alice, then Astrid tries to feed from me. Her little lips make sucking movements as if I have breasts." He sounded aghast.

Shana came over, smiling. "'Tis something babes do from birth, trying to feed. It doesn't mean she thinks you look like a woman, Joshua."

"Well, I don't," he said, smoothing a large hand over his muscular chest.

"So you've decided to name them after your mothers, then?" Shana asked.

Kára glanced up at Joshua with a little grin. "'Twas the only names we could agree upon. Astrid for my mother and Alice for his mother."

"Here," Shana said. "Let's try a different angle under your arms, propping their bodies on pillows."

After another minute of adjustment, the babes settled into nursing. "Your milk's already coming in," Shana said, nodding. "That's a blessing."

"I helped," Joshua said with a mischievous grin, "with the stimulating."

"Good Lord," Kára murmured, shaking her head, but she smiled up at him. The love in her eyes was as obvious as the love in Joshua's face. She'd certainly seen that adoration in Ivy's face this morning when she spoke of Liam.

Shana looked toward the door. "Did Liam go somewhere while you nursed?"

Joshua frowned. "Aye. I asked him to step out while the girls fed." He lowered his voice. "I don't trust him."

"Why?" she asked, wishing to understand the niggling suspicion in her own stomach.

"He's a warrior for certain, possibly a paid mercenary with his build."

"You're not a paid mercenary," Shana said, nodding to his huge form.

"Aye, but I train and battle to protect my clan. An apothecary who has no attachment to the clan he's living with has no reason to build such muscle. His gaze moves about as if searching for threats, and he didn't let the chief of the Sinclairs know he was traversing his lands. He should have stopped in at Girnigoe to tell Cain."

"He was anxious to find Ivy," Kára said.

Joshua crossed his arms. "And I don't like him."

Rap. Rap. "Can I come in?" It was Bàs.

Joshua discreetly laid a thin blanket over the twins as they nursed.

Shana opened the door to stare into the stony face of the Horseman of Death.

• • •

Bàs watched Shana's eyes open wider. He lifted his hands to his face, as if to rub off the anger there, lowering them when he managed to smooth some of the tension from his features. "I need to talk with Liam."

"What's wrong?" Shana whispered.

"Maybe nothing," Bàs said. "Is he inside?"

"Come in and meet your nieces, brother," Joshua called.

Shana stepped aside, and Bàs entered, his gaze moving about his cabin. "Is he above with Ivy?" Bàs asked. He still hadn't checked on his horse since his arrival several hours ago.

"No, he went out while Kára nursed," she answered, tipping her head that way.

Kára was handing one of the girls to Joshua, who laid the bundle over a shoulder to burp. His huge hand patted gently. "Seems they'd rather sleep than eat," Kára said.

"We've named them after our mothers," Joshua said. "Astrid after Kára's mother." He nodded toward the bairn who Kára was raising from under the blanket to lay on her own shoulder.

Joshua walked closer to Bàs. "And this bundle of sweetness is Alice." Joshua's voice was gruff as if an emotion other than anger or mischief choked him. He held the bundle out to Bàs. Bàs didn't move.

Joshua nodded to the bairn. "Alice is the one ye saved with your breath, brother." His gaze connected with Bàs's. "To make up for the Alice ye feel ye killed."

Bàs swallowed past a lump clogging his throat and heard Shana sniff next to him. "Take her," Joshua said.

"Take her?" Bàs asked, his eyes going wide.

"Just to hold, ye fool," Joshua said, grinning. "Then she's all mine."

"And mine," Kára called.

Bàs glanced at Shana, who nodded to him. "You saved her last night," she said. Meaning that his touch apparently wouldn't doom her to an early death.

Bàs extended his arms, and Joshua placed the wrapped bairn in them. "Hold her up against your chest," Joshua said like the expert he'd become since having Adam last year. "That's it," he said as Bàs followed his advice of setting Alice against his shoulder and patting her gently. She didn't cry but made little smacking sounds with her lips.

"Relax a bit," Shana said, coaxing him to sit in a chair with Alice.

He pulled the bairn from his shoulder to look into her wee face. "She has a healthy color," he said, staring at her half-closed eyes.

"Thanks to God and ye," Joshua said, his hand landing heavy on Bàs's shoulder as they both looked down into Alice's face. She blinked to stare up at Bàs. "I think she knows," Joshua said, "that her Uncle Bàs saved her life."

"I think we should call him Sebastian," Shana said. "Uncle Death is not a good name. Or Bast with a *T* on the end."

Kára laughed lightly. "I have to agree about the Uncle Death name, but that's all we've known him as."

"Bast?" Joshua said and tipped his head from side to side. "What does it mean?"

"It means it's not Death," Shana said, crossing her arms.

"I'll ask Gideon to look it up in one of his books," Bàs said but kept his focus on the sweet bairn's face. Alice's wee lips made a perfect *O*, and her nose was little and snubbed on the end. "She's bonny, Joshua," Bàs said.

"I know," Joshua said, pride thick in his voice. "They both are."

The door suddenly opened, and Liam entered abruptly. "Feeding time over?" he asked.

"Yes," Shana said with a quick look over at Kára. "Ivy and Edward are upstairs. Perhaps you two should discuss plans."

He gave a quick smile before striding through to take the stairs. Bàs would have to ask him about his horse when he came back down.

"Ye don't like him either," Joshua said, and Bàs turned to see him studying him.

"He doesn't care for his horse and may have beaten him."

"What?" Shana asked, her voice soft and urgent.

"And ye let him walk past ye without beating him in return?" Joshua asked. He looked to Shana. "Everyone knows that the Horseman of Death will revenge any mistreated animal on Sinclair territories."

"I'll give him a chance to explain. Perhaps the horse is newly bought," Bàs said.

"And there will be no inflicting pain on each other in a room full of babes," Kára said, her voice equally soft and urgent.

They all looked to the stairs. Alice started to fuss,

and Bàs could feel a small rumble under her bottom half. The faint smell of shite lifted in the air. "Your daughter is asking for ye," Bàs said, rising to give Alice back to Joshua.

"Ahh now, come here, sweetness," Joshua said and took the bairn. He paused, frowning. "But ye don't smell sweet."

Bàs turned away when Shana touched his arm. He looked down into her tight face and followed her out of the cabin to the front porch. "You don't like Liam because of the horse?" she asked.

"I don't know Liam, and if ye are to trust him with your sister and nephew, I think ye need to know him," Bàs said. "All I have to go on is evidence that his horse has been mistreated and he failed to attend him."

Her lips thinned into a tight line. "Anyone who mistreats an animal will mistreat a person who is weaker than them."

"I agree," he said. "I took care of his horse. He hasn't once come to check on him."

Shana gazed out at the pasture where Liam's horse rolled as if getting the press of a saddle off his back. "Perhaps he was overcome with seeing Ivy. She's completely in love with him."

"He did come back for her," Bàs said. "Is it a co-incidence he came right after Janet Bell's visit?"

Shana gazed up into his face, her red hair tamed and braided. He liked it better fluffed in disarray or streaming out behind her as she raced with him across the moor. It was wild and free then, framing her smile and beautiful freckled face.

"Maybe Janet knew where Liam was hiding," she

said, "and told him so he would take Ivy and
Edward away to safety from here."

"'Tis possible."

Before she could move away, Bàs stepped closer,
his hand catching a curled strand of hair that lay
along her cheek. He tucked it behind her ear. Even
the thin ridge of her ear had small brown dots along
it, and he had the urge to kiss along them. "I am
sorry we've had no words since this morn."

She pressed into him. "I would have sought you
out, but I want to stay with Ivy and Edward until I
know Liam's intentions."

Bàs's severe anger had lessened each second he'd
been in Shana's presence, and her warmth against
him relaxed the tension in his shoulders. He dipped
his lips to press against hers.

Fast thumps down the staircase made them break
apart in time to see Liam step outside holding
Edward in his arms. Bàs turned away from Shana,
following the man off the porch.

"Where are ye going?" Bàs asked.

"I'm taking my son out for a ride," Liam said
with a false smile.

Bàs shook his head slowly, keeping direct eye
contact. "Nay, ye aren't."

Liam frowned and shifted the bairn to his other
arm, freeing up the one that could grab a sword.
"Aye, I am."

CHAPTER NINETEEN

"…the Midwife must handle [the infant] very
tenderly and wash the body with warm wine, then
when it is dry roul it up with soft cloths, and lay it
into the Cradle: but in the swadling of it be sure
that all parts be bound up in their due place and
order gently, without any crookedness, or rugged
foldings; for infants are tender twigs, and as you use
them, so they will grow straight or crooked: wipe
the childs eyes often, to make them clean, with a
piece of soft linnen, or silk; and lay the arms right
down by the sides, that they may grow right, and
sometimes with your hand stroke down the belly of
the child toward the neck of the bladder, to
provoke it to make water."

THE MIDWIVES BOOK OR THE WHOLE ART OF
MIDWIFERY DISCOVERED BY JANE SHARPE, 1671

Shana held her breath where she stood on the porch.
The babe was only a few weeks old, too young to go
riding on a horse.

Joshua stepped from the open doorway and followed his brother down the steps to the ground. His
hand rested on his sword hilt. "Nay," Joshua said.
"Ye aren't taking the bairn anywhere."

Liam and Edward stood before two of the most
powerful warriors Shana had ever met. If violence
was going to erupt, Ivy's son needed to be taken out
of it. Shana stepped around Joshua and up to Liam.

"He's too young for a ride without his mother," she said. "I'm a midwife and know such things that exuberant new fathers do not." She offered him a smile and pulled Edward slowly from his arms, although she trembled inside. Not for herself, but for Edward, caught between three angry Highlanders.

Liam kept his gaze on Bàs. "Ivy needs to rest. There are dark circles beneath her eyes. So I told her I'd take the bairn out for a bit. I'm his father."

"A father who abandoned him and his mother," Joshua said.

Liam glared at Joshua. "I told ye. Ivy begged me to go. I left so I could come for her once I'd made a plan."

"Or once ye knew she and the bairn survived?" Joshua asked, doing what he'd been raised to do, start wars.

"I'll check on Ivy," Shana said. "If she needs rest, I'll watch Edward while you can check on your horse, Liam."

"My horse?" Liam asked as Shana slid around him under the protective gaze of Bàs and Joshua.

"Aye," Bàs said. "Your horse who ye didn't even consider feeding or watering over the last four hours."

Shana resisted the urge to stay behind and listen to the interrogation. But she had Edward and needed to check on Ivy.

Kára listened through the open door, her daughters sleeping on either side of her. She looked at Shana when Shana hesitated. "I'll let you know what happens," she whispered as if she didn't worry one bit about a battle breaking out before her babes.

With Bàs and Joshua there, any concerns would be extinguished before they could grow.

Shana hurried up the stairs with Edward. Ivy had her eyes closed when Shana entered, but they opened when she shut the door.

"Oh," Ivy said. "Is something wrong?"

"Did you send Edward out with Liam for a ride on his horse?"

Her brows furrowed but she gave a little laugh. "A ride? The man knows little more than I do about infants. He said he would entertain Edward while I rested. I didn't know he wanted to take him riding. Edward's hardly two weeks old."

Ignorant new father or sly abductor? Shana wasn't sure.

"I see you stopped him," Ivy said, beckoning for Shana to give Edward back to her. "I really don't mind having Edward with me while I rest. Our sleep and waking times seem to be connected now."

Shana went to the window that overlooked the yard. She stopped her gasp with a hand across her lips. Liam had a rope around his shoulders, pinning his arms down along his sides. Bàs was leading him to the fence where his horse shied away.

"Liam says we will leave here soon," Ivy said from the bed. "That we can set out together, our small family."

Bàs was gesturing with his hand, and Shana could imagine his furious words. Liam seemed to refute what he was saying with shakes of his head, but the rope prevented him from using his arms. Bàs dropped the end of the rope.

"Do you think Edward will be safe riding against

me?" Ivy asked.

"Uh…" Shana watched Liam shake the binding off. Joshua wasn't out there. Where had he gone?

"Shana?"

"Uh… 'Tis too soon for riding distances," she said, trying to give Ivy a smile. Luckily her sister seemed more interested in her son's tiny fingers as they wrapped around a clump of her hair.

"I think he'll have to hear that from you, Shana," Ivy said. "He's anxious to get us both to safety and doesn't think this place is hidden enough, since he found it easily."

"Oh no," Shana murmured as Liam took a swing at Bàs, but Bàs ducked easily, avoiding the strike.

"Well, he does have a point," Ivy said, sounding distracted. "Keenan told him right where we were. Thank the Lord it wasn't one of Erskine's men pretending to be Liam."

Shana glanced quickly at Ivy, who was bent over Edward, kissing his palms and each little finger. "Was Liam friends with Erskine or his soldiers?" Shana asked.

Ivy smiled at her babe. "I think he had few friends in the village. Everyone needs an apothecary from time to time, especially soldiers. But Erskine never went to him."

Shana turned back to the window as Bàs pulled a long whip from behind a bail, holding it out toward Liam as he spoke, the words too low for her to hear through the glass panes.

Liam's arms were fisted next to his legs. The wavy glass made it hard to see, but Shana thought his cheek was red. Was Bàs shaming him for his treatment of his horse?

Bàs snapped the whip, making Shana twitch. Would he whip Liam? But Bàs threw it to the ground, took two steps forward and punched Liam with an underhanded fist to the gut. As Liam doubled over, he tried to roll away but had a hard time standing. Bàs followed him and kicked him so that he rolled onto his back, and then Bàs walked away like he was finished and had no fear that Liam could jump up to attack him.

"What are you watching?" Ivy asked, finally having noticed Shana's disinterest in her one-sided discussion about how Edward's eyelashes were growing in, curling upward.

"Ivy, how well do you truly know Liam?" She looked away from the window.

Her face pinched. "I know he's an upstanding man, that he loves me, and would die to keep Edward safe."

"But about his family? Does he have siblings? Parents? Did he have a pet growing up? Have you talked about where you will live and how he can support you?"

Ivy kept her frown. "Our times together were usually rushed. I couldn't spend the night away from the castle. I believe his parents are dead, and he's never talked about siblings or pets. He's an apothecary, so I assume he will continue to work as one once we find our way to a safe town. Perhaps in France."

Shana came to the bed. "I think you need to get direct answers. Don't assume."

Tears welled up in Ivy's eyes. "Why are you asking me these things?"

"I want to make certain you are safe and happy. I don't know anything about him."

She glanced at the window. "Do the Sinclairs not like him? Joshua openly blamed him for following my request for him to save himself when Janet told me that Erskine knew the child wasn't his."

"How did *she* know?"

"She heard from someone," Ivy said but seemed to brush off the question. "Does your Bàs not approve of a man who chooses to hand out cures to people instead of battling and killing?" Ivy asked.

Shana blinked at the switch in topics. Did her sister feel the same prejudice people had against Bàs for being the Horseman of Death? "Bàs loves animals," Shana said, switching the topic again. "Maybe more than people."

Ivy's eyes narrowed in confusion.

"If Bàs disapproves of Liam 'tis because..." Shana said, her words trailing. "Well, it looks like Liam has beaten his horse, mistreated it."

"His horse?" Ivy looked confused. "I didn't even know he had a horse."

Could he have recently acquired it to ride away from Wick? But then Bàs wouldn't have hit him. Or could Bàs have raged merely for the horse being forgotten upon Liam's arrival? The apothecary had been easily knocked to the ground. Perhaps Liam wasn't a fighting man at all even though he was built like one.

Shana squeezed Ivy's wrist. "Promise you won't run off with him. Wait until we figure all this out and you have a solid plan that will keep you and Edward safe."

"Of course," Ivy said. "But we must stay ahead of Erskine or possibly King James's forces, so we don't contribute to a civil war or get captured and falsely charged as witches."

Shana knew all this. Time was moving forward, and they were not. But that didn't mean they should race off in a panic. Shana had done that with Edward, and they'd almost been eaten by wolves. Once again, they could be in jeopardy, and not just from Erskine and the king. Wolves lurked about, sometimes dressed as honorable men.

• • •

Bàs ran a hand down the bay horse's sensitive side. Was he bruised from being kicked by Liam's heels in the stirrups? The gelding's side quivered. "Ye're safe here." He hadn't gotten a name from Liam before the arse said the horse deserved to be whipped, and Bàs lost his temper. "I didn't cut off his head or any body part," he murmured.

He walked slowly to the horse's head, giving the animal time to sniff and finally lick up an apple from his hand. "I'll call ye King, because ye need a name that gives ye confidence." Being a bay, he'd ride with Joshua's red army once he'd healed physically and emotionally, but he'd still be Bàs's horse.

Liam could walk out of here, because Bàs wouldn't trust him with a Sinclair horse. Ivy and Edward, however, would be a problem. Shana wouldn't let them set out on foot. "What to do?" Bàs murmured and scratched behind King's ear.

The barn door opened, and Bàs watched as

Shana slipped inside. She looked at him and the horse. "So, he admitted to beating him?"

"Ye saw?"

"Liam try to punch you and then you laying him out flat? Yes."

Bàs studied Shana to see how she felt about his actions, but she kept her expression neutral. "Aye, he said as much. The horse is no longer his, so it will be hard for him to ride your sister and nephew to safety. But we can keep them safe. And ye, Shana."

Shana came closer. "We won't be the reason for civil war and thousands dead."

"Ye won't be the reason. Erskine Oliphant will be."

She sighed. "Bast—"

"And I don't trust that Liam Ross isn't involved somehow."

Her head tipped to the side. "With Erskine?"

"'Tis a feeling," Bàs said, coming out of King's stall.

"Ivy thinks he's a good man. She's in love with him."

"Love makes one blind."

"How would you know about love?" she asked, frowning.

Bàs crossed his arms and leaned against the stall door. "Aunt Merida says my mother loved my father. She was blind to his harassment of those he felt were weak. My father," he continued, "was blinded to anything but battle and blood lust when his only love was killed. And my brothers don't notice anything negative about their wives, and yet no one is perfect. They must be blinded as well."

"Maybe love helps one put up with small annoyances in people," she said, her voice tight. "Make one not care if their husband snores or their wife cooks poorly, but that doesn't mean they are blind to their faults."

"Beating a horse is not a small annoyance."

"Of course not." Shana huffed. "Did he give any explanation?"

"None that justifies mistreatment."

She nodded, looking away. "Ivy didn't even know he had a horse. She's convinced that it was recently given to him and was mistreated by a previous owner."

"He did not just acquire King."

"King?"

"He needed a name."

"So Beò wouldn't eat him?" she asked, her words tinged with a hint of teasing. He continued to wipe down the horse's neglected tack. "Why King?"

Bàs inhaled fully. "He needs a name that will give him confidence."

Her face softened. "Confidence from a name?"

Bàs shrugged. "Liam kept calling him Horse."

"See," Shana said, taking a step closer. "We can rename you to give you confidence, too. Confidence that you aren't all about death."

Bàs's frown deepened. "'Tis not as easy for a man who's been called a name for over two decades."

She patted his arm. "Consider it." She then looked back at the cabin. "I'm not sure what to do. Ivy is convinced she and Edward will be safe with Liam. She wants to leave with him as soon as I say 'tis safe for the babe to travel."

The dogs began to bark in the yard. "Someone's

approaching," Bàs said. In all his years in the forest, he'd had a total of six visitors. So many people visiting wasn't normal by any means.

"Erskine?" Shana asked, whirling around to the door. "With three babes in the cabin."

"Go to them," Bàs said, dropping the tack into the bucket and striding out. "Prepare Ivy and Edward to run. Joshua will protect his own."

Blood surged hot through Bàs's arms as he drew his sword. Beò stood off to the side, half hidden in shadows of the surrounding trees. Apollo and Artemis barked with ferocious vigor at the space that led through the thick bramble surrounding his humble fortress. Even Banshee ran out of the barn, leaping higher into a tree to view the threat.

The sound of horses broke the quiet morning. Joshua came out the cabin door, his own sword drawn. He jogged over to stand beside Bàs, his face grim. Since having a wife and children, The Horseman of War no longer lusted for blood sport. With Kára just giving birth and his two newborn daughters to protect against what was sounding like a small army in the brush, there was no leaping from foot to foot in gleeful anticipation.

Bàs glanced toward the porch when he heard the door open. Kára came out, her simple gown thrown over a clean smock. She held two throwing mattucashlasses and a vicious expression. She met Joshua's gaze, and a determined look passed between them, completely dedicated to keeping their newborns safe no matter what army came through the bramble.

From behind her, Shana hurried out holding the

smaller bow that Hannah had loaned him. As much as he'd rather have Shana safely inside, she looked determined to again protect her sister and nephew with her life. Her gaze slid to him, connecting. He gave her a little nod, which she returned before looking down to nock her arrow and raise the bow.

"Where is the coward?" Joshua asked, obviously meaning Liam Ross. "Did he abandon his woman and child again?"

"He might be inside helping them ready to run," Bàs said, although his tone indicated he didn't give Liam that much credit. "Or he's taking a nap somewhere."

Joshua snorted and drew his sword, his dagger in his right hand to throw first. "'Tis too early to be James," he said. "He couldn't have ridden here in this short time since Erskine sent his lies."

"Agreed." Bàs's gaze slid back to the opening in the briar where the horses must traverse to enter his yard.

Joshua raised his throwing arm. "I say we kill whoever—"

"Ho there, brothers! Friends, not foes, approach!"

The sound of Cain's voice sent a wave of relief through Bàs. Joshua lowered his dagger and leaned forward to prop his hands on his knees in relief, huffing loudly. "Thank the good Lord," he murmured. "I need to get Kára and the bairns up in our tree." He referred to the tree house that he'd built as a refuge for him and Kára. Unless an army cut all three trees under it down, it was inaccessible and quite hard to find. Harder, apparently, than Bàs's cabin.

Bàs noticed Bruce, his hawk, swoop overhead to

perch in a tree. He'd delivered the slip of paper with the news of Kára's successful birth yesterday.

Cain and Ella rode through the pass into his clearing. But they were merely the beginning of the parade. Gideon and Cait followed, along with Keenan, Hannah, Kára's amma and aunt, Aunt Merida, and Kára's brother, son, and best friend, Brenna.

"Bloody hell," Bàs said, his fingers raking his hair to grab the back of his neck where an ache had started. After this, if he wanted any privacy, he'd have to rebuild somewhere else. Maybe in the trees like Joshua.

"Kára!" Brenna yelled, waddling forward. The woman was pregnant with her second bairn. Her first was named Joshua because he'd helped with the birth back on Orkney Isle. From the look of her, and the week Bàs had been having, she would probably go into labor within minutes. "You should be in bed," Brenna said. "Where are they? Two girls! I knew you were too large to be carrying only one."

Gideon walked up to Joshua, his hand coming down hard on his shoulder. "Congratulations, brother. Three bairns already."

Joshua had recovered from the rush of relief. He smiled. "Aye. My seed is so potent I made two at once."

Cain snorted a deep laugh while Ella shook her head.

"What are their names?" Cait asked, her hand sliding down over her own protruding belly.

Daingead. Bàs's solitary life was suddenly filled with bairns and pregnant mothers. Somewhere behind him, Ilsa bellowed as if announcing her own bairn. He turned to see Iona nursing greedily under her. The dogs raced around after Kára's older son, Geir, who ran in to meet his new half sisters.

"Astrid for Kára's mother," Joshua said. "And Alice for our mother."

Where was Liam Ross? He hadn't shown himself since Bàs had punched him in the stomach for saying the horse deserved a strong hand, which included whippings.

"And Bàs saved Alice," Joshua said.

"Saved?" Hannah asked, pausing on her way to the cabin.

"Bàs?" Aunt Merida said.

Bàs turned to see everyone staring at him. He stood still, hands fisted by his sides.

"Aye." Joshua came over to throw his arm over Bàs's stiff shoulders. "Kára was having a bloody messy issue that Shana was being brilliant about stopping, and Ivy couldn't get wee Alice to take her first breath. So Bàs took the bairn from her and blew his own breath into Alice. Over and over until she took her own."

Joshua thumped Bàs hard on the back with enough power to make him stumble forward, but he caught himself. "We named that twin Alice because Bàs saved her. In case he still foolishly thinks he killed Ma by being born. A life for a life."

Hannah came over and hugged Bàs tightly. "You are a hero, brother."

"Perhaps ye should be called the Horseman of Life," Gideon said, his smile broad. "Instead of Death."

Hannah pulled away, smiling up at Bàs. He

rubbed the side of his face that felt hot with the attention. "Doesn't have the same gruesome ring to it," he said.

"The warrior saved the babe?" Kára's aunt was questioning Shana on the porch.

"Yes, he did," Shana said. "'Twas like his breath was magic."

"Don't say that to King James," Cain said, his broad grin dimming as his brows pinched.

Cait's happiness faded, too. "James would be an idiot to bring accusations like that against the Sinclair brothers."

Gideon pulled her closer, his hand sliding protectively over her stomach. "The man has moments of brilliance, but for the most part he's a fool who lets others sway his mind."

Bàs met Gideon's gaze. "Then ye must sway them against Erskine and away from Shana and her sister."

Gideon raised his hands, palms out, as if slowing down a wild horse. "I have written a letter reminding him about our upcoming task in Orkney in his name. To bring up the dispute with the Oliphants would make it seem like more than a mere complaint by a minor lord."

"Where's the man looking for Ivy?" Keenan asked as he turned in a tight circle.

"Without you showing him to me first," Cain said, his voice gruff.

"A mistake I'll not make again," Keenan said with a bow of his head.

Bàs turned to Shana. "Is Liam upstairs with your sister?"

She shook her head, her face pinching into worry.

"I didn't see him, but I'll check now." She turned, running inside. The wives hurried after her to see Alice and Astrid.

The four brothers remained outside along with Keenan. Bàs crossed his arms. "Liam Ross mistreats his horse." His pronouncement made all the brothers frown. "I don't trust him. He has the body of a trained warrior but says he's an apothecary."

"There's no excuse for poor treatment of an animal," Gideon said. "But he could be an apothecary who likes to stay strong."

"I think he's a mercenary," Joshua said.

"Why?" Cain asked.

Joshua shrugged. "A feeling. He's strong and he lies."

"That doesn't mean he's a hired killer," Gideon said, ever the practical brother. Where he thought everything through, Joshua went with his gut on most things. Cain listened to it all to form plans.

And what did Bàs do? He waited for someone to tell him to kill. The thought made his hands clench into tight fists again. Brainless, dutiful, and deadly.

Shana came back onto the porch with both Kára's aunt and grandmother trailing her. Her gaze fell on Bàs. "Liam isn't inside," she said. "Ivy has Edward and says Liam never came to her."

"So, Death saved the babe?" Kára's amma asked, glancing his way.

Shana frowned at her. "I don't call him Death. I call him Bast, not Bàs."

Gideon looked at Bàs. "She's renamed ye?"

"'Tis either Bast or Sebastian," Joshua said with a smirk.

"Bast is Egyptian, I think," Gideon said. "I'll look

up the meaning."

Kára's aunt, Hilda, flapped her hand toward him. "That warrior, there, him? He blew his exhale into the babe's mouth and nose to revive it?"

"Is there enough air in an exhale to do that?" Harriett, Kára's grandmother, asked.

"Apparently so," Hilda said.

Shana looked back at Bàs. "I don't know where Liam went. Ivy's worried."

Would Liam abandon Ivy and his bairn? Bàs rather hoped he would. "I'll look for tracks." He glanced at the barn. "He must be on foot, since I took his horse."

Bàs jogged to the barn first, breathing some relief to see both horses there. With all the chaos of everyone's arrival, Liam might have tried to sneak one out. Bàs circled the edge of his not-so-hidden yard and picked up fresh tracks through the bramble toward the curved river where he'd found Shana and Edward originally. He followed it easily to where the man had forded it. Was he headed somewhere with a purpose or just trying to leave his responsibilities behind?

Bàs exhaled and walked back toward what had been his refuge before pregnant mothers, wee bairns, questioning midwives, and celebrating relatives had infiltrated his peace. Peace? Had he ever had peace? Bàs stopped near the garden of arranged stones around the carving he'd done of his mother's face. How many hours had he sat there searching for peace? Hundreds.

The crunch of a step made him look up to see Shana. She stayed quiet, understanding the reverence of the place. "Is your mother buried here?" she whispered, standing close to him so that he felt her arm brush his.

"Nay," he said. "She and my father are buried side by side in a field next to Girnigoe Castle. I carved her face from a likeness that Aunt Merida drew after she died so we wouldn't forget her."

"'Tis beautiful," she said. "The carving."

Silence hovered over the area for a moment before Bàs spoke. "His tracks lead back the way ye came. I stopped at the river."

"Liam's headed toward Wick?" she asked.

"Not sure. He might veer off." He turned to look down into her concerned face. "He may have abandoned them again."

Shana held her face in her palms. "What am I to tell Ivy?"

"Better that she's not tied to a man who beats his horse," Bàs said. "He'll only turn to beating her or his children."

A scream came from the cabin and then laughter. Shana grasped his hand. "Perhaps Betty found another nut to throw. She has a lot of targets now."

"Daingead," he murmured. "With all the new mothers and bairns, I'll have to move back to the castle."

She laughed softly as they walked toward the cabin. "They'll only follow me if I return to Girnigoe, I'm afraid."

He stopped and looked down at her, his chest tightening. "Ye would come with me? To Girnigoe if I went there?"

She kept her gaze on the path before them but

glanced sideways with a gentle grin. "Someone has
to correct people when they call you Death."

A tremor cracked through his chest. Death was
who he was, had been since he was five years old.
But her words were like a chisel being hammered
against what he'd always been. Could it be strong
enough to break through?

CHAPTER TWENTY

"To be kind to all, to like many and love a few, to
be needed and wanted by those we love, is certainly
the nearest we can come to happiness."
MARY, QUEEN OF SCOTS, 1542–1587

The downstairs was crowded. No one had left the
night before, and pallets had been laid inside for the
women. Kára and her babes occupied the bed where
she'd given birth while Cait and Brenna, both pregnant, slept upstairs in the bed with Ivy. The two
elderly ladies were given pallets above. Shana kept
quiet about their pallets being beds for Bàs's dogs.

Hannah, Ella, and Merida also slept below.
Considering the bodies lying about, it was quiet as
Shana pushed up from her spot on the floor. The
sound of metal grazing the floorboards made her
look underneath the bed. Her blanket had caught
the knife that Kára's friend, Brenna, had placed under it to keep the evil and mischievous sprites away
from the babes. Shana set it straight underneath and
rolled forward to stand, stretching.

She walked to the window where the grayness of
dawn was brightening. Men were scattered, still sleeping around the huge bonfire that Joshua had lit to
celebrate his "powerful seed" at making two babes at
once. Whisky had been involved, but it was curbed by
the other brothers who were ever watchful.

Shana pushed open the glass to let in fresh air

and paused to watch Bàs walk from the creek toward the smoldering remains of the bonfire. He'd probably risen early to take care of his livestock, which were as important as family to him. In the turmoil of his life, the beasts of the world had become his family and only friends.

I'd rather be a beast. His words made complete sense to her now.

He carried his shirt, his hair wet after washing. The way Bàs moved across the yard made her think of his wolf, full of graceful power from keeping his body strong and ready for war. Muscles corded easily up his arms and chest, and his broad shoulders looked as if they could hold the world upon them. Watching him made her wish she'd found a way to sneak out to him last night. Lord, he made her wanton.

"Good morn," Hannah whispered where she leaned against the end of the bed, holding one of Kára's new babes. Shana's heart gave a little start, and she spun away from the masculine beauty.

Shana lowered her hand that had flown to her chest. "Was she fussing?"

Hannah smiled down at the girl in her arms, a look of longing in the tightness of her eyes. "Just wee Alice here and only a little bit. She's precious even when she fusses. They both are." She looked up at Shana. "I will help care for them at Girnigoe." It was obvious that Bàs's sister loved babes. Did she long for one of her own? Was there a man she liked among the Sinclair people? Perhaps people were frightened of her brothers and didn't get close.

Hannah was beautiful and kind, although a bit meek. But that was usually prized in a woman, which was why Shana hadn't remarried. As a midwife who demanded the best care for her patients, she was anything but meek.

"Ella, Cait, and Kára are blessed to have you helping them," Shana said with a smile.

Hannah gave her a small nod and looked back down at the babe who had fallen asleep in her arms.

Shana glanced at the rafters over her head where Betty stared down, her tail flicking in jerky movements as if signaling a code. Light footsteps above told her one of the ladies in the upstairs bedroom was walking around.

Shana began to pick her way through the sleeping bodies toward the stairs. "I better see if Edward is—"

Heavy footfalls down the stairs interrupted her. Cait met her at the bottom, her eyes wide. "Is Ivy down here?"

Shana's body tensed, and she grabbed hold of the smooth wooden rail. "No. Isn't she above with Edward?"

Cait shook her head. "They're both gone."

• • •

Bàs held Shana before him on Dòchas, trying to keep his focus on the fresh marks made by a single horse. Cain, Joshua, Ella, and Hannah accompanied them, following Bàs's lead through the forest.

"Did he take her, or did she run away with him?" Shana whispered.

He didn't answer, because there were no answers. Not yet anyway.

Sitting straighter to keep his face out of her sweet-smelling hair, Bàs looked down at the tracks. Luckily, they were easy to follow, even without Beò trotting ahead to lead their small party.

"Liam must have returned with a new horse," he said.

Gideon had stayed behind with Keenan to guard the pregnant women, Kára, and the twins. It was unlikely anyone would bother Bàs's clearing, but the enemy was often unpredictable. And Liam Ross was the enemy. Bàs was certain of it, not only from the way he'd casually said a horse should be beaten but also the dishonorable way he'd either taken or tricked Ivy into leaving without a farewell to her sister.

Shana exhaled in a small huff. "What do you think we should do? Follow their trail all the way to the end of the tracks?"

"I think ye should have stayed back at my cabin," Bàs said.

She turned in her seat to glare at him. "She's my sister."

"Which makes ye ready to rush into something dangerous to retrieve her."

"Like you would stay behind if one of your brothers or Hannah were in danger."

When he didn't answer, because her point was valid, she made a satisfactory condemning *humph* and turned forward. The truth was that he was worried about Shana. Not that she was a woman, because Hannah and Ella also rode with their search party, and he didn't worry as much about them. They were better trained with weapons, but it was more that Bàs anticipated the coming battle. Shana had started to think of him as something other than the warrior and killer that he must be in battle. The trust that had begun to grow in her was still fragile. He didn't want her to see him war.

Beò jogged around a bramble full of summer blackberries, and Dòchas knew to follow without Bàs's guidance.

"She says she loves him," Shana continued softly. "He's Edward's father, and Ivy deserves to be freed from her marriage to Erskine Oliphant." The path widened, and the tracks were even easier to see. They were fresh enough that Liam and Ivy might be just around the boulders ahead.

"But you don't trust him," Shana said.

"Nay."

Her sigh held weight. "He makes her happy. He helped her cope with living with Erskine. So I will show him kindness until he proves he doesn't deserve it."

"Does he deserve kindness after stealing Ivy and Edward away from ye in the night?" Bàs asked, trying to keep his gaze on the path and not drifting to the red-gold strands of Shana's hair that caught the morning sunlight.

"I don't know yet," she said, her voice tight.

Beò stopped ahead, and Bàs raised one fist in the air, signaling that they should all stop and sit quietly. Nose tilted to the breeze, the wolf sniffed, giving a small bark, and circled back toward Bàs and the party. His ears were back, a sure sign that he smelled danger. And danger to the huge wolf meant humans.

Joshua brought his horse up next to him. "The

woods are silent. No birds." Joshua trusted birds like Bàs trusted Beò's nose.

Bàs leaned his mouth toward Shana's ear. "Call for Ivy. I think she's close."

Shana inhaled and straightened in the seat. "Ivy," she called, her voice cutting through the forest. "Ivy, can you hear me? Are you well? Do you have Edward? We are so worried."

After a long moment, Ivy appeared from around the boulders. She glanced over her shoulder at the tall granite and then ran ahead toward them. "Shana," Ivy called. Her cheeks were flushed, and worry sat in her eyes as she looked at Bàs and then the people on horses behind him. "I am so sorry to worry you. I am well and so is Edward."

Shana turned to Bàs. "I need to get down."

Bàs looked in her eyes. "Liam is behind that boulder," he said. "Stay near us."

Ivy stood several feet away. "He doesn't trust you, either," she said, a bitterness to her words that showed Liam had been poisoning her with tales of the Horseman of Death, tales that were probably true.

Bàs jumped off his horse and lifted Shana down. She turned right away from him to hug her sister. Bàs backed up but could still hear them. Shana looked into her sister's face. "You left with Liam because you wanted to, not because he abducted you?"

Ivy shook her head. "He would never have taken me if I hadn't wanted to go with him. But he's Edward's father, and Shana"—she reached forward to squeeze Shana's hands—"I love him."

"Why would he sneak you away without allowing you to let your sister know?" Bàs asked.

Ivy frowned at him. "He's heard Erskine is coming for Edward and me, and he knows we are at your cabin." Her gaze shifted to Shana, tugging her closer. "And the Sinclair horsemen are dangerous. Everyone knows that." She whispered something else to Shana that Bàs couldn't hear.

"Where is your child?" Cain asked from beside Bàs. He'd brought his horse up on one side of Dòchas, and Joshua stopped on the other.

She glanced toward the boulder. "With Liam." She took Shana's arm, pulling her toward the side as if to shield her from battle.

"He's hiding while sending ye out to greet God's horsemen?" Joshua said, his voice raised in a taunt. He yanked Bàs's skull mask off the back of Dòchas and handed it to Bàs. Joshua felt it, too, this tension that was escalating to battle. Maybe it was the fact they couldn't see Liam and Edward behind a boulder outcropping that presented a perfect spot for an ambush.

"Coward," Joshua yelled.

"He's keeping Edward safe while I talk to my sister," Ivy snapped back.

"Is he alone?" Bàs asked and pulled his shield from Dòchas. He set the skull mask to balance on his head without pulling it on. He didn't want Shana to see him wearing it, becoming the executioner who almost killed her before her eyes.

Ivy hesitated but then nodded.

Bàs walked past them toward the boulder, his sword out, his ears alert for signs of ambush. There'd been only one set of hoofprints, and Bàs looked up along the ridge of the boulder. What did Liam believe he could do against three of the Four Horsemen alone?

Bàs looked at Cain. "Stay here. He may ride away with the bairn if we all advance."

"He's not afraid of you," Ivy replied with acid in her tone.

"So, he's a fool as well as a coward," Joshua called, taunting.

Bàs walked with wolflike silence, treading on moss instead of leaves or pebbles. He rounded the edge of the boulder, his shield in place. His gaze fastened on a man riding away through the woods, but he knew immediately it wasn't Liam. Because Liam sat in the center of three mounted men with bows. He wasn't alone. Had he told Ivy to lie?

Liam's face was more snarl than smile. "Don't pull your clan into a war ye have no business being in. Be on your way," he called.

"Where are ye sending Edward?" Bàs asked.

"Bàs?" Cain yelled.

"Tell them not to come forward if ye want to know where Edward is going," Liam said evenly.

"Wait there," Bàs called back, keeping his gaze on the archers.

Liam tapped his horse, riding forward until he looked down at Bàs. "Edward is going where he can be raised as the next chief of the Oliphant Clan," Liam said, his voice lowered, and he leaned forward so his face was almost level with Bàs. "As was the plan from the beginning."

"Ye're taking him to Erskine?" Bàs guessed.

"When Ivy worries her husband will kill him?"

Liam chuckled, glancing toward the hedge of boulders that blocked his words. "Why would he kill the son he tasked me with giving him?" he whispered with an evil grin.

Liam swung his leg over his horse and dismounted, confident because the three other men behind him held arrows nocked and aimed toward Bàs.

"Ye aren't an apothecary, are ye?"

Liam slid his sword free. "Nay." He kept his foolhardy grin as men stepped out of hiding like rats planning to attack an injured animal. Some stepped from behind thick trees; others rose from wide, green ferns where they'd been crouched low. A quick count added to ten. This boulder had evidently been a meeting place where Liam could hand off Edward to waiting warriors. Some of the men held bows while others brandished swords. Their horses must be waiting farther back or else they'd come on foot.

"Ye would steal Ivy's bairn from her, giving him to the monster who beat her because of his own impotence? She will be devastated to lose her bairn," Bàs said, his voice raised. Bàs slid the skull mask over his head where the cap attached to the back caught it in place. The familiar press of the bone against his cheeks sent warrior's blood rushing through his limbs. They were outnumbered and Shana was back there.

"She won't suffer long," Liam said. The edge of his mouth hitched upward in a sardonic grin.

The plot sharpened inside Bàs's mind. Liam nodded at one of the archers who raised his arrow, aiming it toward the boulder. "Ivy, come quick," Liam called loudly. The slight shake of his head and prideful grin showed his true intent. Liam was going to execute Shana's sister.

Thought slipped away from Bàs, something that he'd trained himself to do over the years of carnage. His body—muscle, bone, and sinew—became a combined weapon. Danger to those he cared for overrode any resistance to becoming the Horseman of Death. He gave in to the familiar feel of transformation, his pulse slowing as worry and resistance slipped away.

He still remembered his father's deep voice as he roared the words from the Bible, making Bàs repeat it with intense feeling. As he matured and his voice had deepened, the words took on the weight of Bàs's beliefs.

"When the lamb opened the fourth seal," Bàs recited. He knew Cain and Joshua would come forward as soon as they heard his words. "I heard the voice of the fourth living creature say, 'Come.' I looked, and there before me was a pale horse." Bàs strode forward, his sword rotating as an extension of his arm. "Its rider was named Death."

After years of practice, he knew the required steps that brought him to a foe who thought he would hesitate, perhaps talk or negotiate. But Bàs was Death, not Justice. He'd been trained for one purpose. He didn't negotiate. As soon as he knew that the man was evil, there was only one outcome.

Bàs swung his sword in a powerful arc. It caught the air, singing its death cry a second before the blade hit Liam's neck.

Bàs's strike continued through its arc, slicing Liam's head cleanly from his shoulders. A scream tore out into the woods from behind him, and he spun around, his shield slung protectively over his back toward Liam's bowmen. But nothing could protect him from the horror on Shana's face as she stood beside Ivy at the edge of the boulder. Shana's lovely mouth, which could banish the coldest shivers with a smile, was twisted in terrible surprise. And her beautiful eyes were wide with fear, fear of the monster Bàs had always known himself to be.

The Horseman of Death.

• • •

Shana had rounded the corner with Ivy in time to watch the most horrific thing she'd ever witnessed. Bàs's voice rang loudly with his biblical words, the skull mask over his upper face, and he swung his mighty sword at Liam. His thinly covered arms bulging with power, Bàs severed Liam's head in one strike.

Liam's face, contorted with painful surprise, balanced for the slightest moment before toppling to the ground. His body, devoid of life, fell to the moss and ferns at his feet. Ivy screamed with the force of her sorrow and fear. And then pain as a flying arrow pierced her shoulder, throwing her backward.

Shana staggered as Ivy fell into her. There was no time to grieve or cry out or even think as Bàs flew down over them like a huge bird of prey. She crouched, staring into the face of Death. Only the eyes, peering from the dark holes in the skull mask, showed any humanity.

"You…you killed him," Shana said, backing away as he stalked toward her. She could do nothing as he picked up Ivy.

"Stay in front of me," he yelled as Cain and Joshua advanced to take on the group of men behind the heap of Liam's corpse.

Shana ran before him as he carried Ivy back around the boulder and straight to Hannah. He lifted Ivy onto Hannah's horse before her. "Get her to my cabin. Tell Gideon we are battling with the Oliphants."

Hannah wrapped her arms around Ivy and, seeming to be as great a horseman as her brothers, whirled her horse around to charge off into the woods from the direction they'd come. Bàs turned to Shana, and she backed away, her hands outward, palms up to stop him from coming at her. Liam's blood had splattered across Bàs's white tunic and mask, marking him as the most lethal creature on God's earth.

"Shana," he murmured, her backward steps seeming to stop him cold. "Ye need to ride to safety."

"You just…" She couldn't get it all out. Not without more air. "You just struck his head off." Her lips remained parted, and her eyes, wide with shock, narrowed as anger and fear twisted inside her like two tangled serpents.

"His plan has always been to give Edward to Erskine," Bàs said, his words coming on heavy exhales.

Shana tried to understand his words, but the chaos made it hard for her to process them. "You…

killed him without hesitation, without hearing his thoughts, his arguments. Edward's father. Ivy's love. You just killed him without…"

Bàs turned his face away from her. "Ella, take Shana back to my cabin."

Without asking her or meeting her gaze, Bàs closed the distance Shana had put between them. She backed up, her breath coming fast. The memory of the inhuman swing of his sword slashed through her mind, the spray of blood, the toppling of Liam's head… She raised her hands to cover her face as he leaped forward, grabbing her. His grip tightened around her waist, and he lifted her, placing her behind Ella on her horse.

"Go," he ordered and ran back to the boulder where shouts could be heard.

When he disappeared, Ella steered her horse to the back side of the boulders. She wore dark trousers and boots. "Let me stand," she said, straightening on the beast's back. She grabbed her bow and full quiver and pulled herself up easily to the top of the boulder. She looked at Shana. "Ride back to the cabin."

"You… You aren't coming?" Shana asked, her voice high-pitched with shock.

"I won't leave Cain," Ella said, plucking one of her arrows and nocking it.

Shana's gaze whipped between the boulders and over her shoulder at the space where Hannah had disappeared holding Ivy.

At the top Ella started firing down at men, her arm moving swiftly to pull arrow after arrow.

Shana had never felt so helpless. What did she

have to offer the situation? Fear? Shock at watching Bàs murder the father of her sister's son? What had Liam said that made Bàs react without waiting for any type of verdict, deciding right there that he was guilty and deserved death? *His plan has always been to give Edward to Erskine.* Why would he take his son to Erskine, the man who wanted the babe dead?

The men behind Liam had fired at Bàs, trying to hit him, but one had hit Ivy instead. If Bàs hadn't attacked, would her sister still be whole?

"Edward?" Shana whispered. Where was her nephew? Was he lying there in the bramble while men shot, slashed, and died around him?

Shana slipped her leg over Ella's horse, tugging her skirts with her, to jump to the ground. She grabbed a rock and ran up to the boulder. The scene stopped her inhale. Three Sinclair brothers stood back-to-back in a tight circle as they blocked arrows and fought the men as they came to strike them down. Ella shot from above, ducking back whenever an arrow soared her way. The three horsemen battled with calm strength, each of them taking their attackers in turn. Liam's body still lay in two bloody pieces in the dirt, men dodging it. Edward was nowhere to be seen. "Edward?" she said, half choking on the name.

Crack. A sharp pain radiated through her head and, like black ink spilled on a page, it spread outward to swamp her with darkness.

CHAPTER TWENTY-ONE

"Wounds and hardships provoke our courage, and
when our fortunes are at the lowest, our wits and
minds are commonly at the best."
PIERRE CHARRON, FRENCH THEOLOGIAN, 1541-1603

"Where is she?" Bàs yelled as he whipped off his
skull mask, throwing it in the low bush. He dropped
his gaze to the broken ground and footprints in mud.
Which were Shana's prints?

"I told her to ride back," Ella said.

"Apparently, she didn't," he yelled, his hand gesturing to Ella's horse standing there. *Shana. My
God, where is Shana?* The look on her face had
hacked through him, but he'd still been able to move
to do what must be done. But the idea that she had
been stolen away by the enemy, an enemy who could
torture and kill her as easily as breathing, made the
demon of hate rear up inside Bàs.

"I'm so sorry, Bàs," Ella said, going to him. Her
hand rested on his arm.

He snapped his face to her, and she yanked her
hand back, stepping away. Cain's arm crossed between Ella and Bàs, putting his wife at his back.
"She's not to blame," Cain said.

Nay, I am.

"I should have left her behind," Bàs murmured.
Then she wouldn't have seen him kill Liam, and the
look of horror on her face would remain in his

nightmares instead of being real.

"She wouldn't have stayed behind with her sister and nephew out here," Joshua said.

Bàs's hands came to his face. He felt the tightness of dried blood there. Not his own, but blood from Liam and his men.

He rubbed at the blood, wishing for his scratchy sponge that would scrape it away until the pain numbed his guilt for what he did, what he was. Someone who brought terror to the world.

No one said anything in the silent clearing. Even the birds remained quiet. Bàs looked down and saw a jagged rock next to the boulder. He crouched to pick it up, seeing blood on it. Shana's? He turned, holding it out to Cain. "She was taken. Erskine has her."

"And the bairn," Cain said, looking at the rock.

A horse came riding through the woods toward them, its hooves thundering on the moss and dirt. Gideon pulled his black horse to a standstill and jumped off. "I've missed all the fun," he said, although his face and voice were serious.

"Is Ivy alive?" Ella asked.

Gideon's gaze swept them, and he walked to glance around the boulder at the carnage on the other side. "Aye. Harriett, Hilda, and Hannah are tending her." He turned to them, waiting in silence while his mind came to the obvious conclusions. "So we are officially waging war on the Oliphants?" Gideon said.

"Aye," Bàs said. The single word ground out with the promise of spilling blood. For once, he welcomed the embrace of his role as the Horseman of Death.

• • •

Cold. Shana was so cold. She watched the blue sky as she floated on a frozen slab in a sea of broken ice, the wind blowing like the howl of a beast. The murmur of voices wavered in and out through the long dream until the words began to make sense.

"Is she awake?" The voice belonged to a man and held scorn. "I need her awake to examine."

"Erskine hit her hard enough to kill her," a woman said. "I'll work to wake her."

"Call me when she's conscious. She must be able to speak her confession and be aware when I prick her."

A witch hunter? They would strip a person naked to look for marks, bumps, or blemishes, which were thought to be teats for an animal familiar to suckle or a mark of the devil. The Prickers would jab those spots and other spots, sometimes the whole body, with needles to see if they bled and were painful. If they didn't bleed or make the suspected witch cry out in pain, they were marks from the devil, and the accused would be hanged, burned alive, or drowned. Torture first, followed by a painful death.

So many women and a few men had been tried and most found guilty. Would she be one of them? *I must save Edward.*

Shana kept her eyes closed and her breathing even as she listened to the man climb a stairway, his footsteps fading. Where was she? Old Wick's dungeon again? The last thing she'd remembered was watching the lethal grace of Bàs as he parried against one attacker and kicked a second in the gut, throwing him backward. And then pain had exploded in her head. She wanted to touch the spot that still throbbed but didn't dare move.

"You're awake, aren't you?" the woman said. Her voice was familiar. She waited, and Shana could hear her draw closer to the bars. "You weren't meant to be drawn into this," she whispered.

Shana opened her eyes slowly to see the woman who'd helped Ivy in the birthing of Edward standing there. Janet Bell.

"Janet?" Shana said, slowly pushing up even though her head throbbed. "Help me out of this."

Janet shook her head with a look of authentic pity. "Erskine needs someone to blame for his wife dying, someone other than himself, or the people won't support his continued chieftainship."

"His wife dying?" Shana murmured.

"Yes. The Sinclairs shot her when she tried to return to Erskine," Janet said.

"That's not—"

"That's what the Oliphant warrior who saved Erskine's son reported."

Had Ivy been the true target at the boulders? Not Bàs?

Shana's head ached, and she touched the back where crusty blood matted her hair. "Where is Edward?" Her gaze shifted past Janet toward the stairs.

"Edward is fine," Janet said, pacing slowly before the bars. "Erskine never wanted to kill him."

"Then why does he want Ivy dead?"

She smiled, the glow from the torch making her

expression into a macabre mask. "Because he loves me, not your sister. I've always been his true love, but he thought he could get a younger wife pregnant when I didn't conceive as his mistress." The woman looked like she truly believed it. Believed a madman could order the murder of his wife and then love her.

Janet's hands slid over her gently rounded belly. "He will marry me now, once Ivy is dead."

"He got you with child?" Shana asked.

"The same way he got Ivy with child," Janet said. "Through his blood-related nephew."

"Liam," Shana whispered.

Janet walked along the bars, and her fingers slid from one iron rod to the next. "Erskine feels bloodlines are very important, so he found his nephew when he couldn't create a child himself. Liam was the perfect substitute. Young, virile Liam." She smiled as if remembering their coupling but then shook her head. "Your sister fell in love with Liam when she was merely to have an affair."

Because her tenderhearted sister would not sleep with someone other than her husband unless she'd lost her heart to him.

"He lied to her," Shana said, pushing up to sit on the stained pallet where she'd tended Ivy after her birth in Old Wick's dungeon. "Liam was kind to her, telling her he loved her."

Janet nodded, pity heavy on her face. "Liam quickly realized your honorable sister wouldn't sleep with him unless she thought he was totally in love with her."

"Why would he agree to do this?"

"Gold, of course," Janet said. "His uncle figured out that he couldn't get a woman pregnant after years with me and then his young wife. So, he hired Liam to impregnate both of us. Now that I'm also having a child, I will replace your sister as lady of Old Wick. Erskine will have two children to inherit from him." Janet frowned. "He'd have had more if Bàs Sinclair hadn't killed his nephew. The Sinclairs will pay for that."

Bàs. The heavy weight of remorse dropped through Shana's middle, from the ache of tears behind her eyes through the tightness of her throat and chest to the lump of guilt in her stomach. She'd judged him guilty when she'd seen Liam topple and then Ivy struck by the arrow.

Shana met Janet's eyes. "Erskine will betray you, too, Janet, eventually. If he's willing to kill his first wife, he will plot to kill you, too, when he tires of you."

"We've been together for three years," she said, smiling. "He won't tire of me."

"Tyrants become more dangerous as they age and become infirm and in pain. Look at England's King Henry and his wives."

Janet frowned, her pretty face pinching. "If that happens, I am clever enough to escape. I learned early on from my mother not to fall in love with a man," she said, her gaze lifting as if she couldn't look Shana in the eyes. "I'll leave before that happens," she whispered, glancing over her shoulder before turning back to Shana. "To survive this life, I won't lose my heart to anyone. I'm sorry your sister was foolish with Liam, and that you now must suffer in her stead. The Witch Pricker is not kind. 'Tis best to confess immediately and die quickly."

"What if you have a daughter, Janet? Erskine will keep Edward and turn his back on your daughter. You cannot trust him to care for you. Help Edward and me escape, and you and your child could find refuge at Girnigoe Castle. The Sinclairs could help you journey abroad if that's your wish."

"My wish is to be lady of Old Wick Castle," Janet said, her voice snapping with determination. "My mother was scorned here in Wick, laughed at for her tender heart by the Oliphants when my father left us. I will be the lady here," she said, gritting her teeth. Janet crossed her arms and began to pace before the cell. "But you're right. Men want sons, even when sons are weaklings or lazy." Her hand went to her belly that looked like she was just beginning to show. "But if my babe was the only child of Erskine's blood, it won't matter as much if 'tis not a son. Even England has a queen on its throne."

Only child? "Then give me back Edward," Shana said. "I'll take him away. Erskine will think he died."

She spun to frown at Shana. "He didn't believe it the first time. Why would he believe it the second time?" She shook her head. "Erskine needs to see Edward dead to believe he has only one child to dote upon and love. One child to become his heir."

"Janet," Shana said, shaking her head. "You wouldn't harm an innocent babe. Let me take Edward away from here. We can…I don't know… find a stillborn boy to show him Edward died."

Janet snorted. "Erskine won't believe a replacement." She strode away from the bars.

"Janet! You can't harm a babe. You aren't a monster." Shana stood, her hand clutching an iron bar to keep her from falling over with the dizziness that accompanied her aching head.

"Newborn bairns are incredibly fragile," Janet said over her shoulder. "He could catch a fever from an open window or fall when he learns to crawl."

Shana watched the woman climb the stairs, carrying her torchlight with her. Shana's gaze swept the dirty, dank cell. One barred window cut high in the wall gave enough light that she could see the hole chiseled out of the bedrock was devoid of anything that could be a weapon. Only the pallet lay there, and a cup of some liquid sat inside the bars that could be poisoned or tainted.

She licked her dry lips and went to the bars across the small window. Moisture beaded there, and she captured the precious drops on her finger, sticking it into her mouth. She must stay strong enough to get out of the cell to get to Edward. Could Janet kill an innocent child, one she helped bring into this world?

All the players in this mess were turning out to be evil. The king, Liam, Janet Bell. All except for the one she'd already judged as guilty. "Bàs," she whispered. He'd sought to save them, save Edward, and she had thought him a monster. Would he turn his back on her and Edward now that Shana had condemned him?

"Dear Lord," she whispered. "What have I done?"

· · ·

"So, you're the accused."

King James stood before the cell holding Shana. He wore hose and voluminous breeches made of satin and gold trim. His doublet came to a point in the front, mimicking his trimmed beard, to make him look even taller than he was.

"I'm not a witch, Your Highness. I'm a midwife who delivered my sister's son. Erskine Oliphant has tried to murder my sister to take another wife and has accused me falsely."

James frowned, glancing at Erskine standing beside him. "'Tis a strong accusation, Oliphant."

Shana looked directly at Erskine. "Janet might kill Edward. You need to protect him."

Erskine's eyes widened slightly. "The witch lies," he said with confidence. "Janet is a docile woman, humble before the Lord, and soon to be a mother herself. Whereas ye are a witch." He looked at James. "Look at all the little dots across her skin. Devil marks to be pricked."

Shana stood tall, but her hands rested on her crossed arms. She tried to hide her shivering, part from the dank cold and part born of the evil gleam in the Witch Pricker's black eyes.

James sighed. "I suppose she must be tested." He turned to the Pricker standing behind them. "Sooner rather than later. I have pressing business with the Sinclairs after this mess."

"The Sinclairs have nothing to do with Erskine's plans," Shana called out. "Erskine had his nephew impregnate his wife and his mistress to father children. He's impotent and abusive and spews lies to Your Majesty, a definite act of treason."

"Treason?" James said, his gaze shifting to Erskine.

"The devil is making this woman clever," Erskine said. "Guard your tongue, devil." He spat toward Shana.

Shana didn't back up but kept her focus on the king. "Erskine Oliphant lured you to Wick with false accusations of witchcraft because he fears the Sinclairs won't stop until my sister, nephew, and I are free of his brutality."

"The Sinclairs are allies of the crown," James said. He turned to Erskine. "Are you hiding behind me, chief?"

"The Sinclairs have no reason to meddle with my runaway wife. I've been informed that they killed her and tried to abduct my son."

Shana glared through the bars. "I do believe that lying to the king is an act of treason, Erskine Oliphant."

James tilted his head as if judging Erskine against Shana. He ran his hand down his pointy beard. "Treason or witchcraft? It seems this situation requires my excellent deduction skills to find the true criminal."

Shana knew from her time in Edinburgh that James was frightened of both crimes. He felt his wife, Anne of Denmark, was opposed by witches who tried to block her with winter storms on her way to marry James. And after his mother, Mary Stuart's, mistakes, James knew all about the danger of having traitors quietly working behind the king.

"The Sinclairs saved you, your majesty," Shana said, making the king pause in his stride toward the exit stairway. "When your own men were turned to strike against you, a man chosen by God to rule Scotland, God sent the Horsemen to protect you."

James turned to her. "That He did. You speak of God easily."

"I do, milord. God sent me to care for my sister in this devil-infested clan, an enemy to the Sinclair Clan."

James looked at Erskine. "The Oliphant Clan is an enemy of the Sinclairs?"

"If the Sinclairs back this witch and her sister, then aye," Erskine said.

James waved his hand as if lost in the many details. "A woven web of half-truths." He glanced at the Pricker. "Hold off on examining her. I would not torture someone who God is using to expose the truth."

The Witch Pricker frowned but nodded, turning to follow the king.

"The truth," Erskine said, following the king up the steps, "is that my wife and her sister are wicked and treasonous."

"Which is it, Chief Oliphant?" James asked as he continued to climb. "Witchcraft or treason? It seems you are desperate to find fault."

They disappeared above, leaving Shana in the cell alone. She rubbed her arms. "Another hour without being stuck with needles," she whispered, knowing that her time was running out. Lord how she hated this cell. With the accusations she'd hurled at Bàs, she doubted very much that he would attempt to set her free once again.

• • •

"I can still throw daggers," Kára said.

"And I can shoot." Ella stood in Girnigoe Castle's Great Hall with Mary on her hip, swaying.

Cait sat at the table. "And I can climb any rope. It seems we should be able to get into Old Wick Castle without alerting the guards."

Cain, Joshua, and Gideon stared at their wives, their mouths slack.

Hannah held one of the twin newborn girls. "I can shoot, too. And I'm small so I can fit into windows."

Bàs turned away, pacing before the hearth that had burned low. They needed a way into Old Wick Castle where one of the Sinclair spies had said Shana was being held in the same dungeon as before. They'd ridden back to Girnigoe to ready their armies but agreed that Erskine might kill Shana if they charged into Wick. *If she's not dead already*. The thought burrowed into Bàs's gut, making him want to slaughter every Oliphant who breathed.

"Ye just had two bairns," Joshua said. "Ye aren't going anywhere except to a cozy bed. Maybe up in our tree where no one can touch ye or our bairns."

"And ye are carrying a child," Gideon said. It was obvious in his tone that he was shaking his head.

"Well, Hannah and I could still sneak in," Ella said. "I've already done it once."

"Erskine will be ready for ye this time after ye got Shana and Ivy out before," Cain said. "I need to think things through."

Bàs turned to Cain. "*We* need to think things

through. Ye can't disappear to contemplate on your own, coming out to tell us what to do without conversation." His voice had snapped out of his silence.

They all turned to him with a mixture of wide eyes and frowns, but he wouldn't hold his tongue. "Shana is in that bastard's grasp. If he's testing her for witchcraft, he could be torturing her *right now*. Or killing her. We need to act, not think." He yanked out his sword that was still bloody. "Within the hour. Ride against them. Crush the walls if we must." Blood lust welled up inside Bàs like he'd never felt before.

Keenan strode in during the last of his tirade. "Ye might want to read this first." He walked up to Cain, handing him a folded missive. "This arrived from Old Wick."

Cain stared down at the seal and glanced at Gideon. "'Tis King James's seal."

"It came from Old Wick?" Bàs asked, striding over. "Ye're sure."

Keenan nodded, his face grim. "The rider wore royal livery with King James's thistle upon it."

Cain broke the seal but held the letter where all four brothers could view the contents.

Chief Sinclair,
I am residing at Old Wick Castle as the guest of Erskine Oliphant to test and condemn a witch. I was unaware that the Sinclairs had anything to do with this foul business until the woman in question said as much. If this is true, your loyalty to me and my judgment is expected and will be forcibly ascertained.
James VI of Scotland

"That foking bastard," Bàs yelled. "I will slaughter Erskine Oliphant." Bàs met Cain's eyes. "James can judge Shana as guilty, but I'm not giving her up to a torturous death. Let him fight the traitors in his Scotland and survive long enough to be crowned King of England without the Horseman of Death standing to protect him." A heavy silence filled the room, as heavy as the stones making up the thick walls.

"King of England," Gideon murmured. "After Elizabeth dies without an heir."

Aunt Merida walked in from the archway. She was wearing dark-colored trousers and a tunic. "I'm here to help, too," she said, pulling everyone's gaze. "In a pair of Ella's trousers." She lifted one leg and then the other. "I see why the lasses prefer them to skirts that wind around your legs."

She stopped, her wry smile turning downward. "More bad news? Well, send me in," she said, looking to Cain. "I'm old, ornery, and I like that lass, Shana." She looked to Bàs. "She's good for you."

Shana made him question everything he'd been told about life and who he was to be. Was that a good thing? Once he got her out of this, though, she'd turn her back on him. *You just killed him.* The memory of the horror on her face made his stomach turn.

"We could send Merida in with food and drink," Cait said. "I doubt anything's been provided."

"Bàs," Hannah said, "you should write her a note to give her hope that we haven't abandoned her."

Bàs's knuckles kneaded the back of his aching neck. If Shana didn't want anything more to do with him, a note from him might cause her pain. *Like the pain I bring to so many other people*. He looked away from his sister. "She will know we haven't abandoned her when Aunt Merida brings her food."

"Do it anyway." Hannah shoved a scrap of paper against his chest.

Without thinking further, Bàs jotted three words, letting Hannah take it away. She snorted but didn't argue, and he turned back to his brothers.

"I'll get Aunt Merida safely there and then find a way into the castle by myself," he said.

Gideon inhaled fully and walked closer to Bàs, exhaling long. His hand clapped solidly down on his shoulder. "We won't wait for diplomacy then. Take a moment for us to form a plan, but I will be by your side."

Bàs stood straight. His wise brother, who knew so much from books, who judged as easily as breathing, had judged him worthy of his allegiance. Bàs felt his world shake from it.

Joshua came forward, stopping before him in a battle stance. He glanced at Kára, who held his second twin, and then back to Bàs. "I'd rip the heart out of anyone who hit the woman I love with a rock and carried her off to be tortured and killed. I would hold his heart up for the bastard to see it beat its last bit of life before his putrid soul was sucked away to Hell." He gave a nod. "I'll ride with ye, brother."

Woman he loved? Bàs's breath paused behind his lips. Did he love Shana? Was love the source of this rage within him? For a moment, Bàs understood his father's blood lust, his father's uncontrollable fury when the woman he loved died. And the madness that followed from not being able to strike down what killed her, his son.

You did not kill your mother. Shana's words beat back his guilt.

Cain stood by the table, the letter still in his hand. He inhaled fully and let the letter fall from his fingers to the floor. He stepped on it as he walked to stand before his youngest brother. "Ye are right, Bàs. Time is running out," Cain said. "I'll ride with ye."

The help from his three brothers humbled Bàs and, at the same time, filled him with strength, readying him for battle. But this battle was different. He battled not because someone ordered him to take up his sword or expected him to do his duty to the clan. For once in his life, he wished for war. To save an innocent woman, a woman he might love.

"Thank ye," he said evenly, giving a succinct nod. "Let's sit together and decide our attack. We ride within the hour." He walked to the long table, grabbing up his discarded skull mask. Only a day ago he'd thought to throw it in the river, but now he clasped it tightly, ready to become the infamous horseman to save Shana. Even if she never looked at him again.

Everyone in the room gathered around. Gideon shook his head at Joshua as he scooped up the royal letter. "Seriously, where do ye come up with your bloody oaths? Who tears someone's heart from them?" Gideon held out his hand as if holding a bloody, beating organ. "And then expects the person to watch it as they die?"

Joshua gave him a pitying look and clicked his tongue. "Ye have so little creativity."

Gideon looked heavenward in supplication and pulled three sheets of blank parchment to set one before Bàs, Cain, and himself. "Judge my creativity after ye read my next letter to James." Gideon looked to Bàs. "Ye gave me an idea."

"Three letters?" Bàs asked.

"I'm expecting that one or two might be destroyed, so I want three copies."

"Clever," Cain said. He glanced at Ella as he spoke next. "Keenan, send word to Chief Sutherland and his regent to ready their warriors for battle." Ella nodded, her face pinched but determined. Cain turned his gaze back to his warrior. "And set the signal fire to call in our own men."

Keenan turned and jogged out of the room.

"My Mackay warriors are already assembling," Gideon said as he shoved his quill into the ink. "I sent word as soon as we arrived back to Girnigoe."

Bàs laid his fist on Gideon's forearm where it rested on the wooden table. Gideon looked up, and Bàs met his gaze before looking to Cain and Ella. "Thank ye."

Gideon gave him a grim smile and nodded.

"With the three clans," Joshua said, standing tall, arms crossed, "we should be five thousand strong."

"James will see us as a threat," Bàs said. "He could name us all traitors."

Cain sat down at the table and leaned his elbow on it, his hand upright in a tight fist. The gold ring, proclaiming him the Horseman of Conquest, sat upright. "So be it," Cain said.

Gideon set his pen down. He dumped the contents of a small pouch onto the table. A few shillings clattered against the wood, and he grabbed his gold Horseman of Justice ring from them. He slid it on his finger and covered Cain's hand with his. "So be it."

Joshua leaned over, his large hand engulfing theirs. His Horseman of War ring sat on his middle finger. "So be it."

Bàs clasped his hand over those of his brothers. "So be it."

Civil war would start over one woman, for that was what this would be if James called them traitors. But this wasn't just one woman. This was Shana, someone who thought he was more than death. For her he would play his part with all viciousness. The irony wasn't lost on Bàs.

Ella looked to the other ladies in the room and all of them nodded, looking to Bàs. "So be it," they said in unison, adding their support. The room agreed. The Sinclairs were going to war against the crown of Scotland.

So be it.

CHAPTER TWENTY-TWO

"The fables of Witchcraft have taken so fast hold and deepe root in the heart of man, that fewe or none can (nowadaies) with patience indure the hand and correction of God. For if any adversitie, greefe, sicknesse, losse of children, corne, cattell, or libertie happen unto them; by & by they exclaime uppon witches. As though there were no God in Israel that ordereth all things according to his will."

REGINALD SCOTT (A RARE 16TH CENTURY
CONTEMPORARY WHO DID NOT BELIEVE IN WITCHES),
THE DISCOVERIE OF WITCHCRAFT, 1584

Shana braided her hair, tying it off with the bit of cord she still had in her pocket from the births. Of course, Erskine's men had taken the small dagger she also carried. She stood up and walked along the bars, feeling thirsty but not daring to drink the cup a guard had left containing foul-smelling liquid.

What would someone do who was dying of thirst? Allow themselves to die or drink what was likely poison in hopes they would stay alive for a bit longer? Eyeing the cup, she kicked it hard, sending it flying back through the bars to wet the dirty floor. "Temptation gone," she whispered, wrapping her arms around herself to ward off the brittle cold.

Silence swelled in her ears. With stone surrounding her in the dungeon, she couldn't hear anyone moving above. Edward was somewhere in the castle.

Was he well or had Janet already acted against him?

Shana paced to the window high in the outer wall. The day had brightened, and she breathed in the fresh air it afforded. Her fingers curled around one iron bar, pulling impotently against it. Footsteps outside along the wall made her yank her hands back inside just as the bottom hem of a skirt stopped before the window.

"Shana? Are you in there?" The woman's voice was familiar.

"I'm here," Shana said. The skirt at the window gathered, and Shana saw what looked like trousers underneath it.

A wrinkled hand pushed something through the gap. A bladder. Of untainted drink? Shana took it, yanking the stopper off, and drank. The weak ale was cold and fresh. *Thank you, Lord.*

"Are ye well?" the woman asked.

Shana wiped the back of her hand across her dry lips. "As well as I can be," she said and drank some more.

"Good. Here, lass, take it," the woman said, working a bundle through the bars.

Shana stoppered the bladder and took the bundle, and the woman walked away. No alarm sounded, and Shana hurried to the pallet to unwrap it. On the front was a torn piece of paper with a slanted script.

I am coming.

Her inhale was jagged, her heart pounding, feeding that bud of hope. Bàs was coming. Even though she'd looked at him with such horrible judgment when he'd killed Liam. Even though her eyes had clearly showed him that she'd convicted him of murder and condemned him as the Horseman of Death.

Could she accept Bàs for who he was, not who she wanted him to be? All sides of him?

She blinked against the tears in her eyes, pulling them back, but sniffing just the same. She was a midwife, a bringer of life. He was an executioner, a bringer of death. Their worlds didn't meet. A huge chasm lay open between them filled with guilt and judgment, remorse, and her condemning looks. What could possibly bridge the gap, bringing them together?

Shana drew in a ragged breath and looked down at the bundle. The package held oatcakes, an apple, and two daggers, which she concealed in her dress. Last was a letter, folded and sealed with a wax dot pressed with the imprint of a horse's head.

To our sovereign, King James VI of Scotland and I of England was scrawled across the front.

King of England? Elizabeth hadn't yet declared James her heir, although he certainly coveted the throne. But what it meant was that Bàs knew James was at Old Wick, and they meant to support him in his claim to the English throne. This was a weapon for her to use, possibly sharper than the two daggers he'd sent.

Shana chewed her oatcake and drank some more ale as hope blossomed fully within her. Senses alert, she waited for the next step in whatever plan had been set in motion.

She'd finished her small meal when the door at the top of the dungeon stairs opened. Standing, she hid the letter in the folds of her petticoat and shoved the bundle under the straw tick. Rapid stomping came down.

Erskine appeared with an Oliphant warrior behind him. "Are the Sinclair brothers fools?" He lifted a letter high, waving it around so that the wax seal flopped, showing he'd opened it. "What do they think will happen if the king receives this?"

"I wouldn't know, since I haven't read it," she said.

Erskine threw his torch into the holder on the wall and glanced at Shana, his lip curling like a diseased hound. "'Tis to King James, but of course my gatekeeper gave it to me first." He held the letter in the light of the torch. "Your Majesty. We have business with Erskine Oliphant about false accusations of witchcraft around an innocent woman he has wrongfully imprisoned. She's a close friend of the Sinclairs."

Erskine looked at her and glared. "And then it goes on to say… 'Ye may wish to inspect the army we plan to send on your cause to bring your traitorous uncle and cousin from Orkney Isle to Edinburgh this spring. We are here at present to meet ye on the field beyond Wick to the west and would greatly appreciate the honor of your inspection of your loyal troops and your help in freeing Shana Drummond and her nephew, Edward Oliphant.'"

Erskine waved the letter in the air and then, with a smirk, lowered it to the flame of the torch so that it caught and burned. "King James will know nothing of this letter."

"Will he know nothing of the army sitting off to the west?" Shana asked.

"If the Sinclairs or anyone is fool enough to attack, or even ride up with an army, while the king is in residence, they will all be labeled traitors to the crown. The rest of Scotland will come to our defense. I might even be able to take over Girnigoe and Sinclair lands." He smiled, brows raised high.

He was right, and Shana's stomach twisted. She would certainly be damned for starting a war that led to so many deaths. *Dear Lord, this is not what I wish.*

"You could let me, an innocent woman, go and prevent any bloodshed," she said, her hand curling around the cold iron bar. "You, Erskine Oliphant, would be a hero, and your nephew could inherit the chieftainship after being raised by his mother."

His eyes narrowed at her. "I am the chief of the mighty Oliphant Clan. I have a son and another on the way."

"They aren't yours," she said. "You are barren like your heart."

"They have my blood running in them from my nephew, Liam. Another dead because of ye."

She felt no remorse for Liam's death. Shock of course, seeing the man her sister loved lose his head, but now she knew Liam's true plans for Edward and Ivy. To take the son and kill the mother.

"He deserved to die," Shana said, venom in her voice.

"I will raise *my* son to hate the Sinclairs for killing their *cousin*, a much-loved man at Wick. A simple apothecary who wished only to help me retrieve the son who was stolen from me."

Shana grabbed the iron bars. "Edward will die by

Janet's hand if you don't let him go. She won't let him stand in the way of her own child."

He seemed to contemplate her words for a second but then shook his head. "Janet is loyal to me. She'll do nothing against Edward."

Erskine beckoned the guard behind him to come forward. The man held an iron mask. It looked sharp and heavy. Shana backed up in her cell.

"Ye can't be squawking to the king about the letter or about your sister." Erskine unlocked her cell. "This is a witch's bridle, and I'll hold the key. Your sister may have mentioned it to ye as a scold's bridle. It's quite effective to keep ye from talking."

The large guard came toward her. Shana could fight him, but then she'd have to drop the letter she held, and Erskine would find her weapons. Shana's heart beat in near panic as Erskine came around back, grabbing her to pin her arms against her sides. She wiggled in his grasp, turning her face away from the warrior, but he caught her chin in his strong fingers.

"Hold still, ye witch," the man said.

Shana reared her head back, but Erskine pushed it forward. She closed her eyes as a bit was forced between her teeth, the iron mask sitting in place over her face.

• • •

Bàs sat on Dòchas at the front of his army of gray and pale green horses. The ridges inside his skull mask pressed in familiar lines across the bridge of his nose and around his eyes. He was thankful he hadn't thrown it in the river.

Not when he could use it to save Shana.

The call to arms had gone out to his men quickly, so not everyone was able to paint their horses before riding out. But it didn't matter. The numbers were enough to make any commander or king pause. Especially when he saw the three other armies of white, red, and black horses led by his brothers.

Each Sinclair brother had spoken to their commanders, who organized the men on horseback as they did during training sessions. The Sutherlands and Mackays had practiced this with them so that they easily added to their numbers on the vast field west of Wick Village. Cain's falcon, Eun, flew overhead with a knotted plaid rag in his beak, the signal for Sinclairs and Sinclair allies to wait.

If battle started, they would play out their parts: the brothers first reciting the biblical verses from Revelation, Gideon's and Cain's armies forming lines much like the ancient Romans, and Joshua's and Bàs's armies flying along in seemingly random patterns to take on small skirmishes, pushing forward and then retreating to pull the enemy farther into Sinclair territory where they would be enveloped and slaughtered.

Cain and Joshua would decide together, Cain as the chief and Joshua as the Horseman of War, as to the changes needed to the plans during battle. The commanders would look toward the sky for Eun to hold colored rags in his talons for orders. Each army and direction had a color, which the men all knew.

"A rider comes," Ella said from her horse next to Cain. She and Hannah had ridden with them, adding their support to the armies. Gideon and Joshua had ordered their wives to stay back.

Bàs squinted against the midday sun filtering through the clouds. "Aunt Merida," he said. "She's alone."

"But I don't see the bundle," Gideon said.

Bàs grunted in frustration, his horse shifting under him, feeling his want to ride. It was nearly impossible to sit still when Shana could be suffering in Erskine's foul grasp.

Aunt Merida pulled her horse to a walk and stopped before them. "She's alive," she said, looking directly at Bàs.

He inhaled. "Is she hurt badly?"

Aunt Merida shook her head, and he closed his eyes in relief for a second. *Thank you, God.*

"Ye delivered the letter and bundle?" Gideon asked.

"Aye. She's in the dungeon. But the bars of the window are too strong to pull from the encasement."

"She won't have to go through the window," Hannah said. "Not with Gideon's clever letters reminding the king that we stand before him in his fight with his uncle on Orkney Isle as well as supporting him as the King of England."

"That bastard, Erskine, hadn't given her any type of blanket and no food or drink," Aunt Merida said.

"Glad we sent the ale and oatcakes," Ella said.

Bàs's hands gripped his reins hard. It was all he could do not to gallop into Wick.

"Another rider," Cain said.

Bàs looked out at the open area before the last copse of trees that hid the village of Wick and Old

Wick Castle that perched on the sea south of their territory. "'Tis Keenan."

Keenan had been tasked with taking one of the copies of the king's letter to Old Wick Castle. He pulled to a stop before them. "They wouldn't let me take the letter directly to the king. The gatekeeper wouldn't raise the portcullis, so I had to hand the letter over."

"Which is why I had two extra copies made," Gideon said with a frown. "I doubt James will see that letter." He looked at Keenan. "Did ye see our man, Richard, about?" Gideon had two Mackay men living in Wick who were loyal to the Sinclairs.

Keenan shook his head. "But your letter to him was delivered earlier. He may be acting without us knowing."

Keenan joined the men behind Bàs, his gray horse painted green. The breeze blew along the field, making the tall grasses and remaining summer flowers undulate in waves like the sea. Even though five thousand calvary stood behind him, only the occasional *clink* of tack sounded as the horses shifted, waiting for the word.

Gideon looked to Bàs. "Let's wait a short while to see if the king comes out first. If we charge up to the gates with the king inside, especially now that we've been officially told he's in residence, it will be an act of treason. Even if James's old steward is gone, he's still surrounded by suspicious men who will assume any large army is ready to take over the throne of Scotland."

Joshua shrugged. "We *are* ready to take over the throne of Scotland."

Gideon frowned at him. "Aye, but we don't want James thinking that."

"That would lead to much bloodshed," Hannah said, "when it could be avoided if Erskine gives up Shana and Edward."

"I don't see him doing that," Bàs said, glancing at Gideon. "Knowing we are out here, he knows Shana and Edward are the only things stopping us from attacking."

"And King James being there," Ella pointed out.

There were so many parts at work, twisted roots that seemed to wrap around Shana. All he wanted to do was cut through the mess to get her free and save Edward.

And then what? The look in her eyes when he'd killed Liam—fear, shock, and judgment—had pierced Bàs right through. Her eyes had mirrored her heart. No matter what, she'd see him as a killer like his father had created him to be.

CHAPTER TWENTY-THREE

A witch's bridle or scold's bridle was placed on a
person's face to stop them from talking and shame
them. A bit (like a horse's bit), about 2 in × 1 in size,
was forced into the mouth and pressed down on top
of the tongue, often with a spike on the tongue. It
functioned to silence the person and caused
extreme pain. The scold's bridle was
overwhelmingly used on women, often at the
request of family members. Witch hunters would
use them if they feared the suspected
witch could cast spells verbally.
DBPEDIA

"A witch's bridle?" King James said as Shana was
led by a long chain attached to the front of the iron
mask. "She has not yet been examined." The bitter
tang of dirty metal in her mouth made her want to
spit, but the bit between her teeth prevented it.

Erskine held the end and stopped before James.
His brute stood beside Shana, holding her back as if
she might lunge for the king.

"Your Majesty," Erskine said. "When I went below to see how she fared, she began uttering satanic
words and spells."

James's eyes widened. "She did?"

"Aye." Erskine, the lying bastard, shook his head
in disgust. "I would not have her bespell ye, Your
Majesty, with her filthy words."

James crossed his arms. "A woman who speaks the devil's words is a witch and must have the demon cleansed from her before she can enter Heaven."

"I think she should be cleansed with fire," Erskine said.

Before another lie or threat could be uttered, Shana drew her hand out of her petticoats. She held the letter that Merida Sinclair had handed her through the window, waving it in the air.

"What is that?" James asked.

Erskine whipped his hand toward her, and the guard grabbed at the letter. Shana twisted, trying to yell against the bit, but it came out as an impotent mumble.

"'Tis a letter, I think. I see a seal on it," James said.

"More spells," Erskine said. "She will try to be-witch ye if ye read it."

Shana had fallen to the stone floor, her face upward and her teeth aching from being pulled and jerked by the chain attached to the bit. The guard grabbed the letter from her hand. Erskine strode directly to it, snatching it away. "I will burn it before it—"

"Stop," King James said. "Bring it here first."

"But Your Majesty—"

"Bring it here, Chief Oliphant," James repeated.

From her position on the floor, Shana saw four royal guards move forward to flank the king. With a nod from James, one took the letter from Erskine's fingers.

Shana closed her eyes and exhaled in relief, letting herself sink into a heap.

"'Tis addressed to me," James said, and she opened her eyes to see him stare first at Erskine and then her.

"It has the crest of the Sinclairs upon it," James said, and Shana pushed herself up into a sitting position. "Did they give this to you to give to me?" he asked her.

Shana nodded, and James looked back at the front. He chuckled slightly. "King of England. With God's help, one day."

With the Sinclairs' help. Hopefully James considered that true even if he didn't say it.

He broke through the seal and unfolded it, reading. Did it say the same as what Erskine had burned below? That the Sinclair armies waited outdoors for him on the field to the west?

King James read it through, his frown increasing. He looked at the front of the letter again, reading how he was named King of England as well as Scotland.

"And this letter came by way of a woman locked in a dungeon?" James asked.

"Someone must have given it to her through the barred window," Erskine said, obviously displeased.

"Gideon Sinclair would have sent the letter directly to me through you, Chief Oliphant." James narrowed his eyes at Erskine, letting the man shift uncomfortably under his royal stare.

"I don't know the mind of Gideon Sinclair, Your Majesty," Erskine murmured, cutting a glance to Shana where she sat without moving.

If the king looked at her, she would nod, but instead he strode toward the door. "Do not harm the

woman, Oliphant. I will get to the bottom of this on
the field to the west." He paused and glanced toward
Shana. "How long ago did this letter come?"

She nodded, but he was no longer asking about a
second letter.

James frowned as if her lack of appropriate answer was somehow her fault. He looked back at
Erskine. "And take that contraption off her by the
time I return. I will question her myself." James
strode out through the door, leaving Shana on the
floor in a room with a furious chief who knew that
he'd be judged guilty when James came back to
question her.

The two daggers might be her only chance to
survive the king's absence, her only chance to speak
to Bàs again. What would she say to him?

• • •

"'Tis been too long," Bàs said. "If the king had received one of the letters, we'd have seen some
movement." Was Shana still in the dungeon? He
hoped she was somewhere behind iron bars keeping
Erskine and his men away from her.

"The letter through the gate probably stopped at
Erskine," Cain said. "He knows we are out here and
that we won't approach dressed for war or King James
will react with fear and fury to mark us as traitors."

Hannah kept her gaze on the tree line at the far
end of the field. "And the second letter could still be
in the dungeon with Shana."

"'Tis why I kept the third," Gideon said, his lips
tight. "But it would be more powerful to show James

our armies that will fight for his cause on Orkney and possibly against any other contenders for the throne in England."

"Then I will ride in alone," Bàs said.

"Ye represent the Sinclair Horsemen," Gideon said, shaking his head.

Bàs yanked his skull mask off, dropping it among the grasses. "I am merely a man making sure an innocent lass is unharmed."

Joshua snorted. "Merely a man, built of muscle and bones of granite, carrying an ax and a sword, ready to slice Erskine Oliphant to ribbons if he gets in his way."

Bàs couldn't promise otherwise if that was what was needed to liberate Shana. Even with horror in her eyes, he needed to get her to safety. Cait needed Shana to tend her during her upcoming birth. Kára needed her to help keep her twins healthy. Ivy needed her to be her champion and protector to heal from this trauma.

And I need her. The thought was powerful, hitting Bàs hard. *I need her.* She made him feel human, more like a man than a beast whose only purpose was to kill. When he'd helped Hamish pass with dignity, she'd made him see how he'd been helping others even as Death. And she'd insisted that his touch wouldn't harm a bairn. He'd believed her enough that he'd tried and succeeded in saving wee Alice when she wasn't breathing.

Bàs looked at Cain. "I need to get her out of there. I can feel it. Shana is running out of time."

"Erskine's not going to let you in his gates," Ella said. "Even Merida was questioned by the guards."

"Richard Mackay is living among the Oliphants,"

Gideon said. He scratched the short beard on his chin. "I sent word to him to leave a way in over the wall on the east side facing the sea. Either an unlocked door in the base of a tower or a rope over the wall. Something to help us get inside indirectly."

Bàs pointed. "I'll go to the east side. Don't follow. I'll act alone."

"Ballocks," Joshua swore. "Ye aren't going alone."

Bàs looked at his brother who had changed from war-loving to war-avoiding during his time on Orkney. Bàs shook his head. "Ye have three bairns now. I'll act alone in case the king sees it as treason."

"I have three bairns because ye saved one," Joshua said. "And the king thinks I'm dead, so I can't be a traitor." He raised his eyebrow in stubborn obstinance and crossed his arms. "In fact, it would be better if I wasn't here if he comes to meet us. Gideon and Cain can wait here for him."

Gideon glanced up at the sun that had begun its descent. "It's been too long. The king may not even know we're here." He huffed in frustration. "I'll go, too. We need to get to Shana."

Cain handed his gold crown, the one proclaiming him the Horseman of Conquest, to Ella. He hated the thing as much as Bàs hated his skull mask. "I'm a brother first," he said. "I ride with the three of ye."

"Keenan," Cain called, and his second in command, under his brothers, rode up. "Spread word to the commanders to wait a bit longer. I won't have civil war started without cause because we're impatient. We will try to liberate Shana and her nephew without anyone knowing we are inside the castle." Keenan nodded and rode off.

Cain whistled long and grabbed a piece of red and green cloth, tying a large knot in it to indicate that the armies were to wait. He put his arm out; Eun, his falcon, dove down to land, taking the fabric in his talons to fly over the men.

"'Tis time," Bàs said. The others nodded, their support more than Bàs had anticipated. They'd always said he was valued, but he'd been the one to cause their mother's death, to cause their father to decide they were the Horsemen. Not only had his brothers agreed to come to Wick, but now they were riding toward it with him as brothers. Their complete support behind him.

Bàs leaned over Dòchas, and his sleek horse leaped forward, feeling the need to do something, anything required to save the woman Bàs had realized he couldn't live without.

• • •

Hannah Sinclair watched her four brothers race off toward Old Wick Castle, leaving their armies of four colors, nearly five thousand horses, waiting behind with orders not to advance. They would show King James their allegiance if he ever came out.

Aunt Merida had ridden toward the back of the black horses to wait by Kenneth Macleod, the regent for Clan Sutherland and Ella's father. Kenneth and Aunt Merida had been spending time together, and he'd wanted her safely back by him when she'd completed her mission to get the food and letter to Shana.

Lord, protect Shana and little Edward. Old Wick's dungeon was horrible. Were there rats in the darkness with her? Hannah shuddered to think of it. At least Shana now knew that they were coming to save her.

Up ahead, at the tree line, a group of riders appeared on the field. Hannah's brothers continued to ride toward them. Were they Oliphant warriors? Her heart sped up, although a quick glance over her shoulder at the thousands of loyal warriors behind her reminded her that she and Ella weren't alone. The men were virtually silent. Only the slight stepping or shifting of their horses could be heard over the breeze.

Hannah watched the riders. What should she and Ella do if they came upon them? Ella was lady of Girnigoe, and Hannah was the only daughter of George Sinclair. They could retreat behind the endless lines of horses and men. *Or I could lead the armies myself.*

Having been raised not to utter a word didn't mean Hannah's mind was quiet. She'd watched and learned everything she could growing up as the daughter of the most feared warlord of northern Scotland. She'd sat silently in her brothers' Latin and French lessons and had Bàs teach her how to shoot a bow with enough power to knock over a stag. Calm and meek on the outside, she raged sometimes as hot as Joshua on the inside. She read all the books in the Girnigoe library, and she used to hide in a dark corner of the library listening to Cain and their father discuss how the Sinclairs could take over Scotland. And now they might be forced to do so.

She sat up straighter on her mare, Loinneil, who shifted slightly as if she were as impatient as Hannah to do something. Hannah's head snapped around when two horses walked up between Ella and her. Kára and Cait. Kára sat on her bay horse and Cait sat on the gentle mare she'd won after helping to save King James's life last winter.

Before Hannah could ask, Cait spoke up. "No, Gideon and Joshua don't know we came." She glanced at her before looking forward. "We're riding slowly and will stay out of any fray, but we wanted to represent the women of Girnigoe and Varrich along with you and Ella."

"And we waited until they left," Kára said. "Or they'd worry." She flipped her hand as if the reactions of their husbands, which were bound to be thunderous, were not concerning.

Ella moved her horse over so that the four of them sat their mounts at uniform intervals like Hannah's brothers did when they stood as the Horsemen. "Who are they?" Ella said, squinting out at the riders. The four Sinclair brothers split to ride on either side of the oncoming group of about twenty mounted men, Bàs and Joshua on one side and Cain and Gideon on the other. Gideon slowed, falling behind, as did Cain, but Bàs and Joshua continued their gallop toward Old Wick.

"What is he doing?" Hannah murmured. She had excellent vision, but the group was far away.

"It looks like Gideon is passing something to the lead rider," Cait said.

And then Cain and Gideon charged forward again, following Bàs and Joshua, who were already riding on the path to the castle.

The man in front turned his horse in a circle,

stopping to watch her brothers race away. He threw his hands up in the air as if he were an unbreeched lad demanding attention.

"Daingead," Cait murmured. "That's King James."

Hannah picked out the pointy beard and feather waving from his cap. "Bloody hell," she whispered.

"And the Horsemen raced past him like he was no one," Ella said, a grim smile turning up her lips. "He's bound to be angrier than a swatted hornet."

For a full minute, they watched the king turn in circles as if not knowing which way to go.

"What do you think he's saying?" Kára asked.

"Nothing good," Cait said.

"And probably in a whiny voice," Ella said. Hannah snorted softly.

Finally deciding, King James rode toward the women. "Well, fok," Kára murmured. "I expected him to go the other way."

"What do we do?" Cait asked, alarm in her voice.

Hannah glanced at the ground where Bàs had dropped his skull mask. She swung her leg over Loinneil and leaped to the waving grasses, her petticoats billowing out. She strode over, grabbed the mask, and held it up to her sisters-by-marriage. "We represent the Horsemen while they're gone." She thrust her foot into the stirrup and mounted as she spoke. "Each of you for your husbands."

"My husband is still supposed to be dead," Kára said.

"James wanted us to find another Horseman of War to hold up the legend," Hannah said. "You're his wife."

"I'll be Penelope then," Kára said with a small

smile. "She was the virtuous wife in the *Odyssey*."

Hannah held the skull mask up to her face, peering through the eye sockets, but it was damp inside and smelled musty. The three women watched her as she held it far from her face and set it with both hands gingerly on the pommel of her saddle. "I'll just set it here," Hannah said. "I don't actually have to wear it."

"Here he comes," Ella said. "Look fierce."

"He thinks all women are worthless except as breeders," Cait murmured.

Kára *tsk*ed. "His poor wife."

"God's teeth! What is bloody going on?" James yelled as he approached.

The four women kept still, sitting straight with neutral frowns in place. Hannah was proud she didn't flinch when his horse came to a thunderous stop before them. "I received the letter to come meet the Sinclair Horsemen." His arm flew out behind him. "And then Gideon Sinclair handed me another, but then they rode past me."

"Your Majesty," Ella said. "There is a situation that required—"

"Why are they not here to meet me?" James yelled with all the indignation of a ruffled monarch. A spoiled child. His gaze moved from woman to woman. "I demand an explanation."

"Well..." Hannah said, drawing his attention. She shrugged, meeting his direct gaze. "You were late."

• • •

The iron mask pressing into the skin of her face made it hard for Shana to see anywhere except directly in front of her. Yet the enemy surrounded her. She kept turning her face from side to side to keep Erskine, the callous Witch Pricker, and the Oliphant guards in her view.

With the witch's bridle on, connected to Erskine's brute by a leash made of chain, Shana could not escape them. But she must try to stay alive while the king was out meeting with Bàs and his brothers.

I am coming.

Those three little words strengthened her with hope. Even with her horrible condemnation and the pain she'd seen in his eyes, Bàs was still coming to help her save Edward and herself. Where was Edward? How could she get to him before Janet did something to him?

With the damn bridle on, she couldn't even ask. She turned around while still sitting on the floor to see the stairway, the chain scraping. Shana saw Janet standing there in the archway, her eyes widening as she saw the full extent of the bridle locked on Shana's face. Janet said nothing, just looked at her with a mix of pity and fear, before stepping back into the shadows.

"Remove the bridle," Erskine said, and Shana turned back to center him in her view. He sneered at her, his hand scratching at his unruly hair. "And what will ye say, witch? Lies?"

He didn't fear lies. He feared the truth—the truth that Erskine had planned Ivy's death from the start. That he'd paid his nephew in gold to seduce Ivy and get her with child along with getting his mistress with child, too. That he'd summoned the king with lies about witchcraft because his presence would protect him from the Sinclair Clan, who'd become involved through an act of God or fate when Bàs saved her and Edward from wolves and then the ax.

Erskine Oliphant did not fear her telling lies. He feared her telling King James all the truths that Erskine wanted buried.

The mad chief's gaze swept to her, his lips pulling back so that his brown teeth showed. "Perhaps if ye were to lose your tongue."

"She may be able to write," the brute behind her said.

"And her fingers," Erskine said. He looked to the Pricker. "Do ye have instruments to do that?"

"Aye," the Pricker said, making Shana swallow around her trapped tongue. "But His Majesty said no harm was to come to the woman while he was gone. I will not tangle myself in your schemes, Erskine Oliphant, and find myself hanged for treason."

Erskine cursed, striding across the room. "Show me the instruments."

Shana's breath was coming faster as she watched the worry and anger mix in Erskine's face. He was afraid now, and fear could change a cruel man into a murderer.

The Witch Pricker opened a leather satchel that held his instruments of torture: long needles used to pierce into every spot on a suspected witch's body, instruments to pinch and open a woman for inspection as he tried to find a teat for an animal familiar, and apparently blades to cut off a woman's tongue and fingers.

Lord, help me. Shana prayed as her bladder

tensed with the ale she'd drank. They probably wouldn't care if she peed on the floor. It would mix with her running blood.

"Perhaps ye should go to another room," Erskine said to the Pricker. Erskine looked at her while holding a type of sharp clamp. "Maybe we removed the bridle and she started calling the devil to kill the king." He took a step closer and tossed the bridle's key to the brute. The man yanked her chain hard enough to whip her around, making her tumble on all fours across the stone floor, bruising her knees.

Erskine's man held her down and shoved the key into the lock, turning it while Erskine kept talking, his voice pushing Shana's heart into a frantic pace as he walked closer. He brandished a clamp in one hand and his short sword in the other. "And perhaps I had to remove her tongue to stop her," Erskine said.

Shana tried to hold the bit between her teeth so he couldn't reach her tongue. Her hands dug down into her petticoat pocket for the blades hidden there, pulling one out.

A deep voice came from behind her. "And perhaps I will cut off your nose and shove it down your throat."

Bàs! He stood in the archway, a short sword in one hand and a dagger in the other, his face full of restrained fury. If she'd removed the bit, she probably would have sobbed her relief.

With a flick of Bàs's wrist, a dagger flew across the distance to stab the Erskine's brute right through his forehead. The sword he'd drawn clattered to the stone floor.

Joshua appeared next to Bàs, looking as deadly with his own sharp blade. "Ballocks, brother," Joshua said over the *thud* of the brute's body hitting the floor. "Ye'll cut off his *ballocks* and stuff them down his throat."

"Bàs is not as gruesome as ye," Gideon said, stepping out of the archway. With a heavy step forward, he threw his own dagger at one of Erskine's warriors who'd run toward them. It hit him in the forehead also, felling him.

Cain stepped into the room, his hand pinching the Witch Pricker's nape as he shoved him into Old Wick's Great Hall. Bàs ran toward Shana, but Erskine grabbed her, yanking her upward until she knelt against his knees. He dropped the clamp but held the sharp edge of his short sword against her throat.

His roughness caused the bridge of the bridle to shove upward, blocking Shana's eyes. She looked down the front of her and found a target. Raising her hidden dagger, she brought the point down, thrusting it into the top of Erskine's foot.

He screamed, and she closed her eyes, expecting to feel the blade cut into her throat. Instead, Erskine's grasp disappeared as he flew sideways as if God's hand had yanked him away.

Shana sat on the floor with the bridle mask still crooked over her head. The sound of men fighting around her ended almost as quickly as it had started. Someone touched her leg, and she jerked it back.

"I won't hurt ye." It was Bàs, his voice low and tinged with something close to pleading. "Let me remove your…this prison. I won't touch ye otherwise."

Shana couldn't talk with the bit in her mouth. As he slowly pulled the bridle off, her tongue pushed against the iron bar, spitting it out. She rubbed the back of her wrist across her damp lips.

Bàs stared at her. "Look only at me, Shana," he said. "Nowhere else."

The silence in the room told her that Erskine and the heinous Oliphant men who'd remained in the room to watch her torture were dead.

"I had nothing to do with any of this." The Witch Pricker's voice shook. "I was hired by Chief Oliphant but left when he demanded that I cut the lady's tongue out."

"How many other women have ye tortured?" one of Bàs's brothers asked.

"I helped them prove that they weren't witches," the Pricker yelled.

"Hold your tongue, else find it cut off," another brother said. "Sit over there."

All the while, Shana stared at Bàs, and he stared into her eyes. "I won't harm ye," he said again, and she realized she was shaking.

She nodded, using what little moisture was still in her mouth to swallow so she could speak. "I know." And she realized that she did. He would never hurt her.

Joshua strode over, his sword bloody. "Where's the bairn?"

Shana stared into Bàs's beautiful blue eyes. "Edward," she said. "Janet has him above somewhere."

"Janet?" Bàs asked.

Shana scrambled to stand, and Bàs helped her.

"She doesn't want him to live. She was Erskine's mistress and wants to be his wife. She's carrying Liam's baby." She jumped as the front door swung inward and more Oliphant men surged inside. His brothers instantly formed a barrier before her.

"Your weak and evil chief is dead," Cain said. "Who among ye will become the next Oliphant chief?"

"We need to save Edward," Shana said, rushing toward the stairs. "Janet is planning to hurt him."

Bàs raced with her. "Go on," she said. "You're faster than me in these skirts. Find him." He rushed past her, flying up the spiral staircase. She blinked against the tears in her eyes. Tears of relief? Of worry? Of gratitude? Her heart was full of it all.

CHAPTER TWENTY-FOUR

"I have found the one whom my soul loves."
SONG OF SOLOMON 3:4

Bàs used his powerful strides to run up the narrow stairs two at a time. Shana's words below echoed in his ears. *I know.* He'd said he wouldn't hurt her. *I know.*

She trusted him? Her simple words added to the fire pumping through him, making him surge up the coiled tower. He heard her following.

Where would Edward be? He threw open the door to the main bedchamber above the Great Hall, the chief's room. But it was empty.

"Is he in there?" Shana asked as she caught her breath. Her face was pale, and she held tightly to the wall.

"Ye don't look well," Bàs said, helping her up the last step.

"My head still aches," she said. She pointed up. "You look in the room above."

Daingead. He needed to find the bairn, but he hated to leave Shana looking so pale.

As if reading his mind, Shana shooed him with her hand. "Go on," she said. "I know you will come back for me. Edward is the one in jeopardy now."

Bàs continued up the stairs and pushed against the door. It was barred. If he slammed against it, the bar might break, but if Janet was intent on hurting Edward, it would give her time to kill him.

Bàs breathed deeply, calmly. *Rap. Rap. Rap.* He thought about Erskine. The man had a higher voice, gruff and with little care in it. "Janet," he said, trying to imitate the man's bark. "Open the door, woman."

"The Sinclairs are here," a voice called back. The thick wood was muffling enough to help his disguise.

"All dead," he said.

After a pause, he heard the bar scrape off the door. His hand waited on the latch until he heard it hit the floor, and he slowly opened the door.

Janet gasped, her eyes shifting to where a cradle sat under an open window. She turned, but Bàs jumped past her, his arm coming out to hold her back from the bairn crying softly in the cradle. Edward lay in only cloth around his hips. Even in the summer, the stone walls held no warmth, and he would die of exposure within hours.

"I was changing his clothes," Janet said.

Bàs lifted the bairn, pulling him into his arms. The poor boy cried. Bàs immediately yanked the end of his tunic out of his kilt and shoved Edward up under it so that he lay against the warm skin of his chest. His other arm pulled the sash of his plaid around Edward. The infant was so small and light that the woolen sash easily held the boy swaddled up against him as he tucked the tunic back into his belt.

"I was protecting the lad," Janet said, her eyes big with fear as she watched Bàs. "If he dies, 'tis your fault for allowing him to touch your skin, Horseman of Death."

"Hold your lying tongue, you evil bitch," Shana said as she pushed into the room. She yanked Janet's arm, making her gasp. Shana flew past her, running to Bàs, her face desperate. "Is he well?"

"I'm warming him," Bàs said, and she pulled back his sash to see Edward's relaxed face. "He was under the window with no covering." He started to lift the bairn from him, but Shana stopped his hand.

"Leave him there," she said. "He's safe and warm." Her eyes turned up to Bàs's gaze, the wetness of tears in contrast to the relief across her face. Bàs's breath caught at the beauty he saw there. Even with smudges of dirt and lines from the heavy bridle in which she'd been trapped, Shana was lovely.

Footsteps sounded behind her. "Janet is fleeing," Bàs said.

"Let her," Shana said, and she stepped in to Bàs, careful not to crush the bairn against him. Her hands slid down his arms. She leaned in to kiss Edward's head and then looked up at Bàs. The tears he'd seen before broke from her eyes. "I am so sorry, Bàs," she whispered. "For what I said…when you had to…kill Liam." She swallowed and a tear ran down her cheek.

Bàs would have wiped it, but he was frozen. Even his breath hovered there as if he waited for a reprieve or the strike of a blade on his neck.

She shook her head, her dry lips opening again. "You were only protecting us against Liam and Erskine. I…I am—"

"I love ye, Shana," Bàs said, not letting her finish. He looked upward where the beams held the stone ceiling. She was grateful, that was all, and he couldn't bear to see it in her face. "But ye are all about life, Shana, bringing life into the world, helping bairns and mothers survive the entry. I am the opposite. I am…" His words trailed off as his heart thudded hard in his chest. It was as if Edward were the only thing keeping it from breaking out of him.

Bàs cleared his throat that suddenly felt too narrow for his words. "I've always been the darkness of death. 'Tis what I am." He shook his head, his eyes shutting. "I know ye can't love me back. There's too much difference between us, like an open chasm."

A gentle pressure on his cheek made Bàs open his eyes. Shana's cool palm lay there, and the gentleness in her face caught his breath. There was no pity. "I've learned from you that death is not always bitterness and horror," she said. "Like with Hamish. And sometimes…" She glanced downward as if looking two floors below. "Sometimes 'tis necessary to protect those you love."

Bàs held his breath as she spoke.

She shook her head. "You are not Sebastian, nor Bast." Her thumb slid across his cheek as she dropped her hand. "You are Bàs Sinclair, warrior for your people." She glanced down at Edward's head. "And protector of those who are weaker and those you love."

He drew in a breath. "You've lost too much to death?" he said, but the words came out like a question. "The difference between us is too wide."

She stared up at him. "Love fills the divide," she whispered. She rose onto her toes, her hands on his shoulders. "We balance each other. And you've proven how you, too, help babes enter this world. I can be part of your helping those who deserve to die with dignity."

She spoke as if they had a future together. "Shana?"

Her hands went to his cheeks, holding him there. "I love you, too," she said, staring into his eyes.

The words were like a shot of light piercing the darkness within him, conquering the shadows that wrapped around his whole life. "Ye cannot mean—"

"I love you, Bàs," she said again. "The rest we will work out together."

She slid her hand down his arm and captured his hand, bringing it up before their faces so that their hands lay palm to palm, their fingers pressed straight together. "Two halves of a whole," she said, and shifted her fingers so that their hands slid together, their fingers interwoven.

He pulled their clasped hands to his mouth, resting his lips on her knuckles. "Ye are sure?"

"More than I've ever been about anything," she answered, and Bàs's heart swelled as if it would burst with happiness.

"Then marry me, Shana," he whispered. "Ye balance me like no other under Heaven." He glanced down at Edward, whose eyes had closed, his lips pursed and moving slightly as if dreaming of suckling. "Have bairns with me so we can raise them—"

"To pick daisies and bluebells," she finished. "If they wish it."

Bàs blinked, a smile forming on his serious mouth. "Aye."

"And to wield a sword and ride a horse," Shana continued, "so she or he can protect those they love, too."

His smile broadened, and he leaned over Edward's head. "Is that an aye? Will ye wed me, Shana?"

"Yes," she said, the word loud in the room as if

she didn't care who heard. She leaned over Edward, kissing Bàs's lips. "Yes, I will wed you."

Bàs wanted to holler and sweep Shana up, but Edward was so content, so he just smiled, letting joy radiate from his face.

Shana's smile was pure and full. She wiped at the moisture gathering in her eyes. "We'll celebrate after we deal with everything below."

The bairn was secured to Bàs's chest, so his two hands captured Shana's shoulders. He leaned in. "We'll celebrate tonight." He let her see the heat in his gaze.

She ran the pad of her thumb across his lips. "Definitely."

"Bàs? Shana?" Joshua yelled a second before he charged into the room. His gaze swung to Shana. "Ye well, lass?"

"Very," she said.

His gaze shifted to Bàs. "Ye should come below. Gideon says we need to deal with the king who must be throwing a fit after we rode past him."

Bàs caught Shana's hand, and they headed toward the door. "Did ye have to battle more Oliphants?" he asked.

"Even without the fourth horseman, those who came running in to find their chief skewered were most amenable to our proposition."

"Proposition?" Shana asked. They descended carefully, Bàs's hand resting on Edward's back.

Joshua looked back up at them. "That we don't want their clan or their castle."

They reached the bottom, and Bàs tried to remain in front of Shana to keep the view of death hidden, but the solemn Oliphant men were already taking their wounded and dead clansmen out of the hall under the watchful gazes of Gideon and Cain. Erskine remained where he'd dropped, a dagger in his foot and his white tunic turned red after Bàs removed his short sword. "Hell has gained another inmate today," Bàs said.

Cain looked their way as they walked into the Great Hall, his grim face relaxing somewhat. "Bàs found the bairn."

Gideon turned, his brow raising. "And he's holding it up against him."

Bàs frowned at the teasing tone. "He was cold."

Joshua's hand clasped his shoulder, moving him slightly back and forth. "Ye seem to have a way with bairns, lit—younger brother. Perhaps ye will have some of your own." He grinned at Shana. After she'd helped birth his twins, Joshua had apparently changed his opinion of her.

They all turned toward the door as several men dressed in the king's colors strode in, swords drawn. No one inside had swords drawn, so the royal soldiers sheathed theirs and formed two lines flanking the doors. The king's new steward, a wiry man with an easy smile that the king liked, came down the aisle.

"Erskine Oliphant," the steward called.

Cain pointed to the corpse on the floor.

The man snorted. "Very well then." He looked to Cain. "Your king is arriving."

Gideon exhaled long. "This will be unpleasant."

They'd ridden right past the king of Scotland. Bàs had thought Gideon and Cain would stop to talk with him, but they'd continued riding with him and

Joshua, showing their loyalty to brotherhood over sovereignty. The simple act was treasonous and there'd be hell to pay.

Shana stood next to Bàs, finding his hand. His brothers lined up in their familiar order as they braced themselves for the king's fury.

Instead, laughter came from the entryway. "Very right, my dear." James walked into the Great Hall with Cait on his arm, both smiling like they'd just shared a good laugh.

"Cait?" Gideon murmured.

"Bloody hell," Joshua said as Kára entered behind them with Ella and Hannah.

"Ho there," James called out when he saw the brothers. His smile soured, but more like a reprimand, not someone who planned to behead anyone for treason. In fact, he didn't seem ruffled at all.

Cain bent his knee and head. "Your Majesty." Gideon did the same, followed by Joshua and Bàs.

Kára came up on the other side of the king, and he offered her his other arm. "My husband took the name Joshua to fill the spot the old Joshua Sinclair vacated."

"Quite appropriate, Lady Penelope," James said, his gaze sliding along Joshua's form. "My but he certainly looks big enough to be the Horseman of War."

"Lady Penelope?" Joshua murmured, his brow rising. "I'm tupping a Lady Penelope now?"

"Not for six weeks at least," Shana said under her breath.

James came before them, glancing at Erskine on the ground. He shook his head. "Foolish man,"

James said. "Lying to the king and starting a war with the Sinclairs. I am sorry that I hadn't time to see him justly punished, but I'm glad that you, milady," he said, looking at Shana, "are out of that terrible mask and looking unharmed."

"Yes, Your Majesty," she said, performing a small curtsy. "And we've saved my sister's babe."

James noticed Edward, pressed against Bàs's chest. His eyes opened wide. "Brave babe to sleep so soundly in the arms of death."

No one corrected him because, first of all, James was the king. Second, Bàs was death, but death on his terms, and Shana had helped prove that his touch didn't doom anyone.

"Your Majesty," Gideon said. "Pardon that we did not stop—"

"Lady Sinclair explained the urgency to save the babe and Shana Drummond from Chief Erskine and the Witch Pricker," James said, motioning with his head to Hannah. "That your impressive army had been waiting for hours because Erskine didn't give me the first copy of your letter." He looked to Shana. "But you, brave woman, managed to deliver a copy to me even while you were handled with viciousness."

Shana bowed her head graciously as if she wore a court gown instead of a wrinkled and stained country dress.

James shook his head as he looked at the ladies. "The Sinclairs have found wives of great courage, cleverness, and beauty. I would have my Anne spend time with you fair ladies, as these are qualities that will make a much-remembered queen."

"We would be honored to meet with Queen

Anne," Hannah said. "And we will send one of our most beautiful horses to her as an invitation and gift."

"Delightful," James said, nodding to her.

James, his smile turning easily to a pinched frown of anger, turned to Erskine on the floor. "Once again, the Sinclairs have given their help to the crown." None of them mentioned that this war with the Oliphants had nothing to do with the crown or James, because to a king's mind, his realm revolved around him. "Does he have no supporters, warriors to subdue?"

Gideon nodded toward the doorway. "Some other Oliphant men removed those foolish enough to raise their swords against us and therefore against ye, Your Majesty."

"Janet Bell may still be in the castle or has fled," Shana said. She touched Edward's head, where he slept against Bàs. "She was Erskine's mistress and was impregnated by Liam Ross as well. She planned to let little Edward die from the cold."

"Terrible," James said, shaking his head. "I did see a woman in the shadows when I spoke with Erskine. She mistakenly thought I didn't notice her, but a king notices everything."

Luckily, Joshua did nothing more than snort softly.

"The Oliphants can find and decide if anything is to be done with her," Gideon said. "We will offer our help if they ask." Bàs's brother had come a long way from declaring her guilt and advising a serious punishment all by himself.

Bàs cradled Edward against him. Did the bairn

listen to the beat of his heart? Was that what calmed him?

James turned away from the mess as if dismissing Erskine's life easily. "Well then, a new leader of the Oliphant Clan must be found, and then I will partake of your hospitality, Ladies Sinclair," he said, nodding to Ella and Hannah, "at Girnigoe Castle." He smiled at Cait, patting her arm. "And I would enjoy another of your free-swinging performances."

Gideon opened his mouth, but the king raised his hand to him. "But in your delicate state, we shall postpone that until after your child has arrived." James smiled broadly at Gideon, having guessed right about Gideon's disapproval of his quite pregnant wife swinging from the rafters.

"We will be happy to host you and your men," Ella said, and Cain nodded even though Bàs knew they all despised royal visits.

"We can discuss our plan to secure your realm on Orkney Isle," Cain said.

"And have a festival in your honor," Hannah said to the king who smiled, nodding.

"Or a wedding," Shana said. Her words were soft, but Bàs's three brothers, their wives, and Hannah all turned to look at her and then him. Joshua's frown broke into a wide grin, as did Cain's. Gideon looked pleased, and Hannah rushed forward.

James looked around as if lost. "Is someone in need of marrying?"

Hannah hugged Shana and looked up at Bàs. "When you don't have a bairn strapped to your front, I'm hugging you until you swoon with blood loss." The love and joy in her eyes glowed as if it were she who'd met her true love. He wished one day she would.

He smiled back. "I'm fair warned."

"Yes," Ella cried, nearly jumping up and down. "We will have a grand wedding for Bàs and Shana."

"And I will bless it with my presence," James said in jubilation that wasn't noted as Bàs's family surged around Bàs to pat him on the back. "I can be an official witness," James called over the chaos and laughter. But Bàs was too full of joy to care about including the king in another event that had nothing to do with him.

He felt a tug on the knot of his sash, and Ella gently took Edward from Bàs with him helping to pull the bairn from inside his shirt. The coolness of his absence was quickly replaced by Shana as she threw her arms around his neck. Bàs pulled her up against him.

"Aye," Bàs said as he smiled down into her joyful face. "A grand wedding."

Shana blinked back tears and sniffed as if overcome with happiness. "And a grand life."

. . .

Pastor John stood beside Bàs at the end of the dock built to stretch out onto Loch Hempriggs. Lily pads floated on top of the water, and dragonflies zipped about. Their friends and family stood around the edge of the lake. Hannah held Edward in her arms, who seemed wide awake for the wedding. Bàs's three brothers stood beside her, dressed in fresh plaids and bleached tunics, smiles on their faces as they watched him sway nervously at the end of the dock.

He was supposed to be the Horseman of Death, afraid of nothing but God, and yet he nearly trembled with waiting. What if Shana changed her mind? Had decided that they did not balance each other? That the chasm between them was too deep to fill? That his soul was too far lost to risk tying herself to him?

A flute began a light tune, and Ivy and King James came from around a privacy screen set up among the trees. They walked arm in arm to the dock in time to the song. Ivy smiled broadly, her head high, as she was escorted by the King of Scotland, something she had celebrated as much as her sister's betrothal. The two would act as official witnesses, signing their names to the marriage contract.

Pastor John leaned in to Bàs. "Her sister is here, so she'll come." The young pastor smiled knowingly at Bàs as if he could see the cowardly thoughts racing through his mind like panicked fish caught in a barrel. "Keep your eyes on the screen," John said and stepped back, nodding to the king and Ivy as they stopped, parting to each side of the small landing out in the loch.

"A lovely day," James said. "I ordered it myself as a wedding gift." He chuckled at his own jest.

But Bàs barely heard his words because Shana emerged from behind the screen. She walked alone to the top of the dock, a vision that captured his breath, his chest full. Her golden red hair reflected the setting sun, making it glow as it lay around her straight shoulders. She wore a gown made of green silk, and a wreath of flowers encircled her head.

Bàs released and sucked in a quick breath.

"Bluebells and daisies," he whispered, and he realized they matched the bouquet she clasped in her hands. His gaze went back to her face and connected with hers. She smiled then, knowing he'd seen them, the same flowers he'd picked that day long ago when his father had made him trade wildflowers for his skull mask.

The wind gusted, and a few leaves tugged free to swirl. Shana's hair floated around her, making her look like a woodland fairy, freckles dappled across her smooth skin. Bàs had never met his mother, but he felt like she would approve.

Shana began to walk toward him, her small boots treading along the boards of the dock. The long green dress spread out behind her, and she used one hand to lift the front. The bodice was in the courtly style, lined with hand-sewn pearls, pointing down the front and lifting the swell of her breasts up where an edging of white lace teased along her soft skin.

The flute played a slower beat, and Shana stepped in time until she reached him. The green of her dress enhanced the color of her eyes. "Och, but lass, ye are the loveliest creature I have ever witnessed on this earth," he said, his voice gruff.

Shana's smile grew with unstoppable joy.

Bàs forgot all about the people watching as he took in every detail of his lovely lass. Her eyes reflected all the plans they'd talked about during the early hours of the morning after they'd loved each other. Wedding, adding on to his cabin, having bairns, and growing old together. It was all there in her eyes, and he couldn't look away.

Pastor John cleared his voice. "Bàs, ye need to

turn toward me now."

The king chuckled and stepped forward to gently place his hands on Bàs's shoulders, turning him to stand next to Shana, his gaze on the pastor. A rumble of laughter circulated around the lake.

They didn't look at each other, but Bàs felt Shana's knuckles brush his leg. His fingers caught hers there, and they intertwined as Pastor John spoke of the seriousness of marriage. Bàs's whole life had been full of seriousness and gloom, but now there would be laughter and light.

The vows were quick and easy as if they both wished to rush through them to get to the point for which they longed.

"Ye may kiss your bride," Pastor John said.

Bàs's fingers trailed up through her hair, and he gently kissed her. She pressed into him, hugging him. His arms wrapped around her. "We are together as one, Shana."

Without releasing her hold, she tipped her head back to look up at him, and he saw happy tears in her eyes. "We are balanced. I love you, Bàs."

"I love ye, Shana lass." He leaned down and kissed her again, and the onlookers erupted in cheers. Bàs picked Shana up and spun her around. She threw her head back, letting the breeze catch her hair, and laughed. Bàs laughed, too, really laughed, letting the joy overtake him. Joy and love.

EPILOGUE

"Where are we going?" Bàs asked. And why did he need to bring his skull mask? She'd insisted, and he let it hang from his fingers as they walked hand in hand.

"Come along," Shana said, tugging him through the wildflowers in the field next to Girnigoe Castle. "We have one more thing to do."

"But everyone's waiting to drink to our health," Bàs said, glancing back at the celebration taking place in the bailey. "I think Joshua is drinking to it already," he mumbled. "And to everyone else's health."

"This won't take long," Shana promised and began to sing.

"Lavender's blue, dilly dilly,
Lavender's green.
When you are king, dilly dilly,
I shall be queen."

It was the lullaby she sang the night of their first kiss, sitting in the darkness on his porch swing.

Still wearing her gown and wreath of flowers, Shana carried her bouquet of bluebells and daisies, their stems wrapped with a blue silk ribbon. She turned as she sang the verses as if she truly were a fairy princess dancing among the green leaves.

"Banish the shadows, dilly dilly,
From your dark dreams.
Rest in the promise, dilly dilly,

That you are seen."

She smiled brightly at him with the last line. Aye, Bàs was seen, truly seen by this amazing woman. And she loved him all the same. Bàs didn't think his heart could swell any more with happiness.

She unwound the ribbon from her bouquet until the stems were free. "Here," she said, thrusting them into his hand. She dodged around him, grabbing the mask from his hand, and ran ahead, her curls streaming out behind her like some nymph in a fairy tale.

Lord, she's beautiful.

Bàs stood holding the bluebells and daisies, their stems poking into his palm. The feeling sent a shiver through him, bringing him back to the Great Hall when he was a boy standing before his scarred and demanding father.

"Come along!" Shana called, waving him to follow her as she ran across the narrow stretch of tall grass to a copse of trees set back from the castle and revelry.

"I am coming," he called, the same quick message he'd scrawled to her that he'd since learned had meant so much when she'd been imprisoned in that dank dungeon. He leaped forward, carrying the flowers in his hand. She halted before the tall oaks where two chiseled headstones sat upright, angels on one and a sword carved into the other.

Shana looked at him, giving him a gentle smile. "I came to talk with her this morn, before the wedding." She walked behind his mother's grave, her hand running over the white granite of her headstone. "Alice Sinclair," she whispered and looked to

Bàs, "loves you very much."

Bàs sniffed, his nose itching. He rubbed at it, not sure he could speak yet. He swallowed and gave a little nod. "She would love ye, too, Shana."

Shana smiled brilliantly. "Go ahead," she said, nodding to his hand.

"Go ahead?"

"Put your flowers on her grave, like the ones you picked before."

Bàs looked into Shana's eyes. Tears sparkled in them. "They were taken from you before," she said, holding up the skull mask. She turned away to set it on George Sinclair's headstone. "But now you have the flowers back."

For a moment, Bàs stood still as emotion engulfed him. Sweat sprang up along his palms as he held the stems. He walked forward. "Mama," he said softly. "I love ye, too." He set the flowers on the neatly trimmed grass covering the earth over her coffin.

"There," Shana said and walked around to Bàs. She wrapped her arms around his middle, hugging him tight while he rested his chin on her head.

Bàs breathed in her smell and the fresh air off the moor and sea. "Did ye talk to my da too this morn?" he asked, glancing at his father's grave where the skull mask had been given back to him.

"Yes," Shana said.

"Yes?" he asked, looking down at her, his brows raised.

"I did quite a bit of scolding, but I think we came to an understanding." She tipped back her head to meet his gaze and nodded, her face serious.

Laughter rolled up through Bàs, and he pulled her tighter. "I bet he yelled back."

She smiled broadly. "A bit."

The two of them laughed heartily, the air filling with the sounds of their joy. He looked down at her upturned face. "I love ye, Shana, with every bit of my being."

She blinked, a happy tear escaping. "I love you, too, Bàs, my sweet beast."

He growled low, and she yelped, pulling away to run through the field laughing, her skirts raised so she wouldn't trip. He gave her a head start but ran after her, growling more when she shrieked, laughing harder when he caught her to spin her around in his arms.

Each Sinclair brother has found his happily-ever-after. But there is one Sinclair who grew up ignored, and now 'tis time for her to shine. Follow the Sinclair saga to the conclusion with Hannah Sinclair, sister of the mighty Horsemen of Caithness, Scotland! When a descendent of Viking warriors is tasked with conquering the famous Sinclair brothers, he hits them where they're vulnerable. But when he abducts their sister, he doesn't realize that Hannah Sinclair isn't the meek mouse she was taught to portray.

HISTORICAL NOTE

Fears about witchcraft flourished in sixteenth-century Scotland. King James VI was certain that witches were responsible for preventing the safe sea crossing of his bride, Anne of Denmark. Anne was forced to return to the coast of Norway at least four times before she sent word that she could not cross to marry James until the storms calmed down in the spring. James sailed to her instead in pretty much the only romantic gesture he ever made toward his wife.

These events, plus his time in Norway, where superstitions about witches abounded, prompted James to write a book on witchcraft. *Daemonologie* describes witches, along with other paranormal subjects like vampires and werewolves. It was published in 1597 in Scotland and 1603 in England when he inherited the

crown of England from Elizabeth I. It is thought that William Shakespeare used *Daemonologie* to help him describe the Weird Sisters in *Macbeth*.

James personally witnessed witch trials and the killing of convicted witches. Hired Prickers would poke long needles into moles and growths on the accused's body to see if the subject felt the pain and bled. If they didn't, the spot was thought to be a mark of the devil or teat for the witch's familiar. Victims were usually strangled by hanging and then burned.

Around 1599, James's views on the subject became more skeptical, and he warned his son to investigate with vigor to prevent false accusations sentencing an innocent to death. Unfortunately, this didn't prevent 1,500 people from being killed in Scotland as witches during James's reign, 75 percent of them being women.

ACKNOWLEDGMENTS

Thank you so much for journeying with me through the Sons of Sinclair stories! I've fallen in love with this family, and your excitement for this "last" book in the series, helped me win a contract for a fifth book about Hannah!

Thank you to my mother, Irena, for sewing me fabulous gowns from different time periods so I can feel how my heroines feel living with stays and heavy petticoats. I was able to wear one when I visited castle ruins in Scotland to get an authentic feel for climbing stairs up cliffs and surviving the cold wind off the sea. The layers really did keep me warm.

Thank you to my high school friend, Hilary Biesecker, certified nurse midwife and owner of Loudoun Homebirth and Healthcare, for answering all my questions about midwifery. You are amazing, my friend!

A huge thank you goes out to my fabulous agent, Kevan Lyon, for her constant support and guidance. Thank you also to my talented editor, Alethea Spiridon, who gives me just the right amount of push without pressure to get me to the finish line. And thank you to the Entangled production team who puts together such a beautiful package.

And of course my heartfelt gratitude goes out to my own Highland hero, Braden, who reminds me that I can write fabulous stories on a constant basis, even when my confidence has fallen off a cliff. Thank you, Braden, for getting me to Scotland, taking me everywhere, and getting me home when it felt way too hard. You are the love of my life and my happily-ever-after.

Also...

At the end of each of my books, I ask that you, my awesome readers, please remind yourselves of the whispered symptoms of ovarian cancer. I am now a nine-year survivor, one of the lucky ones. Please don't rely on luck. If you experience any of these symptoms consistently for three weeks or more, go see your GYN.

Bloating

Eating less and feeling full faster

Abdominal pain

Trouble with your bladder

Other symptoms may include: indigestion, back pain, pain with intercourse, constipation, fatigue, and menstrual irregularities.